SWEET
RECKONING

SWEET RECKONING

WENDY HIGGINS

HARPER TEEN

An Imprint of HarperCollinsPublishers

HarperTeen is an imprint of HarperCollins Publishers.

Sweet Reckoning
Copyright © 2014 by Wendy Higgins

Library of Congress Cataloging-in-Publication Data
Higgins, Wendy.
  Sweet reckoning / by Wendy Higgins. — First edition.
    pages cm
  Sequel to: Sweet peril.
  Summary: Anna Whitt, daughter of a guardian angel and a fallen one, join forces
with her true love, Kaidan Rowe, as the Nephilim gather together one last time to
fight against the demonic Dukes for their freedom.
  ISBN 978-0-06-226597-5 (pbk. bdg.)
  [1. Angels—Fiction. 2. Demonology—Fiction. 3. Good and evil—Fiction. 4. Love—
Fiction.] I. Title.
PZ7.H534966Swr 2014   2013021528
[Fic]—dc23   CIP
                                                                      AC

Typography by Michelle Gengaro-Kokmen
14 15 16 17 18 LP/RRDC 10 9 8 7 6 5 4 3 2
❖
First Edition

For Autumn and Cayden
My best, sweetest works in progress

CONTENTS

PROLOGUE

Not a soul in the Vegas cocktail lounge had any idea demons were in their midst. Not a soul would believe the four gentlemen receiving appreciative stares and envious glares were some of the best workers of hell ever to walk the earth. Humans could sense their allure—the power and mystery in their handsome faces—and were drawn to them like butterflies to bright, poisoned nectar.

Pharzuph, Astaroth, Mammon, and Melchom sat unsmiling in crisp new suits, sipping martinis and scotch, discussing events from the night before. They'd taken four women to Melchom's private island off the California coast, ruined them, and then abandoned them at the docks after promising transportation back to Vegas.

"I'd love to see those cows explain this one to their husbands and fiancé," Astaroth, the Duke of Adultery, had said, laughing as they sped away.

But the fun and games were over now, and it was time for business. They sat contemplating all they'd learned last night about traitors in their ranks and among their children.

Mammon, the Duke of Greed, absently swirled his scotch in the melting ice, thinking about the son he'd killed on the island. Flynn had been his favorite Nephilim child in centuries, and he'd turned out to be an ungrateful Judas. The shock of his betrayal still stung. It'd been many years since Mammon had killed, and it left a bad taste in his mouth—not that he'd ever admit that to his brethren of hell.

"He showed no signs of rebellion before last night?" asked the Duke of Envy, Melchom.

"None." Mammon tilted back his drink and emptied it before slamming it to the table with a grimace.

"It's time to tell the other Dukes. We'll gather tonight." Pharzuph's arms were crossed as he thought.

"Some have already left town," Melchom said. "Like Belial."

"We'll call them back," Pharzuph said with a sneer. "We can't let Belial know we're on to him. Let's make him think we're only suspicious of a Neph uprising."

Astaroth ran a hand through his shoulder-length blond waves and pulled out his cell phone, dialing. The others listened in on the conversation with their keen supernatural senses.

"Yes?" said a voice with French inflection.

"Brother Rahab. Call the Dukes back to Vegas. We have news."

Rahab paused. "Very well."

"And one more thing," Astaroth continued. "The old prophecy."

"What about it?" Rahab snapped.

"Can you recite it for us?"

"To my knowledge . . ." His voice went gravelly with disgust. "A Nephilim pure of heart shall rise up and cast demons from earth to the depths of hell, where they will remain until the end of days."

The table quieted, and the demon men appeared momentarily ill.

"How certain are you of its validity?" Astaroth asked.

"Lord Lucifer himself told me of the prophecy."

The four Dukes exchanged silent looks as the lounge bustled around them. Pharzuph cleared his throat and took the phone from Astaroth, speaking low.

"How did our Lord obtain this information?"

Rahab's voice was a dangerous whisper. "You dare to question him?"

A carefully blank look remained on Pharzuph's face, and his smooth English accent never wavered. "Don't be ridiculous. I question his source."

Rahab was quiet. Then, in a tone of reluctance, he admitted, "It was a whisperer. One of the Legionnaires."

Again the Dukes exchanged skeptical looks. *This* was the reason nobody had ever taken the prophecy seriously. It seemed unlikely that a worthless Legionnaire spirit could acquire important information and recite it back correctly.

"The prophecy is valid!" Rahab shouted through the phone. "I've been telling you fools for two millennia not to trust the Nephilim race! Why are you bringing this up now? What has happened?"

"We will discuss our findings soon, brother," Pharzuph assured him.

Rahab let out a low grumble before disconnecting.

"Right, then. What's the plan?" Astaroth asked.

"First we find out if Belial and the girl followed through with the orders given at the summit. See if she's still a virgin. She's number one on my suspicion list. The angels of light had never intervened for a Neph until her."

Melchom leaned his elbows on the table. "How will we find out if she's pure?"

A wicked grin spread across Pharzuph's face. "Leave that part to me."

"And if she is?" Melchom asked.

"We kill her immediately before the damned angels can stop us." Pharzuph finished his martini and eyed a woman who kept stealing glances at him. "And wait to see Belial's reaction to gauge whether they're working together or if this is a Neph-run operation."

"None of it makes any bloody sense." Mammon rubbed his forehead. "We had the lot of them tailed after the summit."

"Only for the first six months," Astaroth clarified. "Apparently they've been busy in the year since then."

"We'll have them tailed again. For as long as it takes."

Melchom shook his head. "Lord Lucifer won't be happy

about this—using his Legionnaires to babysit the Neph again when they should be focusing on humans. He was livid about the wasted efforts after the summit."

Pharzuph sighed. "Fine. We won't sic the whisperers yet. We'll wait and see what we find out about the daughter of Belial."

They all nodded their agreement, and Pharzuph stood.

"Let's enjoy a few hours of Vegas before our meeting." He walked toward the woman with the red aura, who was locked in his blue gaze. "Best job in the world," he whispered to himself.

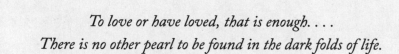

To love or have loved, that is enough. . . .
There is no other pearl to be found in the dark folds of life.

—*Victor Hugo*, Les Misérables

CHAPTER ONE

ON FIRE

The moment I left L.A., a fire began kindling inside me—a satisfying burn of purpose and drive unlike anything I'd ever experienced. Never again would I sit back in silence and watch the Dukes take a life. We'd lost our ally Flynn, the son of Greed, killed by his own father when he was discovered as a traitor against the demons. I would never forget the helpless feeling of being submerged in the water under the dock at that island while the Dukes worked their evil. Never again.

We, the Nephilim, were going to rid the earth of demons, and I was slated to lead the way.

This knowledge sparked, caught fire, and spread through my veins. Despite all the unknowns, I'd never felt stronger or more focused. And love was to blame . . . that very essence of life believed to be a weakness by the Dukes of hell. They had no idea of its fortifying power.

I loved Kaidan Rowe, and he loved me.

I loved Patti and my father, and I knew they were willing to die for me.

I loved the Nephilim, and wanted to see them free from the terror of their fathers.

I loved the inherent goodness in humanity and the potential for a better future on earth without demon interference.

For the first time ever, I didn't doubt myself. When Patti met me at the curb at the Atlanta airport, I held her close, feeling different from the girl who'd left her a week before. She pulled away and searched my face, brushing hair away from my shoulder and giving me a single nod as if she understood. It was time to take my place in the world. Time to fulfill my task. Patti's eyes watered, but her shoulders squared with motherly pride.

Yes. It was time, and her support meant everything.

On the drive home my cell rang. Seeing Dad's number made my heart race.

"Hello?

"Another meeting's been called in Vegas tonight," came his gruff reply. "This might be the last safe time you have to talk to the others. I'm emailing you information. Be careful."

He hung up before I had a chance to say a word.

Another meeting. The Dukes weren't wasting any time. That knowledge made my earlier confidence waver ever so slightly. I just hoped the other Neph and I could survive what was to come.

I texted Kaidan, who was listed in my contacts under *James*, for James Bond. He'd chosen it. He had me listed as *Hot Chick From Gig.*

Video chat in 30.

His immediate response made me shake my head and blush.

Clothing optional?

It was nice to know he could keep a sense of humor in the face of calamity. Or maybe he wasn't joking. . . .

"Are you two flirting?" Patti asked, her eyes darting to me from the road.

I hurried to delete his message.

"It's so weird," I said.

I'd waited two years for Kaidan to return my affections. Now he was my boyfriend. My boyfriend! Unbelievable.

Patti reached over and squeezed my hand. "Enjoy it, honey. Every second."

I definitely was.

The first thing I did at home was open my email to see Dad's message:

You've been granted late acceptance to Virginia Tech in Blacksburg, Virginia, four hours from where I'll be in D.C. You will be in a single dorm room. Patti will have a fully furnished house in the next town. Pack only the essentials. You leave in less than three weeks.

"Patti! Come read this!"

She ran in and read the message over my shoulder, then she hugged me from behind.

"The Virginia mountains," she whispered. "That sounds nice, college girl."

The whole thing sounded nice, especially the fact that Patti would still be nearby and in her own house, far away from Duke Pharzuph here in Atlanta. I wondered how long Dad had been working on this plan, and how many strings he'd had to pull.

Now I just needed to break the news to Jay and Veronica, the people I'd miss most in Georgia.

Patti left to make dinner, and I leaned against my pillows, pulling the laptop closer on my lap. I logged on to the video chat server. Butterflies danced inside me as I dialed Kaidan. His image popped up, and I sucked in a breath.

"Ah, there's my bird." He sat at the desk in his bedroom with no shirt on, wavy wet strands of brown hair around his angled face, five o'clock shadow lining his jaw, blue eyes heating me through the screen.

Wow. Just . . . *wow*. I kind of wished I'd taken time to reapply my lip gloss or something.

"Hey," I said in a small voice, because even through the screen he reduced me to gooey girliness. I eyed his chest and the top of his firm abs. "You're not really naked, are you?"

He waggled his dark eyebrows. "Shall I stand?"

My eyes widened. "Seriously? You're not naked."

"I just got out of the shower, luv." He wore an unapologetic grin.

No way. He was just messing with me.

"You should try it," he said. "It's safe fun." When he winked, my chest, neck, and face heated. I glanced toward my closed door, and Kaidan laughed. "You're considering it, aren't you?"

"No," I said, trying not to smile. "I just don't want Patti to overhear your naughty mouth. Now hush, and listen."

I told him my college news and he nodded, running a hand through his damp hair to move it back from his face.

"Good. Glad you'll be away from there. I wish you could leave sooner."

"Yeah." I chewed the inside of my lip. "When do you think they'll come after me?"

His entire face darkened. "I don't know. Maybe you should leave sooner than three weeks. Stay in a hotel or something."

"I'll see what Dad says after their meeting tonight."

We stared at each other.

"You're so bloody cute," he whispered, his voice all low and yummy.

Blood whooshed through my body. A Kai buzz. Oh, he was totally using the bedroom eyes . . . all heavy lidded and seductive. I don't even think he was trying. I suddenly felt shy. Even from the other side of the country, this boy was dangerous.

"Behave, Kai." My voice sounded more sultry than I intended.

"I didn't say a word." He wet his lips, and I thought of that mouth on my body several days ago. We'd only been apart one day, and already it felt way longer.

"Okay, stop," I said.

He grinned. "Stop *what*?" As if he didn't know. Kaidan Rowe was anything but innocent, and well aware of his charm.

His phone rang from the nightstand behind him.

"Just a sec, luv."

He spun in his chair, and when he stood I got a flash of toned, bare-butted hotness. I let out a yelp before dissolving into a fit of giggles and covering my eyes.

"It's Blake," he said.

I whisper-yelled, "You're really naked!"

"I told you I was. . . . Hey, what's up, mate? . . . Talking with A. . . . No news. Maybe tonight. . . . Yep. Later."

I heard movement, and Kai said, "You can look now."

I peeked through my fingers and saw only his handsome face. Dropping my hands, I tried to look serious. "You are so bad."

"You like it." He leaned back and kicked up his big feet on the desk. "You should try it sometime, little Ann. Just with me, of course."

Without taking his eyes off me, he picked up a pen and began weaving it through his fingers. Only Kaidan Rowe would sit naked on the other side of the camera, completely nonchalant. It was rather . . . distracting.

I watched his chest slowly rise and fall in a sigh. He set the pen down. "I dreamt of you last night. That you were still here with me."

I rested my cheek on my hand, letting his words settle over me like warm sunlight. I still couldn't believe he was letting this happen—letting us be together—letting me love him.

"Thank you," I said.

"For dreaming of you?" He chuckled, and I smiled.

Talking via camera was weird. Ironically, I felt exposed.

Every word and expression seemed magnified.

"Just . . . for everything."

"No, gorgeous. Thank *you*."

Again we stared in silence. For a millisecond I even forgot he was nude. And then I remembered.

"What?" he asked. "What's that look for?"

I wished I didn't embarrass so easily. He rolled his chair to the side and I heard him get up.

"Okay, luv. All better."

He'd put on some running pants, slung low so I could see the V at his hips.

Drool.

"It's not fair, you know," he said, sitting again and leaning in.

"What's not fair?"

"That's twice you've seen my arse. And zero times I've seen yours."

I shook my head. My face was permanently on fire now.

"Come on," he urged. "Just a quick peek."

I laughed. "No!"

Now he laughed, too. "You know I'm taking the piss with you, luv."

I shot him a fake glare and he kept chuckling, with those sexy, crinkly eyes. He hadn't teased me this much in person, but I guess technology provided a safety net that made him more brazen.

I could maybe get used to it.

I *needed* to get used to it so I'd stop freaking blushing and wanting to hide.

My phone dinged, and I opened the text message. It was a single question mark from Marna.

"Who's it from?" Kai asked, sounding tense.

"Marna. Hang on. I'm gonna call her real quick." The girls had no idea what had happened on the island, that we'd been extremely close to being caught and captured. I shivered at the memory of how cold it'd been in the water under the dock as the Dukes walked above us with their prey. And how they'd killed Flynn and dragged his body out to sea . . .

My stomach churned as the vision hit me.

The twins had to know something was up, since their father left for a lengthy summit and none of us Neph—Blake, Kaidan, Kopano, or me—had been available for days.

She answered immediately.

"Hey," I said.

"Are you all right, then? What the bloody hell is going on?"

Even knowing the Dukes were meeting tonight, I still didn't trust a phone conversation.

"It's not good," I told her. "One of our . . . *pieces* fell."

It took her a second to figure it out, and then she gasped. "Oh, God . . ." I could tell she wanted to ask who, but she didn't. Instead she said, "We're in Miami, and we've got two days off. Can we come up?"

"Yes. Please." I was relieved I'd get to tell them everything in person.

When we hung up and I gave my attention back to Kaidan, all humor was gone.

"Everything will be okay," I said quietly. "The sooner we get rid of them, the better."

His jaw worked from side to side. I wanted him to talk to me.

"What are you afraid of, Kai?"

"I'm only afraid of one thing." His blue eyes hit mine. "Losing you."

Pained fear showed on his face, and it wrung my heart. We both knew what we were up against.

"Swear you'll be careful, Anna. No unnecessary heroics."

"I promise. I'm not going to run out and make a martyr of myself. I want to survive this thing. I want to get rid of them, and keep living. With you."

Judging by how the pain eased from his face, he seemed to like that idea.

My phone dinged with another text. "Jay," I said.

U home yet?

Yes, I replied.

Come over plz?

My eyebrows pushed together in worry.

"What's wrong?" Kaidan asked.

"I don't know. He wants me to come over."

"Right, then. I'll be here all night. Ring me when you get back."

I looked up at him with a grateful smile. "You're a good boyfriend."

He smirked. "Hurry home, luv. Oh, and give Jay a message for me. Ask him why DJs can't play pool."

"Okay. What's the punch line?"

"Because they always scratch!" He raised his eyebrows, hopeful.

17

"Um, sure." I put on a fake smile.

His eyebrows dropped. "Not funny?"

"No," I said with a laugh. "But he'll appreciate it."

We were smiling when we logged off, and I hurried to Jay's.

CHAPTER TWO

AND SO IT BEGINS

I let myself into Jay's house and found him and Veronica sitting apart in his room—her in his computer chair, and him on the bed against his headboard. Both wore auras of navy blue sadness, with a fizzle of gray nervousness in Veronica's. I knew from the distance between them and the tension in the air that they weren't together anymore.

"Hey," Veronica said.

I sat on the edge of the bed. "Hey."

Jay raised his eyebrows at Veronica. "You wanna tell her?"

She bit her lip. "So, I got this really cool opportunity. I didn't tell anyone 'cause I wasn't sure at first if I'd take it, but I decided to do it. I'm going to Spain to study abroad this semester."

"Spain!" I couldn't help but smile. That was so awesome. I

could totally picture Veronica there. And then I saw the lack of joy on Jay's face, and my excitement waned. "Oh . . ."

Silence.

"I guess it'd be hard to keep a long-distance relationship, huh?" I asked.

"There's the time difference," Veronica explained. "With Jay working nights, and me probably busy with school stuff. . . ."

I knew it was more than just the time and distance issues. All signs had been pointing to breakup for months now. Neither of them seemed surprised or angry. Just sad.

"You guys are both okay, though?"

Jay picked at his jeans. "It's a good opportunity, you know? She shouldn't pass it up."

I looked at Veronica and a stream of light-gray guilt swam around her before dispersing.

I patted the spot on the bed across from Jay and me, and Veronica came over on shaky legs to sit with us. We sat in a semicircle facing one another. Being closer lightened Jay's aura.

"I love you guys," I said quietly.

Veronica kept biting at her lip. "You're not mad at me about school? I know we were going to room together. . . ."

"No, I'm not mad." This was terrible timing, but I had to tell them now. "Actually, I kind of have some big news, too."

They stared at me, waiting.

"I'm not going to Georgia Tech after all. My dad is moving to Washington, D.C., and we want to live closer, so he pulled some strings and got me into Virginia Tech. Patti and I are both moving."

Their eyes bulged. Jay said, "What?" just as Veronica said, "Wow!"

"I know. It all happened so fast, but I think I need a change. My dad, too."

"Dude, this is crazy." Jay's eyes glassed over for a second. "You're both leaving me."

At the same time Veronica and I leaned forward and hugged him. He wrapped his arms around us. Our last group hug.

When we pulled away, there was a strange shift between us—a change stemming from knowing we'd never get the old us back. We could either embrace the inevitable and work to stay friends through the changes, or we could let go, and allow time and miles to slide between us. Jay gripped my hand hard, and I knew he'd never leave me. Not in the ways that counted. Veronica, on the other hand . . . her eyes were already kind of far away. I could never hold it against her. She was excited for her future and ready to fly.

I wiped the corners of my eyes, and Veronica leaned over to poke my shoulder.

"So," she said. "Are you and Kaidan really together? Like, really really?"

The change of subject lifted some of the awkward tension in the room. I tried to rein in a smile. I'd forgotten I texted Jay and Veronica from L.A. in a drunken state to tell them.

"I know, right?" Jay sat up, suddenly animated. Orange sliced through the darkness of his aura. "How did this happen? I didn't even know you were going to L.A."

"It was crazy." I pulled my feet in and sat cross-legged. They thought my dad lived in California, and as much as I

21

hated telling them half-truths, sometimes that was just what it came down to. "My dad flew me out for a visit, and I went to see Blake, but Kai was there, too."

They were both gaping at me.

"And?" Veronica asked.

"And at first we were fighting, because we needed to clear the air, and he was jealous because I'd kissed Kopano—"

"*What?*" they both hollered.

Whoops.

"When did you guys kiss?" Veronica was practically in my lap now, trying to yank all the details from me.

"Over Christmas break."

In a closet in Australia when we were there to talk Flynn into being an ally. The memory of the whole extraordinary experience was tainted now by Flynn's death.

"I can't believe you didn't tell me this!" Veronica crossed her arms, a shot of dark anger shooting out from her aura, but when I eyed her, reminding her she'd withheld the possibility of Spain from me, she uncrossed her arms and guilty gray seeped around her.

"I felt bad," I admitted. "He was just a friend, and I didn't mean for it to happen. I kind of messed things up. Plus, I knew Kaidan would be pissed if he found out."

"Bro drama," Jay said. But he looked rapt.

I let out a dry laugh. "Yeah. Majorly. But when Kai and I finally made ourselves talk . . . I don't know . . . I guess we both decided we were tired of being scared."

"And now you're together," Veronica said, her voice sounding distant.

We all got quiet. Now Kai and I were together, but Jay and Veronica were not.

Her cell phone chimed, and she groaned.

"It's my dad. I have to go. He's having people from his work over for dinner, and the whole family has to be there."

Her father. A major reason she'd want to be far away from home.

"Call me later," I whispered.

"I will. And I want every detail."

She turned to Jay, both again showing navy auras of sadness tinged with anxious gray. "I'll see you later?"

"Yeah. Course."

A slow beat passed before Veronica turned and left.

"You okay?" I whispered to Jay. He looked tired.

"I don't know. I mean, I knew we probably wouldn't last forever, but it still sucks."

I could feel the steady pain of loss pushing out from his aura, and I wanted to cheer him.

"Kaidan gave me a joke for you."

This lightened Jay's colors real quick. He watched with interest as I told the joke. At the punch line he blinked, straight-faced. "He should really stick to looking good and leave jokes to the normal guys like me."

I fell sideways on the bed laughing, and Jay laughed with me.

"Man, I'm so glad there's something he's not good at," Jay said as I pulled myself together.

I didn't want to leave him yet. "Wanna go get a pizza or something?" Patti was making dinner, but I was sure if I called her she'd understand.

23

"Dude, I wish, but I can't. I'm supposed to mow the lawn. You don't need to worry about me, 'kay? I'll be all right."

He gave me a playful shove.

"I'll call you later, then?" I asked.

"Yep." He stood and pushed his feet into some old tennis shoes. Then he grabbed his faded Braves hat and slipped it on his head. He stuck out his fist and I bumped it before hugging him good-bye.

On the drive home I thought of the good days Veronica and Jay had had together. I recalled Veronica showing me pictures on her phone last summer, and when she got to one she screamed and pulled the phone close, a burst of hot gray embarrassment blasting from her aura.

Yeah . . . for one split second I'd seen a whole lot of Veronica skin. I'd never seen her blush like that.

"Oh, my gosh. I totally thought I'd deleted all those," she said.

"Uh . . . why do you have . . . Wait . . . did you send pictures to Jay?"

"It's not like. . . I mean . . . we were just playing around. He's my boyfriend!"

I started giggling first, and then we were both laughing, killing the shock and tension.

Veronica had obviously trusted Jay, and I wondered. Could I do something flirty like that to surprise Kai?

I was still thinking about it as I walked from my car up the concrete stairs of our apartment complex. Patti's car wasn't there. She was probably out getting boxes for the move.

I stopped at our door and got a weird prickly sensation.

The thought of a demon whisperer caused my heart to pound and my eyes to search all around me, but nothing was there. I glanced down the stairs. Nothing.

With a shaking hand I slid my key into the bolt lock, only to find it already unlocked. Weird. Patti never forgot to lock the door. My heart rate jacked up as I reached into the pocket of my shorts for the small switchblade I kept there. My other hand went into my purse and wrapped around the leather-clad Sword of Righteousness hilt. I pushed the door open and stood in the doorway without going in. Scents from the Crock-Pot drifted out.

"Anyone home?" I called out sweetly.

Nothing looked out of the ordinary. I gripped the knife handle and peeked around the corner. All clear. I went in and closed the door behind me, then moved in slow steps around the apartment—kitchen, balcony, bathroom, coat closet—all clear. It wasn't until I stepped into my bedroom that a surge of panic burst through my system.

My laundry hamper was lying on the floor with dirty clothes spilled out. My body went into some sort of protective mode, clearing my mind in preparation for a fight. It still came as a shock when a short-haired man in all black tore out from behind the door, and months of training prompted me into action.

I lunged forward, lowering myself so that his balance was thrown off when he hit me. My purse with the hilt inside hit the wall. I managed to keep on my feet as he rolled to the floor and kicked himself up with grace that depleted a bit of my confidence. I swiped my knife through the air, and the blade sliced his bicep. He hissed, and I tried not to think about the fact that I'd just purposely drawn blood from another human being for the first time in my life.

His foot kicked up with lightning speed and I yanked back, but his boot still caught my fingers, forcing me to release the knife with a sharp, searing pain. And now I was mad. Instead of retreating, I pushed forward, taking him by surprise as my shoulder and head rammed the soft part of his torso beneath his ribs. He groaned and grabbed at my waist, but I moved fast, wrapping my arms around his knee and yanking him onto the floor.

He caught my wrist in his strong hand and I went crazy, kicking and stomping anywhere I could—his groin, chest, knees, hips. He moved around, grunting, and we were both too filled with adrenaline to stop. But one hard kick to his armpit made him drop my wrist and cry out. I turned to run, but he grabbed my ankle and I fell onto my elbows. In a split second he was on my back. I tried to buck and throw him off, but he used every bit of his body to control mine.

"Get off!" I ground out, my face in the dirty clothes.

"Stay still, you stupid girl!"

His accent was something European. I spotted my knife, so close, only a few feet away. And then I saw feet rushing in through the doorway. My attacker must have seen, too, because I felt his body weight lift and heard a sound of protest escape just before a reverberating *WHAP!*

He rolled off me, grabbing at his head and yelling in pain. I looked up and gaped at Patti standing above us, a frying pan in one hand and a gun in the other. When the heck did Patti get a gun?

She dropped the pan and pulled me up with her free hand, then used both hands to point the gun at the guy. Her hands trembled, but her face was deadly.

"Is he one of you?" Patti whispered to me under her breath.

I looked him over. No supernatural badge at his sternum to signify a demon or Neph. I shook my head. "He's definitely not from around here, though."

"Call the cops," she said.

I did as she asked. While we waited, the guy began to murmur. He was a mess, bleeding from his arm, with a purpling lump on the side of his head. Patti shifted her stance, appearing as uneasy with the sight as I was.

"Please," he whimpered. "Don't turn me in. He'll kill me."

My pulse, which had finally started to settle, went wild again.

"Who?" I asked.

I wanted to naively believe this was a random break-in.

"He'll kill me!" he said again.

The door to the apartment opened and I heard footsteps.

"Mrs. Whitt?" a man called. "It's the police."

"Please," the perpetrator begged.

"Back here!" Patti yelled. And to the man on the floor she said, "It's too late."

The police took him away and spent over an hour questioning us and examining the apartment. The bolt lock was not broken, so he'd somehow picked it. A definite professional.

"And you have no idea why this man would break in and attack you?" he asked. Again.

"No," I said, and it was the truth. I was baffled. He hadn't been trying to kill me; of that I felt certain. It was as if I'd taken him by surprise and forced him to attack. He'd been there for something, but it wasn't me.

Just as the officer was putting away his pad of paper, another cop walked in and approached. He held out a plastic bag with a small, pink wad of cloth inside. It looked vaguely familiar.

"I think we figured out why our perp broke in," said the cop. "Panty thief."

Gah! My freaking underwear!

Patti gasped, and the interviewing officer sighed, shaking his head. "Well, you two gals sure put a hurtin' on him. I don't usually suggest that people fight intruders if they can avoid it, but I commend you both."

"Thank you, officers," Patti said.

After they left, we stood there in the silence staring at each other, her curly strawberry-blond hair askew. I was glad we'd be moving soon, because our home was now tainted. Everything about the place felt violated and unsafe.

Where did you get the gun? I asked her, using my hands to sign in case any Dukes or enemy Neph were listening nearby.

Your dad.

Well, that figured. I was glad she had it, though.

Who sent this man? The second she finished signing the question, my stomach dropped, and I knew.

In slow letters I spelled out, *Pharzuph.*

The Duke of Lust, my boyfriend's father, was behind this. He was checking to see if we'd followed through with the lie Dad had told them at the New Year summit seven months ago. Pharzuph wanted to know if I was still a virgin, a state of being that was unheard of for a Nephilim of my age. Only Pharzuph would have the ability to smell someone's virginity in such a way. A disgusted shiver raked up my back. I shook it off and stood up straight.

All right, Dukes, I thought. *It's on.*

CHAPTER THREE

CRAZY DAY

After I calmed myself and worked up enough nerve to return to my trashed room, I dialed Kaidan on video chat and told him everything. He might not have shown any emotional colors, but the murderous look on his face said it all. He rubbed his palms roughly over his eyes, then dug his fingers into his hair.

"They're meeting in Vegas tonight. He must've sent someone before they even started. I want you out of there."

"I know," I said. "We're going to a hotel. Not that we can hide for long, but at least we can make them work for it if they're after me. I want to tell my dad, but I'm afraid to text him while he's in the meeting."

"Wait a bit and see if he contacts you."

I nodded and chewed my lip.

"Are you all right?" he asked.

"Yes, but he scared the crap out of me," I admitted. "Then I just felt determined, and it sort of overrode my fear, so that was good."

"Good. I'm glad you didn't freeze up. And Patti is a rock-star under pressure, yeah?" His words were light, but serious anger still clung to his features.

"Yes. She is."

"What did Jay want?"

I told him the whole story about Jay and Veronica, but he didn't seem surprised. Neph were used to seeing relationships crumble. In fact, they were the cause of many breakups.

"They'll be all right, luv," he said.

"Yeah," I whispered.

My plan had been to stay up that night chatting with Kaidan—to make use of every second we had—but I felt skittish after the attack, like staying stationary was too dangerous.

"You should go," Kaidan said, reading my mind.

I stared at him on the screen, his handsome face with slight worry lines between his eyes.

"I love you," I said.

His head tilted and the worry line smoothed. "I love you, too."

Those words, in that voice, from that mouth, did so many things to me.

I kissed my fingers and touched his cheek on the screen. He did the same, and with reluctance, we disconnected.

It didn't take long for Patti and me to grab our emergency bags with all the essentials and get out of town. We stopped at a hotel one hour away.

We entertained ourselves playing Skip-Bo and Yahtzee. We were just starting to get sleepy when my phone rang. My heart banged against my ribs when I saw Dad's number.

"Hello?"

"Where are you?" His voice was low and quiet.

"Hotel in Georgia."

"Alone?"

"With P."

"Separate. From here on out, you need to be together as seldom as possible."

"Okay." I looked at Patti, who sat across from me on the bed, watching me and taking shallow breaths as she waited for news. "Something happened tonight."

"Go on."

I told him about the attacker and his thwarted attempt to steal my underwear. Dad's stewing silence was like a ticking bomb.

"Stay away from the apartment." His raspy, violence-filled voice gave me the chills.

"Is anyone working the Atlanta area tonight?" I asked, referring to demons.

"No. Everyone'll be heading out in the morning, but keep your eyes open. I'll be in touch soon."

I hung up and looked at Patti. "He wants us to separate tonight. I'll come get you in the morning."

Her chin quivered for one second before she cleared her throat and nodded. "Please be careful, Anna. I want you to take the gun."

She reached for her bag, but I stopped her. "No. You keep it. I've been training with the knives and always have them on me."

Patti hugged me hard, and I set off with a lump in my throat.

I drove without purpose or direction. When my phone rang I was happy to see Marna's number.

"We're in Atlanta. Where are you?" she asked.

I made a split-second decision and said, "I'll come to you." Normally I stayed in the outskirts of Atlanta and avoided the inner city because of Pharzuph and heavy whisperer counts, but the demons were in Vegas tonight, so the coast should be clear. We agreed on a hotel, and when I met the twins in the lobby an hour later I squeezed Marna around her thin shoulders. I planned to give Ginger a quick hug, if she'd let me, but to my surprise she held on when I tried to let go.

"Is Blake dead?" she asked in a dry voice.

"What? No!" I pulled back, and she closed her eyes, puffing up her chest. "I'm so sorry, Ginger. I didn't mean to scare you." I lowered my voice. "It was Flynn."

The sisters looked simultaneously dejected and relieved by the news of whom we'd lost. Marna smoothed her flight attendant uniform down and let out a giant breath.

"Come on," I said. "I'm getting a room, and I'll tell you everything."

The girls and I got comfortable in the hotel room, and I told them the entire story of L.A.—everything from me staying at Kaidan's place, to Kai and Kope going to Syria to save Zania, to the island—and then the attack in my apartment today. I left out the fact that Blake had a girlfriend who he'd soon be forced to marry per his father's orders, because I didn't think Ginger could take it.

They were speechless for a long while.

"It's starting," Marna finally said.

"Yep," I whispered.

"Bring it, arseholes," Ginger said.

In a rare moment of camaraderie I stuck out my fist and Ginger bumped it, causing Marna to say, "Aww!" Ginger rolled her eyes.

My phone rang, once again sending my heart into my throat. Would it always be like this now? Constant trepidation?

I let out a breath when I saw the screen. "It's just Jay."

Marna's beautiful gray eyes got big when I answered. It was loud in the background.

"What are you up to tonight?" he asked.

"Nothing much." I winked at Marna. "What's up?"

"I dunno. I kinda don't want to go home after work and be alone. I thought maybe if you were at a party or something, I'd hit it up and hang with you."

I couldn't remember the last time Jay wanted to hang with me. I mean, naturally a guy should want to hang with his girlfriend, and I always understood that, but it felt kind of nice. I'd missed him.

"Where are you?" I asked.

"I'm deejaying in Atlanta, but I'm done in half an hour."

I grinned. Marna grinned. Ginger rolled her eyes again.

"What if some friends and I come to you instead?"

"For real? That's cool. This club is eighteen and up."

He gave us the name of the place, which was only fifteen minutes from the hotel.

I felt bad on the walk over. Jay and Veronica hadn't been broken up a whole day, and I was bringing his dream girl straight to him. Veronica would be offended and hurt, even though the breakup had been mutual. I had no idea if Jay would still be appealing to Marna now that he was single. Maybe I was worrying about nothing.

Jay looked super cute from across the club in his backward hat and freshly shaven face. The DJ booth was raised up at the edge of the dance floor, and Jay held headphones to one ear with his shoulder while he changed CDs and adjusted dials. From the corner of my eye I saw Marna staring. Hard.

A group of guys in tight shirts flanked us when we walked in.

"Piss off," Ginger said.

Apparently American guys were just as magnetized by an English accent as we American girls were, because they went a little goofy.

"You're British?" one of the guys asked, starry-eyed.

Judging by the look of annoyance on Ginger's face, she didn't think it was cute. She grabbed Marna's hand, who in turn grabbed mine, and we moved past them. I shot an apologetic look over my shoulder, because, well, I understood.

As Ginger wove us through the crowd and onto the dance floor, my mouth watered at the sight of people's drinks held high. After the week I'd had, my system was begging for alcohol, but as the daughter of the Duke of Substance Abuse, one drink would only fuel my longing for a whole lot more.

I focused on the DJ booth instead.

Ahead of me I heard Ginger ask Marna, "Are you sure about this?"

Marna's head nod was small but certain.

The girls stopped just as a dark, sensual song with a thumping bass beat came on. It was the kind of song that made you want to move your body, but all I could do was stand there and gawk with everyone else as the twins broke into a smokin' hot dance.

Red auras popped up in fizzing bursts all around them as they moved against each other in perfect sync. I glanced up at the DJ booth and found Jay's aura blowing up like a firecracker, orange, yellow, and red. He tore his eyes away from the girls and found me, which seemed to settle his aura a little. And then a strand of grayish guilt crept in.

He gave me a wide-eyed look that seemed to ask, *What are you thinking?*

I gave him a small smile and shrug. The twins were only here for a night. It wasn't like Jay and Marna were going to fall in love or do anything crazy in a matter of hours.

When the song ended and the twins were applauded, we left the dance floor and found a table.

"I'm getting a drink," Ginger said. She gave us pointed looks, I suppose as her way of asking if we wanted anything.

"One for me, as well," Marna said.

Yes. "No, thanks," I told her.

As Ginger left, Marna lifted the hair off her neck and fanned herself. "Jay's looking fit."

The way she gazed at him was sweet. "He's single. In case you're wondering."

She dropped her hair, and her big, rounded eyes sparkled. "Are you being serious?"

"Yes. But Marna . . . it just happened today."

Her face fell. "Oh." Brokenhearted boys on the rebound were not a good idea.

Ginger came back with two identical red mixed drinks and set one in front of her sister. They made a silent toast and both drank. I allowed myself a few seconds of envy before looking away.

Fifteen minutes later Jay was handing over the reins to another guy and joining us. Marna didn't try to hold back her beautiful smile. She stood, bouncing on her toes, and ran to hug him.

"Way to play hard to get," Ginger mumbled.

Jay held her with his eyes closed. He was a good bit taller than her now. They pulled back enough to look at each other, and my heart gave a squeeze at the way they gazed with open adoration.

"This kid is not good for her," Ginger said under her breath.

I didn't respond. What Ginger meant was that Jay *was* good for Marna, but in our world, good was bad. Marna couldn't afford to fall in love when she was expected to work as an adulteress. Kaidan and I posed a huge danger to each other, but we'd chosen to be together anyway. Jay knew nothing about angels, demons, or Nephilim. Starting something with him would only end up in heartache for Marna and him both.

I should have probably thought this through better.

"What are y'all doing here?" Jay asked. He looked down

at Marna's uniform. "Layover?"

"Just a quick one. We leave at five a.m."

Jay whistled. "Well, this is a nice surprise. It's great to see you." He smiled, but the edges of his eyes drooped from the day's emotion.

Marna patted his cheek. "Come on, gorgeous. Let's get out of here."

The four of us left together, Marna never letting go of Jay's hand. Ginger glared down at their joined hands from behind them. I understood her worry about Marna, and I had my own worries about Jay's vulnerable, human heart, but I also knew it would do no good to try to come between them.

We exited into the hot, muggy night, and Ginger wrinkled her nose.

"It's bloody stifling here in the summer."

"Yep," I agreed, though I was used to it.

"What do you guys wanna do?" Jay asked. "There's a diner on the corner that makes awesome milkshakes."

"Ooh!" Marna clapped her hands.

"I'm beat," Ginger said.

"You can go back to the room," Marna told her.

Ginger narrowed her eyes. "Not without you."

I expected Marna to cave to her sister's forceful wishes, as usual, but she held her ground. "You can stay or leave, but I'm not ready to go." Marna lifted her chin.

Ginger's little nose flared in annoyance as they battled in a silent stare-down. Then she snapped, "Don't stay out late."

"Bye, Ginger," I called as she sashayed away.

"See ya," she answered, not looking back.

"You seem tired, too," Marna said to me with a sympathetic tilt of her head.

Dude. I was pretty sure Marna had just told me to get lost. I *was* beyond exhausted, now that she mentioned it.

"Yeah, I am." I looked at Jay. "You okay?"

His mouth went up on one side in a half grin. "Sure." He threw an arm around me and pulled me in, then the three of us walked to the diner, which was a few blocks from my hotel.

"I'm gonna head out," I told them. "Please be careful."

"We will," they answered together.

"I'll call you tomorrow," I said to Jay, then I walked to the hotel with a dainty switchblade in my closed fist, eyeing every shadow until I was safe in my room. I checked the bathroom, closet, and under the bed before flopping down on it.

I texted Patti to let her know I was safe, and she texted right back. We kept the messages brief and generic, but I still deleted them.

Without bothering to stand, I stripped off my jeans and tossed them to the floor. As I was about to climb under the covers and call Kaidan, I got a devious thought.

I turned on the camera feature of my phone, struck a pose, and took a picture of the bottom half of my body. It was so silly-looking that I started laughing at myself. How in the world had I landed Mr. Sexy?

Determined, I struck different poses, shaking my head, laughing, or groaning at each picture, and deleting them immediately. And then I took one that made my whole body go still.

Wow.

That one was kind of . . . nice. I was lying on my side, one leg hitched up with my feet tangled in the covers, and it was a great shot all the way from my lower back down. I was wearing panties with black lace trim, nothing crazy, but the whole angle really worked.

I stared at the picture for a long while. My thumb hovered over the Send button, then over the Delete button. I chewed my lip. Kaidan loved me. He'd be shocked if I sent this pic, but he wouldn't think less of me. Still, each time I envisioned him opening it, I felt a hot wave of embarrassment. I hit Save and dropped the phone next to me, falling back on the pillows. Maybe I'd send it someday. Maybe.

CHAPTER FOUR

HELLOS AND GOOD-BYES

A light, persistent knocking woke me at four in the morning. I saw Ginger through the peephole and let her in. My eyes darted down the hall, but there was no sign of Marna. It was the first time Ginger had ever looked less than perfect. Small purple bags rested under her eyes.

"What's wrong?" I asked. "Where's Marna?"

"She went home with your friend last night," Ginger spat. "We had a row about it over the phone, but she wouldn't listen. You have to rein in that bloke of yours, Anna."

"Ginger . . ." Man, she was prickly this morning.

"No, Anna. This is bloody serious, and you know it. She's already talking about coming back to see him next week!"

Anxiety spread through me like nettles. This was the worst time for any of us to veer off our paths. The Dukes and whisperers would be watching. If she started making frequent trips to Atlanta, her father was likely to notice.

"You can use your persuasive ability thing," Ginger said.

I shook my head. "It won't work if they want to be together. They'll fight it."

Marna was desperate for love. And Jay was a relationship kind of guy, who was on the rebound with a girl he was wild about.

"I'll talk to Jay," I promised.

Ginger pulled out her phone and shoved it under my nose, asking, "By the way, have you seen this?"

I took the phone from her. It was an article from a Santa Barbara newspaper. The headline read LOCAL EXTREME SPORTS STAR ENGAGED. It had a picture of Blake and his girlfriend, er . . . *fiancée*, Michelle, sitting on one of his motorbikes, beaming. They looked gorgeous. And in love.

"Oh no," I whispered. I looked into Ginger's broken face. "His father is making him."

"Whatev." She snatched the phone back and shoved it into her purse with a shaking hand.

"Ginger—"

"Gotta go. Take care." She slung her purse over her shoulder and left.

I tried to go back to sleep, but I couldn't relax. Ginger and I weren't exactly friends, but I still hated to see her upset. Marna and Blake were the only people she cared about.

At five I pushed myself out of bed. By seven I was parking outside of Jay's house, greeted by the scent of wild honeysuckle bushes. His home was quiet, everyone sleeping in since it was a Saturday. I let myself in, like everyone did at Jay's place. He was conked out on his rumpled bed, lying diagonal across it. I sat next to him and gave his shoulder a gentle shake.

"Jay," I whispered.

He didn't budge. I shook him harder and said his name louder. With his eyes closed, he grinned and flung a heavy arm over my lap.

"Jay, it's me. Anna!"

His eyes cracked open and he pulled his arm away.

"Dude. Sorry." His voice was groggy. "What time is it?"

"It's seven. I need to talk to you."

He sat up and scrubbed his eyes with the back of his wrists before giving me his sleepy attention.

"I don't think it's a good idea for you to jump right into something with Marna."

He blinked and scratched his short hair with both hands.

"It's nothing to worry about. I can't believe you came all the way out here to say that."

"I'm serious, Jay. I love you both, and I don't want to see either of you hurt. Plus, if Veronica found out . . ."

"She dumped me. I'm allowed to have a little fun, right?" Guilt spun around his chest. "We're just hanging out."

I gave him my "yeah, right" look, and he gave me a sheepish grin.

"You're not gonna tell Roni, are you?" he asked.

"No way." The breakup was mostly her doing, but she'd still go ballistic with jealousy if she found out he'd immediately moved on with her nemesis.

"Do you hate me?" he asked.

"Of course not." I needed to talk sense into Jay, but I knew how it felt to fall for somebody. Nothing anyone said could stop it. "It's just that Marna lives in England," I explained. "And her dad is *really* controlling. He'd never let her move here."

"Yeah, I know. But she's a flight attendant, so she can come here on her days off and stuff."

He sounded way too hopeful.

"That's such a long trip, Jay. It's going to get really tiring."

"You're the one with a boyfriend on the other side of the country, so you don't have much room to talk."

Hmph. Well, crap.

"Anna," he said, searching for words. "There's just something about Marna. I didn't think we'd ever be able to be together, you know? But I've always thought about her. Probably too much. Roni used to test me. She'd ask stuff like, 'What would you do if that British girl came back right now and tried to get you to break up with me?' And I'd tell her she was crazy for asking, 'cause I knew that would never happen, but really . . ." He cleared his throat and dropped his eyes. "I knew what I'd do. As much as I loved Roni, I always thought about Marna. Everything feels different with her. Bigger. I can't explain it. Like she's my soul mate or something—and I don't even believe in that crap."

"I get it, Jay. I really do. But Marna isn't at a time of her life when she can settle down with you. I don't want you to get your hopes up about her."

"You worry too much." He slid back down into his bed and closed his eyes.

I rubbed the top of his thick blond hair and sighed. "Go back to sleep."

"Nigh'-night," he mumbled.

And he fell asleep. How nice would it feel to be so free of worries you could slide into sleep that easily? I hoped Jay's life would always be like that.

Outside in the warm morning I climbed into my car and called Patti.

"You doing okay?" I asked her.

"Fine. You?"

"Yeah. Just tired. I think you should stay where you are until it's time to move."

She sighed. "You're probably right. There's plenty of stuff in walking distance. I should go over to the store and get a couple novels to keep me busy. I'll need my car eventually."

"Yeah. Once I get word, I'll come get you and we can run back to the apartment to grab our stuff and leave."

"All right, sweetie. Be safe."

A sudden chill slid up my spine. My thumb hit the End button and I heard the Legionnaire chuckling inside my head—a rattling, insidious sound. I turned and jumped at the sight of the dark whisperer behind me in the car. Its ugly face grinned in gleeful malice, and its giant wings stretched through the sides of my car. How long had it been there? The hearing of demon spirits wasn't very good, but in this small, quiet space the whisperer would've had no trouble. I went over the conversation in my mind, searching for anything incriminating I might have said. Any little thing could be used against me at this point.

45

"What do you want?" I asked, letting my irritation show.

Again, it chuckled, and without answering flew away. What the heck was that about? Just a checkup? I had to be more careful—constantly on guard. This was why Marna needed to stay away from Jay. Hopefully she would do the smart thing. For once I was siding with Ginger.

Not knowing if or when Pharzuph might come back to town, I got out of Atlanta and drove to a mall. I walked around all day, buying a few things. At four o'clock I went to see a movie by myself, which was lonely, but it passed the time.

I never stopped looking for demon spirits.

Veronica called to see if I wanted to hang out, but I told her I couldn't. The incident with the whisperer in my car was too fresh on my mind. I promised her we'd see each other before she left in five days. I hoped I could keep that promise.

My anxiety was rising. Dad hadn't contacted me or sent his ally spirit, Azael, with any messages. I hated waiting. By the end of day three I'd bitten off all my pretty fingernails. I'd seen a whisperer every day. Each day one would find me, swoop down, circle me, and leave, as if monitoring my location. The only good thing was that after they spotted me, they left me alone.

On day four, after my daily whisperer sighting, I went to see Veronica.

"I can't stay long," I said. All of her bags were packed in her room, and stuff was lying around with the look of someone in the midst of moving. Something inside me ached at the sight.

Close to Veronica's chest, like a thin band around her,

was a deep, blue sadness. On top of that was a fizz of orange excitement with a sprinkle of gray nervousness. Emotions were funny things.

I reached for her hand and she took it, then looked down at my fingers.

"What did you do to your nails?"

"Oh . . . I've been kind of stressed."

"Sheesh, Anna! You could've at least cleaned them up with a file. Can I do your nails? For old times' sake?"

"Sure," I said.

Her dark, thick hair had been recently cut and blown out in a voluminous style around her jawline. I memorized the look of perfectly drawn eyeliner around her almond eyes, the slant of her regal nose.

We sat down on the floor with her basket of polishes.

Veronica talked to my nails. "Don't worry, you poor things. Roni'll take care of you."

She gently filed the messy nubs, and I bit back a wave of emotion.

"How's Jay?" she asked without looking up.

I cleared my throat. "He's . . . okay. How are you?"

"I'm okay, too, I guess. It's weird, though. I miss him. But I feel like I don't have the right to call him anymore. It's hard to stay friends after you've been together."

"Yeah," I whispered. "I wonder if you'll meet someone in Spain."

She grinned up at me. "We'll see. I don't want anything serious, but I'm counting on a lot of hotties in my near future."

"I'll miss you," I said.

She patted my hand. "Don't get sappy. No tears. Just think of me when you do your nails, 'kay? And for God's sake, don't bite them anymore."

My poor nails were the least of my concerns.

CHAPTER FIVE

MARNA

I missed Kaidan like crazy. It'd only been five days since our video chat, but it felt so much longer. We were trying to stay cautious—to chat only when we knew it was safe—but it was hard.

I was tired of bouncing around to different hotels every day, hanging out in their gross bars sipping Cokes so that if whisperers came I could jump into action. I was only eighteen, but I had a fake ID to buy alcohol if necessary. I was bored, lonely, and impatient, waiting for Dad to give me the thumbs-up to leave for Virginia Tech.

I was surprised to see Ginger's number calling me that afternoon as I sat in my hotel room, reading about a swoony alien guy. Books were about the only thing that could distract my anxious mind.

"Is she with you?" Ginger asked, sounding frantic. "She" was obviously Marna.

"No."

"Shite! She snuck off when we got stateside."

I set down my book and sat up. "Are you here?"

"No. I'm in Newark, the armpit of the bleedin' world. Will you find out if she's with your friend and call me straight away?"

"Okay."

We hung up, and I called Jay. It rang so many times I thought voice mail would pick up, but then he answered.

"What's up?"

"Is Marna with you?" I asked.

"Um . . ." He got quiet.

"That's a yes." I sighed. This was not good.

I heard Marna say in the background, "Argh! Just tell my sister I'll be back in time for our morning flight!"

"She just wanted to know where you were," I said.

"Well, she's suffocating me. I don't have to answer to her."

"Dude," Jay said. "How can you two hear each other when the phone's at *my* ear?"

We both got quiet.

"I'll tell her she's okay," I said, and then hung up.

Ginger answered immediately and I told her, "She's fine. She's working here tonight, but she'll be back in time for your flight in the morning."

"*Ugh!*" Ginger screamed into the phone, and disconnected.

Four hours later I was sitting on a stool in a bar, playing a game on my phone and ignoring the stares from two men when Ginger called again.

"We need to meet so you can take me to them," she said. "This has to stop."

"You're here? I don't think this is a good—"

"Just meet me." She sounded desperate.

We met in front of the superstore in Cartersville. We both stepped out of our cars into the humidity, searching the skies and crossing our arms.

"Take me to her," Ginger demanded.

I hesitated.

"I think Marna needs to get this out of her system," I told her. "I'm worried that the more you try to stop her, the more she'll cling to him."

She appeared to be barely containing her anger. "I swear, Anna. I'll chain her up if I have to, but she is not staying another night with him. I won't let her endanger herself for some stupid human boy."

I took a deep breath. These were touchy circumstances. If whisperers caught Marna hooking up with a boy, just for fun and not for the purpose of making him cheat, her father would have her killed. Worse yet, the Dukes would probably make a spectacle of her death as a lesson to the other Neph about the importance of working.

"If I take you to her, will you promise to try to stay calm?"

Ginger gave me a tight smile. "I'll be calm."

I so did not believe that, but while I couldn't tell her how to deal with her sister, I *could* tell her how to deal with my best friend.

"I can't have you yelling at Jay. He doesn't understand."

"Fine."

51

"All right. Let's go."

She followed me to Jay's house and I texted him from the gravel driveway to let him know we were there. I didn't want to walk in on anything.

Ginger came in behind me, wearing a face of stone.

Jay opened his bedroom door as we came down the hall. He wore jeans and was pulling a shirt over his head. I opened my senses to feel the anxious confusion in his gray aura.

"What's going on?" he asked, looking back and forth between us.

"It's hard to explain, Jay," I said.

His guardian angel stood close, protective as ever.

Ginger never stopped moving, so Jay stepped out of her way and we all went into his room. Marna sat on the bed with one of Jay's pillows on her lap. Something about her seemed . . . off. I couldn't put my finger on it. I searched the room, wondering where the strange vibe was coming from.

Jay walked over and stood next to Marna, who gave her sister a defiant stare as Ginger's sharp eyes went from Marna to Jay, and back to Marna.

Oh man. She did not look happy. The twins could sense romantic bonds between people—everything from attraction to love and marriage. Was that what was happening to me? I'd never sensed bonds between people before, but I couldn't place the awareness I was experiencing.

"I'm sorry," Jay said. "But I don't see what the big deal is. We're both adults. We're just . . . hanging out."

"Just hanging out?" Ginger asked sweetly. "Not falling in love?"

My heart kicked with surprise. Was that what she saw between them? But . . . he'd just been in a relationship with Veronica! I felt light-headed. This was so like Jay to let his heart be snatched up by another so quickly.

I watched Jay and Marna exchange a tender glance, and sure enough a fluff of pink floated up around Jay. Then he looked at me and his eyes dropped to the floor, a wave of gray guilt covering over the pink.

"It's time to go," Ginger said in her don't-mess-with-me voice.

Marna lifted her chin. "I'm not leaving, Gin. I'll take the red-eye to New York and be back in time for our flight."

"Don't do this," Ginger warned.

Jay looked at her like she was crazy. Marna flung the pillow aside and stood face-to-face with her sister. I rocked back on my heels and gasped, slapping a hand over my mouth. My body reacted—heart pounding, limbs shaking, a chill of disbelief zipping down my spine.

"Anna?" Jay came over and grasped my arm to steady me.

"What?" Marna asked. "What's wrong? Why are you staring at me like that?"

She brushed a hand down her flat stomach, where my eyes had locked.

God, please. Don't let this be happening.

The faintest recognition of buttery light pulsed from her abdomen.

I felt like I might hyperventilate as the reality of the situation crashed over me. Marna would be gone within the year. Dead. Because she was pregnant.

"You guys . . . had sex."

It was a rude comment under any circumstances, and I couldn't believe it was the first thing to leave my mouth. But I had to know if it was Jay's. If it wasn't, he didn't need to be a part of this.

"Dude." Jay's cheeks reddened.

They'd definitely had sex.

Marna and Ginger converged on me, pushing Jay back, searching my face for answers.

"What is it?" Ginger asked.

"Yeah, you're freaking me out." Marna crossed her arms, and I forced myself to stop staring. When I looked up, I could feel the wetness of tears on my cheeks.

"I'm so sorry," I whispered.

I was scared to say it. Scared to put the words out there and make it real. A sob rose up in my chest and I covered my mouth again. Sweet Marna.

"Anna." Jay squeezed in and whispered to me, "Don't cry. We didn't plan for this. I know it's fast, and . . . I know Veronica's going to be hurt—"

"It's not that." I made a spontaneous decision. Jay needed to know what he'd gotten himself into. I gathered all the courage I had in me, trying not to cry harder.

"Marna." I took her hand. "You're pregnant."

The three of them stared at me. Ginger was the first to react. She grabbed my shirt in both fists and shook me, screaming, "*Shut up!* You shut your bloody mouth!"

Jay tried to pry her off me, and I grabbed her wrists, staring her in the eyes. "I'm sorry, Ginger."

She shoved me away like I'd burned her, and stumbled back into Jay's desk, looking rabid. Marna stood still with her eyes wide.

Jay glared at me. "This is not cool. Why would you say that?"

"She can't be," Ginger whimpered. "She had the surgery. We both did."

Jay's head swung toward her, a look of confusion on his face. I'd worry about him in a minute.

Right now, my mind searched for a possible answer. "We heal fast. Maybe the surgery corrected itself before it had a chance to take? But . . . I wonder why you never got pregnant before this?"

"Anna!" Oh, man. Jay looked appalled, and I couldn't blame him.

"I usually don't . . . ," Marna whispered. Her eyes were glazed when she looked up at me. "I do other things, if I can help it. You know . . . anything but?"

"A half-arsed worker, just like you," Ginger mumbled.

"What the hell are you guys talking about?" Jay sounded frustrated now.

Ginger ignored him and yelled, "This is stupid! You can't possibly know she's pregnant, Anna. She'd be less than a week!"

"I've always been able to sense it," I said. I opened my mouth to explain and became very aware of Jay's stare. He looked at me as if I were a stranger. "Jay," I whispered, "I have a lot to tell you."

"You're being weird, Anna. You've always been weird, but this ain't right."

My eyes watered again. His words hurt. I knew what it must sound like to him.

Ginger stepped up to Jay. "I need you to shut up and stay out of this while we figure it out. Then we'll all leave you alone and you won't have to see any of us *freaks* again."

His face scrunched in bafflement.

"Stop it, Gin!" Marna grabbed Jay's arm, and he wrapped it around her, glancing at our faces like he'd found himself in another dimension.

"I'm not going anywhere," Jay said. "I just want to know what's going on."

"I can sense a warmth," I said, pushing on despite the overwhelming awkward tension. "It's like an aura, but different. I can feel the extra life force—"

"It's a multicellular freaking zygote!" Ginger screamed. "Not a life force! Not a *soul*!"

"I didn't say . . . I meant, I just don't know." It was so hard to explain. "It's like . . . an extension of Marna, only a tiny, separate entity."

Ginger started pacing. "Oh, God. Oh, God. We need one of those morning-after pills."

Marna's eyes widened. "I'm not taking any pill!"

"An operation, then!"

Marna shook her head. "It doesn't work, Gin. You know that! Other Neph have tried it, and it kills them just the same."

Jay dropped his arm from Marna's shoulder and stepped back. I'd never seen him so freaked out. The twins kept arguing.

"Those other Neph couldn't have been as early on as you," Ginger reasoned. "If there's no soul in the thing yet, then you're safe. When do babies get their souls?"

Both sisters looked at me, and I shook my head. "I have no idea."

I knew souls were created in the heavenly realm, and the Maker knew every detail of our earthly lives and our purposes, starting from conception, but it was never specified at what part of the process the soul was embedded in the flesh.

"I'm not having an abortion," Marna said. "I don't care if there's a soul yet or not. I'm not having one."

"Why the hell not?" Ginger's voice reached an all-time high. She got in Marna's face. "Don't be an idiot! There could still be time!"

Marna blinked and tears streamed down her cheeks. "And I could die today! I'm not doing it!"

Jay and I stood watching, silent.

Ginger was shaking. Marna covered her mouth, her eyes spilling over as she sat on the bed.

"I'm . . . I'm going to have a baby, Gin," she whispered.

"You will be dead, Marna. *Dead!* You won't get to enjoy it. You can't be a mother!"

"But you can raise her and tell her about me—"

Ginger reeled back, scowling. "I don't want anything to do with this creature! And how will I raise your stupid baby when I'm working? Shall I ask Grandfather Astaroth to babysit?" She looked wildly around the room, then grabbed Marna's wrist. "We're going to a clinic. Now."

Ginger turned, and Marna twisted out of her grip. "I'm not going!"

A vicious, crazed scream tore from Ginger's lips. Marna

tried to reach for her, but Ginger slapped her hand away.

"Gin, please," Marna sobbed.

Ginger turned to me, and I froze. "You! Fix this. Pray."

"I am," I promised her. "But I don't get everything I ask for, Ginger."

"You're His little prodigy child, aren't you?"

"No. I don't have any more access than you or anyone else! Maybe we could all pray together?"

I reached for her hand, but she yanked it away.

"I am *not* praying. He let this happen! He bloody hates us!"

Ginger made a sound that broke my heart, and then reached for her keys and ran from the room. Marna covered her face. I pulled her to me and we hugged, both of us crying. My heart was in shreds.

"Give her some time," I whispered. "She just needs a minute to herself."

I glimpsed Jay backing himself against the wall. Marna and I pulled away and faced him. He didn't look scared anymore. He didn't look anything. Just kind of blank and pale, like it'd been too much for him and he'd shut down.

"Jay?" Marna whispered.

We didn't step any closer to him.

In a robotic voice, he asked, "Can you please tell me what's going on now?"

Marna and I looked at each other. She gave me a nod. I turned to Jay's guardian angel, half expecting him to shake his head, but he only watched me sadly.

"It's going to sound crazy," I told Jay. "Even worse than the conversation you just heard."

"It could not get any crazier. Just tell me."

I took a deep breath. "There are angels on earth, Jay. And demons, too."

He didn't move.

"Most of them are in spirit form, and you can't see them," I continued. "But twelve of the demons are in human bodies. They're called the Dukes."

I looked at Marna's pinched face, and she nodded for me to keep going. Jay was still in zombie mode.

"Our fathers are two of the Dukes," I whispered. "Same with Kai, and Kope, and Blake. We're children of demons."

No reaction whatsoever.

"We're called Nephilim," Marna said. "But we usually just say Neph."

Still he was unresponsive, eyes glazed. Marna looked worried.

"We can prove it to you," I said. "Come with me. We'll leave our cell phones here. Marna, you stay and listen, okay?"

She nodded. I motioned for Jay to follow, and he did. We got into my car and drove down the street, almost a mile away. I felt his eyes boring into the side of my face the whole time. I stopped the car and parked.

"Tell me something nobody else knows," I said softly. "When we get back to your room, Marna will tell us what you said, because she can hear us right now."

"How can she hear us?"

"We have supernatural abilities—heightened senses."

At first I didn't think he'd play along. His eyes widened, but he was silent.

"Uh . . ." He finally spoke, and his voice came out quiet and dry. "Okay. I used to dream of Marna when I was with Veronica. I always woke up feeling guilty, but I couldn't help it. And I'm pretty sure I'm still dreaming now. Only it's not such a good dream anymore."

Oh, Jay.

"I know this is a lot to take in. I only found out when I was sixteen, and it's still hard for me."

He looked at me now, really looked at me.

"Angels and demons aren't real, Anna. They can't be."

"They are," I whispered.

He stared at me. "I just don't get it. You're both *sweet*. How can you be . . . part demon?"

"We have urges, Jay. Worse than any human could understand."

"Urges." He continued to study me.

"Drugs and alcohol for me." He sort of swayed backward as understanding rocked him. I kept going. "The twins deal with adultery—cheating. We're meant to hurt people."

His brown eyes swelled while he pieced everything together. "The night I was deejaying . . . New Year's Eve . . . when we . . ."

"Yeah," I said. "She saw a bond between you and Roni. There were demon spirits watching, and she worked on you, but she liked you. Genuinely. And it says a lot that she loves you, now, completely single."

"She really loves me?"

"The twins can see bonds. Ginger saw love between the two of you today."

Poor Jay. He looked so overwhelmed. His eyes shot to mine again.

"Is Patti . . . ?"

"No." I shook my head. "She's human. All the other Neph were raised by their fathers and Neph siblings, but my dad was in prison and I don't have siblings."

"What about all the mothers?" he asked.

I swallowed hard, feeling the burn behind my eyes again. I had to catch my breath.

"They all died during childbirth, Jay." My eyes held his, waiting for the terrible moment when he'd understand. "Earthly bodies aren't made to be able to release a Nephilim soul."

"Even . . ." He stared down the street in the direction of his house.

"Even Marna," I whispered.

"That's why her sister's so upset."

I watched Jay grow up in that moment. He sat up straighter, and his eyes cleared. He wore an expression of bravery. It was a sad and beautiful thing to see him so serious.

"Take me back to her," he said.

I turned us around and did just that. He leaped from the car when I pulled into the driveway, and ran into his house. When I got to his room I found them sitting on the bed, Jay holding her, letting her cry into his chest until she quieted.

"You dreamed of me?" she whispered.

"Yes." He kissed her forehead.

Marna gazed up at him. "I can see that you're afraid. But happy. Me, too."

"You can see it?" he asked.

She pulled back and ran her fingers through the haze at his chest. "Your aura."

Jay shot me a questioning look.

"We see emotions as colors," I explained.

"Anna can feel them, as well," Marna added. "She's different from the rest of us."

Jay raised his eyebrows, and I shrugged. He came forward and hugged me more gently than normal, like I was fragile. I squeezed him until he squeezed me back. I didn't want him to treat me differently.

He pulled away and stared down at me as if seeing me for the first time. "All along . . . you could always see this stuff? And you had, like, superpowers?"

I dropped my eyes. The heightened senses had been a struggle for me. "It's not as cool as it sounds. I've always hated it, and I'm still not so good at it."

"And Kai!" Jay's eyes widened. "*Duuuude* . . ."

"Yeah," I said.

"It's all making sense now."

He sat on the bed next to Marna again. Their hands immediately linked. "So, what makes you different from them?" he asked me.

"Their mothers were all human. My mother was a guardian angel. That's why I can see the pregnancy when other Neph and the Dukes can't. It's an angel ability."

"Nuh-uh." I saw in his eyes that his perception of me fully changed in that moment, from the silly, strange Anna he'd once known to an Anna who elicited awe. "So, your mom was an angel, but your dad's a demon?"

"It's complicated. They knew each other in heaven, before he became a demon."

Jay stared at me.

"I'm still just me," I promised him.

"No . . . you're more."

I shrugged again, embarrassed by the attention.

"And wait," he said. "There's really guardian angels? Here on earth?"

"Yes," Marna said. "All humans have them."

Jay got still. "I have one?"

Marna and I nodded, and then giggled as Jay's head swiveled side to side, searching.

"You can't see him!" I said.

"No way! No way!" He jumped up and spun now, looking right past his guardian angel, who stared down at him with a look of mirth on his celestial, misty face.

"I think he's laughing at you," I said. Marna giggled and nodded.

Jay went into spaz mode. "For real? I got a cool angel with a sense of humor!"

"He loves you," I told him. "He's always watching over you."

"Like . . . as in, *always* always?" His eyebrows went up. Marna giggled again.

"Yep," I said.

"Oh, man. This is crazy." His face paled, and he started babbling. "Holy crap. Demons. What do they do, exactly? Never mind. I probably don't wanna know. I knew there was something messed up about your dad, but dang."

I didn't want to talk about our fathers. Jay would learn soon enough about the demons. He'd have to know everything he was getting himself into. Even mentioning the demons gave me the creeps. Dark thoughts raced through my mind, followed closely by a tumbleweed of emotions.

Jay was in danger.

Marna had less than forty weeks to live.

If the Dukes or whisperers found out about this baby, the child would be killed.

I pressed a hand to my chest. What were we going to do?

"You all right, Anna?" Jay asked.

I nodded and shot him a quick smile. "Yeah."

"Do you think your sister's okay?" Jay asked Marna.

Marna's face darkened. "I've never seen her that upset. She's always been protective of me, but this isn't something she can save me from. I know she feels like the world is ending, but if I give her a little time and space, maybe she'll be okay. . . ."

Marna met my eyes, and I could see we both knew. Ginger, the mama bear, would be wrecked by the loss of her twin. I couldn't imagine the world without Marna, so I couldn't begin to understand how it felt for Ginger.

"I'll talk to my dad and ask what he thinks we should do."

Jay jumped to his feet, a terrified look in his eyes. "You can't tell him!"

"Her dad is good," Marna explained.

We spent the next hour explaining everything to Jay. From meeting Kai, to my parents' story, to the Great Purge when demons killed all the Neph, to Sister Ruth and the prophecy that said I'd rid the earth of demons. By the time I got to the

64

events on the island, Jay looked ill.

"Is there anywhere I can take the baby to be safe?"

Those words made me dive forward and hug him, getting choked up.

"Oh, my gosh. You're going to be such a good daddy."

I heard Marna sniffle.

"You'll take good care of the baby, Jay," she said.

We were a mess. I wiped my eyes and thought.

"We took Zania to a convent. What about a church? Demons avoid places where two or more people convene in prayer."

"I'm on it," Jay said. "I'll contact every church I can find and see if they have something, like a room to rent or a basement, or *anything*. I don't know. I'll figure out something."

Marna beamed up at him.

"It'll be okay," he said to her. He sounded strong and sure.

He sounded in love.

CHAPTER SIX

LIE DETECTOR

Like every other night in the hotels, I couldn't sleep well. I spent a lot of time begging for peace and clarity, and now I had the Marna situation on my mind, too. I couldn't think too hard about losing her. I just couldn't. I wanted so badly to talk to Kai about it, but for all I knew he was flanked by whisperers at any given time.

I wanted to cry with relief that night when I received a text from my father.

Where are you?

I gave him the name of the hotel and the city: *Marietta, Georgia.*

I waited, but he didn't respond. After an hour I was starting to get worried, and considered leaving the hotel in case someone else had gotten ahold of my father's phone. Just as I was shoving stuff into my bag, I heard a familiar, gritty voice in my head.

"Greetings, daughter of Belial."

I'd gotten good at controlling my reactions, even while my innards liquefied with fright.

"Azael," I responded telepathically.

He peered down at me, his heavy feline features fixed in an intense glare. My pulse slowed as I watched our spirit ally, but my nerves were still shot as I waited to hear his news.

"You will have Nephilim visitors. Be careful what you say."

Neph visitors? Oh, heck no. I shoved the last of my things into the bag and ran to the door as Azael flew away. I lost my cool, letting out a scream when I swung the door open and found two people standing there—a young girl with dark, slicked-back hair, and a blond man with sharp cheekbones and icy eyes. Both had black badges at their sternums.

"Going somewhere?" the girl asked in a high-pitched voice, her accent replacing *w* sounds with *v*'s and rolling her *r*'s. Her identity hit me with a sickening slap.

Caterina. Daughter of Jezebet, the Duke of Lies.

I fought to control my breathing. Caterina may have looked young and harmless, but I knew better. Up close, the evil glint in her eyes made my stomach turn. She had no idea I'd been hiding under the dock on Duke Melchom's private island. She had no idea I had witnessed the part she'd played in the death of Flynn. She was the one who'd told the Dukes he was lying.

"What do you want?" I asked.

"We aren't here to hurt you." The man's accent was thick

and European, sounding something like Russian to my untrained ear.

"Who are you?" I asked.

"I am Marek, son of Shax. From Czech Republic." Son of the Duke of Theft. I held the shoulder strap of my bag a little tighter as he continued. "And this is Caterina, daughter of Jezebet, from Romania."

He smiled warmly. She didn't.

"What do you guys want?" I asked again.

I had to be careful, just as Azael had said. Caterina could sense lies and she was absolutely no friend to fellow Neph.

"We just want to talk," Marek said, never losing the pleasant smile. "May we come in?"

I remembered back to last week when I'd seen Dad in L.A. He'd mentioned looking into the possibility of the son of Shax being an ally. That made me feel slightly better . . . but only a smidge. For a possible ally, he didn't keep very good company.

"I was just leaving. We can talk outside."

The last thing I wanted was to be stuck in a room with them. I felt the light weight of the knife in my pocket, though I didn't like the two-against-one odds.

They crowded the doorway, but I pushed my way out. The door was almost closed behind me when Caterina slapped her tiny palm to my chest.

"We prefer to speak in the room," she said.

I smacked her hand away on instinct and yanked the door shut.

"Sorry, but I prefer to speak outside."

"You are not sorry," she scoffed.

Dang it. Stupid lie detector. I'd have to watch every word I said around her.

"Fine. I'm not sorry."

"It's all right, Caterina." Marek smiled at me. "You can hardly blame her for being cautious, yes?"

He gave her a look that said something along the lines of *Chill out, you're scaring her.* She rolled her eyes and started moving to the exit door down the hall. She looked like a soldier the way she marched in her black pants and stiff button-up white shirt.

"Come on then," she called brusquely.

Marek shot me an apologetic glance and gestured for me to go next. I went, looking over my shoulder at him several times with distrust. I had the hilt inside my bag since I was wearing shorts, and I wasn't letting his stealthy hands anywhere near it.

When I slowed near the door, Marek bumped me from behind and I let out a little screech, turning on him. He kept a hand on my shoulder to steady himself, and I had to shove him away with an elbow.

"My apologies," he said, all innocence. He slipped his hands into his pockets and nodded down at the paper outside someone's hotel-room door. The caption was about a huge pawnshop robbery in Atlanta. "The headline caught my attention."

Not knowing whether or not to believe him, I pulled the bag around from my back to my chest as I pushed through the doors. I felt the shape of the hilt through the bottom of the bag and breathed a sigh of relief.

Outside it was dark, but the air still held the heaviness of the day's heat and humidity. I didn't walk to my car, opting instead to stand in a patch of grass at the side of the hotel, away from prying eyes. I faced them with my stance wide, sliding the book bag onto both shoulders in case I had to fight, which I prayed I wouldn't.

"Strange things are happening," crooned Caterina. "Would you not agree?"

I kept my hands loose at my sides, prepared. "You have one more chance to tell me why you're here before I leave."

She narrowed her beady dark eyes at me, and Marek stepped forward to speak.

"We have a few questions, daughter of Belial. That is all."

"Questions from you? Or questions someone sent you to ask?"

I was losing patience, feeling overly anxious.

"Are you a virgin?" Caterina blurted.

Great.

"Okay, so something you've been sent to ask," I said.

She smiled, a malicious show of teeth. Dread pooled in my belly.

Marek glowered down at Caterina.

"I'm not answering your questions," I said. "I don't trust you."

Her smile was one of genuine amusement this time. "It's true—you don't trust me. But evading questions is almost always a sign of guilt."

"Almost," Marek pointed out, speaking to Caterina. "But not always. You've cornered her like an animal, and she obviously feels threatened."

"If you can do better, do it yourself!"

The look she gave him was frightening. He had over a foot of height on her, but she stared at him as if she could take him down one-handed.

"Forget it!" I yelled. "It's bad enough I have to deal with whisperers following me around. I'm not dealing with a couple of Neph, too. I'm out of here."

I turned for the parking lot, walking fast.

"We are not finished!" Caterina spat.

Marek said something to her in a different language, using a scolding tone, and she responded in kind. I heard them following me, and I was shaking by the time I got to my car. I reached into the stretchy side pouch of my bag for the keys.

They were gone.

A jingle sounded behind me. In a flash I dug my knife out of my pocket, slid it open, and turned, jutting it out.

Marek and Caterina were five feet away, at the back of my car. He dangled my keys in front of him, a pleading look on his face. How the heck had he taken them? Freaking magician!

Caterina's eyes widened at the sight of my knife.

"Give me my keys," I said.

Marek spoke calmly. "I will, but I had to be sure you would speak to us before you left."

"Throw them to me," I demanded.

Caterina crossed her arms. "Not until you answer our questions. If you prefer not to speak with us, I'm certain the sons of Thamuz would be more than happy to pay you a visit."

The mention of the sons of Thamuz made me dizzy with fear. Thamuz was the Duke of Murder, and I knew their methods of extracting information. They'd broken sweet Marna when she was still just a child, hurting her in unthinkable ways until she opened herself to seeing the demon whisperers.

A knowing smile lit up Caterina's face. "I see you know of them. Do you know what they do for a living, daughter of Belial? They assist in kidnapping-for-ransom heists in South America."

I had to shut her up before she said another word about those two psychos.

"I don't appreciate you showing up unannounced. I don't answer to you or any other Neph. I do what my father tells me. He's not the kind of Duke you want to cross, so I suggest you give me my keys and leave me alone."

Caterina began to laugh but quickly stopped when she saw Marek toss the keys to my free hand. She gave him a disbelieving look.

"She hasn't answered our questions!"

"And she won't now that you've treated her as our enemy."

I pitied Marek. I'd hate to have to deal with the enraged mini-vamp girl.

I hit the Unlock button, opened the door, and threw my bag in.

"Good luck," I said to Marek before I quickly slipped in, locked the doors, and cranked the engine on.

"Wait!" he yelled, grabbing the door handle. His face looked panicked. "Don't leave yet!"

What did he expect when he threw me the keys? Caterina made a run for the front of the car to block me, but I hit the accelerator and she jumped back as I sped away. They'd have hell to pay with the Dukes for letting me go.

At the first stoplight I opened the bag and felt around until the hilt was in my hand, then I breathed a sigh of relief. I texted Dad with my information code: *A411*. I tried to keep my hearing around the two Neph, but they were both silent, and I wasn't great at following sounds of cars when other cars were around. Just to be safe, I kept driving for the next three hours until my body demanded rest.

I pulled into the back of a supermart's parking lot and used my backpack as a pillow. I never heard back from Dad. That night, I fell asleep haunted by the look of regret in Marek's eyes as I sped away. What did he regret, exactly? Was he an ally or a foe? I didn't know, but I intended to find out.

CHAPTER SEVEN

JAY'S FUTURE

I was certifiably grumpy when I woke in the car the next morning. If those restless moments of dozing could be considered sleeping.

I texted Patti first thing. *U ok?*

Yes. You?

Fine, I texted back.

We said nothing more, and I deleted the conversation from my phone, wishing it was safe to tell her I loved her. I would have given anything to sit out on our balcony with her this morning, sipping coffee like we used to, discussing college plans and other normal things.

I texted Dad again.

He never responded, which made me antsier. I felt stuck in limbo and I didn't know what my next move should be. I decided to swing by our apartment in Cartersville to check the mail. It probably wasn't the smartest move, but I tried to be careful. I stopped as I neared the neighborhood and did surveillance. No strange cars or people. I pushed my hearing into the apartment. The place was silent, but I wouldn't be going in. I got the mail and left as quickly as I could.

I drove to Jay's house and sorted through the envelopes as I sat parked in his driveway. I was glad I'd gotten the mail, because there were things from Virginia—information about checking into campus housing at Virginia Tech, and letters from the bank and realtor about Patti's new house in the small town of Riner. I shoved everything into my backpack, slung it over one shoulder with a quick glance for whisperers, and walked into Jay's house.

His parents were at work, and I could hear clicking on a keyboard in his room. The door was open, so I knocked and peeked in.

"Hey," I said.

He tried to smile, but he looked stressed. "I think I found something, but I don't really know what I'm doing. I—"

I put a finger to my lips and motioned toward a pen on his desk. He picked it up and wrote in messy handwriting, *There's a church in Atlanta that needs a night janitor and they offer lodging.*

Janitor? I wrote.

He shrugged, seeming so much more unsure of himself than usual. He bent over the page and scratched out another message. *I'll have to give up DJ stuff at nights, but I don't know what else to do. I can get one of those carrier things for when I'm sweeping and stuff.*

I underlined *carrier things* and put a question mark.

He pointed at the computer screen full of different baby carriers, and tears of surprise sprang into my eyes.

"Aw, come on," he said softly. "Don't do that."

I wiped my eyes dry. So many things ran through my mind that I wanted to say: How proud I was of him. How awful this situation was, and how sorry I was that it was happening. But none of that was necessary with Jay. Though a navy blue stream of sadness and gray worry ran steadily through the underbelly of his aura, the rest was a pastel swirl of pink love.

Jay was going to be a daddy. Despite his trepidations, he was being proactive about it. The thought of anything happening to him scared me to death. It wasn't safe for him or the baby to be in Atlanta, but I hated asking him to leave the place he'd always known as home.

I took the pen. *Would you consider moving to a place where there are no Dukes?*

He didn't immediately refuse, like I thought he might.

You mean Virginia, with you?

Hm, there was a thought, but I shook my head. *I have to live on my own, but maybe you could be nearby?* A lightbulb went off, and I wrote faster. *Maybe you could live with Patti! Or near her. You could help each other, and you'd only be a town away from me.*

The idea grew on me as I stood there thinking about it, and a grin spread across Jay's face.

Patti's awesome. I'm okay with it if you think she'll agree.

I'm sure she will! She needed someone to mother, and she hated being alone.

We both smiled. Maybe this could work. I leaned over to write more.

She and I are leaving soon, but you wouldn't have to come right away. You have some time before . . .

Our smiles vanished and we both looked down. One thought hovered over us.

Marna.

Jay's jaw tensed as he slowly wrote. *I swear I had no idea. If I knew what could happen—*

I took the pen from his hand. *I know. We all know.*

Not her sister. She hates me.

I shook my head. *It has nothing to do with you. She doesn't think she can live without Marna.*

My heart twisted every time I thought about the broken look on Ginger's face when the truth sank in. Ginger, who'd always been so strong.

Everything was changing.

It was time for me to leave. *I'm going to give you Patti's number and I want you to get in touch with her. Things are starting to happen. I'm under investigation, and they're determined to bust me this time. I don't want to put you guys in danger, so I'm going to keep my distance.*

He looked worried as he wrote, *I wish there was something I could do.*

Knowing Patti has you to lean on will be helping me more than you know. I gave him a hug and was about to leave when his phone went off.

He showed me the screen, which said *Marna*.

I zoomed my hearing toward the earpiece as he answered.

77

"Jay?" Marna's voice held a thinly veiled panic. "Have you seen my sister?"

His eyes darted to me as he shook his head. "No."

I held my hand out and he said, "Here, talk to Anna real quick."

"What's going on?" I asked her.

"She wasn't here in New York when I arrived, and she missed our flight back to England, so I made an excuse to miss it, too. Now we're both on probation with the airline. But I can't find her!" Marna sniffled.

Crap. We shouldn't even be having this conversation over the phone. I felt fairly certain that creepy Caterina had left the area, but anyone could be listening. Even coming to see Jay one last time wasn't smart.

"Okay, don't panic. She couldn't have gone far. She wouldn't leave you."

"Do you think she was taken? Oh, God—" She let out a sob.

"No . . . I don't think that." My mind went straight to the one person in the world Ginger cared for other than Marna. "What about . . . ?"

California. Blake.

Marna got quiet. "That would be royally stupid."

Now we were both quiet. It would be dangerous for Ginger to abandon work to see Blake, especially when he was right in the middle of one of his biggest assignments—planning a grand-scale wedding with the gorgeous Michelle to provoke the envy of many.

"Oh, no." Marna whispered my exact thoughts.

That was exactly where Ginger had gone.

"I have to go get her!" Marna said.

"No," I told her. "You get back to work. She probably just needs a day or two to get past this and she'll come back."

"What if she doesn't?" she whispered.

"Then we'll have to intervene. But I think between the two of them they have enough sense of self-preservation to work it out."

Blake wouldn't let her stay long. We had to trust them to be smart. I'd get ahold of Kai and ask him to drag Ginger away if I had to, although I really didn't want him involved.

We hung up and Jay bear-hugged me. As we released, a dark blotch appeared on his wall and slowly grew. I felt paralyzed as the dark spirit flew into the room, an ugly face I didn't recognize. It looked back and forth between us. Jay's angel darted between him and the spirit.

A million thoughts ran through my head—the notes we'd written to each other were sitting right on the desk, and there were freaking baby carriers on his computer. Thankfully Jay was blocking it, but I needed to get the whisperer away. I reached into my pocket and pulled out a wad of cash, handing it to Jay.

"Use this toward the keg," I told him.

His eyebrows went together and I smiled big.

"Uh, yeah. Sure." Bless him for playing along.

"See you at the party!" I said, before turning to leave. Just as I'd hoped, the spirit followed me into the hall, and I was so relieved I winked at the ugly thing. It gave me a suspicious look before flying ahead of me, gruesome wings spanning through the walls of the hallway, until it was out of sight.

At the car I texted Jay. *Destroy notes. Delete msg. Get P and go. Stuff in mailbox.*

Hopefully he'd have a chance to say good-bye to his parents, though I had no clue how he'd explain such a sudden move. He'd figure it out. Poor Jay. I deleted the message from my phone's memory and pulled Patti's new housing information from the backpack. With a quick scan of the skies, I stuffed the fat envelope into Jay's mailbox, then got into my car, kicking up gravel as I got the heck out of town.

When you start to live outside yourself,
it's all dangerous.

—*Ernest Hemingway,* The Garden of Eden

CHAPTER EIGHT

TAKING THE INITIATIVE

I drove up the interstate feeling tired of hiding and evading—tired of doing nothing.

Dad was nowhere to be found. The fact that he hadn't responded or shown his face was bad news. He could be chained in hell for all I knew—a thought that made my confidence and hope threaten to slip away.

I'd always relied on his advice. His inside knowledge. Now I just felt useless and timid. So, what would Dad want me to do if he were here?

It was time to take the initiative. The first thing that came to mind was Marek, the son of Shax. Was he or was he not an ally? With a sense of resolve, I decided it was time to find out.

He could still be in the U.S., or he could be back in Europe. Was I willing to fly to the Czech Republic to find him?

Yes.

What I needed was more information. An address or phone number to reach him. Who had Neph or Duke contacts that I could trust?

Kopano. His brothers still lived in Africa with Duke Alocer. Maybe they could get their hands on some information for me.

I pulled into a rest area in North Carolina, parking as far as possible from the other people—families traveling on their summer vacations.

Dad had warned me over and over that phone lines weren't safe, despite his military-grade equipment and all the fancy technology he used. At moments like this, I just had to trust in the precautions he'd made for us and hope for the best.

I dialed Kope. He answered quickly, sounding worried, probably because I hadn't called him in ages.

"Are you all right?" It was good to hear his soothing voice.

"Yes. But I need some help." I took a deep breath and rehashed the story of Marek and Caterina's visit, and how I wanted to track him down.

"Let me make a call. I will be in touch."

I hung up, loving his willingness to jump right in without argument. I got back on the road, not wanting to stop for too long. He called back half an hour later.

"I have his number. I will text it to you."

I smiled. "You freaking rock, Kope."

"I am flying down to accompany you."

Oh, no.

"You don't have to do that. I know after last time you said . . ." He'd said he couldn't travel on missions with me anymore after what happened between us that winter, and the subsequent jealous rage from Kaidan. But saying it out loud felt too uncomfortable.

"That was a long time ago, Anna. Much has changed."

"I'm not afraid of Marek. He didn't seem very threatening—"

"He is with the sons of Thamuz. And the daughter of Jezebet."

"Oh." Icy fear slithered up my spine. That changed things. "Do you know where they are?"

"Moving north, as are you, according to the last whisperer who spotted you."

Creepy-crawly sensations pricked my skin.

"How do you know all this?"

"Father told my brothers they are to be prepared to help search for you, if necessary. The Dukes are using Neph to hunt for suspicious persons. I believe they hope that by putting Neph together they will be able to draw out which ones are guilty and innocent."

That made sense since Neph were naturally wary of one another. I looked up at the next exit sign.

"I'm at Mooresville, North Carolina, off I-77. I'm going to text Marek and see if he can meet me alone."

"No!" The alarm in his voice made me wonder how stupid I was being. My gut told me I wasn't in danger from Marek, but what if I were wrong?

"I promise I won't do anything crazy. I'll try to find a hotel with a bottom-floor room that has a sliding door I can exit through if he tries to bring anyone."

"Anna—"

"Kope, I feel like we're running out of time. I'll be careful."

"I do not like this."

"Neither do I, but I have to do something. I'll call you as soon as I've met with him. Promise."

Kope was quiet for a long while before he asked, "Do you have your knives?"

I patted my pockets. "Yes."

"Do not let down your guard. Even if he claims to be an ally. The others will be near."

"Okay."

We said our good-byes, and I felt bad for stressing him. I drove around Mooresville, which turned out to be NASCAR city, until I found a hotel with what I had in mind. Then I texted Marek.

Can u meet me alone? —Daughter of B.

My heart raced and I doubted my own sanity.

His response came too fast. *Yes. Where are you?*

My thumbs hovered over the letters, hesitant. *Where are you?* I countered.

His response this time took longer. *Blythewood, SC.*

I did a quick search. They were an hour and a half away.

With a deep breath and a prayer, I texted him my location. Then I headed to the gigantic outdoorsman store. I'd never before considered purchasing a gun, but I was scared enough to do so now. The line at the gun counter was outrageously long, and the background-check stuff would probably be time-consuming as well. Instead, I browsed the knives counter and other weapons until something caught my interest—a stun gun disguised as a flashlight.

It was dark out by the time I left the store with a fully charged stun gun and a slick new pocketknife. Super sharp and quick to open. Then I settled into my hotel room for the wait. I stared out through my sliding glass door at the parking lot with my hands in my pockets, turning my knives over and over. I decided not to wear the hilt on me. If it came down to a fight, I didn't want Marek discovering it. I'd stuffed the hilt between the mattresses as far as my arm could stretch.

An hour and a half had passed. They'd be in town by now. I was pacing and listening hard when a text from Marek came.

Cannot meet alone.

Alarms sounded in my brain.

Forget it then, I responded.

Later tonight?

I thought about it. If he wanted to trap me, he could've come straight to the hotel with the others. Maybe he really was an ally, and he couldn't lose the three Neph. As much as I didn't want to stay in town knowing that Caterina and the sons of Thamuz were nearby, I was also desperate enough to have another strong Neph on our side.

Fine, I texted, deleting our messages. And the wait began.

I couldn't relax. All I could do was stare out the window at the people coming and going from the parking lot. My extended hearing surrounded the hotel's entrance, and it took complete concentration to keep it there and make sense of what people were saying.

An hour after my texts with Marek, something caught my attention in the lobby. A preteen-sounding girl said, "That creepy guy bumped me and didn't even say sorry."

A woman, presumably her mother, responded with a terse whisper. "Stay away from that man. I don't like the look of him."

My heart flew to my throat and I fell to my knees next to the bed. I shoved my arm between the mattresses until I felt the hilt. My instincts were screaming for me to get out of there. Shoving the hilt into my backpack, I ran to the door and stuck my head out. Sure enough, at the end of the hall was a wiry-looking man with black hair pulled in a low ponytail. At his sternum was a black starburst. It grew when he saw me, and he smiled.

I slammed the door and locked it, then ran for the patio door. As soon as I slid it open, a tanned hand gripped the edge. Half a scream escaped my mouth before his hand barreled down in a hard slap across my face. Blood covered my tongue and I stumbled to the side long enough for him to shut the back door. My bookbag fell off, but I had no time to worry about it.

Ignoring the pulsing pain in my mouth, I shoved a hand into my pocket. My reflexes must have been slowed from the slap, but his were fast. He grabbed my wrist and twisted it behind my back, ripping an agonizing screech from my throat, which was quickly muffled by his hand. He did all this while moving us toward the door as I struggled like mad. For a short, slender guy, he was strong. He held me against him as he walked, taking my kicks to his shins like they were nothing, his hand clamped too hard around my mouth for me to open it and bite him.

As he released my mouth to unlock the door, he yanked up on my twisted wrist and I sucked in a breath, ready to shriek again. In a heartbeat he had the door unlocked and his hand was clamped back over my mouth and jaw, muffling my scream. His brother pushed his way in. They moved fast and fluidly. I went ballistic.

In a fit of terror I threw my head back and butted his nose. I heard the crack and he yelled, letting me go long enough for my hand to plunge into my pocket and pull out my knife, since I couldn't reach the stun gun. My blade came out and my arm began slashing. I felt the steel connecting with flesh over and over, and saw the blood, but they never backed away or gave me an inch to run. Within seconds the knife was extracted from my hand and my arms were pinned behind my back.

One of them chuckled, and that was when hysteria set in. I remembered what Caterina had told me about the sons of Thamuz's kidnapping involvement. They were pros at this. I never stopped struggling, but it seemed useless and I was tiring. I'd have to do more than physically fight them. I had to use my brain, too.

My self-defense instructors held me tightly, but it was always apparent that they didn't want to hurt me. The sons of Thamuz had no reservations. I felt their fingers digging, bruising, scratching. When I fought, they fought—punching, smacking, kicking, yanking hair. They took pleasure in my sounds of pain. They never ceased smiling, their eyes shining with zeal.

When my struggling slowed, I was shoved face-first onto the bed, on my stomach, and both men held me down. My body was spent. I was sweating and whimpering, because even in my beat-up, nearly passed-out state, I still had enough sense to be scared for my life.

"What do you want?" I managed to ask between panting breaths.

"We're taking you on a li'l trip, *chica*," one of them said close to my ear.

They would bring me to the Dukes. Pharzuph would smell me. My instructors always warned me never to let myself be taken to the second location. My thrashing began anew as my brain flared with panic. All I needed was to get my hand to my other pocket. Just a few inches . . .

One of them grabbed my hair and shoved my face into the mattress so hard I couldn't breathe. The other beat me with a round of punches to my shoulders and back. I screamed into the mattress as his fist connected to my shoulder blade with a crack.

Dear God. I'd never felt anything like it. My whole body tensed with shock as searing pain lanced through my shoulder. I couldn't take in a breath with my face smothered against the bed. I thought surely I was dreaming it when my head was released and the weight from the man behind me suddenly lifted. I rolled, dazed, and pain bolted through my upper back.

For one fleeting moment I thought I was imagining the scene before me through clouded eyes.

A third man was in the room, and he was fighting the two Neph. He wore all black, including a face mask and black gloves. The way he moved and the shape of his body were familiar to me.

Kopano. My head swam with gratitude.

I'd never seen him fully unleash his wrath until now. The sons of Thamuz stood no chance. He must have managed to sneak in and get the drop on them while they were in their bloodlust over me, because they both seemed disoriented, trying and failing to escape from his fists. Kope threw one of them to the floor and was whaling on him when the other reached into his pocket. I saw the flash of silver, and I was on my feet despite my body's protests.

I grasped the stun gun protruding from my pocket and shoved it into the guy's rib cage as I pressed the button. A high-pitched snarl escaped him as the jolt of electricity zapped through his nervous system. He fell to the ground as if paralyzed. I turned to Kope and nearly vomited at the sight of so much blood.

My sweet friend was lost to the beast of wrath.

"Stop!"

I stumbled to his side, trying to avoid the fast swing of his elbows. I didn't want to say his name, because even if the other two had noticed his badge, they hadn't seen his face.

"Stop it!" I grabbed the back of his neck from behind and stumbled forward, righting myself with my other hand on his big, moving shoulder. "*Stop!* We have to go!" I shook him hard.

The combination of my touch and my voice made him still. A strangled groan left his throat as he took in the sight of the bloodied man beneath him, barely alive. From the corner of my eye I saw his brother stirring, trying to sit up.

"Come on," I whispered to Kope. My vision became spotty. He caught me just as I was about to fall. I blinked until the room came back into focus. "My bag. Let's go."

The two of us exited through the back sliding door. I pointed to my car, which was blessedly right outside the room, and he led me to the passenger side. He then got behind the wheel, squealed tires out of the parking lot, and ripped the mask from his face.

"Thank you," I whispered once we were miles away. I worked hard to focus and not pass out. I leaned against the door because when my shoulder touched the seat I wanted to cry in agony.

"I am sorry you had to see that."

"It's okay," I whispered.

"You were being suffocated. And then when I saw him hitting you . . ."

"You did good. I'm so thankful you came. I should have never tried to do it alone." I winced when we hit a bump in the road.

"Do you need a doctor?"

"No." Even if something were broken, going to a doctor was too risky in numerous ways. I hated taking medicine, because something as simple as aspirin made my body long for more. In this case I'd have to make an exception. "I need ibuprofen."

Kope stopped at a drugstore in the next town. We used napkins and wet wipes from my car to clean his hands. He fed me four painkillers every half hour as we drove north. He also got bandages for the cuts on his hands, though they healed fast.

"What happened with Marek?" Kope asked.

I closed my eyes and rehashed the story.

"Do you think he set you up?"

"No. I don't know. Why would he have bothered to tell me he couldn't meet me alone? He could have just sent them to ambush me unexpectedly in the first place."

"But how did the sons of Thamuz know you were there? Perhaps they are using Marek to earn your trust and deceive you."

That was a depressing thought.

"Maybe," I admitted. "Or maybe they saw the texts somehow. Or maybe they scouted for me on their own. Either way—"

"Down!" Kope hollered.

I held in a wail of anguish as I scrunched my body down, out of sight.

"A dark one. It's gone now."

I stayed down, gritting my teeth. "Did it see you?"

"No. It was flying in the other direction."

I slowly sat up. "Where are we going?"

"I will leave from Roanoke airport."

"Virginia?"

"Yes. But not until you are well enough. Where shall I take you?"

I had no clue. "Just . . . take me to the airport with you. I'll find somewhere to go after that. I'm already feeling a little better."

I felt the brief warmth of his hand touch my shoulder blade.

"It's swollen," he said with worry.

It still hurt, but between my quick healing and the painkillers, each span of minutes was increasingly better. "I'll be okay."

We passed Blacksburg, Virginia, on our way to the airport, and though the signs for Virginia Tech should have made me happy, they only served as reminders of how far removed I was from the world of humans.

"There's my college," I said quietly.

Kope made no reply other than a sad glance my way.

As we neared Roanoke, I wasn't 100 percent, but I was feeling more like myself.

"I wonder how Z is doing," I said.

And darned if a shy smile didn't fill his face.

"Your father found her a place in Boston. I do not know how he did it, but a nearby monastery agreed to rent a room."

I sat forward. "She's in Boston now? That's awesome!"

"Yes. She is . . . thriving away from her father and alcohol."

"And near you."

His badge thumped and he kept his eyes straight ahead on the road. He wet his lips, and I had the urge to ask if he'd used those lips on Zania yet. The thought made my face heat. Marna would have asked him, but he and I didn't have that kind of relationship, especially after he'd used those lips on *me*.

Our trip to Australia seemed like a million years ago, not a mere eight months.

"Well, I'm glad she's doing better, and I'm glad . . ." I rubbed my shoulder. "I'm glad she has you. And you have her."

He finally looked at me again, those hazel eyes searching mine. I hoped he saw the truth, that I wanted him to be happy.

"You like her a lot, don't you?" I asked.

"I like her very much, Anna." His words held enough passion to make me shiver.

When he looked back at the road, I smiled out my window. He may or may not have kissed her yet, but he definitely wanted to.

My pulse jumped at the sound of an incoming text message. I pulled my phone from my bag. The message was from Marek.

Cannot rid myself of Cat. Cannot locate two other companions. Not safe to meet.

My heart thumped as I tried to figure out his guilt or innocence. I read the text to Kope, and we pondered in silence. My angel side wanted so badly to trust him, but my demon side was shaking its head and telling me not to be stupid.

"I'm not going to answer him. And I won't contact him again."

"Good," Kope said.

It was after midnight when we got to the airport.

"Do you have a red-eye flight?" I asked.

"No. I leave at five, but it's better if we are not seen together."

"Yeah." I agreed, but I still felt a gaping loss at the thought of him leaving.

He parked at the curb and turned to me, the streetlamp catching a glint of green in his light eyes.

"You saved me. They were going to take me to the Dukes."

Or worse, depending on whether they could keep their murderous urges in check. I somehow doubted they'd have been punished for "accidentally" killing me.

"I had a terrible feeling after we spoke. I had to go to you."

"Thank you." Without thought, I reached across the seats to hug him. He pulled me close, careful of my shoulder. For one second I worried that this contact might spark his lustful side, but it didn't. He held me gently and let me go.

"Are you certain you are all right?" he asked.

"I'm better already. Maybe one more dose."

Kope shook four tablets into my hand and put the bottle in his pocket. I imagined begging him for the bottle, but he would never give in.

"Good-bye, Anna. Stay safe."

"You, too, Kope. Give Z my love. Miss you."

I hadn't really meant to say the last part, but it was true. He was my friend and I missed him. I was rewarded with a flash of his grin and dimple before he left me. Alone again.

CHAPTER NINE

KAIDAN OR THE WORLD

What now?

Still hadn't heard from Dad. Desperately wanted to talk to Kaidan. Was worried about Jay, Marna, Ginger, Blake, and Patti. And here I was driving aimlessly around Virginia.

A foolish part of me wanted to be near Patti and Jay, even if we couldn't actually be together.

I stopped for gas in a tiny town, admiring the view of the Blue Ridge Mountains against the deep blue night sky. The scenery was abruptly ruined as two vile winged beings flew down and circled the car, watching me. Crap. Ignoring them, I started the car and got back on I-81.

They would never leave me alone.

There would be no hiding or escaping from the whisperers. I was being watched and followed. I could try to find a church like Jay. But they'd still know where I was, and they'd send their human lackeys in after me. All I could do was try to stay one step ahead.

Even on the open roads, surrounded by immense earthly beauty, I felt trapped.

Where are you, Dad? What am I supposed to do now? My brilliant plan to speak with Marek had been a whopping failure.

I wouldn't cry, but my eyes burned and my breathing felt ragged.

The last thing Dad had advised, and all we Neph agreed to, was to pretend to work. Maybe that was what I should do. Instead of running and hiding, I could head to college. It was Dad's plan for my life. My next "duty station," where I'd put on a show of being a student while partying it up. Would it throw the Dukes off if I kept with the working charade instead of running and looking guilty? Anything was worth a try at this point.

I headed to Blacksburg, checking into a hotel since the dorms weren't open.

Dorms. College. Ha. It was all in my grasp, and yet it wasn't. I couldn't even be excited by the cute town or fun atmosphere.

I tossed and turned all night, sweating despite the blasting air conditioner. My whole body hurt, and I fought the urge to go out and buy more painkillers, worried I'd take more than I should. I woke at six a.m. from a dream that was blurred and faint.

The sheets were still tangled around my hips when the knock at the door came, and my heart rate rocketed. I disengaged myself from the blankets and grabbed the stun gun and knife from the nightstand. This hotel had no window or door through which to escape. My brain whirled.

Was it the sons of Thamuz? Kope had hurt one of them pretty badly—I couldn't imagine they'd be on the go already. Hotel staff wouldn't knock at the door this early. It had to be a Neph or Duke. Whisperers must have found me while I slept. Was it Marek and Caterina again? With great effort I forced my extended hearing outside the door and whispered, "Who is it?"

"Kaidan Rowe. Son of Pharzuph."

My breath stuck and my internal organs somersaulted. It was his voice. But why did he sound so formal? And what the heck was he doing here? I sprinted to the entrance—no peephole!

I stood in front of the door, shaking. "What do you want?"

"I need to speak with you. Open up."

Either it was really him, and something horrible was happening, or someone was doing a dang good impersonation.

"I'm not here to hurt you." He spoke softly, but his tone sounded dangerous.

I didn't want to be scared of Kaidan. My Kai. But instincts made me clutch the knife harder.

Swallowing down the moisture of emotion, I turned the doorknob. When I pulled the door open, my heart soared. It was definitely Kaidan, looking like he'd been up all night. His chin-length brown hair hung disheveled around a blast of bright blue eyes and a hardened face. Next to him, hovering with a malicious grin, was a whisperer.

I was confused, nervous, elated, sickened. He'd brought a whisperer straight to me . . . or perhaps the whisperer had led Kaidan. The human panty thief hadn't worked. Neither had Marek or Caterina or the sons of Thamuz. So the Dukes sent Kaidan. That fact made me relieved in one major sense—they must not be suspicious of him. He was safe, for now.

So, what was Kaidan's plan?

My pulse would not settle. Kaidan grabbed the edge of the door over my shoulder and stepped forward, moving us both into the room.

I realized I'd completely let down my guard when I felt his hand wrap around mine, successfully snapping my knife shut and slipping it into his own pocket. He gave the "flashlight" a funny look before pulling it from my grasp and dropping it to the floor. The door shut, and the whisperer pushed its way through it, watching as Kaidan backed me against the wall.

With the spirit watching, I had to pretend I didn't love him, just as he was doing, even if it hurt. In normal life I couldn't stomach lying. But where whisperers and Dukes were concerned, all bets were off.

I put my palms on Kaidan's chest and straightened my arms, giving him my fiercest look. His red starburst pumped.

"Back off, son of Pharzuph," I warned.

A predatory grin spread across his handsome face, and the repulsive whisperer sidled closer.

"I'm only here as a precaution," Kaidan crooned. "To be sure our little daughter of Belial is behaving properly." His voice sounded as it had during our first meetings—contemptuous and dark. It was so appropriate that they'd sent him, the

100

son of Lust, to make sure I wasn't a virgin. Letting my lust for him overcome me was something I could *not* do. If the heavenly hilt, the Sword of Righteousness, sensed any lack of purity of heart, it wouldn't allow me to wield it. I had to be angelic to use an angel relic.

"I heard you don't even like Neph girls," I countered.

He laughed, swishing hair from his eyes with a flick of his head and stepping forward again. "I don't. But I'm willing to make sacrifices for the greater evil."

I swallowed hard. He was convincing. Too convincing.

He's just putting on a show, I told myself.

"So, what are you saying?" I asked. "The Dukes don't think I'm working? Is that why they're sending every Neph to question me and fight me?"

His pause at my mention of other Neph was minuscule, but I knew him well enough to catch it.

"Just covering all the bases. They know you're pushing alcohol, but you weren't exactly a well-rounded worker at that summit, yeah?"

"That was a year and a half ago," I ground out. "I'm *very* well-rounded now."

"Prove it."

His mouth hit mine with a wave of warm, citrusy pheromones and his body pressed me to the wall. I'd forgotten about my shoulder blade until a dull crest of pain coursed through me, and I whimpered. I felt him hesitate, as if he might stop to ask what was wrong, but then he kept going.

I wanted to sink into the touch of him, but a disgusting gurgling purr sounded in my brain from the whisperer, who was watching way too closely. Kaidan broke from the kiss long enough to glare at the spirit.

"Bit of a turnoff when you do that," he told it. "Mind shutting up?" The whisperer snarled, and Kaidan was kissing me again—hard, firm kisses.

This was nothing like the making out we'd done at his apartment in L.A. He was all physical business now—nothing more. I trusted him, but my feelings wavered as clothes began to shed. He took his shirt off in one swift move. When he reached for my shirt, I wanted so badly to stop him because I wasn't wearing a bra. I forced myself not to protest or cover myself as he unceremoniously yanked the top over my head and kissed my mouth again, roughly, pure lust, our bare chests touching.

The desperate, self-conscious part of me wondered what he thought of my body. It was strange not to have him taking time to savor me like I knew he could. Like I knew he enjoyed.

At that moment I imagined I could smell the rancid breath of the whisperer in our space, making me bitter and nervous. We had to get that thing away from us.

Kaidan's mouth found the curve where my shoulder met my neck, and I felt his warm hands dip fully into the back of my pajama bottoms, his hands cupping my butt, pushing my underwear down my thighs.

My heart rate tripled. How far was he going to let this go?

"Take them off," he said.

For the first time I hesitated and wanted to cry. I'd always wondered if I'd be naked with Kaidan someday, but never under these circumstances. Unleashing my emotions, I snapped,

"You don't have to be such an ass."

Kaidan's brief laugh was a dark sound as he turned me and pushed me onto the bed. He grasped my bottoms and pulled them down my legs, tossing them away and leaving me bare. His whole body tensed as his eyes landed on the faded, greenish bruises across my shins. A quick survey of my skin showed I had bruises everywhere. Kaidan recovered quickly, his jaw set in hard lines.

He kept his eyes on my knees or stomach after that. The red badge at his sternum was as large as I'd ever seen it, spinning and pulsing. I wished for one soft glance from Kai—one glimpse of the boy who loved me. When his gaze finally met mine for the briefest second, it was all heat and anger.

I pressed my knees together, shocked that I lay naked in front of Kaidan Rowe and he seemed not to care. He stood at the end of the bed, unclasping his belt, which made his cargo shorts droop low on his hips. I had to swallow as he unzipped them.

This isn't happening. I took a cue from his playbook and appeared slightly uninterested, keeping my eyes on his chest as his shorts dropped to the floor. *Don't look, Anna*, I told myself.

Kaidan Rowe was nude, in all his glory, and I had to pretend to be unfazed. I couldn't be caught gawking as if it was something I'd never seen. Which I hadn't, and didn't want to now. Not like this.

He won't do it, I told myself. *He won't. Not like this. He loves you.*

This was exactly the position Kaidan and I swore to never let ourselves get in. Naked. Together. I had no doubt in my mind that his father had sent him and the spirit. The consequence of refusing his father's will would be death. Was I willing to go all the way in this moment to save him? Even if it meant I couldn't wield the Sword of Righteousness—the only weapon that would help us get rid of the demons? Kaidan or the world. What kind of choice was that?

Please, please, please, I begged. *Get us out of this.*

Kaidan came toward me. When the whisperer made that gross, guttural purring sound again, I scrunched my nose. Panic and frustration made me speak out.

"Do you have to be here?" I asked it. "You're really distracting."

"*Shut up,*" it said to me. "*As if I want to be here with you boring Neph.*"

"Then leave," Kaidan said. "We're almost finished here. Anyway, I think you'd find room 108 far more interesting."

This seemed to catch the spirit's interest, and for the first time since Kai and the whisperer entered, I felt a spike of hope. The demon froze and then bobbed up and down.

"*You won't tell?*" it asked.

"Tell what?" Kaidan said with impatience. "You did what you bloody came to do—you saw me find the girl and assure she's impure. Your job is done, and I can finish mine much better if you're not hovering."

The spirit pondered this a few seconds before it turned with a swish and flew through the walls, disappearing.

I was afraid to breathe. We stared at the blank wall in silence for a full minute before Kaidan collapsed on the bed next to me, shoving his face into a pillow and hollering. I climbed beneath the blanket and tossed a pillow over his chiseled, naked butt.

My heart was beating too fast, and the thoughts in my head were too murky to decipher. When Kaidan reached an arm over and pulled himself closer, burying his face in the blanket at my lap, I was afraid to touch him.

"I would have stopped, Anna." His voice was a thick whisper, causing tears to streak down each of my cheeks. "I swear. I'd die before I took you against your will. Please tell me you believe me."

"I believe you." And I did, but it had still been a scary, desperate moment that left me trembling. I was furious with the Dukes for putting us through this. What if we hadn't been able to talk the whisperer into leaving? Things were going too far. Something would have to give. And soon.

I swiped the tears from my cheeks and pushed my fingers into his hair, knowing full well the whisperer could return at any moment. We couldn't keep touching like this.

"Get under the covers with me," I said. "We need to lie here for a little while in case it comes back."

Kaidan looked up at me, showing all the emotion he'd so expertly kept hidden in the presence of the spirit. His expression made everything inside me come to life.

"There you are," I whispered, stroking his cheek until I was awarded with a tired, small grin.

He sat up, shifting the pillow over his lap until he was under the blanket. We lay side by side, quiet, both our chests rising and falling too fast. Kaidan trembled before seeming to suddenly remember something. He shot up and took my arm, running a hand over the bruises.

"Anna . . ." *Here we go.* "What. The bloody hell. Happened? Who did this to you?"

I swallowed hard. "Listen, Kai. I'm all right now, okay?"

"*Who?*"

His breathing became faster, a raging storm brewing.

"The sons of Thamuz."

His mouth went slack. "What did they do? I swear to God—"

"Nothing. They tried to take me, but I fought. And . . . Kope showed up."

"Kope?"

"Yeah." Kaidan was not going to like this story. I braced myself, and told him everything. He looked ready to blow a fuse.

"You should have called me," he said.

"I thought you were in L.A. There wasn't much time, and I didn't want you to be worried. I was going to tell you everything afterward."

He rubbed his face. "I can't . . . I just . . . Anna, swear you'll never engage another Neph like that. You're bloody lucky Kope showed! God, what would I do? Look at you!"

He pushed my hair aside and cursed at the sight of my shoulder and back.

"I'd no clue you were injured," he whispered. "I was too rough. . . ."

"I'm okay. I swear. You had to be rough. It was more convincing that way."

"I'll kill them."

"Sh." I pulled Kaidan back down to lie next to me and

watched him breathe as he worked through his anger.

After ten minutes I said, "We can probably get up now, right? I think that's long enough to get the job done."

My words pulled him from his dark thoughts enough to make him chuckle. "Ah, luv, I'd certainly hope not."

It was a relief to hear him joking. We sat up, and just as I was about to ask if he thought the spirit would come back, he turned and kissed me for real, cupping my face. I gripped his shoulders, gasping at the feel of our bare chests meeting as our passion urged us closer. I forced myself to pull back.

"Oh, God," he said. "Clothes. *Now.*"

"You first," I said.

"Look away," he advised. "Unless you want an eyeful."

I turned my head, partly out of embarrassment and partly because if I let my curiosity get the best of me and he caught me staring, he might attack. And I might let him.

My head snapped up when I heard Kaidan curse, and I found him standing there shirtless, facing the same hovering spirit that had left us ten minutes earlier.

"Yes, I'm obviously done," Kaidan said to it, sounding bored.

The spirit turned toward me, and even though my chest was covered by the blanket, I wanted to pull it up higher. I didn't dare move.

The spirit must have said something else telepathically to Kai, because he responded in a snide tone, "You do that."

When the spirit flew away, Kaidan let out a breath and said in a low voice, "He's gone to tell Pharzuph."

I swallowed a dry lump and nodded. Kai bent to pick up

my discarded clothes and tossed them to me before disappearing into the bathroom.

The whole time I dressed, a question continued churning inside me: Kaidan or the world? I'd been spared making that choice today, but it seemed inevitable that I'd have to eventually. Could I do the right thing if it meant Kaidan would lose his life? Tears threatened to fall again, but I fought them back, putting on a strong face and closing my eyes.

Please, God. Don't make me choose.

CHAPTER TEN

WORRIES APLENTY

We opted to stay in the hotel room awhile longer now that the whisperer was gone, but we knew we'd have to leave soon.

Kaidan stretched out on his back and looked longingly at my lap, which was at the perfect level to lay his head. I would have loved to run my fingers through his hair again but didn't want to take any chances. Having him there with me felt unreal. I expected him to be snatched away at any moment. I never fully relaxed, always tense and waiting for a dark spirit or enemy Neph.

"What happens now?" I asked.

"I have to go back to L.A." His voice mirrored my sadness. "But I don't want to leave you."

"You must be tired."

He pulled my hand under the covers and twined our fingers together. "I'll sleep on the plane."

I needed to be strong, but after experiencing how easily two Neph could overpower me, the thought of being alone was more frightening than ever.

"I haven't heard from my dad," I said. "I'm starting to worry. He's gone a long time without calling before, but never when things were this serious."

Kaidan sighed, sitting up and facing me, never letting go of my hand.

"I have news about that. They're trying to get him kicked off earth."

My stomach sank.

"Father flew me to Atlanta yesterday morning. He said you and Belial are suspected traitors, and that there were Neph and whisperers tracking you. I was sent with that bloody demon to confirm your lack of purity. I imagine they've got other trackers on your father, giving him hell."

I rubbed my forehead, the twinge of a headache coming on. I felt like Kaidan was giving me the abridged version by the way he stared off in thought.

"What else did he say to you?" I asked. I studied his serious face.

He hesitated.

"Tell me."

"There was nothing more about your father."

He was staring at my hands, not meeting my eyes. I scooted closer and forced my face into his line of sight.

"I don't want any secrets between us."

"It's not a secret, Anna. Just something not worth upsetting you about."

I crossed my arms and sat up straight. He took in my stern face. If there was anything I couldn't stand, it was being left in the dark, and he knew it.

He shook his head, eyes staring at the ceiling as if exasperated.

"Let's just say my father expects you to have no trace of purity left after our meeting today."

The prophecy called for a Neph who was pure of heart. Kaidan's father had sent him to be sure I would never be able to fulfill the prophecy. So when the truth came out, someday, that I was still pure of heart, still able to fight the Dukes and send them back to hell, Kaidan would be to blame. And just like with Flynn, they wouldn't hesitate to kill him.

I couldn't breathe. I had to stand up. I paced in front of the bed.

"Anna . . ."

"Pharzuph will kill you as soon as he gets a whiff of me, won't he?"

"*You'll be dead on the spot* were his words," Kaidan deadpanned.

I stopped and leaned my palms on the desk, letting my head hang.

Kaidan came up behind me, cupping my shoulders with his warm hands.

"It doesn't matter," he said gently. "You won't see him again anytime soon, luv. Not until it's time to fulfill the prophecy, and by then it won't matter."

I turned to face him. "But what if I do see him? He'll go after you right away. They're not taking any chances this time, Kai."

I felt caught in an invisible net. Kaidan's life was linked to my ability to use the sword. We were all intricately involved, like it or not.

"So much has happened," I whispered.

"Tell me everything."

I told him about Marek and Caterina being sent, and the constant barrage of whisperers in the few days since we'd spoken. Worst of all was Marna—my eyes burned when I thought about her.

Kaidan had no idea.

I wrapped my arms around his waist and pressed my face to his chest. His arms went around me as well.

"I need to tell you something else," I whispered.

I felt the muscles under my hands and cheek tense. I held him tighter.

"Say it."

My phone rang, startling me, and I yanked myself away from Kaidan to grab it.

"Marna," I whispered. What timing.

Kaidan and I stood there, watching each other. I knew he'd be using his heightened hearing to listen.

"Hey," I said.

"Oh, Anna." She sounded like she'd been crying. "She's still not back and she won't answer her phone. It's been over a day, and I'm too scared to wait any longer. I'm going to her."

Kai stepped closer, his eyebrows tightly knit with concern and confusion.

I thought about Dad and what he'd done when our ally Zania was in trouble. Her own father, Duke Sonellion, had

112

given up on her because of her alcoholic ways, and he left her to be beaten and sold into slavery somewhere in the Middle East. But Dad sent a group to help bail her out. Of course, her rescue had led to the eventual death of one of them. . . .

"Are there any Dukes in California?" I asked. "Blake's dad?"

Kai shook his head just as Marna said, "No. It was on the news. He died last night and left his fortune to his only son."

I shivered. Blake's dad, Duke Melchom, was most likely spiriting his way around China, his new duty station, looking for a new body to possess.

"All the Dukes should be back in their respective areas," Kaidan said. "What's going on?"

"Is that Kai? What's he doing there?"

"Yes, it's him. Hold on." I looked at Kai. "Can you call Blake and see if he answers? We think Ginger's with him."

Now he raised both eyebrows, starting to understand, though he had no idea what had sent her running there. Kaidan turned and dialed Blake. It rang and rang, then went to voice mail.

"Ring me back straight away," Kaidan said to the machine, then hung up and shook his head at me.

"Listen," I said to Marna. "I'm going to meet you out there. I think it's going to take more than just you to break the two of them apart."

"Are you sure you want to do that?" she asked.

I was sure it was dangerous, but at this point nowhere felt safe. I couldn't sit back and watch Blake and Ginger get themselves killed. Whisperers were bound to find them together soon, if they hadn't already.

"I'm sure," I said. "I'll leave right away and call you when my flight arrives. We'll go to Blake's together."

"I'm going," Kaidan said.

I bit back a smile and said to Marna, "Make that three of us."

We disconnected and I fired up my laptop to buy a plane ticket. Kaidan and I decided we'd drive to the Roanoke airport separately to avoid being spotted together, but it was a small airport with a minimal number of flights, so we'd have to take the same one. I remembered Dad once saying that the whisperers stayed low to earth, so I felt remotely safe at the idea of being in the skies with Kai.

"Did Gin go mad when she found out Blake's engaged?" Kaidan asked.

I stopped shoving stuff into my bag and faced him.

"She was upset about that, but it's not what sent her over the edge."

"So, what did?"

It felt like a boulder was weighing down my chest. I'd been selfishly avoiding this moment. I saw the tick of nervousness in Kaidan's jaw. It was going to break his heart to lose one of his oldest and dearest friends.

"The twins had a . . . disagreement."

"About?"

I swallowed, barely able to get the words out. "Marna's pregnant."

Kai stared at me with big eyes and a slow shake of his head like he wanted to argue the possibility. And then his eyes glassed over.

"I sensed it," I said. "And it's Jay's."

114

"Bloody *hell*." He fell back to a sitting position on the bed, raking a hand through his hair as his body tensed from the shock of the news. He searched around the room as if lost before putting his elbows on his knees and letting his face fall into his hands.

For one horrified moment I thought I'd see him cry for the first time, which would have obliterated my heart, but when he looked up, his eyes were red and dry. I felt horrible bearing this news to everyone. In a way, this whole thing was my fault. If I hadn't taken the twins to Jay's club that night . . .

"Come here," Kaidan said, reaching out a hand.

I took it and let him pull me to his lap. I hugged him around the neck.

"It's not your fault."

I choked up. "How did you know what I was thinking?"

"You have that sad, guilty look on your face, but you're guilty of nothing. It's better to know these things sooner rather than later."

It was true that Jay'd been able to start preparing right away, which was good, but every other aspect was tragic. I couldn't imagine a world without Marna's smile. And it was horribly unfair that they'd fallen in love, only to be soon torn apart. And the baby left without its mother, just like we'd all been. I couldn't help but feel guilty.

I wondered if Jay and Patti were in Virginia now, staying safe.

"It's my fault they got together. I didn't think they'd move so fast, and if I'd known she could get pregnant—"

"Sh, Anna. Those two always fancied each other, yeah?

115

This whole thing is horrid, but you can't stop the inevitable."

Even in his heartbroken state over Marna, Kaidan sounded reassuring and strong. I let myself hold him while I got my emotions in check. So much was happening, and everything was at stake. We needed to get to Santa Barbara as soon as possible.

"We better go," I whispered. I promised to tell him everything on the plane. And then we'd both have plenty to worry about.

The only way to get rid of a temptation is to yield to it.
—*Oscar Wilde,* The Picture of Dorian Gray

CHAPTER ELEVEN

GINGER AND BLAKE

A distraught Marna met us inside the Santa Barbara airport. It was the roughest I'd ever seen her look—an off-center
ponytail and flats instead of heels.

We rented a sedan with the darkest windows possible and
drove to Blake's cliffside mansion. I shouldn't have been surprised to see a news van outside of his closed gates, considering this was major local-celebrity gossip. Blake's father, a
billionaire, had just died, leaving his massive fortune to the
city's extreme-sports star, who just last week had got engaged
to a gorgeous girl from a prosperous family. Speaking of
Michelle . . .

"Pull the car over," I whispered.

There wasn't much of a shoulder, but Kai squeezed to the
side and we stopped to watch. We were half a mile away, so I

had to push my sights out to take in the scene clearly.

"Just what we need," Kai mumbled.

Parked in front of the news van was a sporty red car and a beautiful, pacing blonde.

"Whoa," I said when I focused on her aura—an ugly mix of thick forest green envy and dark swirls of gray.

"Is that her?" Marna asked.

I nodded and we eyed each other. Michelle was stuck outside, clearly not being allowed entrance, which could only mean one thing. Ginger was definitely in there, and judging by the overwhelming jealousy in Michelle's aura, she knew it.

"Can you get us a little closer?" I asked. "I'll try to persuade them to leave."

Kai drove closer, stopping in the driveway of Blake's neighbor. It always felt wrong using the power of persuasion I'd gained from my double angel parentage, but sometimes it was necessary. I honed my sights on the driver of the news van and silently repeated, "*Nothing is happening here. There's no story. Leave now. . . .*" He started looking around, nervous-like. Finally after a minute of my nudging, he started the van and drove away.

The three of us grinned. Now for Michelle. When I started chanting the words to her, she slowly walked to her car, reached for the handle, and then grabbed her temples. She let out a mournful wail and began bawling.

"It's not working," Kai said. "We've got to go in. Hope the git hasn't changed the code."

We drove up to the gate, and Michelle ran to the car.

"Don't you dare roll that window down," Marna warned

me, but my finger was already on the switch. I couldn't just ignore this brokenhearted girl.

"I know you," Michelle said to me thickly. She still managed to be gorgeous, even in her exhausted-looking state.

"Hi, Michelle," I said gently. "Listen, Blake's going through a really hard time. . . . He's sort of pushing everyone away—"

"He let a girl in!"

Crap.

"I know," I said. "She's an old friend, like me. We're going to try to calm him, okay? Why don't you go home and rest? Give him a little time to digest everything."

The gates began to swing open, and the car inched forward.

"No!" Michelle screamed. "Something's going on! I'm going in!"

Go to your car, I silently urged her with my angelic will.

She ran to her car. When she realized the gate wasn't going to stay open long enough, she ran back but was too late. She was left crying at the closed gate, even angrier than before.

"She's gone mad," Kaidan said without humor. He sped up the driveway and parked directly in front of the doors. The three of us jumped out, but the door was locked.

Kaidan banged with his fist. We waited. He banged again. "Open up, idiot! This is bloody stupid!"

After what seemed like forever, the door opened, and the three of us gaped. Blake wore only low-slung basketball shorts and the hardest expression I'd ever seen. Then his sights slipped down the long driveway to where Michelle stood holding on to the gate, bawling. His green badge grew.

"Stop that," I said. "She's really hurting, Blake."

A vicious giggle sounded from behind him, and Ginger strode up wearing just Blake's shirt, which stopped at her midthigh. Her badge was circling. The two of them appeared wild, lost to their natures of envy and cheating, and probably high on the rebellion of being together after holding back so long.

Ginger rested her elbow on Blake's shoulder and fluffed her bedhead. Blake reached an arm around her waist.

Marna stepped up. "It's time to go, Gin."

Ginger kept her arm around Blake's neck, giving her sister a stare. "You're one to talk. I seem to recall that line not working on you. I'm quite fine where I am, thanks."

"Like hell," Kaidan murmured, pushing past them. Marna and I followed him into the immaculate stone-tiled foyer, and Kai slammed the door, turning on the couple. "Have whisperers seen you together?"

"Course not." Blake sounded smug.

Marna and I let out our breaths.

"You're bleedin' lucky!" Kai said.

"Back off, brah." Blake dropped his arm from Ginger to step up to Kaidan. "What, you're the only one who can be with your girl?"

"The Dukes were at their summit when we were together. This is sheer madness!"

"Guys," I said, moving closer. But they were too fired up.

"Why do you care?" Ginger spat at Kai.

"Because we're this close, Gin." Kaidan held his finger and thumb an inch apart. "This close to fulfilling the prophecy, and the two of you are likely to get yourselves killed!"

Next to me, Marna's hand went to her mouth, silent tears streaming down her cheeks.

"As if you care!" Ginger yelled. "You only give a shite about yourself. You want everyone to be willing to sacrifice themselves so you can finally be with your precious Anna. Well, I'm not waiting around anymore. I'm taking what I want from this damned life while I can!"

Ginger and Kaidan were inches apart, both angry as they shouted.

"It's about all of us, not just me and Anna!"

"Oh, right!"

Kaidan grasped her small shoulders, and when he touched her they both seemed to soften. "I don't want you dead, Gin."

Her eyes watered. "I've nothing to live for now, don't you see? She'll be *gone*. My sister is dying! And Blake will be married off to that cow. I'd rather be dead."

Kaidan wrapped his arms around her just as she broke into choking sobs, her knees buckling.

Marna started crying, too, and I took her hand.

Kaidan held Ginger up, stroking her hair like a big brother, and I could see the understanding and concern born from sharing a childhood together.

Marna stepped to them, and Kaidan reached out, pulling her into the embrace. Blake and I made eye contact and nodded, moving together to the next room so the three of them could talk. We sat on the leather sofa. Blake leaned back, pressing his fists to his eyes.

"Damn," he whispered. "Everything is so messed up."

That was an understatement. I had no words. When Kai

and the twins came back in, the five of us sat there in sad silence. Every moment we were together brought more danger. We all knew it, yet it was hard to force ourselves apart.

Kaidan's phone rang, and we all froze. His tan face paled as he looked at the screen and held it out for us to see.

Pharzuph.

The four of us held our breath and listened as he answered.

"I assume you took care of the girl then?" Pharzuph asked in his silky accented English.

"Of course, Father. She wasn't a virgin anyhow."

"Interesting." There was a long, expectant pause. "The spirit I sent to oversee the operation has been sent back to the pit of hell, never to return to earth. Do you know why?"

Kaidan's eyes darted to mine. "No, Father."

"Because he admitted he did not stay to see your mission through to the end. He says the two of you persuaded him to leave."

"Bollocks!" Kaidan stood. "That disgusting wanker was distracting. It's hard enough to try to bang a Neph without a spirit interfering."

"A whisperer should hardly distract you from your task, Son." The suspicion in Pharzuph's voice made my blood run cold.

"You're right, Father. But the deed was done, and the whisperer left on his own. Obviously I couldn't force him."

"Hm." Another pause swelled the tension in the room. "I think I'll pay the girl a visit myself. A lot's riding on her lack of purity."

Goose bumps covered me.

Kai's jaw clenched. "Do what you must, Father, but I hate to see your valuable time wasted."

"Good of you to care." It was the last thing Pharzuph said before he hung up.

Kaidan let out an enraged sound and kicked the coffee table, flipping it with a giant crash.

We all stood.

"Everything's going to be okay," I said. "We just all need to get back to work. At this rate the prophecy's bound to go down soon, and we can't afford to lose anyone."

"What about you?" Marna asked. "Where will you go?"

I looked at Kaidan, feeling the pain in his gaze. "I don't know."

"Well, I don't think you should be alone," Kaidan said.

"We're all gonna have to be alone if we want to convince them we're working," Blake said.

He was right. Kaidan and I couldn't stay together, especially after we'd come all this way to keep Blake and Ginger from doing that very thing.

Kaidan shook his head. "Anna can't pretend to work now that my father's searching for her. She's got to stay hidden."

"Well, perhaps—" Marna was cut off by her own giant gasp as a dark, ethereal form with the largest wingspan I'd seen yet dove through the window and halted above us.

Our group instinctually recoiled as one. I fought to breathe and appear unafraid. We were caught. Ideas and excuses began tumbling through my mind, none of them feasible.

The huge spirit swooped down, his horned head looming over the group before seeing me and advancing. This demon's face appeared as a ram, thick horns curling downward. The closer he got, the stranger I felt. I waited for fear to engulf me, but a familiar warmth filled my chest instead—the feeling of safety.

"It's me, baby," the spirit said.

The voice was different in my mind—not as gruff, but still deep.

"Daddy?" My voice cracked.

He moved nearer. No wonder he hadn't called. He'd shed his body. As a spirit, his giant chest and arms were bare, and he had a strange cloth wrapped around him from his waist to his knees. His body was humanesque, and yet not. Swirly and hazy. Too graceful. I felt a sense of loss knowing I'd never see that big, scary-looking man again. I pushed away the strangeness and sadness and lifted my chin to him.

"Thank God it's you," I said. "So much is happening. Pharzuph is hounding me, and I don't know what to do or where to go."

"That's why I'm here." His voice was unlike those of any of the dark whisperers. His was a soothing rumble. *"You don't have much time."* He turned his head to Kaidan, who came and stood at my side. The others watched, on edge.

"What do you suggest?" Kaidan asked.

"You have only one safe option," Dad answered. *"Get married."*

CHAPTER TWELVE

Dream Within a Dream

The room stilled as his words cartwheeled around in my head. I had that distant feeling that came with dreams—first at the realization that Dad's body was forever gone, and then the unbelievable words he'd just uttered—giving voice to a dream that I'd long since buried.

"We can't." I shook my head. It wasn't possible. If there'd been a glaring loophole, we'd have thought of it by now. Dad failed to notice one *major* issue. "I have to stay a virgin. The sword—"

"No. You have to stay pure of heart, Anna," Dad said. *"What's more pure than committing yourselves in love?"*

"But . . ." I looked toward Kaidan.

My insides twisted at the dread on his face as he stepped back.

"No." His voice was low. "It won't work."

I wanted to reach for him, but he stepped back even farther. His face hardened into the mask I knew all too well, concealing emotion.

"I'm sorry, Duke Belial," he said to my father. "I can't marry."

I said nothing, but my heart shattered into a million shards as his rejection slammed into me.

"Don't be stupid, Kai!" Ginger said. "There's no time for this. If it can save you both, you need to do it!"

"Duke Astaroth will be able to see the bond of marriage," Kaidan pointed out, sounding frustrated.

"Well, he'll see the bond of love between you anyhow, which is nearly as bad," she countered. The twins' father was the only Duke who could see relational bonds. We'd need to avoid him at all cost.

Kai thrust his fingers through his hair and faced away. He looked poised to run, his back muscles tense.

Obviously, being a husband had never been in the forefront of Kaidan's mind, but his reaction still burned like an acid bath. If he loved me, why wouldn't he want to take this step? Yes, we were young, but we weren't *normal*. Yes, these were perilous circumstances, but the romantic part of me wanted him to want it all, peril or not.

"Dude, come on—," Blake started.

"Don't pressure him," I said. "If he doesn't want to do it, he shouldn't have to."

"Anna . . ." Kaidan kept his back to us, dropping his head. I hated seeing him like this. Especially with a roomful of others watching.

"It's okay," I said. "It was a bad idea."

Dad watched our conversation play out, silent above us.

"It's not a bad idea," Marna said to me, then looked at Kaidan. "Really, Kai, why the hell not?"

"Marna—," I began, but she shook her head and cut me off.

"That's pants! What's the problem?"

Kaidan turned now, a storm in his eyes. "She can't tie herself to a bloke like me and expect to come out of it white as snow. *It won't work.*"

I sucked in a breath, stunned.

"She loves you," Marna whispered. "And you love her. You're not going to soil her soul, babe."

He shook his head. "My past has to be taken into account."

"Your past is in the past," I said, staying calm. "And it's not going to . . . rub off on me or something. You know it doesn't work like that."

His jaw ticked as he glared at the wall.

I started to move forward just as my father's weightless form lowered toward Kaidan and encircled him. Kai stilled, as if listening. What was Dad saying? More listening and head shaking. They seemed to converse for hours. Now Kaidan gave an almost imperceptible nod. I wanted to stop their silent conversation. For all I knew, Dad could be threatening him, like he'd once done when he wanted Kai to stay away from me. He'd gone from using all his power to keep us apart to wanting us to get married?

"I need some time to myself," Kaidan said. Without a backward glance, he left the room. I let my special hearing trail after him until he stopped on the deck outside.

I looked to the other three Neph. Blake raised his pierced eyebrow.

I turned on my dad and spoke to him telepathically.

"You'd better not have threatened him."

"I tried to reason with him and reassure him."

"But . . . if this was a possibility all along, why didn't you tell me?"

"I assumed you'd figured it out for yourself. This is what I hoped would happen with you and the son of Alocer."

Hold on. He'd wanted me to marry my friend Kope? Ugh! I turned my back, irritated. Dad's massive spirit form moved in front of me.

"I knew the son of Pharzuph would have reservations. I tried to back off and give the two of you space, but there's no time for that now. I've told him that if he loves you, he needs to marry you."

"Gee, no pressure, Dad," I said out loud.

"Sometimes people need to be pressured to do the right thing," he said only to me, completely unapologetic.

"I need to talk to Kai." I walked away from my dad and past the others. I took a couple wrong turns, Blake's house being so huge, and when I got to the back doors, Kaidan was coming in. He must've heard me. To my relief, he reached out his hand and took mine, leading me down a flight of carpeted stairs and into a cave of darkness.

"This is my favorite room," he said quietly.

I adjusted my sights and saw that it was a mini movie theater with four rows of stadium seating. The walls were covered in old movie posters and pictures of pinup starlets from long ago when it was considered unsexy to be skinny.

The room was atmospheric and cozy. We took seats in the back row, never letting go of each other's hands.

"Look," I began. "I don't know what my dad said to you, but don't let him pressure you. You don't have to do this. I'll find a way to hide from Pharzuph."

He looked resigned. "You can't hide from him forever."

"Yes, but I don't want that to be our sole reason for getting married."

He dropped his eyes to our hands, letting strands of dark hair block his face.

I tried to tell myself not to be disheartened, but it was hard. Talking about marriage like a business proposition or a means to an end . . . it was depressing. Yes, it would keep us safe to a degree, but *both* our hearts had to be in it or it would be a farce, not an arrangement born of love.

I began to stand. "I'm telling him no."

Kaidan's eyes shot up, wild, and he held my hands tighter. "You don't want to get married?"

I sat again. "Of course I want to, but you have to want it, too. And it has to be for the right reasons."

"I'd do anything for you—to keep you safe."

His words were sweet, but he wasn't getting it. Tears of disappointment filled my eyes, and he kept going.

"When I think of what those sons of Thamuz could've done—"

"Wrong reason," I whispered. "We can't do this." I tried to pull my hands away, but he wouldn't let me.

"Anna—"

"Let me go, Kai." I didn't want to bawl in front of him.

"No, please. God . . . I'm just not good at this, luv. Any of it."

I closed my eyes and let my head fall back against the tall seat.

"I know this is something you've always wanted," he said.

I shook my head. "That was a long time ago. When I thought I was normal. I never wanted it to be like this."

Kaidan was so tense. I wished I knew what he was thinking. I hated this whole stupid situation. The pressure. The rush. The unknown.

"That's what I tried to tell your father," Kaidan said. "We've no time to plan a fancy ceremony or to have a gown tailored—"

"Whoa, stop." I held up a hand. "I don't need any of that fairy-tale stuff. It's the marriage that matters to me, not the wedding. As long as our hearts are in the right place, we could be in pajamas for all I care."

A mass of tension seemed to roll away from him. His eyes softened as he looked at me. "But . . . I wanted to give you all that."

Sparks of love lit up behind my eyes. I tried to gauge the jumble of emotions inside me—but it was hope that rose up and caught wind.

I'd always thought marriage was special—a partnership of challenge and love. What Dad was proposing was a secret wedding. A bond between us that no one would know about except our small group and the Maker Himself.

A tingle of joy circled my soul as the possibility of it all became real.

"Kai, please, tell me what you're thinking right now. We don't have much time, and we have to make a decision." He knew I wanted it, so the ball was in his court.

He froze. "I . . ." Then, as he searched my face with wonder, he slid from his seat and down to one knee. "My sweet, lovely Anna. I love you . . . and I want to marry you. But only if you want to. Do you? I mean, will you? Marry me?"

Be still my heart. His proposal was so adorably awkward that I had to laugh, sliding out of my chair so I could face him on my knees, too. I grabbed his face and kissed him for saying exactly what I needed to hear. We kissed once, twice, three times before he pulled back.

"Does it always take this long for someone to answer? It's making me bloody nervous."

I looked into his eyes. "Yes, Kai. I'll marry you."

And as we kissed again, a cheer rose up outside of the door, making us laugh.

"So much for privacy," Kaidan said with a grin.

His genuine happiness sealed the deal for me, and I was warming to the thought of marrying him. Okay, I was pretty much hot for it. This was Kaidan Rowe on his knees for me. *This* was my desire—our mutual love and devotion.

We stood when Marna came bouncing into the room, throwing her skinny arms around our necks.

"Brilliant!" she said.

Blake and Ginger came in behind her. Blake slapped his palm into Kaidan's, and they shared a back-clapping hug.

"Man," Blake said, "you almost screwed it up. I thought you were smoother than that."

Kaidan gave him a shove and said, "Shut it." But they kept grinning.

Ginger was the only one not smiling. I felt bad celebrating when everything in her life was falling apart. She crossed her arms, appearing anxious. Time to get back to business.

"Where's my dad?" I asked.

"He's scouting the area," Blake said. "He'll be back."

And sure enough he flew down into the room from above, sending my heart into pounding mode.

"All clear," Dad said, speaking telepathically to all of us. *"I've worked out the details with the son of Melchom."* We all looked at Blake, who gave us a wink as Dad continued. *"You'll need to go somewhere remote this evening, and then head back to your individual homes tomorrow to avoid further suspicion."*

Only one night? Well, we'd have to make the most of it.

My insides flipped in nervous anticipation.

"Everything has been prepared. I must leave now."

"Thank you for everything," I whispered to him.

Dad moved forward, wrapping his wings around me and bringing his head down as if to kiss my head. Though I couldn't physically feel him, my soul felt whole and full.

I raised my hand and signed, *I Love You*, and a smile lit up his otherwise frightening face. He kept his eyes on me as he flew up and away.

"All right," Blake said, motioning us into a circle. "I've got some things to take care of. Let's meet at the regional airport in three hours."

Nerves zipped through me again. "Where are we going?" I asked.

"You're getting married in the sky," Blake said. "Courtesy of moi."

"You mean . . . ," I started.

"You're flying us?" Marna finished, looking doubtful.

"He's got a pilot license," Ginger said proudly.

"That's right." Blake beamed. "I've been shopping for a small jet the past few months, and I've got one waiting on me now. It's a beauty."

"Nice," Kaidan said.

There was a long lull in which we all kind of stood there looking around at one another in disbelief.

"So, yeah." Blake clapped his hands and rocked back on his heels, seeming to think the awkwardness was funny. "You know what this means, right? Our little Anna's gettin' some tonight."

Oh, my gosh! My face lit on fire and I could not look at Kaidan. I wanted to crawl away from the twins' and Blake's laughter.

"I totally hate you," I said.

"Nah, you love me." Blake tried to put me in a headlock, but I wriggled away and shoved him, laughing despite my horror.

"Get off, mate." Kaidan slid his arm around my waist. "You're just jealous you can't have me."

"That is the truth, brah." Blake grabbed Kai and pretended to latch on to his neck. The two of them wrestled while Marna took my hand and pulled me and Ginger away.

"We should break up for the three-hour wait so we're not seen with each other," Marna said.

The boys got their acts together and followed us to the doors. We were all set to leave when I thought about poor Michelle.

"Guys . . . what are we going to do if she's still out there?" I looked pointedly at Blake.

"She's gone," Blake and Kaidan both said. So, they'd been listening. Blake had the good sense to appear guilty while Ginger stared down at her thumbnail.

I opened the door to the bright, hot sun. Blake led Kaidan and me to the garage and handed me keys to a cherry-red convertible Mini Cooper. I couldn't help the little *"Ooh!"* that escaped.

"Yeah, it's cute," he said. "I bought it on a whim, but it's too girly for me. I was gonna give it to . . ."

He froze as we realized he was referring to Michelle, and we braved glances toward the twins just as Ginger yanked the door of the rental car open. Blake shook his head, probably cursing himself for the slipup.

Kaidan looked out over the clear skies, on alert. "Thanks, mate. Let's get moving."

"Yep. See you in three hours." As Blake walked back to his front door, he winked at Ginger, who flipped him off before letting the tiniest smile grace her lips.

The twins drove away. Now it was just Kaidan and me. We stood there shyly avoiding each other's eyes.

"What will you do for three hours?" he asked.

"Maybe shop, since I didn't bring anything. I thought I'd be flying back today."

It felt surreal to have a casual conversation when our lives were hanging in the balance and a huge event was about to take place between the two of us.

He gave me a shopping center's name, which I put in my

phone's navigational system for directions.

"Cool," I said.

More shyness.

"So, I'll see you soon?" he asked. The blue of his eyes shone through strands of hair.

"Yeah. See you soon."

"Right, then." He cleared his throat, walking backward now, away from me, with a flick of his head to clear the hair from his eyes. I loved the way the sun made him squint a little.

I loved everything about this boy. And I was going to marry him.

Oh. My. Gosh.

I was about to marry Kaidan Rowe.

If I get married, I want to be very married.
—Audrey Hepburn

CHAPTER THIRTEEN

SKY HIGH

I went straight to the mall and stood in front of the lacy nighties. I didn't even realize I was wearing a dreamy, dorky smile until a sales associate came up and asked if I needed any help.

Embarrassing.

I said, "No thanks," and hurried off. Kai wasn't the type of guy to be impressed by frills, anyway.

My nerves were building—jitters of the monstrous variety. Not the sickening kind of anxiousness the Dukes gave me, but precarious, dancing nerves that made me light-headed and giddy. Drunk on anticipation. High on Kai. Okay, that was incredibly cheesy, but that was the kind of mood I was in.

I kept an eye out for dark whisperers or creepy Neph kids. If anyone or anything tried to ruin this amazing plan of ours,

141

my demon side would definitely be coming out to play.

I bought some travel toiletries and an outfit for the next day. Then, on a whim, I decided to purchase a sundress. I may not have needed a grand, elaborate gown, but I also didn't want to get married in grungy jeans if I didn't have to.

The white dress had a halter top with an open back, and it flowed down to my ankles in a light, silky material that made me feel pretty. I was glad to see that my bruises were mostly gone. I ran to a hair salon for a quick style, changed my clothes in the mall restroom, and got to the airport just in time. Shaking. My teeth were all but chattering.

The twins were waiting for me in the entrance. Marna let out an excited squeal and bear-hugged me, praising my dress choice.

"I wish Jay could be here," she said.

My heart dropped. "So do I. And Patti, too."

"Ah, Patti." Ginger smiled, causing Marna and me to halt and stare at her. "What? She's lovely. She'll be sad to miss this madness."

"She will," I whispered. So would Veronica. I wished they all could be here, and I hoped I could see them and tell them our news soon.

With a sigh, Ginger picked up the pace through the terminal. Marna and I followed.

"Kai and Blake are on the plane," Marna explained as we speed-walked to an exit ramp. A man in uniform led us outside to the jetway. "Blake's been doing all the safety checks and whatnot. I'm sure they're ready for us by now."

"I can't believe this is happening," I whispered to Marna, feeling shy and shaky again.

"I know!" She let out a squee and linked her arm through mine. I clung tight.

Only Marna could be thrilled for me when her own situation was so grim.

Outside was loud with the sounds of prop planes. We were led to a beautiful white jet, bigger than what I'd envisioned. I should have known Blake wouldn't settle for one of those rickety things.

"Have a nice flight," said the airport personnel as we climbed the jet's narrow steps.

I took one last look for peeping spirits before the door swung up and sealed shut behind us. I closed my eyes, waiting for doubt to creep in about what we were about to do, but I felt only excitement and sureness. I could only hope Kaidan felt the same. His face would tell me the truth.

I wasn't sure what I was expecting when I opened my eyes, but the inside of the jet was even more gorgeous than the mini yacht we'd taken to Melchom's island two weeks prior. That horrid night felt like eons ago. Life had continued, moving us along at top speed.

I stood in the aisle and absently ran my hands over the soft leather seat backs, losing myself in the poshness as the twins moved ahead of me. The plane seated six, with three rows of cream seats on each side. The back half of the plane was a lounging area with a big television screen and mini bar. Ginger crashed into a window seat and closed her eyes. My trance was broken then, leaving one thing on my mind.

Kaidan.

He lounged on a bench seat in the rear of the plane, leaning

143

back with one hand behind his head. His red starburst badge pulsed wildly as he looked me over, and I stood at the edge of the seats, holding my breath. Only a few feet separated us, but I was frozen in place.

He didn't look scared or doubtful, that was for certain. He looked like he wanted me, which sent my pulse into a frenzy.

Kaidan lifted two fingers and beckoned me closer. Marna, who'd taken a seat across from him, cleared her throat and stood, moving past me with a smile and flopping into the seat next to her sister, facing away from us.

I moved nearer until my knees were touching Kaidan's and I was looking down at him. My heart threatened to dance right out of my chest.

"Hey," I managed.

"Hey, yourself." His melty voice and darkened bedroom eyes were not helping to calm my pulse any. "You're stunning. I feel like a slob."

He was wearing the same low cargo shorts, fitted T-shirt, and skater shoes he'd been wearing all day.

I felt like useless warm putty when I said, "You always look good."

Ginger made a barfing noise behind me, and Marna shushed her. Kaidan took my hips, pulling me to sit next to him. I lifted my hair from my neck, feeling too warm, and my hand shook.

Kai lifted my hand to kiss my palm, then signed to me. *Don't be nervous.*

I forced myself to meet his eyes, but he looked so serious that I had to look down again. I couldn't stop being nervous.

He pulled me close and I climbed onto his lap, burying my face in the crook of his neck. His hand stroked the length of my hair and down the silky material at my lower back.

"Are you sure about this?" I whispered against his warm skin. Without pausing, he whispered back, "I am. Are you?"

"Yes."

We stayed like that, his arm around me and my face in his neck until Blake said it was time to buckle up and get ready for takeoff. Kaidan and I took our seats across from the twins.

It was slightly unnerving to know that wheelie-popping Blake was about to fly our plane. But he looked focused and mature sitting up at the gears with the small doorway opened for us to see. I caught Ginger leaning into the aisle and gazing at him as he worked.

Blake said something into his mouthpiece then gave us the thumbs-up, and I felt us push back from the gate. I said a prayer as we lifted. It was the smoothest takeoff I'd ever experienced. Kaidan raised his eyebrows, impressed.

When we leveled out, Marna stood and went into the small server alley, making drinks for everyone. Nobody had alcohol. I knew they probably wanted it, but they were being thoughtful about not displaying my temptation in front of me. Or maybe they were worried because I looked nervous enough to drink the whole bar myself.

I nearly choked on my Coke when Blake stood up from the pilot's seat and walked back to us, making Marna scream, "What are you doing? You have to fly the plane!"

Blake laughed. "It's all good! I got this baby on autopilot. Don't your pilots ever come out of the pit?"

Marna frowned. "They have copilots, so even when some-one gets up, the cockpit's never empty."

"Chill. It's under control. Everyone up," Blake announced. "Time to have us a wedding."

My stomach wobbled.

Marna cheered. I loved that girl.

I stood, never letting go of Kaidan's hand, and for the first time I wondered how exactly this wedding was going to go.

"I didn't prepare any vows or anything," I said. "I guess we're just winging it?"

Kaidan appeared as clueless as me, and a little nervous now.

"I got you covered." Blake grinned, pulling out a piece of paper and clearing his throat. "Just call me Reverend Blake."

"You've got to be kidding me." Ginger snatched the paper from his hand, scanned it, and then bent at the waist to laugh.

Kaidan took it and we read together. Sure enough, Blake had been ordained. Online. Technically the marriage wouldn't be legal since we hadn't applied for a marriage license or any-thing like that. We couldn't leave a paper trail, but the marriage would be valid in all the ways that counted.

"A half-demon minister," Kaidan said. "That has to be a first."

"Yup. And I've got the traditional vows here. I thought that's what you'd probably want." He looked at me and I reached for-ward, pulling him into a hug. *I will not cry*, I chanted to myself.

"Thank you, Blake," I told him. "You thought of everything."

It was miraculous how fast it all had come together. Like it was meant to be.

I let him go, trying not to get emotional, but—*GAH!*—this

was really happening! We all moved to the open area in the back. It was still a snug fit, so the twins sat while Kaidan and I held hands facing Blake, who was wearing a silly mock-serious look on his face.

"Dearly beloved," he said in a booming voice.

We all burst out laughing. It must have been nerves because all five of us laughed way too long, and it took several minutes to get ourselves together again. Now that the tension was broken, we all began to calm.

Blake turned his attention back to Kaidan and me.

"All right, for real this time." He looked at Kaidan. "Keep your eyes on Anna and repeat after me. You ready?"

Kaidan ran his hands through his hair and blew out a breath before taking my hands again. I rocked back on my heels a little when he held me with his most intense stare. He nodded, and Blake told him what to say. Kai's voice was rich and velvety as he repeated the vows, punctuating each word with a passion I felt down to my toes.

"I, Kaidan, take you, Anna, to be my wedded wife. To have and to hold from this day forward, for better or worse, for richer or poorer, in sickness and health . . . till death do us part."

He whispered the last promise with pain in his voice, and I let the silent tears I'd been holding back slip down my cheeks. He wasn't just repeating the words. He meant them. This was real. No one could ever take this moment from us. I swallowed, and before I could wipe my cheeks, Kaidan was wiping them for me.

"No tears," he whispered.

Deep breath.

I nodded and took his hands again. It was my turn. I took a few more breaths before saying my vows with all my heart, trying not to cry.

"I, Anna, take you, Kaidan, to be my wedded husband. To have and to hold from this day forward, for better or worse, for richer or poorer, in sickness and health. Until death do us part."

His eyes were a soft blue as he watched me in wonder, his warm thumbs running back and forth over my hands. I smiled, and when he smiled back at me, I'd never felt such pure joy.

"Time for the rings," Blake said.

Rings! "Oh," I began, "I didn't—"

But Kaidan surprised me, reaching into his pocket.

"This is what I did during my three hours," he said quietly. He looked almost bashful and hesitant as he pulled out a platinum men's band with black tribal markings—something that a rocker boy would totally wear. Next he brought out a platinum women's band that appeared woven with vines, studded with a small round emerald. Gorgeous and delicate. It didn't look like a traditional wedding ring, which was smart of him.

"I figured we'd have to wear these on our opposite hands after today," he explained, "and since it's our secret, I decided on your birthstone instead of a diamond. I had to guess your ring size. You have small hands."

"I love it." I beamed and he gave me a relieved grin.

He handed me the heavy men's band.

"Kai, you first," Blake said.

Kaidan slid the ring onto my finger and held it there. It fit perfectly.

In a low voice he repeated after Blake, "With this ring, I

thee wed. Wear it as a symbol of our love and commitment."

At that point the moisture from my eyes was gone and I couldn't stop smiling. I put Kaidan's ring on his finger and said, "With this ring, I thee wed. Wear it as a symbol of our love and commitment."

We clasped hands again. The plane was quiet except for the buzz of the engine. We looked at Blake.

"Well, you know what they say, guys. What God has joined together, let no man put asunder."

Or demon, I thought.

I felt Kaidan watching me, and I soaked in the moment.

Blake clapped Kaidan on the shoulder. "Here's the good part. You may now kiss your bride."

"'Bout time," Kaidan said. He leaned down.

"No tongue," Ginger called out.

"Yes tongue!" Marna countered.

Kaidan was still waiting for them to shut up when I threw my arms around his neck and pressed my lips to his. It didn't take him long to sink into me. I felt his tongue for a moment, soft against mine, before we were pulling away and pressing our foreheads together.

We were married.

"Did we really just do that?" he whispered, eyes wide. I smiled, nodding, bursting with a crazy, all-consuming happiness. The cabin buzzed with hyper energy.

"Should I be this turned-on by a wedding?" he asked.

Ginger snorted. "You get turned-on when the wind blows."

I giggled, and Kai grinned at me.

"I now present Mr. and Mrs. Kaidan Rowe," Blake said.

"Aw," Marna said with a sigh.

"Words I never thought I'd hear," Ginger murmured.

"Me neither." Kaidan pecked my lips once more. He looked more alive and content than I'd ever seen him.

"Now to your final destination," Blake said as he headed for the cockpit.

"Which is where?" I asked.

"Ask your *husband*," Blake answered as he took his seat.

"Husband!" Marna squeaked.

"Weird," I whispered.

Kaidan's half grin was killer. "Am I less sexy now?"

"Um, no," I assured him.

"You have to live together and start seeing each other's annoying, nasty little habits before that happens," Marna informed him.

Ginger nodded. "And have your first row."

"We've had loads of rows," Kaidan said.

"Yep. We're like an old married couple when it comes to fighting."

Kaidan and I pretended to push each other, but it ended with him holding me. I looked up at him.

"Where *are* we going?"

"Somewhere I should have taken you years ago. The Grand Canyon."

I buried my face in his chest as yet another wave of emotion and memories crashed over me.

The road trip when I'd wanted to detour to the Grand Canyon, but we didn't, because he sent me home alone.

The postcard he'd mailed from the Grand Canyon when

he cut me out of his life and moved to L.A.

So many ups and downs. So many months of wondering how he really felt, and not knowing if he was okay. And all along he'd loved me. All along we were going to be together.

"You okay, luv?" he asked.

"Yes," I whispered. I was far better than okay.

"Time to buckle up," Blake said, getting fancy by using the intercom system. "We are now beginning our initial descent into the Grand Canyon area. Please, uh, stow all your luggage in the, uh . . ."

"Overhead compartments," called out the twins in sync as Blake fumbled his way through the landing spiel.

While they chattered, Kaidan and I linked fingers and held tight, impromptu husband and wife headed for our one-night honeymoon at one of the world's natural wonders.

"Oh, man, look out your windows," Blake said.

A collective gasp sounded as we all leaned over and took in the great expanse below—a massive crevice in the earth's surface as far as we could see and deeper than we could fathom. The enormity of it was spooky. I looked up into the blue depths of Kaidan's eyes, which held warm promises that sent a shiver to my core. It was a day for beautiful, unfathomable, wondrous things.

With each dip of the plane, my heart soared, and I thanked heaven for loopholes and long-lost dreams come true.

CHAPTER FOURTEEN

IMPATIENT FRECKLES

Kaidan and I said our good-byes to the others and took a cab together, all the while searching the skies. This seemed too good to be true. I didn't want to think that way, but I'd never wanted anything as badly as I wanted this night with Kaidan. After two years of longing, we could finally be together, and it would bring us some measure of safety.

I still couldn't believe this was possible. I'd been so paranoid about the hilt and its unforgiving judgment that I hadn't taken into account the power of love and loyalty, for which the Sword of Righteousness could not fault us. It seemed so obvious now. So right.

"Grand Canyon's right over there," the cabbie said, pointing to the left. "Your place ain't far. You could probably walk."

As we drove past, we stared through patchy trees and saw railings along a dry, rocky ledge, and then nothing. Just a massive drop and a sky darkening into dusk. Kaidan and I cuddled closer as we leaned toward the window to peer out together. It was almost enough to make me forget everything out there in the world that wanted to hurt us. But Kaidan never forgot. He peered around at our surroundings again in that protective, cautious way, and it brought me back to reality.

Minutes later we were parked outside a modern log cabin. An uncontrollable grin split my face as nerves overtook me once more.

Kaidan and Blake had been busy boys during our wait this afternoon. Along with getting the rings, Kaidan had scored an amazing resort cabin.

The cabbie drove away, leaving us standing on the front step in silence. I stared at Kai's badge for what felt like a long time before he touched my chin and I met his eyes. The night was warm, and yet I found myself shivering.

Without warning, Kaidan picked me up, cradling me in his arms.

"What are you doing?"

"Er . . . carrying you over the threshold. That's what I'm meant to do, right?"

I giggled and he gave the cutest sheepish grin. "I think it's supposed to be the threshold of our home, but I like it."

He held his face an inch from mine. "This is our home tonight. Anywhere with you is my home."

Love for him lit every corner of my soul. I held myself up with my arms around his neck, giving him a soft kiss. "Take me inside," I whispered. The scent of sweet and spicy citrus filled my nose.

"Yes, ma'am."

Inside, I drew a deep breath as he set me on my feet and closed the door. I said a silent prayer that no whisperers would find us this night, and I vowed to myself not to spend our time together worrying. I would focus on Kai and let him distract me.

The cabin was exquisite. Everything from floor to ceiling was natural stone and wood beams. It had a rustic atmosphere, with the added luxury of modern amenities.

We walked into the single room with its steepled roof, and I covered my mouth to stifle an excited squeal. The bed. *The bed!* I'd never seen anything like it. The headboard was part of an enormous tree, and the branches jutted out high over the top of the king-size bed like a canopy. I ran to it and jumped onto the fluffy comforter made of soft fall colors.

"This is so awesome!" I bounced on my knees, grabbing a silky brown pillow with turquoise trim and squeezing it. Kaidan stood against the wall with his hands in his pockets, looking amused.

I leaped off the bed and grabbed his hand, pulling him to the bathroom, where I clapped my hands at the sight of an oversize claw-foot tub. A sliding door caught my attention next and I opened it, walking out and gasping.

"An outdoor shower!" I said. The area was enclosed by stone walls for privacy, but open to the darkening sky.

Kaidan stood in the doorway. "I'm having flashbacks of the sixteen-year-old girl I took on a road trip who got excited over every little thing."

I blushed and he stepped out onto the stones, cupping my cheek and then sliding his hand into my hair. "It's adorable, luv," he whispered. And then he kissed me.

My heart started pounding as his lips moved against mine. For the first time ever we wouldn't have to be careful or hold back, and it sent a nervous jolt to my core. I didn't know what to do. I knew how he made me feel, like we could never be close enough, but I didn't know how to channel those instincts.

"What's wrong?" he asked.

I shook my head, feeling foolish. "I don't know what I'm doing."

"Anna?" He stayed close, not taking his hands off me.

"Hm?"

"Have you ever felt as if you were fumbling around awkwardly when we're together?"

"Um . . ." I thought about it. "I guess not."

"Exactly. Some things come naturally, so don't overthink it. I'm going to take care of you."

Oh, my. Major chills.

"But," I whispered, "I want to take care of you, too. You have to show me what to do."

His smile was wickedly sexy. "I'm not as hard to please as you might imagine. But don't worry—I'll show you anything you want."

I swallowed a dry lump in my throat.

"Also . . ." He cleared his throat and sounded serious now. "Two days ago when Father told me he was sending me to seek you out . . . I went to the doctor first. Just in case anything were to happen with us—not that I thought it would, but I just wanted to be sure."

"Oh," I said as it dawned on me and I thought of Marna. "To make sure you're really . . ."

"Sterile, yes. And I am."

The thought of getting pregnant hadn't crossed my mind. Even after everything with poor Marna and Jay. I was grateful he'd thought of it.

"Thank you," I whispered. My knees were trembling. Seriously, I could not get my body under control. Those bedroom eyes were short-circuiting my functioning abilities.

"Anna . . ." Uh-oh. His voice was low and gravelly.

"Hmm?" I cleared my throat.

"Remember when I told you I wanted to introduce myself to every freckle on your body?"

Mesmerized, I nodded, not trusting my voice.

"Well, it's time."

I couldn't breathe. Kaidan closed his eyes and inhaled. When he opened them again, they were half-lidded, and a rumble came from the back of his throat.

"You smell so damn good."

He grasped my hand and led me back through the bathroom to the main room. Blood rushed through my body. I stared at his strong back and shoulders. My *husband*. The boy who'd stood at the summit, ready to die for me when my life was threatened.

He let go of my hand and went to his bag.

"I asked Marna to pick up a few things for us—some clothes for tomorrow, food and whatnot. She said she downloaded mood music as a gift. I'm a bit frightened." He pulled out a music dock and set it up, clicking an MP3 player into place and pushing Play. A popular romantic song came on.

Kaidan made a face. "Country music?"

"I love this song!" I laughed when he groaned.

"Maybe we should listen to my playlist instead." He reached into his pocket, but I shook my head, not in the mood for heavy metal.

"Come on, Kai . . . my freckles are getting impatient."

He straightened, standing tall, and his eyes crashed into mine as his badge spun and pulsed. My heart banged at my own bravery, then stumbled inside my ribs as he came closer, bringing with him a cloud of incredible earthy, citrusy pheromones.

"Well, then. Let's not keep them waiting."

I expected the tearing-off of clothes to begin, but instead he kissed me like we had all the time in the world, his mouth and tongue warming me, then heating me. He moved me backward as we kissed, until my bottom hit the edge of the bed. A tickle began at my hips—the feel of his fingers gathering the silk of my dress upward, slowly.

I was breathing hard when he finally pulled it over my head. I kicked off my shoes, sending them flying. He let me lift his shirt off him, but stopped me when I went for his shorts.

"Not yet." Again with the wicked grin.

He reached behind me for the clasp of my strapless bra, and as it fell a rush of self-consciousness made me cover my chest. He narrowed his eyes, and I felt like I needed to explain, even though he'd seen me naked already.

"They're . . ." I couldn't even say it. No doubt Kaidan had seen all kinds of rockin' bodies in his time. Mine would not be one of them—at least not in this department.

He put his hands over mine and looked at me very seriously. "I assure you, they're *perfect*."

He gently pulled my hands away. My chest heaved with nervous breaths as his eyes trailed down, took in the sight of my nearly naked body, and then closed. When they opened they were as stormy as ever.

"Like I said. Just right. On the bed with you now."

Nerves. So many nerves.

I climbed onto the bed and the sweet torture began as he lay on his side next to me and continued taking his time kissing me. I tried to squirm closer, but he laid his hand firmly on my hip to keep me in place. When his mouth moved down to my shoulder, I let out a moan and saw him smile. He kissed a tiny freckle there I'd never paid attention to in my life. Then, slowly, he made his way across my collarbone and down my chest from one side to the other. My fingers were buried in his hair.

Kaidan made good on his promise. My freckles were very happy, spoiled rotten even, but the rest of me was desperate and jealous. And he'd barely gotten started. When he got to my lower stomach, I was breathing way too hard.

He bypassed my lacy white panties, keeping them on, and I was certain now he was trying to send me into a state of insanity. His mouth landed on my inner thigh. My hips bucked and I made a really embarrassing sound of yearning.

He chuckled and pushed my hips firmly down. Again. Not funny. Then continued working his way down my leg.

I whispered, "Please," needing so much more.

"Not yet," he said, all maddening slowness.

I whimpered when he rolled me to my stomach and brushed my hair aside. My back felt ultrasensitive to the caress of his warm mouth. Using my heightened sense of touch was absolutely not necessary tonight. I clutched the downy covers and tried to control myself. How was he not going crazy? I knew he must be because I could smell his pheromone cloud of zesty, sweet oranges and limes around us, but his self-control was incredible.

My lower back was particularly sensitive and I gasped as he kissed me there. When he got down to my panties I felt his teeth gently bite through the lace, and he emitted a low growl. His fingers tightened on my hips and I smiled into the downiness. Ah, finally. His weakness.

"Take them off," I said.

He didn't hesitate, pulling down the lacy cloth.

I dared a peek over my shoulder and saw him staring at my naked body.

"My *God*," he breathed.

I flipped over, and he loomed above me, both of us breathing hard. I stayed very still as Kaidan gave me a stare, starting from my rumpled hair all the way to my red-painted toes. I curled my finger through his belt loop and tried to pull him down to me, but he released my finger, lifted it to his mouth, and nipped it with his white teeth.

"I'm not done yet."

I fell back, as his mouth lowered to my stomach again, working his way down.

Oh, wow.

Over that next hour I learned Kaidan was true to every claim he'd ever made about being good at what he did. It wasn't fair to the rest of the world that a man like him existed. My body was spent as if I'd run a marathon, and considering that Kaidan was still mostly dressed, I knew he was just getting started.

System overload.

As he lay next to me now, leaning over me, placing angelic kisses on my lips, I was barely conscious enough to unscramble the single thought running through my mind.

I'm still a virgin.

"You can nap, luv," he whispered.

That cleared my head. This was no time for napping! I pushed up on my elbows and glared at him. It must not have been scary enough because he chuckled.

"It's your turn," I said.

His chuckling stopped and turned to a heated stare as I moved closer to him. I leaned in and nuzzled his ear. He pulled my hip closer.

"My sweet little vixen." I heard the arousal in his voice, so I licked his earlobe, and he hissed, trying to roll on top of me, but it was my turn to push him back.

No sex yet. I wanted to do to him what he'd done to me.

This time when my shaking hands went to the buttons on his shorts, he didn't stop me. I could feel his racing heart against my shoulder. He let me undress him, and in that moment, as I acquainted myself with all of him for the first time, I learned the power of being a woman—the weakness in his eyes brought on by my touch—and the underlying trust and love I saw there. My nervousness disappeared, replaced by curiosity and a desire to make him happy. It brought me tremendous satisfaction as he reacted and lost himself in the caress of my hands and my lips.

Afterward we showered in the moonlight, lost in our new knowledge of each other. But each kiss and touch was overshadowed by one repetitive thought.

I'm still a virgin.

We wrapped ourselves in towels and went back in, eating sandwiches on the bed while Kaidan made fun of the pop love ballads on Marna's playlist. Funny how he knew the words to so many of them.

When we finished dinner, I looked at the clock. Kaidan had walked to the window and stood staring out, towel still around his waist. I refused to let him think too much. I didn't want any insecurities of his to rise up between us.

"Hey," I said softly. "It'll be midnight soon. Our wedding day is almost over."

His face clouded, and my stomach tightened.

I stood on the far side of the bed. "Come here."

Kaidan walked over slowly, keeping his eyes on me in my towel. When he got to the other side of the bed he put his joined hands on top of his head and eyed me across the king-size expanse. He made me feel crazy in so many ways.

I reached for the edge of my towel, and before I could think too much about it, I pulled it off, letting it drop to the floor. The cloudiness in his gaze turned stormy. I crawled across the bed toward him. I watched the surprise and lust flash across his features as I reached him and raised up on my knees to face him. My heart was beating overtime.

"Are you scared?" I asked him.

The master of lust seemed to have lost his cool because his response was a grunted "Hm?"

"Been too long?" I cocked my head to the side. "Out of practice?"

He hadn't been with anyone in eight months. For Kaidan Rowe, that was an eternity.

His eyes got wider than I'd ever seen them, full of indignation, and I felt a rush of mean potency in my blood. Acting as the vixen he often called me, I reached out and pinched his nipple. Hard.

He let out a small holler and grabbed my wrist. With my other hand I tore off his towel. In a movement too quick for me to comprehend, he was on top of me, pinning me to the bed.

"You win," he ground out, breathing hard.

I wanted to laugh at the thrill of my victory, but his seriousness snuffed that urge. I tried to move my hips up to him, but his body pressed me down. I stroked his cheek, which had grown a five o'clock shadow, and he rested his forehead against mine. I felt his worries creeping in—the deeds of his past haunting him.

"This is right, Kai. We love each other."

He closed his eyes. "I'd do anything for you."

"Just love me," I whispered.

"I need you to know this is different for me. I've never felt like this with someone. I don't just love you, Anna. I adore you."

I kissed him, and when he pulled away, his hair hung around his eyes in sexy strands. I knew from the deep look he gave me that this was about to happen.

"Don't look away from me, Anna," he said.

I nodded. Nervous. Excited. "Okay."

"If you need to stop—"

"Kai. I'm not fragile."

"Right."

I watched him swallow, then close his eyes as a shiver ran through his body. When he opened his eyes again, color poured through the air around him—the vivid, hot pink of passionate love.

Kaidan was showing me his colors.

It was my turn to swallow hard as I beheld the special gift he was offering. Under his thick aura of love was a strand of gray worry and even darker self-loathing. I wished I could make those go away, but only he held that power. Still . . .

"It's beautiful," I whispered.

"*You're* beautiful," he whispered back.

I hitched a leg around him to pull him closer. He shifted above me, his body powerful and graceful. His hips curved toward mine and I moved to meet him, gasping at the contact. I never took my eyes from Kai as we became one.

CHAPTER FIFTEEN

DANCING WITH LIGHT

My goal had been to stay awake with Kaidan all night, but I must have dozed off because I woke at three a.m. with that eerie feeling of being watched. Moonlight streamed through the curtains, and I found Kaidan sleeping soundly next to me. I looked around the room but saw nothing out of the ordinary.

It must have been a full moon because the night seemed brighter than normal. There were no streetlights. And then, suddenly, the light shifted and dimmed. Something was out there. My heart raced as I climbed silently from the bed and went to the window.

In the darkness, trailing through trees away from our cabin, was a spirit of light. An angel! Wonderment swirled through me like a windstorm. I didn't want it to leave. I wanted to know why it'd been at our window and what it wanted—who it was.

I slipped on a pair of shorts and a T-shirt, and slid my feet into flip-flops. Kaidan didn't wake up. He must have been really tired, and I couldn't say I was surprised. Hopefully I could sneak out and make it back without disturbing him. I left our cabin in silence and took off running toward the woods.

The spirit was fast, only a dot of light now. I followed it in the direction of the Grand Canyon. I could see the nearest cabin down the road, but no lights were on. Only a crescent moon and a huge sky full of stars lit my way, so I opened my night vision to get me through the pine trees on the dirt trail. I couldn't see the angel anymore.

This was really stupid of me. I knew better than to go out in the open at night. As I berated myself, the trees tapered off around me and I stopped and stared.

Whoa.

Fifteen feet away from me was a wooden railing, and then darkness. Nothing. It could have been the edge of the earth. I moved closer and felt a dizzying sense of vertigo until my hands grasped the rail. It was monstrous. Eerily majestic. Scary, even. Deeper and wider than I could comprehend. With my supernatural vision I could just barely make out layers of earth in the canyon walls. I wished Kaidan were at my side to see it.

From the corner of my eye I saw a shooting star. My heart thumped and I stared at the white light as it moved with graceful speed through the sky. Definitely not a star. It seemed to be dancing its way toward me, loving the open space provided by the canyon.

I held my breath as it got nearer, feeling that same awe I'd felt when angels had entered the summit in New York. Such indescribable beauty and peace, like everything was okay, and all of my worries were silly and inconsequential.

As its gossamer form neared, a song blossomed in my mind—a sound more enchanting than children laughing and choirs harmonizing. My heart grew wings.

The angel descended until we were face-to-face and I was overcome with clear, pure emotion. The spirit wore a fine cloth around its body, golden hair long and windswept. I met its perfect, angelic face, and while I didn't recognize her visually, my heart cried out. . . .

Mother.

Through our telepathic bond I asked, *"Are you . . . Mariantha?"*

She smiled. *"Yes, my darling girl. We finally meet."*

Her voice was the most tender sound in the universe. I felt a brief flashback to my days in the womb when I heard her singing. It was her human voice, but her angelic soul had been shadowed within it.

Words couldn't express what it meant to have her there at that moment. I could see why Dad's soul had been drawn to hers. She was like a sweet wind of comfort that beckoned and pulled, sweeping me closer.

"I keep watch over you when I can, Anna, though I've only been given permission to visit this special night. We have been celebrating your marriage."

"You have?"

I must have looked stunned because she giggled. At least I think it was a giggle—it sounded like light, jingling chimes ringing, and it made me smile.

"Oh, yes. We rejoice when love endures. I believe you already know the truth of life, my dearest Anna. That love is the strongest force. The binding substance. The element worth existing for. That is what makes you pure of heart."

I didn't know what to say. I felt buoyant and light, lifted by peace. Because she was right. I did know the truth.

"Never doubt it," she said, and her voice sounded like a song in my ears.

A bright star flashed far out in the sky, making my heart jump. Mariantha noticed it, too.

"I cannot stay." She circled me again like she was dancing, and I turned to follow, together, spinning. Then she looked up toward the trees. "Your young man searches for you. He is frightened."

Oh, no!

"Kai!" I called to the air. "It's all right. I'm at the canyon."

I pushed my hearing into the trees and heard him running down the path. I met him at the edge as he emerged barefoot, wearing only a pair of shorts. He looked around wildly, eyes landing on my mother.

"It's okay," I whispered. I went into his arms. He was short of breath as he stared at her. I took his hand and led him to the lookout point.

"Kaidan . . . this is my mother, Mariantha."

His eyes got huge. He bowed his head and said, "It's an honor to meet you."

I couldn't hear her, but she must have been talking to him, because he looked up at her shyly and thanked her. Then she spoke to us both.

"*I must go. Guard your love, for it will lead you through the darkness.*" She turned to me. "*You are ever in my heart, Anna. I love you always.*"

"And I love you," I whispered to her as she drifted farther out above the canyon.

My fingers clutched the railing as she rose high with a magnificent flap of wings that took her out of view.

Kaidan and I grabbed hands and hurried back to the cabin so we weren't in plain sight. When we got there, he grasped my face in both his hands and backed me into the wall.

"You scared me to death," he said. "Don't ever leave me like that again."

"I'm so sorry. You were sound asleep, and I saw her. . . . I know it was dumb, but she was like . . ."

"A beacon to you?"

"Yes." I reached up and held his wrists, feeling horrible that I'd scared him.

"Were they really celebrating us?" he asked. "Up there?"

I smiled. "They really were."

His eyes glassed over, as if he couldn't fathom anyone in heaven talking about something he'd done, much less celebrating him. His astonishment made me kiss him, wanting to capture his sensations and mingle them with mine. Kaidan responded, not holding back a single part of himself.

"Let's not sleep tonight," I said between kisses. We had to leave in a few hours. I didn't want to waste a minute.

"I'm going to let you make all the rules in this marriage, Anna."

"Good boy."

He laughed, a delicious sound that turned his gorgeous face into that of the happy man I wanted to see. We spent the rest of our wedding night loving each other and trying to forget about the things we'd soon be facing. For those last few hours we wrapped ourselves in each other and forgot about the world.

CHAPTER SIXTEEN

ALL-AMERICAN BOY

Leaving Kaidan in the past had never been easy. Leaving him this time felt like I was ripping out some vital part of myself. We lingered at the airport too long, risking too much, waiting until the final calls for our flights and barely making them.

As I flew to Virginia, I couldn't help but smile to myself. In this one way we'd outsmarted the Dukes, taking something special for ourselves. And it had been the best night of my life.

My only regret was that Patti hadn't been there when we exchanged vows. I wanted so badly to see her—to tell her everything and be filled with her loving energy.

I'd received a text from Jay early that morning that simply said: *All good*. I hoped they were keeping each other safe and sane. Maybe even having a few laughs.

I bit my thumbnail and stared out at the wisps of clouds as we flew through them. Could I chance a visit to Patti and Jay? My heart accelerated in happiness as I imagined it, but I wasn't sure I was willing to take the chance. I would never forgive myself if I drew attention to them and they were hurt.

My head spun with details and I knew I needed rest. Kaidan and I had not gone back to sleep.

Ah, my Kai . . .

I closed my eyes and allowed only happy thoughts until sleep found me.

The dorms of Virginia Tech opened that day. I adored the castlelike gray stone buildings and mountainous landscape. Campus was a wild rumpus of minivans and families with armfuls of stuff. I felt like an outsider. An impostor. No family. No belongings. Just a book bag with a laptop and a few changes of clothes. I had spent most of my life feeling like I didn't belong, so I should have been used to it, but that desire to fit in and be like everyone else never went away. Especially on a day like today.

I tried not to get in anyone's way as I walked across the grassy quad to my dorm. I glanced at students playing a pickup game of touch football—guys and girls laughing, flirting, being young with their yellow and red auras. No immediate concerns for their lives. As much as their happiness made me mourn for the youthful experiences I'd never have, it also brought me joy to see people *living*. And to think how their lives could be even richer if we rid their world of demons . . .

A weird thought suddenly hit me as I walked through the multitudes of students and their families.

I was freaking married. My eyes got big and I stumbled a little. Then I giggled and shook my head at the craziness of it all.

At my dorm I held the door open for a mom and dad carrying a futon while their daughter walked behind them, texting on her cell phone. She let me hold the door for her as well, barely glancing up at me.

"You're welcome," I said brightly.

She looked at me like I was crazy.

I passed them and took the stairs up to the sixth floor, letting myself into the tiny end room, a single. As the door shut behind me, I thought for a moment that it must be the wrong room. Someone's stuff was already there. And then I saw the note.

I didn't know if you'd have much time for shopping, so I figured I'd help. ~P

My eyes welled up as I scanned the things: a fuzzy purple papasan chair and matching throw rug, lavender bedding, a new fridge and microwave, food and drinks, a bathroom kit with all the necessities, and a box of my clothes with a roll of quarters for laundry.

I wondered if she'd had it all delivered or if she'd brought it herself. I ached inside from missing her. Wiping my eyes, I unpacked everything and set up the room. It felt a little more homey, but I was far from feeling at home.

I set up my music station and put Marna's romantic playlist on, then flopped onto the bed for a hopeful nap. As the music played, I remembered last night—the silly faces Kaidan made at certain songs, and his serious look when he was solely concentrated on my body. Each song was a memory, replaying our honeymoon through my mind in vivid recollection.

A naughty thought crossed my mind as I recalled the picture of myself I'd saved on my phone. I pulled it up and found it to be just as sexy as I remembered. Now that he'd seen every inch of me, it didn't seem like such a big deal to send it. It probably wouldn't even affect him.

With a nervous, half-delirious giggle, I sent it.

Right away the giggles disappeared and panic set in. What had I done? Kaidan Rowe had, no doubt, received hundreds of sexy photos in his day. Suddenly mine seemed lame. Would he laugh? I wished I could unsend it, or that there was a way to cancel a message if it had yet to be opened.

Stupid, stupid, stupid! I climbed under the covers and pulled them up to my neck. I must have been crazy from lack of sleep. What was I thinking? I rolled over and squealed into the pillow.

And then my phone dinged with a text message. I shut my eyes as my heart went into overdrive. Would he throw me a bone? Say something like, "Aw, that's cute, luv—thanks"?

With reluctance I picked up my phone. Another text dinged. I opened it—both were from Kaidan. Another dinged. Sheesh, what was going on?

OH GOD.

What r u doing to me??

I can't believe u took a pic.

Killing me. DYING.

My worry began to subside, and the laughter rose up again. Text messages poured in, one after another.

CANNOT STOP STARING.

Just wait little vixen.

F me. Ur so fn hot.

Ur in serious trouble when I see u again.

Serious. Trouble.

Whew, dang, it was hot under the covers. I kicked them off, feeling relieved, giddy, and so tired. When a minute passed with no messages, I texted him back.

Baby steps for your nerdy girl.

I smiled at his quick response: *Nerdy my arse. All the cold showers in the world can't cure what u've done to me.*

Sorry, I texted, still smiling like an idiot.

U r not. Leave me alone. I'll b busy 4 a bit.

PS . . . ilu.

I texted back, *ilu2.*

Letting out a long breath, I deleted the conversation and cuddled my pillow. Poor Kaidan. I hadn't meant to work him into a frenzy, but I had to admit I was glad I could.

A knock at the door woke me from a hard sleep sometime later. I blinked groggily toward the window. It looked like early evening. Another knock sounded. I turned off the music and went to the door without opening it.

"Yes?" I asked through the wood.

"Anna Whitt? A delivery for you from the front desk."

I opened the door a crack. A large, gorgeous blond guy stood there with a box—it looked like another box of my stuff.

"I'll set it down for you," he said.

"Oh, sure." I stepped aside. "Thank you."

Yes, I was married to a total hottie, and no, I wasn't lusting after this guy, but it was hard not to take him all in. He was tall and broad like a football player, with an all-American smile and wavy hair. He carried himself with total confidence, like Kaidan, exuding a presence that drew people in.

And then the guy turned to me and my heart nearly stopped.

At his sternum was a bright red badge—the biggest badge I'd ever seen on a Neph . . . as large as a Duke's. My heart banged a painful triple beat.

Red. Lust. Who was this?

With one grand step he stood over me, looming, taking in a deep breath through his nose as if smelling something.

All at once, whisperers came in a dark whoosh down the busy hallway, weaving through parents and students. My room was at the end of the hall and nobody was looking my way. There were so many spirits, at least six of them. For one horrible moment I was shocked into inaction. And then the handsome Nephilim's eyes shone red.

What the . . . ? A Neph's eyes could *not* do that.

I made an involuntary sound of fear and ran for the open door, but the kid was faster. He actually chuckled as he caught me by the arm and closed the door, pressing himself against my back and nuzzling his nose into my hair.

"Don't make a sound," he warned in a calm voice.

He moved fast, capturing both of my wrists in one of his hands and holding them above my head against the wall while his other hand circled my throat.

Red badge. American accent. Did Pharzuph have another son? Why did he feel so powerful? The room darkened as the spirits piled in, making sounds like hissing and scratching that echoed in my head.

He moved my hair aside with his chin and placed a warm kiss on the side of my neck. I shivered, but not in the good way.

Again, he inhaled deeply.

"So, you're not *the one* after all," he said. "And I'd been so certain. I even hoped. I should teach you a lesson for all the trouble you've caused."

What was he talking about? My mind swirled with confusion.

He ground his strong body against my backside. Every instinct inside me flared with the need to fight my way to freedom and run, but a deeper part of me told me to be still. The whisperers hovered around us, shifting.

"Let me go," I said, struggling for any wiggle room and finding none. He squeezed my throat harder and I made a strangling sound.

My resistance only seemed to turn him on, and he chuckled again. His hand blessedly eased off my throat, only to start wandering down my body. I was about to bite his arm and stomp his foot when he spoke again.

"You smell so much better than the last time I saw you. If you weren't a disgusting little Neph, I'd take you right now."

I froze. No way.

With a grunt he released me. My eyes felt big when I turned to face him.

"D-duke Pharzuph?" I whispered. Had I fallen into a warped universe?

The whisperers bounced with anticipation. Pharzuph waved an impatient hand and growled at them as if they were pesky gnats.

"No show for you right now. She's not a virgin. Go tell the others." With that, they shot out of the room from all angles, making my head spin.

"How do you like it?" He grinned, motioning to his grand physique, and I swallowed. "I was going to wait a couple years, but with all the excitement going on, I wanted a change. This poor kid had a logging accident up in Oregon. Parents were already dead. It would've been a shame to let this go to waste, wouldn't you say?"

I just wanted him and his ego to leave. This whole thing was incredibly weird and creepy. He sounded nothing like his old self.

"It's . . . a good body."

"Better than good!" He laughed. "I can have any girl on this campus tonight, and I think I will." He rubbed his hands up and down his chest and abs, obviously high on his born-again youth. "I always forget how much energy and stamina a young man's body has."

Ew.

My stomach turned at the thought of him tearing through campus and hurting these girls in any way. He looked so innocent on the surface with that farmer-boy grin. And then his eyes flashed red again with his evil intentions and I jumped as he stepped closer.

"I still don't like you," he said. "Or trust you. But at least I can check my son off the suspicion list now."

"Suspicion list?" I asked, trying to keep my eyes down and appear meek. "Sir, please. If this is about the summit in New York, I was just as shocked as you all when those angels came—"

"Just mind your own business and work for the cause. This place is fertile for a Neph of your type. You're lucky Belial's given you such a good setup after all the trouble you've been. And speaking of your old man . . ." He eyed me. "Where is he?"

He was trying to sound light and disinterested, but I wasn't buying it.

"I don't know, sir. I assume somewhere in Washington, D.C., now."

"Hmph." He continued to stare me up and down. How had I thought he seemed like a regular, nice guy at first? His eyes were so clinical and calculating. Even when he was grinning he had a menacing quality.

He pushed past me to the door, turning to speak one last time in a hushed voice. "Never forget you're expendable. If you give us trouble again, you will disappear with no questions asked, angels be damned. Do you understand, Neph?"

My heart thumped. "Yes, Duke Pharzuph."

"And when you see that father of yours again, tell him hell's looking for him."

Keeping my eyes averted, I gave a tight nod. My throat was

too dry to swallow. I was suddenly paranoid about how long he'd be here on campus and what he expected of me.

"Excuse me, Duke. . . ." I hated how weak my voice sounded, although it was best that he knew I feared him. "I was just wondering, do you need me to, um, work with you tonight or anything?"

He laughed. Loudly. A patronizing sound.

"No, I don't *need* you to work with me. I don't work with Neph." He practically spat the words. "I'll only be here one night and I want to enjoy it. Find your own bar and send the drunks my way."

He laughed again, low and lewd.

I felt his stare roaming my body before he finally left, and I collapsed onto the bed, shaking.

CHAPTER SEVENTEEN

Darts

It was a true testament to how strange my life had become that the best night of my life was followed by the most uncomfortable. Knowing that Kaidan's father, a guy who was now the same freaking age as him, was leaving a trail of broken hearts all over my college campus made me ill. And not just broken hearts. That would be too tame for Pharzuph. He would push people to do things they weren't ready for, and all the while he and the whisperers would mess with their minds—filling them with guilt and self-loathing that would plague them for years to come. He wasn't just a campus player out for sex. He was an evil bastard out to hurt souls. A weapon in a very beautiful disguise.

All night as I sat at the bar, my knee bouncing a thousand miles per hour, I thought about what Kaidan and I had shared—how special and beautiful it had been. And then I thought of Pharzuph. My stomach turned.

Did Kaidan have any idea that Pharzuph had changed bodies? Had he received a call about his father, Richard Rowe, dropping dead at work in New York City or at his posh home in Atlanta? He knew Pharzuph planned to find me and give me the sniff test—trying to catch the scent of virginity. I wished I could call Kaidan and reassure him that it had happened and I was okay.

What a freaking mess.

But at least our plan had worked, and for that I allowed myself to smile into my beer glass. Kaidan and I were momentarily off the suspicion list. Unfortunately, my father was still on it. Big-time.

My smile disappeared.

"Hey, can I buy you another?"

I looked up at the cute boy who'd spoken. The bar I'd chosen had gotten crowded and loud, but it was mostly groups of friends, so nobody had talked to me yet. Pharzuph was probably too busy to keep an ear out on me, but I didn't want to take any chances. Plus, there were at least six whisperers prowling through town tonight, so I had to work.

"How about this?" I asked the guy. "Let's play darts, and the loser buys the next round."

He sucked in air through his teeth. "I don't know. I'd feel kinda bad making a pretty girl I just met buy my drink. . . ."

"Oho, so it's like that, huh?" I hopped off the stool, surprised by my own ability to feel lighthearted at the moment, but sometimes boys needed to be taught lessons about underestimating girls.

And so the night passed with me kicking the butt of every guy in the bar. The girls, after realizing I wasn't interested in their boyfriends, became my cheerleaders. Yeah, I got a few people drunk. Between the beers and shots, I pushed glasses of water their way all night, hoping to keep them hydrated.

I never forgot who I was, or the fact that I wasn't one of them, but I still let myself enjoy their company and the feeling of being embraced by friendly strangers. We were having a great time until someone turned up the television for a breaking news story. A popular rapper had been shot after his show in D.C. while greeting fans. He had a colorful past, serving jail time, but had turned his life around and become an education advocate—an inspiring American success story. And now he was in a coma, probably going to die.

Everyone in the bar shook their heads, muttering, "What is wrong with this world?"

If they only knew.

The mood was somber after that.

At closing time I managed to evade the cute boy who'd been at my side all night. I slipped the bartender a note to call cabs for my drunken buddies, giving my credit card number as payment.

As I shuffled back to the dorm at two in the morning, a knife in my pocket and the Sword of Righteousness strapped to my ankle under my jeans, I imagined that Kaidan went to school there with me and we were a normal couple. Students. Sometimes it was fun to pretend, but I didn't let myself long for impossible things, because there were Nephilim who would do anything to have the life I led.

Calling my life blessed was ironic, considering, but when it came down to it, I was loved, and that made life worth living. Just like my mother, Mariantha, said.

As I was having that lovely thought, my dorm in sight, a dark shadow flew into my path on the narrow sidewalk, causing a shriek to stick in my throat.

"Baby . . ."

I pressed a hand to my chest. *"You scared me half to death, Dad!"* My telepathic voice screamed at him, and I looked behind me, searching for signs of whisperers but finding none. *"Pharzuph is here tonight with a ton of spirits!"*

"I know. Hurry up and get to your room so we can talk in private." He flew ahead of me, disappearing into the side wall of my dorm.

I huffed a little, my nerves still on alert, and sped to the entry door. It was strange passing the night-watch girl at the desk. I gave her a small smile and she nodded, oblivious to the gigantic ram-horned demon at her side.

In my room, Dad practically took up the whole space, and I felt too edgy to sit. I told him about Pharzuph coming and how Kaidan and I should be safe from him for now.

"But I don't understand something," I said. *"I didn't recognize anything about him—he didn't even talk the same anymore. Has he been an American before, or did he train himself to have a new accent that fast?"*

"No, this is his first time in a U.S. body, but there's certain knowledge a body retains, even when the souls switch. The brain and body hold on to habits like language and gestures. It's still going to talk and act the same until you train it otherwise. It's always

strange at first because it's hard to control, but it ends up being a benefit for us Dukes."

Yeah, how convenient for them.

I told Dad what Pharzuph had said about him being in trouble. Dad laughed. Always a scary sound, deep and guttural, even in spirit form.

"They would've been suspicious of me one way or another, and damned if I was gonna let them capture me. I'll be hunting for a body next, but I came to tell you that Pharzuph and the others have called for a summit tomorrow night—probably to talk about their findings and figure out what to do next. They'll be in Switzerland."

"Switzerland?"

"A ski town. They like to make a vacation of these summits, you know. And since they were just in Vegas, they wanted something different." Dad, being all business, naturally disagreed with the other Dukes' idea of mixing fun with work.

My hopes lifted.

"Wait. Does this mean we Neph have a couple safe days?" I asked.

He grunted. *"Yes, but be careful. I'd say you have forty-eight hours starting tomorrow afternoon when they're all traveling. Some will stay there longer than two days, but don't take any chances. If you need to gather your allies or be in contact with them, this is your chance."*

"And I can see Patti!" I clapped my hands and smiled. This seemed to soften him a little.

"Yeah, you can see her. Give her my regards."

I wished I could hug him, but all I could do was beam up at his frightening face, making him chuckle.

"*And guess what else?*" I said. "*I got to meet Mariantha.*" He became still in front of me. "*She came to congratulate me on my marriage. She was beautiful, Daddy.*"

He drifted back a little, weightless, whispering, "*Yes . . . beautiful, and full of love. You're so much like her, baby girl.*"

I held up a hand, splaying my fingers, and he lifted his big, clawed mass of cloudy hand to mine, overlapping it.

"*I love you, kid,*" he said.

We shared a long, quiet pause.

"*Be careful,*" I told him. "*Wherever you go, I hope I see you again soon.*"

I closed my eyes as he surrounded me with a hug, and when I opened my eyes again he was gone.

CHAPTER EIGHTEEN

MAKESHIFT HOLIDAY

It was three in the morning, Pharzuph was somewhere nearby terrorizing the campus, and I was devising a plan. The Dukes were meeting tomorrow night, so the Neph would have to meet, too.

The thought of seeing Kaidan again after our night together gave me tingles. We wouldn't be alone this time, but being near him was all I needed.

I knew it was safe texting Kaidan since his father was "busy," but my hands still shook with nerves. I didn't want to reveal too much. Each message I sent and received, I deleted immediately.

Book a flight to Va tmrw.

With pleasure. U ok? It's been insane here.

Insane? I wondered if he meant his father's "death."

Here too. Lots to tell.

Same.

I texted him Patti's address and told him I was contacting the others. I knew I'd piqued his interest and concern, but I didn't feel comfortable sharing anything else until the Dukes were all convened on the other side of the world.

Next I texted the twins, then Blake and Kope, telling them where and when to meet. Kope would bring Zania. Everyone was a go. I contemplated texting Jay and Patti, too, but that could wait until the morning.

I was so excited about seeing everyone, and nervous about Pharzuph being so close, that I was restless all night. I finally felt myself pulled under just as the sun was rising. A couple hours of solid sleep would have to hold me over.

When I emerged, groggy and craving coffee, I wished I was better at using my supernatural sense of hearing. I wanted to know if Pharzuph was gone, but when I attempted to scan the area, everything sounded like a jumble to me—too hard to discern. Other Neph were good at it, having trained for years.

After showering and dressing, I walked downtown to a busy coffee shop, keeping my eyes peeled. It was a hot morning, but pleasant compared to the oppressive humidity I was accustomed to. I'd just paid for my latte when everyone got quiet and broke into whispers.

The hair on the nape of my neck went up.

"Oh, my gawd . . ."

"Is he on the football team?"

I turned and bit down to lock my jaw as a tall, sexily

disheveled Pharzuph sauntered up to me, flanked by a dark cloud of whisperers, knowing every eye was on him and clearly basking in the attention. His blond hair was damp and he had a light dusting of morning scruff. His critical eyes lessened his attractiveness, though I doubt anyone else picked up on it.

"And how was your first night of college?" he asked in a low voice, a partial lascivious grin showing.

"Successful, sir." I gripped my coffee to keep from shaking. "And you?"

His grin grew. "One for the memory book. I'd stay another night if I didn't have business to attend to. I'm almost jealous of you." He laughed at the ridiculousness of his statement and glanced around at the myriad of eyes locked on him. I swear, the room seemed to sway with all the swooning and red auras popping up. The spirits dipped and glided among the people.

"It's a great place," I said lamely.

He looked back at me, disappointment flashing across his face as he remembered with whom he'd been conversing. He pushed past me to the counter and I stood aside. But once he had his giant coffee in hand, he left the shop without looking my way again. From my view I watched him making eyes at every girl along the way, and even a couple guys. Then they all turned to look at me. I exited quickly through the side door and went around the corner, watching as Pharzuph caught a cab, his procession of dark spirits flanking the vehicle as it drove him away.

Thank God.

I made the long walk to my car and sat inside, sipping my coffee and feeling oddly safe and content. In a few hours my six

Neph allies would be making their way to town for one night. It could be our last chance to see one another before it was time to fulfill the prophecy. With the Dukes convening that night, our time was short. We'd have to act soon.

I wanted today to be special.

I smiled to myself and started the car. I knew what we were doing tonight.

Patti had no idea I was coming. When I got to her address, I almost rolled my eyes. Of course Dad couldn't have picked out a low-key home. He'd put her up in a huge house on a golf course. It was seriously the only new neighborhood around, and it was smack in the middle of farm country. As I pulled into her driveway, I sent a text.

Don't freak. It's just me.

I knocked on the door and she swung it open, pulled me inside the house, shut the door, and proceeded to squeeze the air out of me. I hugged her back just as hard.

"Anna!" I heard Jay say, coming up behind us.

Patti released me and pulled Jay in until we were having a group hug. She repeatedly kissed my cheek before letting us go.

"I'm so glad you're here!" she said. "You're sure it's safe, though?"

"Positive. All the Dukes are flying to Switzerland right now, so the Neph are coming here."

"All of them?" Jay's eyes got big. I guess Marna hadn't had a chance to tell him yet.

"Yep," I said. "All the allies."

He jumped up and punched the air.

I felt euphoric. "Come on, I have groceries."

They followed me out, and the three of us loaded our arms with bags.

"A turkey?" Patti asked. "Oh, honey, I like the sound of this."

I thought she might. I'd gotten all the fixings for a Thanksgiving meal.

We took everything into the kitchen and I looked around at the stainless steel appliances and stone-tiled backsplash.

"Wow, this house is . . ."

"Overboard?" Patti asked. "Ridiculously huge and fancy? Yes. Your father is a nutcase." But she was smiling as she unpacked the pies.

"Yams," Jay said. "Nice." He was a bit more subdued than normal, but it was understandable, given what he was up against.

"So," I asked the two of them, "do you want the big news first, or should I tell you everything that's happened in order?"

"In order," Jay said.

Patti's eyebrows came together with impatience and she eyed Jay before saying, "Oh, all right then, in order. But make it fast!"

Marna hadn't been able to talk to Jay at all yet, so they had no idea what had happened since Ginger went missing. We made our way into the cushy family room. They were rapt as I talked.

"And then this *huge* spirit showed up," I said, making Patti gasp and her eyes widen as I described its ramlike appearance. "And you'll never believe who it was." They stared at me, on edge. "Dad!"

Patti pressed a hand to her chest. "You mean . . . he doesn't have a . . . he's . . . ?"

"He had to shed his body," I said quietly.

"Dude," Jay said. "He's scary *with* a body. I can't imagine him as a spirit."

"Yeah. It's so weird. He's looking for a new body now," I said.

Patti closed her eyes. When she took a deep breath and nodded, I forged ahead.

"We knew Pharzuph was searching for me, so Dad came up with the idea that me and Kaidan—"

Patti squealed, jumping to her feet. "You're married! Aren't you?"

Jay's shocked face swung back and forth between the two of us. "Nuh-uh! Are you?"

I felt so emotional about my news that I could only nod.

Patti screamed, pulling me to my feet for another bear hug. Her excitement should have felt strange, given the reason why Kaidan and I had decided to marry, but I knew Patti wasn't focused on that. She was focused on the love we shared, and the fact that we were able to have this life experience, despite our circumstances.

"Oh, sweet girl," she said into my hair. "I knew they couldn't keep you apart."

When she let me go, Jay hugged me, saying, "That is crazy. But cool. Congratulations."

"Thank you."

We sat down again, still wired from the big reveal.

"So what happened next?" Jay asked. Then his cheeks got

splotchy. "I mean, not, like, *next* next, but, you know, *after*?"

I picked up the story, telling them how Pharzuph had come to my dorm room in his new form. They were shocked and disgusted.

When I was done, Patti let out a giant sigh.

"I'm so thankful we'll have this night. I'm gonna pop that turkey in the oven and start prepping stuff. Why don't you two go to the pool and try to relax? I think your bathing suits are in one of those boxes upstairs still."

"I can help you with the prep," I said.

"Nah." She smiled. "Let me. I've got plenty to occupy my mind now. You two go be young or something."

She was humming to herself as she went to the kitchen.

We changed our clothes, grabbed towels, and headed down the street to the neighborhood's pool. A couple of families were at the shallow end, so we took lounge chairs at the other end of the pool and lay down. The sun felt glorious.

"I can't believe you're married," Jay said next to me.

"I can't believe you're gonna be a dad," I countered.

"Aren't we too young for all this? Weren't we just learning to drive or something?"

"I know, right?"

We both got quiet. He stared off, and the burdens he carried were apparent in his distant eyes.

"Jay . . . how are you feeling?"

"I don't know. Man. It's like, I'm not really afraid for myself, but I'm scared for Marna and the baby. I want to keep them safe, but I feel like this little nobody. Powerless or something."

"You have more power than you realize. Knowing you love

192

her gives Marna strength. She's happy, Jay. I know it seems crazy, but I think she feels loved by someone other than Ginger for the first time in her life, and she's thankful."

"But I don't want her to die." His voice thickened as he choked up, causing my own throat to swell with emotion. I couldn't respond. All I could do was reach over and link my fingers with his, connecting us in our fear and sorrow.

Lying there next to my oldest and dearest friend felt right—the stretch of silence between us was soothing.

Some kids came over, calling Jay by name. He seemed to cheer a little, getting into the water with them. Of course he'd made buddies in the short time he'd lived here. The kids took turns climbing to his shoulders and jumping off. I lay back on the lounge chair and rolled to my stomach, content as I watched them.

Sounds of splashing faded as I dozed.

And then I heard a beautiful voice. . . .

"Cover your arse, and nobody gets hurt."

I lifted my head to see Kaidan crouched next to me. *He was here!* Just as I was about to get up and throw my arms around him, his gaze slid down my body to my butt and stayed there. Hello, stormy eyes.

I felt twice as hot under the sun as I had one minute ago.

I threw the towel over my body, which forced his eyes back to mine.

"Hey," I whispered.

He touched my face, and I leaned into his palm.

"I feel like it's been a year since I saw you," he said softly. "I've missed you."

I reached up and cupped his hand. "I've missed you, too."

"But you're still in trouble." His voice was low and gravelly. "I need you."

"Um . . ." I looked around.

"Come with me." He was serious. He took my hand and I sped to keep up, holding the towel around my body. Jay caught sight of us and waved from the middle of the pool, but when he saw Kai's determined face, he raised his eyebrows. I shrugged a shoulder innocently, and Jay shook his head. My cheeks flushed.

Kai led us to the women's dressing room, and when he started to push the door open, I pulled back, looking around.

"You can't go in there!" I whispered.

He pulled me forward. "It's empty."

Next thing I knew, we were in a shower stall, kissing behind the closed curtain.

"What if someone comes in?" I asked.

He pressed my back against the smooth tiles. "I'll be listening." He pulled off my towel and dropped it to the dry floor with a growl.

We kissed again and my body reacted. I pulled him closer, loving the feel of his hands across my sun-heated skin. Were we really doing this? In a public place?

Oh, just shut up, my body told my mind. Just a few minutes together before the seriousness began wouldn't hurt.

I heard a sound outside and we both went still.

"Shite, someone's coming."

Two seconds later a woman's voice sounded in the bathroom. Kai pressed his forehead to the tile next to me and squeezed his eyes shut.

"In here, sweetie. Good girl." Oh, great. A mom was taking her little girl to the potty. I felt like a perv.

When I heard their stall door close, I peeked out and pulled Kaidan, tiptoeing out.

I chanced a backward glance at him. His eyes were heated with intensity.

"Later," I promised.

He stopped us under the awning just before the pool area and faced me, lowering his forehead to mine.

"I can't go back out there yet. I'm having a bit of a focusing problem."

I gave a dry laugh, though I knew he was being serious. I was feeling tight all over, too.

"I know, baby," I whispered, squeezing his bicep. Yeah, touching him wasn't helping my frame of mind much either. I dropped my hand. "Let's get back to the house so we can tell each other everything and then . . . yeah."

"Yeah," he breathed, eyes blazing.

I shivered.

"This is all your fault, you know." A naughty smile appeared on his lips, and with a flush to my cheeks I remembered the cell-phone picture.

The mother and daughter came out of the restroom, passing us. Kaidan gave me a hopeful look and I shook my head. I was not going in there again.

"Come on, Kai. I have stuff to tell you. Big stuff."

He studied me. "Are you all right?"

I wanted to tell him everything, but not out in the open like this.

I pulled clothes on over my bathing suit, got Jay, and we headed back to the house. Kaidan kept catching my eye in long gazes, conveying wordless promises that made my blood rush faster.

"Focus," I told him under my breath.

At the house Patti hugged Kaidan, and it'd been a long time since I'd seen her so happy. She continued to hum as she bustled around the kitchen, her mouth tilting up while she chopped and shredded.

I sat with Kaidan and Jay, and we talked.

Kai said, "I suppose my father decided to make the change of the guard, because Richard Rowe died three days ago."

"Change of the guard?" Jay asked.

"It's when they get rid of their bodies," I explained. "The old body dies when their spirit leaves it, and they have to possess a new one—start a new life."

"Nasty," Jay whispered.

"My father was going to wait a few years, but he must've changed his mind," Kai said, looking at me. "I've worried he'd come to you as a spirit and you wouldn't recognize him, but he'd need a body to smell you, so I'm guessing we still have time. It can take a while."

"Yeah," I said. "About that . . . he found a body."

Kaidan bolted upright. "You've seen him?"

"Yes. He's about your age, maybe a little older. Tall. Blond."

His jaw tightened. "When did you see him? What did he say? Did he touch you?"

I told him everything. He stared at the wall and pulled out his knife as he listened. He continued to open it. Close it. Spin it on his palm. Weave it through his fingers. Jay and I gave it nervous glances.

"Bloody hell . . ." Kaidan thought for a while then shoved the closed knife back into his pocket. "Would you say he's better looking than me?" Oh, geez.

Jay laughed. "Dude. Weird."

"I'm only curious," Kaidan said with a half grin.

"Ew, Kai, no. I can't even think of him like that. His eyes are pure evil. I don't know how anyone can look at him and not get a bad feeling."

"They probably do get a bad feeling," said Jay. "But they like it. They feel like he's dangerous or something."

Oh, he was dangerous, all right. I rubbed my temples.

The doorbell rang, and Jay practically tripped over his own feet jumping up.

Kaidan slipped an arm around me. "You did well. That's over, and we'll be safe for a bit now." He kissed my temple, then bit my earlobe, pulling me closer. I lifted my face to kiss him since we were semialone. As soon as his hot mouth met mine, I wished we were really alone.

"I can't stop thinking about you," he whispered. His words and touch held an urgency that was stronger than it had been before we married, like his self-control had lessened now that we'd been together. This was going to be a long day.

From the kitchen I heard Patti set down her stirring spoon with a clatter and say, "Well, hello, Kope. And you must be Zania! I'm so happy to finally meet you."

I smiled up at Kaidan's handsome face before getting to my feet.

"Z!" I ran, crashing into her in the kitchen. We hugged tight, and I smiled at Kopano over her shoulder. He gave me a nod and smile. More people were coming in behind him.

"Well, if it isn't my sweet Ginger!" Patti said now. "And Marna! And you're Blake, right?"

I couldn't even bring myself to scoff at the "sweet Ginger" comment. We had a house full of friends, and the kitchen smelled divine. The holiday had officially begun.

CHAPTER NINETEEN

LOVE IN THE AIR

We all stood in the kitchen talking over one another. Marna and I noticed at the same time when Zania made her way back to Kopano's side and slipped her arm snugly under his. And then they shared a look so tender that Marna turned and gave me a hand-over-her-heart *Aww!* face. She then wrapped her arms around Jay, and they stood there holding each other with their eyes closed. So much emotion filled the room, but one stood out above the rest. . . .

Love was in the air.

Among other things. Like lust. And the smell of turkey. A weird combo.

Kaidan finally made his way into the kitchen with a serious demeanor. He greeted everyone, but whenever his eyes met mine, the air got hotter until a palpable tension had woven its way around the room. I could feel the warm sunbeam of his stare on me, though I pretended to ignore it. Our friends kept eyeing us. Even Patti noticed.

She regarded Kaidan with curiosity, as if trying to figure him out. When she saw him looking at me, her brow went up. She cleared her throat and dropped her eyes, mumbling, "All righty then," and busied herself basting the turkey.

Okay, this was seriously getting embarrassing. I eyed Kaidan as if to say, *Behave yourself!* He cocked his head as if to say, *I can't bloody help it!*

When Patti left the kitchen to make the guest bed, I suddenly smelled his citrusy pheromones from across the room, and they made me light-headed. I hoped no one else would notice.

"Blech. The newlyweds are hot for each other," Ginger said.

So much for that hope. Heat traveled from my neck up to my face.

"Perhaps the whole lot of you can take a walk," Kaidan said, dead serious.

My eyes got huge. "Kaidan, no!"

Blake, Jay, and Marna started laughing. Ginger rolled her eyes, and I couldn't bring myself to look at Kope and Z.

But Kopano, choosing to ignore the sexual tension despite his own inclination toward lust, stepped forward and held out his hand.

"Congratulations, brother. I am happy for your blessing."

Kaidan took his offering and shook. "Thank you, mate. I'm glad to see you happy, as well." He nodded to Zania, who returned his nod and gifted him with one of her regal smiles. When Kope came to me with an outstretched hand I ignored it, going up on my toes to hug him instead. He chuckled and hugged me back before returning to Z's side. Kaidan watched the whole time but thankfully didn't get upset.

I wish I could say the tension dissipated after that. Kaidan leaned against the counter watching me, his thumb running back and forth over his bottom lip. My whole body prickled with a flush of heat, and I tried not to look at him. His need for me became the elephant in the room that everyone pretended to ignore. I thought about sending him upstairs for a cold shower.

Patti bounded back into the room, and I plastered the fakest smile ever on my face.

"How much longer until the feast?" I asked.

"About one hour," she said. She was busy peeling potatoes into the sink. "Did you get any whipped cream for the pies? I didn't see any."

"No." Rats. I knew I was forgetting something.

"We'll go to the market!" Kaidan suggested quickly. "Anna and I. For the whipped cream." He sidled up to me, putting his arm around my shoulder. He felt like a heater.

I closed my eyes for a brief moment, the fake smile still in place.

"That'd be great," Patti said. I saw some of the snickers being held back, people on the verge of laughing. Marna waggled her eyebrows at me. Even Kope and Zania shared a quick bashful glance before looking down. Patti's attention remained on the potatoes. If she had any idea what was going on, she

201

kept her knowledge hidden, and for that I was glad.

"Just don't be *too* long," Patti said, never looking up.

Yeah, she totally knew.

This wasn't awkward at all. I glared up at Kaidan, but he only smiled adoringly. Blake and Jay were still trying not to laugh as I grabbed my keys and headed out of the house with Kai hot on my tail.

No sooner had we climbed into the car than Kaidan was on me.

"Not in the driveway!" I whispered, slapping away his hand as it sneaked up my shirt. His mouth found my neck and that place under my ear that made me crazy. I threw the car into reverse and sped away from the house.

"I haven't stopped thinking about you," he said against my skin. "It's worse than ever. Now I have these images of you that play through my mind nonstop, driving me mad."

It was really hard to concentrate on driving while a hot mass of passionate boy was all over me, saying things that made my brain fuzzy.

"What if people at the house are listening?" I asked.

"Don't care," he said, still nuzzling my neck.

At the end of Patti's neighborhood were three lots of new houses under construction. It was early on a weekend evening, so nobody was there. I parked out of sight in the cul-de-sac.

"How's this?" I asked.

His response was to lift me as if I were weightless onto his lap to straddle him. We kissed hard, yanking down clothes and leaning back his seat with a jolt.

"God, you're so beautiful, Anna. I can't even think."

"Then don't," I said, bringing my mouth down on his again.

Afterward I lay on his chest, our touches more gentle. Kaidan's eyes seemed to clear, and he sat up on his elbows, frowning down on me.

"I'm a right prick."

"Kai . . ."

"A complete bastard." He sat us both up all the way and took my face earnestly in his hands, pressing his creased forehead to mine. "I'm sorry, luv."

"It's okay."

"We're in the bleedin' car, out in the open in your mum's neighborhood! You can't possibly have been comfortable with that."

"Nobody saw. It was kind of . . . nice." *Hot.* I dropped my eyes, feeling shy for saying it. "I wouldn't have done it if I didn't want to."

His forehead smoothed. His cheeks were a little flushed, and he looked so cute that I wanted to kiss him again.

Better not.

"Seriously, though," I said, leaning down to grab my bottoms from the floor of the car, "you have to get a grip in front of the others." I kissed his cheek and pulled my clothes back on, which was hard to do in his lap, but I managed.

He wrapped his arms around me, setting his chin on my head.

"I know. I'm sorry. I've been a disaster since the Grand Canyon, and cold showers aren't cutting it. You're all I think

203

about—and not just the sex. I thought it was bad before, but now . . . I feel you with me all the time. I'm like one of those obsessed lads."

Giving his handsome cheek a pat, I slid into the driver's seat.

"Well, I've felt like that about you since, like, forever." He smirked as if he thought I was exaggerating. "Let's go to the store and hurry back."

"You know," Kaidan said as I drove, "if it makes you feel any better about my behavior, Blake and Ginger are going at it in the upstairs bathroom right now."

"Agh!" I cringed. "Please tell me you're not listening!"

He laughed and crinkled his nose. "No, I stopped when I realized . . . Gin's like my sister." He shuddered. Then I shuddered, and we both laughed.

We were quick at the store, rushing home afterward, where thankfully Blake and Ginger were back with the others. Kaidan and Blake gave each other nods.

In the kitchen it was time to put the toppings on Patti's myriad of casseroles. Ginger was crushing crackers while Marna grated cheese. Kaidan leaned in the doorway with his arms crossed, watching with a look of contentment. Patti basted the turkey and checked its temperature. I was whipping lumps from the mashed potatoes when Kaidan came up behind me and slipped his hands around my waist, laying his chin on my shoulder.

"No boys allowed," Patti teased. She reached up to ruffle his hair. "Unless you want to cook."

He made a pouty face, which made everyone except Ginger

giggle. But when they went back to working, he shot me a serious glance from the doorway, looking me up and down with a pained expression before disappearing into the other room with the guys and Zania.

I sighed. My man really needed to stay out of the kitchen.

"I think we should play games tonight," Patti said. "What do you girls think?"

Ginger smiled. "That sounds lovely!"

It did? Had she been possessed by an angel or something?

Patti bumped her hip to Ginger's and they both looked happy. Marna smiled from her opposite end of the counter.

"How are you feeling, Marna?" Patti asked her. Ginger stiffened.

"I'm . . . all right. Bit hungrier than usual is all."

Patti watched her carefully. "And how are you holding up?"

Marna swallowed, and for one second her happy face slipped to reveal the turmoil underneath. "I'm okay," she whispered. "I don't want anyone to worry about me."

"I know you don't, dear. But everyone loves you. And it's okay to lean on others when you need to."

"Thank you," Marna whispered, and with a single sniffle she would say no more. Ginger never looked up. The beaters trembled in my hand. Marna didn't want us to make a big deal about her circumstances, and I respected that, but we surely all felt the ache inside about what was to come.

Patti leaned in next to me when I finished the potatoes. "Those look great, honey. Time to set the table." She smacked a kiss on my cheek.

I opened the cabinet and looked at the full set of dishes.

"Did you buy all this?" I asked. They looked fancier than something she would have chosen.

"The entire house was stocked and furnished when I got here."

I couldn't place the faraway look on her face, but I knew it had to do with Dad's thoughtfulness.

I counted plates while Marna took out silverware. Zania came in and got out glassware. Ginger gave the gravy a stir, seeming to enjoy the springy whisk. It was funny how the guys and girls had congregated separately, sort of like Patti gave off feminine vibes that drew us girls under her wings. Laughter sounded from the family room, where the guys were watching something, and Patti's eyes sparkled. She finally had herself a big family to spoil, even if only for a day.

We brought the dishes to the massive oak dining table in the adjoining room, and Patti showed Marna and Ginger the proper layout. I approached Zania as she was filling a pitcher with ice water.

"How are you feeling?" I asked.

She held out her hand for me to see. "No more shaking. I still crave it. Every day. But I will never drink again."

I knew that feeling. I nodded and rubbed her back. "I'm proud of you, Z."

"I have all of you to thank. And your papa."

"How are things in Boston? Do you like it there?"

Zania bit her lip. Her olive cheeks reddened. "Things are very well in Boston. Brother Kopano is only allowed in the garden area, but he visits every day if he can."

"I'm so glad," I said. I wondered about her relationship with

Kope, if they'd talked about their future, but I didn't want to pry, especially with listening ears around. I also wondered if he had told her about the kiss he and I shared, and, with a pang, I hoped he hadn't.

Together we filled the water glasses and set the feast of food around the table. I could feel myself being watched, and sure enough, when I turned around, I had a perfect view of Kaidan sitting on the love seat, one arm over the back of it, capturing me with a hot stare. Why did he always have to look so dangerous and alluring?

"All right, guys!" Patti called. "Dinner's ready!"

The boys wasted no time piling into the room. Patti sat at the head of the table. Down one side were Jay, Marna, Kopano, and Zania. Down the other side were Ginger, Blake, Kaidan, and me. Ginger had bumped me aside when I tried to sit next to Patti, so I let her. I couldn't bring myself to be jealous. Sitting on the end next to Kai, across from Z, I couldn't complain. I loved seeing all eight of us in couples. Everyone except Patti, that is. She looked around the table, that motherly grin of satisfaction never leaving her face.

"Do y'all mind if I pray?" she asked.

Silence.

Blake, Kaidan, and the twins were frozen stiff, and though Patti had to sense it, her warm smile never faltered. I saw Kopano give Marna a small nudge, and she cleared her throat.

"Um, whatever you'd like, Patti."

In awkward movements, everyone looked around hesitantly until Patti said, "Let's hold hands." So we reached out for each other. My heart thumped, hoping the awkwardness in

207

the air would pass. Kaidan twined his fingers with mine, and his palm felt clammy. I bowed my head and closed my eyes.

Patti's voice was soft. Almost immediately a blanket of peace seemed to drape itself over the room. "Heavenly Father . . ." She sighed as if already overwhelmed. "You're certainly asking a lot of these precious children, and I can see why. The possibilities in them are endless, and I hope they can feel that strength in themselves. We don't know exactly what's in store, but we know the battle won't be easy. I beg you to fortify their hearts, prepare their minds, and free them of fear." Her voice got thick, and I heard Marna sniff. The moment felt so peaceful. So right. "And while you're at it, please help me not to worry. Thank you for this day, and bless this meal. Amen."

Amens were whispered around the table. When we lifted our heads and opened our eyes, I sucked in a surprised breath, and I wasn't the only one. The room was bathed in bright light that shone down through the ceiling. I had to squint. It stayed with us only a few seconds before lifting, leaving us Nephilim gaping.

"What is it?" Patti asked.

She couldn't see the light.

Jay looked around at our wide eyes, too. "What just happened?"

Marna leaned into his arms. "Everything's going to be okay," she said, letting him rub her arm and kiss her head.

Ginger stared down at her empty plate, emotions warring on her face, still holding hands with Blake. Kaidan looked at me, his eyes like rushing waters that couldn't contain the powerful feelings.

We were all anxious about what was to come.

"Yes," Kopano said to us all. His face was stoic. "Everything is going to be just fine." Zania let out a breath next to him and nodded. Marna wiped her eyes and sat up straight.

"Good," said Patti, still appearing confused about what she'd missed. "That's the spirit. Let's eat."

CHAPTER TWENTY

BIG ROTTY

Halfway through the meal, while we were all laughing and telling stories, I made the mistake of placing my hand on Kaidan's upper thigh without thinking.

He let out a groan loud enough to silence the room. I slipped my hand back into my own lap, and Kaidan cleared his throat.

"Wow," he said. "The corn pudding is *fantastic.*"

I snorted, which started a round of snickers. Patti smiled at Kaidan like he was a precious boy.

"Isn't it good? Anna found the recipe a few years ago. She's a great cook."

"Mm-hm." Kaidan gave a tight-lipped smile. "That she is."

"I made the yams!" Ginger said.

Blake put an arm around her. "And they are *awesome*, girl."

He winked, and she eyed him suspiciously until he took a huge bite of the gooey yams. His eyes rolled back and he moaned as loudly as Kaidan had. We all laughed, and Ginger backhanded his arm, whispering, "Git."

Patti looked like she was in heaven. "They're perfect, Ginger. Thank you—thanks to all of you for your help. This was the best holiday meal of my life, and I've had some pretty good ones." She winked at me.

"Everything was wonderful, Miss Patti," Ginger told her, earning a pleased smile.

"Well, everyone eat up."

Every guy at the table reached out, not hesitating.

"Anna," Marna said. "Pass the potatoes, please."

I reached for the bowl just as Ginger snorted a laugh. "You can't be serious. You've already had a serving. That's enough for you."

Marna's cheeks reddened. "I know, but I'm still hungry."

Ginger pursed her lips, giving her sister a challenging glare.

Kaidan took the mashed potatoes from my hand. "Give it a rest, Gin. Let her eat."

He passed the bowl across the table. Marna was too upset to take it now, so Jay did. He gave Kaidan a grateful look before spooning more onto Marna's plate for her. Then Jay kissed her cheek. She stared at her plate without moving.

"If you so much as gain a pound, Astaroth will notice." Ginger's voice was steely.

Patti wiped the corners of her mouth with her napkin, clearly not comfortable with the direction things were heading.

Still staring at her plate, Marna said, "We all know I'm

going to gain a lot more than a pound. I'll just have to find ways to avoid him. We rarely see him as it is."

"So, you're just going to let your appearance go and hope for the best?" Ginger challenged. "Fine. Have at it. *Enjoy.*" She waved a hand toward Marna's plate.

"Ginger—" Kopano eyed her, and Zania placed a hand on his forearm.

"No, it's fine, Kope," Marna said, standing. She dropped her napkin onto her plate. "I need the loo." She rushed from the dining room, and every set of eyes at the table went to Ginger.

"What?" Ginger said to us all. "Would you prefer Marna and the stupid baby be killed before she even has a chance to have it?"

"Don't ever say that again," Jay said in a low voice.

She glowered at him. Kaidan reached down and took my hand.

"It's the truth," Ginger said, her voice rising. "And don't presume to understand things you can't possibly. You're just a stupid human boy, and this is all your bloody fault!"

"I know she's in danger! I know it's my fault, and I know what's at stake—"

"You've no clue!" she screamed.

"I know she needs her sister now more than ever, and her last memories are going to be of you yelling at her!"

"I'm the only damn person trying to keep her safe!"

"Okay," Patti said. "Both of you. Please . . ."

Jay and Ginger were seething, shaking. Sadness swept across the room.

"You both love Marna," Patti said. "And you have different ways of showing it. Ginger is right that Marna needs to be careful and keep the pregnancy hidden as long as possible, in a healthy way. And she's going to need everyone's love and support, especially yours," she said to Ginger. "Emotions are running high, for good reason. But you've got to stick together."

Jay clenched his jaw and nodded. Ginger let out a breath through her nose, visibly calming a fraction, but her face was still stony.

"Sweet Ginger," Patti said. "I know she's your world. Please make the most of your time with her."

Ginger's jaw trembled.

Patti said, "Come on." She put an arm around Ginger and led her from the room.

Jay was still breathing hard. I swiped a stray tear from my cheek.

"This bites, man," Blake whispered.

"Let's put this behind us and try to have fun tonight," I said. Everyone nodded.

When we finished eating, we took the plates and dishes into the kitchen. Kope and Jay both started rinsing.

"I got this," I told them, nodding to the sink.

"Y'all cooked," Jay said. "It's only fair that we clean."

"What should we do?" Blake asked. He and Kaidan looked lost as they glanced around at the mess.

"You can put away the leftovers and wipe down the counters," I told them.

They looked at each other with big eyes as I took Zania's hand and left the kitchen, trying not to laugh.

They made surprisingly quick work of the cleanup then joined us in the family room. Z sat next to Kope on the Persian rug. Patti was standing, explaining the game of charades, as I squeezed next to Kaidan on the love seat. He immediately twined his fingers through mine. I was happy to see Marna nestled between Ginger and Jay on the couch, looking cozy under Jay's arm. Blake sat on Ginger's other side, leaning forward with his elbows on his knees and paying close attention to Patti's instructions.

"So," he said, "we just have to act out the word for our team to guess?"

I watched his competitive nature emerge.

"You've never played charades?" I asked.

He shook his head. In fact, all the Neph shook their heads.

"Heard of it, but never played," Kaidan told us.

"Wow," Jay said.

"We'll do girls versus boys, and I'll be the judge," Patti explained. "Anna will go first to show you how it's done."

Kaidan gave me a little push to my feet, grinning big at my discomfort. I'd never been outgoing enough to enjoy games.

"Only the girls can guess," Patti reminded the room, holding out the stack of cards with charade subjects.

I picked one: *Pirates of the Caribbean*. Oh, great.

Patti flipped the sand timer, signaling me to go. An immediate rush of adrenaline hit me as I pretended to wind a movie camera by my eye.

"A movie!" Marna said. I gave her the thumbs-up.

I held up four fingers, and all three girls yelled, "Four words!"

I nodded and held up one finger to show that this was the first word.

I closed one eye tight and made a circle like a patch over it, then made an "Arrgh" face, which was difficult when you couldn't make any sounds. The room broke into laughter. I pointed to my shoulder and made a hand gesture like a bird talking.

More giggles.

Did I mention I sucked at games?

"Dude, I know it," Blake said, sitting back and crossing his arms.

"Me, too," Jay chimed in. They both looked smug.

"Hush." Ginger smacked Blake's thigh.

I made the eye-patch gesture again and swung my arm in that ridiculous pirate gesture.

"That's sexy," Kai said, making the room laugh. I glared at him.

"*Pirates of the Caribbean!*" Zania shouted.

"Yes!" I pointed at her, and the girls all cheered.

"About time," Blake teased.

I fell back onto the love seat and sighed with relief. Kai patted my knee.

Oh, if the Dukes could see their children now.

"I'm next!" Blake stood. Just as he made his way to Patti, his hand stilled on the top card. I felt Kaidan freeze next to me. Across the room, Kope sat up straighter. I recognized the glazed-eye look they got when they were listening to something from a distance. The whole room quieted, and my heart rate spiked.

Kaidan signed silently to the room: *Hide.*

Patti rushed the twins, Zania, and Jay up the stairs. Kaidan tried to push me to go with them, but I shook my head, unstrapping the hilt from my ankle. If it came down to a fight, the others could come down and join us, but we needed to keep our allies secret as long as possible. Together the three guys and I silently went to the front of the house and peeked through the curtains.

A nondescript small gray car had parked in the driveway. An African American man who appeared way too large for the vehicle stepped out, making the car bounce upward with the release of his weight. In the span of one second my mind took in a myriad of details about our visitor. He was one of the biggest men I'd ever seen—extremely tall and stacked with muscle like a bodybuilder. He wore a fitted black do-rag on his head, a sleeveless muscle shirt, baggy jeans low enough to show half his black boxers, and he walked with a serious swagger. But the thing that stood out most was the amber Duke's badge at his chest. And the fact that he looked really familiar . . .

Oh. My. Gosh.

"Nuh-uh," Blake whispered.

Kaidan let out a deep breath of relief and said, "It's Belial."

I ran to the door and opened it, looking up as he approached. He had been a large man in his former body, but now his presence was overwhelming. And it was driving me nuts that I couldn't place him. I would remember meeting this body in real life. Why did he look so familiar?

"What's up, baby girl?" he said from the front step. His

voice was deep, but not gruff anymore. Definitely a smooth baritone.

I felt the presence of all three guys behind me now, and Kaidan's hand on my shoulder.

"Dad?" I said.

"It's me. You ain't gonna hug me?" He held open his giant arms.

I wasn't scared, even though it was completely strange. But as I went into his embrace, I couldn't shake the strange feeling of familiarity. Dad squeezed me and I squeezed him back, letting myself feel safe.

When we turned to walk back inside, Kaidan and Blake stood in the doorway with shocked expressions.

"What?" Dad asked, sounding impatient.

"Sir," began Kaidan. "You're . . . did you mean to . . ."

"You're Big Rotty!" Blake blurted.

I gasped, staring up at Dad. Holy crap! Blake was right!

"Why's everyone keep saying that?" Dad asked. "What the hell's a Big Rotty?"

Rotty, as in rottweiler. Big and intimidating.

"You better come in," I said. We walked in and shut the door, but stayed in the foyer. "Don't you remember anything about this body's past?"

He shook his head. "The human soul takes the memories with it. You gonna tell me what's up?"

"Dad . . . did you get this body from a hospital in D.C.?"

"Yeah." His giant brown eyes looked down at me, pinched.

"You took the body of a famous rapper."

He stepped back from me.

217

"It's all over the news, sir," Blake told him. "He was in a coma and they said he died last night."

Dad dropped a big curse. I hadn't seen the news since last night at the bar when Big Rotty was shot.

"Well, at least they think he's dead," I said.

"He wasn't gonna live." Dad's whole forehead was pinched now. "No family was in the room this morning. I just let his soul go long enough for the monitors to show he was gone. They pronounced him dead, unplugged him, and I jumped in. Brought the body back to life. Waited till they wheeled me down to the morgue, then grabbed some scrubs and left. Damn . . . I didn't have time to do research on 'im. Stopped at a store to get some clothes, and everyone kept staring at me." He cursed again.

This wasn't good. He couldn't have picked a more conspicuous body. Big Rotty's family, friends, and fans would want a funeral, but now his body was mysteriously missing. If this hit the news, and people started spotting Dad . . .

He rubbed his giant hands across his face, a gesture that was distinctively John LaGray.

"All the kids upstairs can come down." Dad sighed.

Right away we heard footsteps. Jay was first at the bottom. He did a double take, and his eyes widened.

"Wha— *Big Rotty*? Oh, man! I have all your albums!"

Uh-oh. Music fanboy alert.

"Jay," I warned.

He ran over to us then stopped, suddenly confused. He turned to the twins, who came down behind him. "I thought you said her pops was here."

He looked around, now thoroughly confused as his eyes landed back on the gigantic newcomer.

"My dad possessed Big Rotty," I deadpanned.

Jay literally swayed and had to put a hand on the wall.

Zania came down the steps and went straight to Kopano's side, eyeing the Duke with distrust.

Dad nodded at her. "Daughter of Sonellion, you're looking well. The son of Alocer taking good care of you up in Boston?"

She cleared her throat and nodded. "Yes, sir. Thank you, sir."

"Good. That's real good." His eyes went toward the stairs. "I see you there, Patti. You gonna say hi, or what?"

Patti was standing at the bottom of the stairs, grasping the rail and staring at Dad. Her aura was a mix of excited orange swirled with dark and light grays.

"Hi," she whispered.

He made a path through all of us as he stalked over to her. Patti's eyes went up, searching his face.

Despite her obvious nervousness, she managed to say, "You're looking young and fit these days, John. I hope it's okay if I still call you that."

"You can call me whatever you want, girl."

Ugh, Dad. Time to get the new body and its language under control.

He kind of surprised us all by pulling her into a hug. Patti let out a startled laugh, and her arms slowly went around his wide waist. I was pretty sure Dad smelled the top of her head and quite positive that she rubbed his back for a second. The whole thing lingered a bit too long for my comfort. Everyone in the room shifted. Kaidan raised an eyebrow at me and I crinkled my nose.

Patti pulled away from him, blushing as she tried to get her frazzled aura under control. I prayed for no red to show, and it didn't, to my utter relief.

"Well." Patti crossed her arms and stepped back. "The new you is sure . . ."

"Touchy-feely?" I offered pointedly. A few chuckles rose and died around the room.

Dad actually turned his head to me and gave an embarrassed laugh.

"My bad. Still getting used to this body."

Apparently, Big Rotty had had some affectionate mannerisms. He was known for being a reformed player as well as a gangster, after all.

Patti ran her hands over her hair, getting ahold of herself. "Well, I'm glad the scare's over. Everyone come back in and sit down. It's almost dessert time. Who wants pie?" she called over her shoulder as she headed toward the kitchen.

"Aw, hell yeah!" Dad said, grinning wide as he strutted in his way to the family room.

All of us stood there stunned for a moment before following. Jay wore his same goofy look of awe as he gazed after my father.

This was going to take some getting used to.

"So, where'd you get the money to stop and buy clothes?" I asked Dad.

We were all sitting around the family room, plates of

different pies on our laps. Except Patti, who was too nervous or freaked out to eat.

"Before I ditched my old body, I stashed money in a locker at Union Station. That's another reason I needed to get a new body in D.C."

"Maybe if you change your look just a bit, sir," Marna suggested. "Wear something that Big Rotty might not've worn?"

"Yeah," Dad said, nodding. "Get myself a suit. Straight-up gent." When he grinned, I could see exactly how he'd earned himself a reputation with the ladies. He had a famous scar above his eye from a knife fight, and a scar on his neck from a bullet graze, but he had a roguish handsomeness that made you want to stare.

"I can take your measurements," Patti offered. "We'll send one of these guys out to get you some clothes."

"I will go for him," Kopano said.

"Perfect." Patti grabbed the remote and turned on the television. "Let's see if they mention anything about this on the news."

So far there was nothing. Maybe the police were keeping it quiet.

I looked down at Kaidan's empty plate. He'd had three pieces of pie: cherry, pumpkin, and apple.

"Which pie was your favorite?" I whispered in his ear.

His eyes hit mine and I felt my neck heating, the warmth spreading up to my face. All at once we both realized Dad was watching us, giving Kaidan a murderous glare.

Kaidan quickly amended. "Erm, apple was my favorite, luv."

"Oh," I said.

Dad looked away and Kaidan shot me a big-eyed "oops" glance. I choked back a laugh. Patti came up behind us and kissed Kai's head.

"How you doing, son?" she asked.

He gave her a boyish smile and said, "Very well, thanks." She pushed the hair from his eyes before moving along.

"So, tell me what's been going on around here," Dad said to me. "You seen Pharzuph again?"

"No," I told him. "Nothing's happened since you came to my dorm room."

"When'd you see Pharzuph?" Blake asked.

I told them about the surprise visit and Pharzuph's new body.

"Yeah, brah," Blake said to Kaidan. "We've both inherited fortunes and new-looking daddies we haven't even seen yet. How many people get to say that?"

"Awkward," Jay said. "Acko taco . . ."

"With a side of guaco," Marna finished, and they chuckled together.

"You haven't seen your father's new body yet?" Jay asked Blake.

"Nah. Probably won't now that he lives in China, and that's fine with me."

"Do you have any news?" I asked Dad.

He shook his head. "I just know they're having a summit tonight in Switzerland. Still got my boys looking in on the son of Shax to see if he's ally material. He seems legit, but I'm not sendin' you to have words with him till I know for sure. How'd he seem when you met him?"

Everyone looked at me, and I thought about it.

"Well, compared to creepy Caterina, he seemed normal, but I still wouldn't turn my back on him. He's slick."

Dad nodded, and ran a hand over his do-rag. "I was hopin' to have more allies by this point. I think we all know it's going down soon."

We sat quietly, an intensity blanketing the room. It felt like things were happening too fast.

"What are we going to do?" I asked.

"We roll with it," Dad said. "All we can do is be ready, mentally, for whatever they throw at us. Be strong. Keep your wits. They're not expectin' a team of you like this. We gotta fight smart." He tapped his head.

He was right. We couldn't formulate any kind of plan when we didn't know when or how the Dukes would attack. But that didn't have to mean we were weak.

"So . . . we wait," I said.

"We wait," Dad confirmed, glancing at his empty pie plate. "And eat."

As always, Dad couldn't stay long. Patti and I measured him and then sent Kopano and Zania to the nearest mall with his credit card for new, less conspicuous clothes.

Kope and Z returned with big bags.

"These look good," Patti said, pulling out the clothes for Dad. "But your hair . . ."

"Hot mess," he agreed with a low chuckle as he ran a big hand over his hair, which needed a good brushing or cut.

Patti stepped up and handed him a Miami Heat ball cap. He fitted it on his head and grinned.

"Yeah. That's nice, right there."

The three of us walked back into the family room, where everyone was sitting, and even from the corner of my eye I could see Dad's larger-than-life walk—the kind of body movements that forced people to notice him.

As Dad started talking to Blake, thanking him for pulling off our recent plan, Jay approached me.

"You know, since he still knows how to talk and walk like Big Rotty, I bet he could still rap if he tried."

I could only shake my head, giving him my "you're crazy but I still love you" look.

"What?" He laughed. Marna smiled at him from the couch.

Kaidan walked to my side and I linked my arm through his, hugging his bicep. Dad came over and put his hands on Kai's shoulders. They shared a serious look.

"You take care of my girl, you hear me?"

Kaidan nodded. "I will, sir."

Dad patted his shoulder and then looked at me. Deep in those eyes I saw my dad—his love and concern for me that stemmed from his soul. I let go of Kai and reached for Dad. His arms went around me, and I felt the same pit of sadness I always felt when he had to leave, never knowing when we'd see each other again.

He kissed the top of my head and said, "You make me proud. Every day."

"Love you, Daddy," I said into his shirt.

He turned to Patti, who stood behind me. Dad pulled a

strand of her curly hair, like a little kid, then let his hand rest on her shoulder. They said nothing. She patted Dad's hand and tried to smile. Good-byes were never easy.

Without looking back, Dad picked up his bags of clothes and walked out of the house into the dark, leaving us in silence.

CHAPTER TWENTY-ONE

No Girls

It was late when Jay and Marna went for a walk. Blake and Ginger played video games on Jay's game system, and Kaidan and I chatted with Kope and Z. A tiny strand of discomfort still permeated the air among Kaidan, Kope, and me—a leftover from the time I'd shared with Kope and the jealousy between the two of them.

Kopano made a solid effort to get past the tension, wanting to hear more about my interactions with Marek, the son of Shax.

"He'd be a great ally," I told them. "He freaking stole my car keys from under my nose. But I couldn't get a good read on him with Caterina there. He definitely isn't a fan of hers, which gives me a little hope about him."

"Strange to think her father is an ally," Kaidan said.

"Yeah," I agreed. It was also strange to think of Jezebet as

Caterina's father at all. He was now a woman. Jezebet was the first Duke to ever take a female body. His change of guard must have happened just after he'd fathered Caterina. As far as I knew, Jezebet was Dad's only ally among the Dukes, but Dad was known to keep his secrets close.

When Jay and Marna returned from their walk, Jay took out his guitar. He was decent at it, but the piano was his best talent. He couldn't get a certain riff right, so he handed the instrument to Kaidan, and my heart flipped.

I recalled him saying he played guitar, but I'd never actually seen or heard him play. Kaidan began to pick at each string, testing and tuning with his full attention. I watched the way his hands moved across the wood and strings, gently, reverently, his body seeming to curl around it as if it were a part of him. . . . I felt my hands getting sweaty, because watching Kaidan get lost in music did crazy things to me. My breathing became ragged and I couldn't take my eyes off him.

He looked up at that moment and caught me staring hard. He *knew*. He knew what it did to me! I could tell because his badge expanded.

He angled himself away from the others and signed to me, *I want to be alone with you tonight.*

Patti *did* have a lot of guests staying in the house. I signed back, *I'll work on it.*

"Excellent," he whispered, a hot grin sliding onto his face.

"Hey, Kai," Jay called, across from us.

"Yeah, mate?"

"What's the difference between a drummer and a large pizza?"

227

Kai held back a smile. "I've no clue."

"A large pizza can feed a family of four!"

Everyone cracked up.

Blake said, "Thank God for Daddy's money, huh?"

"Bloody right." Kaidan turned his attention back to the guitar. When the first rich notes of a popular ballad met my ears, I stared at his forearms and lower biceps, then his fingers as they moved, seemingly without effort. The way he concentrated and fell into his own world fascinated me. Each sound was clear and vibrant, stirring my blood until I had a dizzying head rush. *Yep, I was taking this guy home tonight.* He was all mine.

I went upstairs and found Patti making the second guest bed. I got on the other side to help straighten the sheet. "So . . . I was wondering if you minded if Kaidan and I went back to my dorm tonight, since you have a houseful and all? We'd be back first thing in the morning."

She tried to keep a straight face, but I could see her fighting a smile. "Sure thing, honey." She may have been the woman who raised me, but she was also a romantic.

Kaidan and I weren't the only people walking across campus close to midnight, but we might have been the only sober ones. At one point while we were walking I heard distant cheers, then Kaidan busted out laughing next to me. I followed his eyes and the sounds until I spied the backs of three naked guys streaking across the quad.

Kaidan covered my eyes, but we were both cracking up.

We passed a big group of girls who were talking at top

volume, giggling like crazy. They got quiet when they saw Kaidan, putting all their energy into staring as hard as they could. Kai didn't even glance their way, but his fingers tightened around mine as if to reassure me.

The moment we passed them, they broke into another round of giggles and began talking over one another about how all the hottest guys were taken. It was strange to think we looked like an average college couple. Kaidan released my hand to put his arm around my shoulder, and mine went around his waist, my thumb linking through a belt loop. We threw all caution to the wind, but Kaidan's eyes stayed always on alert. Always searching.

When we got closer to the building, I wondered if I was allowed to bring him in. Probably not since it was after hours and he wasn't a student. I made Kaidan wait for me at a side exit while I went in and then came to get him. As soon as the heavy door clicked closed behind him, he pinned me to the wall with a hard kiss. I let myself pull him close and melt into him, savoring our aloneness. I forced my mouth from his so I could talk.

"For the record, you can play guitar for me *anytime*."

Dark hair hung in his eyes as he loomed over me, so hot. "Liked that, did you?"

He took my mouth again and I groaned just thinking about his hands on the guitar. His hands on *me*.

He grinned and said, "I love it that you have to sneak me in."

"I'm such a rebel," I joked. "You're getting the college experience without having to take any classes."

Kai crinkled his nose. "Something smells bad." He looked at the floor suspiciously.

"See? The full experience. Come on." I pulled him up the stairs, careful not to step in any mysterious puddles along the way.

When we got into my room, Kaidan reminded me of everything I'd been missing since our wedding night, and more.

At two in the morning we lay half asleep, spooning on the twin-size dorm bed. I ran my fingers up and down his arm.

"Do you ever let yourself dream?" I asked him. "Like, imagine what the future could be like?"

Kaidan paused. "No. But I'm betting you do." He placed a kiss on my bare shoulder.

"Yeah." For a while after I found out I was a Nephilim, I had laid my dreams to rest, but since finding out about the prophecy, they'd been reignited. Dreams gave me hope. "I want you to dream big with me."

Kaidan was contemplative, having grown up believing that these kind of wishful thoughts were dangerous.

Finally he said, "Tell me your dream for us, sweet Anna."

I smiled into the darkened room. "It starts with us defeating the Dukes. We survive and they're gone. We can do whatever we want with our lives. I know you love music, so I figure you'll still work with music in some way. When I finish college, I want to be a social worker. I'd be able to gauge the danger kids are in better than a human could since I can see their emotions. I'll be able to rescue children from bad situations."

"I can picture that." Kaidan brushed hair off my neck. I felt his lips running up and down over my shoulder and the dip of my throat, but I sensed he was still paying attention, so I kept going.

"We could live wherever you wanted. Patti would probably follow us. After a few years of working, we could think about adopting. I know Patti would just die to babysit while we work."

"Wow. Kids."

"Yeah . . . like five or six."

"*Five or six?*"

I held back a giggle.

"You're a nutter," he said, laughing. "One boy. Maybe two boys, but even that's pushing it."

I couldn't believe he was playing along.

"We have to have girls, too!"

Behind me, he stiffened and the room went silent.

"No girls." He was deadly serious.

I rolled over to face him. Before I could say a word, he sat up and shuddered.

"What's wrong?" I asked.

He dug the heels of his hands into his tired eyes. "I can't even . . . just the thought of having to care for a girl, watching all the bloody gits sniff around her with their red auras . . . it would kill me and I would deserve it, because I was the worst offender of all."

"Kai . . ." I touched his arm.

"No. I'm sorry, luv, but kids are not my dream. Especially girls."

"Okay," I whispered. I scooted closer and ran a hand down his forearm. "Let's try to get a little sleep."

"I'm sorry," he said again.

I rolled over so we could spoon once more, gently pulling him down to lie behind me. I felt his breath on my hair.

"Are you angry with me?" he whispered.

I quickly flipped over to face him, saying, "No, Kai." I placed my hand on his scruffy cheek. "I understand your feelings. It was only supposed to be for fun."

I gave him a peck on the lips and he searched my eyes.

He sounded so sad when he said, "I ruined your dream."

"No, you didn't. We're gonna face our future together, and that's more than I ever thought I'd have. I love you."

I kissed him again and finally felt him soften.

"Let's rest," I said. "We have to be back at Patti's by eight for breakfast."

I kissed him one last time before rolling over and feeling his heat against my back as he reached around my waist and pulled me closer.

As I drifted to sleep, from a state of semiconsciousness I heard him whisper, "You're my dream. My only dream."

Seven o'clock came *waaay* too early. And then it took us forever to get out of bed. Kaidan totally started it, but I can't say I was eager to end it. He was flying back to California that afternoon, and I didn't know when I'd see him again. We clung to each other, desperate for every touch. We were running so late that we only had time for me to take a shower. We hurried to Patti's so the nine of us could have this morning together before it was time to go our separate ways.

The mood in the house was somber when we got there. Marna and Jay wouldn't unlink fingers. Patti's eyes were red, but she held back any tears, trying to cheer us all with omelets and potato cakes. I went straight to the coffee maker, pouring two cups for Kaidan and me—his black, mine creamy and sweet. He took his coffee from me graciously, and as we sipped I ran my eyes over his five o'clock shadow and messy hair, disheveled from sleep and my fingers.

He caught me looking, and I stared down into my mug and smiled.

The others discussed their plans. Blake was flying the twins to D.C. at ten, then Zania and Kopano to Boston. He offered Kaidan a ride back to California, but Kai had a flight booked to Atlanta at noon. He had to retrieve Richard Rowe's ashes and sign estate paperwork giving permission for everything to be sold.

It was time to say our good-byes. Watching Marna leave Jay was heartbreaking. It took Kope's strong arm around Marna to get her to leave.

I stood silently in the foyer with Kaidan, Patti, and Jay as the others drove away.

"We were lucky to have this time together, weren't we?" Jay asked.

"Very," I whispered.

Patti rubbed his back for a second before giving him a small, sad smile and slipping into the kitchen.

Kaidan cleared his throat and looked at Jay. "So . . . got any new tracks for me to hear? Stuff by you?"

"I do have one. . . ." The two of them walked toward the family room, talking music, and I went to help Patti with the dishes.

She was scrubbing and rinsing, but kept leaning her head down to wipe her eyes on the shoulder of her shirt. She gave me a watery smile.

"Lordy, I'm a mess. Can't stop crying lately."

"It's okay."

Patti reached for me the second I sidled up beside her, wet hands and all. I went into her arms, breathing in her comforting oatmeal scent.

"I love you so much," she said, still holding me tight. "Thank you for bringing everyone here and letting me be a part of it."

Just as I opened my mouth to respond, a dark spot crept into the side of my vision, near the window. Panicked adrenaline flooded my system. I jumped back from Patti, causing her to yelp, but when I ran to the window there was nothing there.

Kaidan rushed in, scanning the room. I took a deep breath to calm my frayed nerves, then signed, *I thought I saw something, but I was wrong. It was probably a cloud or a bird.*

His lips tightened. *I'm going to check*, he signed.

Jay came in with a worried look and he put his arm protectively around Patti. I motioned for them to stay where they were. If there were whisperers here, we were all busted. We had no good reason to be together.

Kaidan went out the front door and I inspected all of the rooms, looking out the windows. Nothing. Kai came back in and shook his head. I let out a relieved breath.

"Sorry," I said. "I'm paranoid."

"You have every right to be," Patti said. Still holding Jay's arm, she led him into the family room.

Kai and I studied each other, both of us tense and edgy. Switzerland was six hours ahead of us. The Dukes could be headed back to their homelands now. The whisperers could have been spiriting around the world for hours already.

Kaidan signed, *You're sure you didn't see anything?*

A dark spot, I signed. *It was gone so fast, like a blur. They usually*... I didn't know the sign for *linger*, so I spelled it out. I could see the pulsing in his temples as he ground his teeth together.

He'd be leaving in just over an hour, and then I'd go back to campus. Classes would start in a couple of days. We'd continue living our facades until it was time to act.

The four of us stayed together in the living room, surrounded by a worrisome tension. We turned on the television.

Patti gasped and sat up straight, pointing the remote at the television to turn up the volume. Big Rotty's picture was on the screen. We all sat on the edge of our seats, staring at the news report. A D.C. officer came on.

"We're not sure what the motives of the perpetrator might be, but this is not the work of an amateur. Body theft is a serious, rare crime. Psychologists on the force warn that the person or persons who generally commit this type of crime are not mentally stable. If you have any news about the theft of the body of James F. Cooper, known to the world as Big Rotty, please contact the authorities immediately. Do not approach the suspects on your own."

"Oh my gosh," I whispered.

Big Rotty's mom was on-screen next. She had long, elaborate weaves of curls around her made-up face, and she didn't look sad like I'd expected. She was glowing. "I got my own theory. I don't think my boy's dead. Mm-mm." She closed her eyes and shook her head. "I think he planned all this. He pulled a Machiavelli, and now he's at some island living the good life!" She laughed with pride, like her son had hoodwinked the world.

"Wow . . . ," Jay said.

"I still can't believe he chose that body," I said. "He's always so careful about every detail."

"He's got a lot on his mind," Patti said.

"He'll shed the body if it becomes an issue," Kaidan assured us.

Patti put the television on a cooking show and I snuggled close to her like old times, letting her play with my hair. Just that contact meant so much. I watched Kaidan and Jay on the other side of the room. Jay with his guitar, and Kai patting a beat on his knee. They'd work one line at a time, mapping out the notes and rhythm. Within an hour they'd written a gorgeous ballad.

Jay stared over the chord chart with amazement. Kaidan gave me a wink. He'd helped get Jay's mind off Marna's absence in the only way possible.

"I should probably shower and get ready," Kaidan said with reluctance.

My stomach dropped at the thought of him leaving.

"I'll come show you where everything is," I said.

He followed me upstairs, and I pulled a towel and washcloth from the linen closet. He could have done it himself, but I wanted one last moment alone with him. I set the towel on the sink in the bathroom, and I heard the door shut.

Kaidan pressed up against me from behind, placing his hands over mine on the edge of the sink. I looked up and caught his eyes in the mirror, smoky and intense.

His voice came out a low rumble and he never looked away from my reflection. "I don't want to leave you."

"I don't want you to go either," I whispered.

He wrapped his arms around my waist, still holding my eyes with his. I turned and kissed his warm lips, then pulled away despite his reluctance to let go. I couldn't keep him any longer.

I left Kaidan to shower and went downstairs to join the others.

My foot had just hit the bottom step when I heard a strange gargled sound from Patti, like she was being strangled.

Jay yelled her name. I'd never heard him sound so terrified.

Panic flared in my chest, and my body roared into action. I bent at the waist, hiking up my pant leg and ripping the hilt from its case. I ran into the family room, barely feeling the zing of the sword against the palm of my hand.

Nothing could have prepared me for what I saw.

Jay was swarmed by demons. They overlapped one another, but I was able to discern three whispering at him, and a fourth hovering in front of the couch a few feet away. Patti was nowhere. Jay stepped backward, moaning, clutching his hair and shaking his head. His guardian angel tried to fight them off but was pushed aside repeatedly by the demons.

A current of power ran up my arm, and blood rushed through my ears so fast I could hardly hear. I moved forward, ready to attack, but stopped at the sight of something writhing on the floor in front of the couch.

Patti.

The whisperer I'd seen was hovering above her, and another spirit was *halfway inside her body*. Her guardian angel was going ballistic, unable to stop the dark spirits. A gagging noise came from Patti's throat as she fought, trying to sit up, then convulsing.

As my arm swung toward the demons, a brilliant golden light poured from the end of the hilt, hot and sharp, piercing the top half of the spirit that was trying to possess Patti. With a resounding *crack*, the dark spirit imploded and disappeared. Patti's head fell to the carpet and she coughed. Her guardian angel immediately covered her as the dark spirit above them seemed frozen in shock and fear, its face ugly and contorted.

I lunged forward just as it spun to flee, but all it took was a slice from the tip of the sword as I swung it through the air, and the spirit arched in pain before imploding and vanishing. Maybe the sword returned the spirit to hell, or maybe it vanquished it—I didn't know or care.

A commotion sounded from upstairs, and I realized Kaidan had heard and would be down any second, but I didn't want the whisperers to know he was here.

"Don't come down!" I screamed.

In a swift move I crossed the room, stabbing the other spirit that had left Jay to join the attack on Patti. With a loud *snap*, it was gone.

Jay jumped back, appearing terrified when his eyes landed on the sword. The two other whisperers finally looked up, like two oblivious birds of prey torn unwillingly from their fresh meal.

They wore twin expressions of realization, then shrieked inhuman sounds, high and grating, a shrill whistle that only demons and their children could hear.

I yelled, "Move!" to Jay, who obeyed without question as my arm began an arc through the air. The light sliced into the first spirit and narrowly missed the second as it dove backward through the wall to the backyard.

I could hear Kaidan running down the stairs now.

"Crap!" I sprinted for the back door and threw it open, racing outside. I glimpsed the demon whisperer as it flew into the trees, out of sight. Away.

No!

In the absence of danger, the sword's light faded into nothing, leaving my hand and arm cold and numb.

I was in trouble now. Big trouble. Because that spirit was on its way to rat me out to all the Dukes and whispering Legionnaires. They'd know about the Sword of Righteousness. I wanted to freak out, but there was no time for that. Running on legs that were still buzzing with adrenaline, I found Jay and a shirtless Kaidan crouched next to Patti, who had propped herself against the couch. Her face was pale and damp with sweat.

I fell on my knees next to Patti and took her in my arms. She held on to me, weakly.

"Are you okay?" I whispered.

"I don't know what happened. I felt so sick and scared . . . and . . ." She shuddered, and I held her tighter.

"Who was here?" Kaidan asked.

The sight of him crouched there with wild eyes made

me realize how fast everything had taken place. His hair was soaking wet and he had water droplets on his chest and shoulders.

"I have no idea," Jay said, thoroughly freaked out. "It was so weird, dude. And you should have seen Anna! What *is* that thing?" He pointed to the hilt, which I still clutched. "It was all lit up. She moved so fast. I've never seen anyone move like that!"

It hadn't felt fast to me. It had felt horrifically slow, like a nightmare.

Kaidan crouched next to me, all coiled tension, taking my face in his hands. "What happened?"

"Three whisperers were on Jay. Two on Patti. One was trying to possess her." Patti's shaking hand flew to her mouth and she made a strangled sound of disgust. I kept going. "I killed four of them . . . but one got away."

"One got away . . . ," he whispered.

We stared hard at one another as the danger pressed down on us. Kaidan stood, shoving his hands through his hair, and paced to the wall. He leaned against it with both palms, whispering at first, "Shite. Shite, Anna . . . ," then yelling and punching a hole through the wall.

Jay stood as if ready to calm Kaidan, but Patti grabbed his hand.

"It's okay," she told Jay. "They need to go."

"You all should go somewhere, too," I told her. Inside I trembled. I'd put them in danger. "I saw one earlier in the kitchen. I thought I was imagining it, but it must've been a whisperer. It saw us hugging. You two need to go into hiding.

240

Just keep moving. Don't stay in one place more than a night."

I helped her to her feet. She and Jay ran upstairs to pack their bags. I turned and found Kai leaning his back against the wall, the palms of his hands pushing against his eyes.

"Kai."

He dropped his hands and stood, looking at me with the same kind of fear that had filled his eyes the night of the summit in New York City. Fear for *me*.

"I don't think they know you're here," I said. "That's to our advantage."

He thought about that, nodding.

We needed to move fast. "You're not on the suspicion list, so you can stay in the know. We'll go our separate ways and—"

"No." Kai's hard voice carried an end-of-discussion ring to it. "I stay with you."

Oh, no. His attitude was grim and unyielding. I wanted to stay with him, too, but it wasn't smart.

"As soon as they catch you with me, they'll know you're on my side and you'll be an immediate target, too. Think this through—"

"We stay together." His steely eyes warned me not to argue. I'd never seen him more dead set on something. I knew he'd follow me if he had to, and there was no time to argue.

I sighed and looked away. "Okay. Let's get our stuff and get out of here."

He softened a fraction with relief.

We grabbed our bags. Jay gave me a quick hug as Patti embraced Kaidan.

"Please be careful," I whispered to Patti.

"You don't worry about me." She talked fast, her voice shaking as she took my face in her hands. "Just remember you can do anything you put your heart to. I'd do anything for you, Anna. I'd fight this battle for you if I could."

Patti and I squeezed each other equally hard.

My throat constricted as I whispered, "I love you."

"I love you, too, sweet girl. Now go."

With a gentle shove from the strongest woman I knew, we were gone.

CHAPTER TWENTY-TWO

MERCENARY

Kaidan reached for my car keys and took the driver's seat. I sat next to him, fitting one of Jay's ball caps on my head as Kai peeled out of the neighborhood. He looked down at the speedometer as if impressed.

"This little thing has some power."

"Yeah, my dad probably had that in mind when he bought it." It was sad to think that Dad had bought my car knowing I'd have to make an escape in it someday.

Kaidan did a double take at me in the hat. I wondered if I looked stupid, but then his red badge gave a widening pulse. He tore his eyes away and hit the gas harder, pressing me back into the seat. I was afraid to look at the speed as we merged onto Interstate 81.

"Where are we going?" I asked.

He shook his head, and when he spoke he sounded angry.

"No idea. Deeper into these mountains, I suppose."

I rubbed his shoulder to try to calm him.

"This is my fault," he said. "I should have taken an earlier flight, then you would've been back at school. None of this would've happened."

I shook my head. This was the peril of loving—wanting more time together, taking risks. I hated knowing we'd put ourselves in danger, but it was impossible to regret the time we'd had together.

"It's not your fault. You could have left early, and I might've still been caught hugging Patti. It was bound to go down eventually, Kai."

"But it didn't have to be *now*." His hands went white as he gripped the wheel, and his jaw tightened. I felt sad for him because I knew he was going into this without any belief we would survive.

"We have to have hope," I whispered.

As he opened his mouth to say something, his phone rang. My heart sped as he pulled it from his pocket.

We both glanced at the unknown Oregon number, and Kaidan cursed.

Pharzuph.

I stayed completely silent while he answered.

"Hallo."

"It's Pharzuph. This is my new number, so program it into your phone."

A chill zapped up my spine.

"Yes, sir."

"Are you in Atlanta?"

Kaidan glanced at me and I watched, holding my breath. It was still weird to hear Pharzuph speak with a young American voice.

"Not yet," Kai said.

"Meet me at our former home tonight at nine p.m. I'm flying in, and we have some things to discuss."

Kaidan cleared his throat. I watched the pulse jump in his neck.

"I'll see you at nine o'clock, sir."

"Don't be late." Pharzuph hung up.

Kaidan's hand curled around the phone so hard I worried he'd crush it. "He sounds like a right prick. Even more than usual."

"Oh, he's obnoxious in this new body. You're gonna want to beat the crap out of him the whole time."

He huffed at that and almost smiled. I pried the phone from his hand and twined my fingers with his. We both held tight.

I turned in the seat to face him. "If we can manage to make it to Georgia without being seen together, I want to stay within a mile of the house to listen."

"Anna—"

"No. You were the one who wanted us to stay together, so you need to let me do this. If anything happens to you, Kaidan, I swear I will show up there. And I will kill him."

At the seriousness of my voice and words, his eyes slammed into mine.

"Keep talking like that, Anna Rowe, and I'll have to pull this car over."

I grinned. "No time for that. I'm gonna lie down and try to stay out of sight."

I crawled into the backseat, earning a smack on the bottom as I went, and covered myself with a blanket I'd grabbed from Patti's. At least this way, from the outside, Kaidan would appear to be alone in the car. His head turned long enough to run his hot gaze over me curled up on the small seat.

I reached up to poke his shoulder. "Eyes on the road, you."

He obeyed, reaching for the radio. "Try to sleep."

The odds were stacked against us. A year and a half ago I had held my hands up to the heavens and told them to deal me in, and they had. Now the prophecy was about to happen—this war on earth between the demons and their children—with me leading the way. My stomach was in knots.

I closed my eyes for Kaidan's sake and pretended to sleep.

Kaidan made the trip to Atlanta in seven hours, stopping once for gas. I was on edge, expecting to hear Kaidan shout, "Whisperer!" at any point, but he never did.

We stopped talking as we neared Atlanta, and Kaidan turned off the radio. When he pulled the car into a parking lot, I sat up and was surprised by our location. A Catholic church? I gave Kai a questioning look, and he signed to me, *Legend says holy water does more than repel evil—it's like poison to demons.*

I raised my eyebrows. I liked this idea.

We silently entered the church, searching the skies and seeing nothing but summer clouds. Inside, it was cool, quiet, and empty. We saw the angel statue at the same time, holding a giant shell—the vessel for the holy water. Kaidan moved fast, filling an empty flask that he'd pulled from his pocket.

Someone is coming, he signed. *Take out your knife. Quick.*

We both pulled out our knives. I followed his lead, dunking the sharpened blade into the holy water, all the while feeling guilty for tainting the blessed liquid in such a way.

We rushed from the church just as footsteps sounded down a nearby hall. As we jumped into the car and sped from the lot, I looked back and saw a collared man with his guardian angel watching us go. In a gentle gesture, the priest made the sign of the cross in the air, as if blessing us. I lay down in the backseat and exhaled.

Kaidan's next stop was a rental car place. It was seven o'clock when we stood in the parking lot facing each other. We didn't dare touch in case any whisperers were out. I tried to pour all my love and support for him through my eyes, and he let out a silent sigh before signing, *Are you as hungry as I am?*

I held back a laugh and nodded. Now that he mentioned it, I was starved. We absolutely couldn't eat together. It was time for us to separate until Pharzuph left. I was overcome with nervousness. Kaidan's eyes gave the skies a last scan before he leaned forward for a quick, chaste peck on my lips.

I'll be in touch once he's gone, Kaidan signed.

I tried to hide my fears as I signed back, *I'll be nearby, listening.*

I hated the idea of him meeting with Pharzuph. What was his father planning? Did he really trust Kaidan, or was this a trap? Kaidan had his knives and the holy water, but those couldn't contend with a gun if Pharzuph suddenly decided to shoot him, like Mammon had done to his son, Flynn, on the island.

Don't worry, Kaidan signed.

I shook my head, slightly amused that he could read me so easily. Kaidan slowly stepped backward, and a painful pit opened in my gut. Taking his lead, I moved toward my car as well. With sad reluctance, we left each other. All I could do now was pray for the best. I'd be ready to jump into action if needed.

I grabbed dinner and then found somewhere to park in the Rowes' old neighborhood. I stopped behind a grove of trees up the street, a place Pharzuph wouldn't pass as he came in. I meditated, trying to calm the nerves that burned like acid. If anything happened to Kaidan . . .

No. I could not, *would* not, allow myself to think like that.

Deep, quiet breathing. Silence all around.

I pushed my supernatural hearing into Kaidan's former house and searched around until I found him in his old room in the basement. I jumped at the sudden onslaught of ear-slamming music blaring from his sound system—his way of decompressing.

Through the trees spilled bright headlights coming up the street. I held my breath, and my heart rate kicked into over-drive as the car pulled in to the long driveway. Kai must have been listening, too, because the music's volume went down a small fraction.

When the car's headlights turned off, I could see nothing but the patch of trees separating me from the house. I had to rely solely on my extended hearing, which was my weakest sense, especially when I was nervous. I held the hilt in its case on my lap, ready to jump from the car and run to help Kaidan if necessary. With great concentration I kept my auditory sense surrounding Pharzuph, honing in on his footsteps.

My heart quickened again as Pharzuph began making his way down the stairs to the basement. A blast of chords and drums hit my ears when Kaidan's door was opened. I stretched my hearing wider to encompass both of them.

"Shut this racket off," Pharzuph demanded. As the music silenced, he muttered something about missing the days of wooing lovers with classical music and gentlemanly facades. I pictured him rubbing his temples like the drama king he was.

Apparently even demon parents suffered from the generation gap.

Kaidan's voice sounded low and steady when he said, "Good to see you, Father. Excellent choice on your new host body."

"Yes, it was," Pharzuph agreed. I heard the crinkle of a folded paper opening. "You sign the estate paperwork tomorrow?"

"Yes, sir. In the morning."

"Here is my new account information. You'll receive your own funds from the life insurance and inheritance. Everything else needs to be transferred to me. If a penny is missing, I will know it."

Kaidan's voice sounded tight when he responded, "I understand."

"Good." It sounded like Pharzuph took a deep, sniffing breath. "Smells like old lust in here. You were always a good worker."

My stomach turned.

A surprised pause filled the air. "Thank you, Father."

"But things are not always as they appear, are they?" Pharzuph's voice held a tone of challenging amusement.

Oh, crap.

"In what way?" Kaidan asked.

"Something's not right." Pharzuph began to move in slow, but confident, steps. It sounded like he was circling Kaidan. I imagined him prowling, trying to intimidate his grown son. "I haven't been able to put my finger on it. Ever since that summit when the damned angels showed up, we've been watching the daughter of Belial."

Kaidan made a scoffing sound. "Her? No offense, Father, but I don't see why an unremarkable Neph like the daughter of Belial would warrant such attention. I've worked with her. She's excellent at her job, but on a personal level she's rather . . . boring."

Ouch.

"So you took no pleasure from your time with her?"

"Oh, I took my pleasure. I also got out of there as quickly as I could. She's got zero personality unless she's wasted."

Double ouch. I knew he didn't mean it, but the words still cut.

Pharzuph chuckled. "I know being with her was a chore, but it was necessary. She's somehow been able to fly under the radar. Now we know for sure that she's a threat."

"A threat?" Kaidan laughed.

"You think this is funny?" His voice seemed to get closer to Kai. "You think I have time to joke around?"

"Of course not, but having spent a good bit of time with her, it seems preposterous. She cares about nothing except where she'll find her next drink."

"Then she's fooled you well." Pharzuph's voice turned deadly, making goose bumps sprout on my arms. "That boring Neph who you think's so benign was caught being affectionate with her human mother-figure this morning. We sent five Legionnaires to get more information, and the girl took out four of the spirits! She's a mercenary of heaven."

"Wha—? How is that possible?" Bravo, Kaidan—he sounded genuinely shocked and confused.

Pharzuph seemed to hesitate, then said with reluctance, "She's somehow able to wield a Sword of Righteousness. Only angels of light have been able to do that."

A beat passed before Kaidan said, "But . . . why would an angelic weapon allow her to use it? I've watched her lead souls astray, and I nailed her myself. She's hardly angel material."

"I . . . we don't know." It was the first time I'd ever heard a Duke sound less than confident. Defeated, even.

"Is it possible someone is trying to deceive all of you? Point you in the wrong direction? I mean, how do you know about the sword and the spirits she supposedly killed?"

Kaidan sounded convincing, and it seemed like his father was buying it.

"One of them escaped."

"I hope that spirit isn't misleading you."

"They're too stupid to come up with something like that," Pharzuph said. "Unless they're being led by someone. But I haven't seen a spirit that terrified since the Fall. We sent it down to Lord Lucifer for further questioning. He'll get the truth out of it."

I shivered as Pharzuph kept talking.

"We've got Legionnaires on the hunt for both her and her father. Belial's been eluding us for a while now, so he's definitely up to something."

"I see you're keeping several whisperers with you to keep an eye out. That's good."

"I'm not going to let that girl get in a sneak attack. The other Dukes and I are staying armed and ready. We'll find her and hold an emergency summit to learn the truth and get rid of her once and for all, angels be damned."

"What can I do to help?" Kaidan asked.

"Do you have her mobile number?"

"No."

Pharzuph cursed. "Then search for her. If you find her, she becomes your prisoner and you'll notify me immediately. Do whatever is necessary to keep her with you and get her to the location we choose for the summit. And most important, disarm her. Under no circumstances should she be allowed access to the Sword of Righteousness."

"Of course. I'll begin immediately. I have a few ideas where she might be."

"Good." His next words were spiked with coldness. "It's in your best interest not to fail me in this endeavor. Do you understand?"

I felt the chill between them from a quarter mile away.

"I understand," Kaidan said, his voice low and deadly.

Finally, Pharzuph spoke again. "I'm going to Marissa's tonight, and I leave in the morning. My new duty station will be in New York City, so it's time for me to get settled there.

Don't waste any time getting to work on your task."

"Yes, sir, but . . . you're going to Marissa's, you say?"

He sounded confused, and it took me a second to realize why. Marissa would have no idea who this young guy was. Her underground trade was highly secretive.

Pharzuph chuckled. "Marissa is a special human. She knows about our kind. She's expecting me, and can't wait to get her claws into my new skin."

I nearly vomited.

Kaidan cleared his throat. "She must be an exceptional woman if you've been able to trust her in such a way."

"Exceptional, yes. And I still expect you to be at her service if she calls on you, regardless of whether or not we live here."

"Of course, Father. Enjoy your evening. I'll begin my search for the Neph straightaway."

"If you need to involve the son of Melchom to help you, then do that. He has a lot of resources at his disposal on the West Coast."

Blake. Oh, he would be involved, all right.

"Brilliant idea," Kaidan said.

Nothing else was spoken. Just the sound of footsteps as they both walked from the room, up the stairs, and out the door. Pharzuph started his car and drove away.

I let out a silent breath, and I rolled the conversation around in my head, pondering all I'd learned and feeling proud of Kaidan.

Mercenary of heaven. Was that really how they saw me? A dangerous demon assassin? Actually, I kind of liked that image. I was determined to find a way to secure our safe futures. If only I *felt* like a merciless assassin.

Nerves zapped inside me. Kaidan couldn't keep the demons waiting. They'd be expecting him to bring me in soon so they could "deal with me." This was huge and it was happening so fast. I had no idea how we'd fight so many of them. Would more allies rise up at the sound of our battle cry? If not, we were throwing ourselves into the mouths of the lions with the sheer hope that we'd be able to keep their jaws from clamping shut. I'd been saved by a miracle once before, but it didn't feel feasible to wish for that fate again. This time it had to be us. We had to fight.

CHAPTER TWENTY-THREE

STRATEGIZING

Pharzuph had been gone ten minutes before I saw Kaidan's headlights pull out of the darkened driveway. I followed, keeping distance between us. I wondered about Patti and Jay—where they'd gone and how they were. The image of Patti half possessed made everything churn inside me. I had made Jay swear that if he saw something like that happening again he would call me immediately. We may have been separated by states, but I would get there.

We'd been driving for half an hour. I watched Kai's taillights in silence, and just as I began wondering where he was taking us, he exited for Lookout Point.

Wow. I had to shake my head. He was leading me to the very place his father had ordered him to take me two years ago to begin my "training."

Two cars were parked at the top of the peak with space between them. The interiors were dark, but I was willing to bet they were occupied. Kai and I parked next to each other and we both got out and stood without speaking. The stars shone bright above us. Crickets serenaded from all around. Kaidan walked to my car and opened the back door, signaling me to get in. I came around the car and stood as he held the door open, giving me a look.

"What are we doing here?" I asked, half teasingly.

His face was serious. "We're going to talk strategy."

I bit my bottom lip and tried to look equally serious. "It's a little snug back there for strategizing."

When he still didn't smile or take the opportunity to make one of his infamous innuendoes, I ducked into the car and he followed. I turned to face him and we stared at each other for a long time. Our circumstances were dire, and his mood reflected it.

"So," I said quietly. "Am I your prisoner now?"

My words did not have the desired effect. His face only tightened, so I reached up to push hair from his eyes.

"Kai . . ."

"We don't have to do this." He spoke with sudden urgency. "You can stay hidden, like Zania."

My heart broke to see his fear for me and hear it in his voice. As much as I wished I could ease his mind, there was no escaping the truth of our situation.

"I can't hide forever. And what would that mean for you? Your father will expect you to be working. Marissa will be calling you."

He gave a light shudder. "I'll go into hiding with you."

"That's no way to live."

"Are you truly not afraid?" He searched my eyes. "At all?"

"Of course I am," I admitted. "Mostly because I don't know how it'll go down. I don't know how to face the Dukes. But the chain of events has started, and we can't stop it."

"We can try." In the moonlight his eyes shone with the passion of his words.

I shook my head, feeling torn. I was scared, and I didn't know if I was ready for this monumental, mysterious task, but I needed Kaidan's support in order to come to a sense of peace about it.

His voice was hard. Adamant. "I finally have you, Anna."

"And every second we've had together is a blessing I never thought we'd get."

I ran my hands across his strong shoulders and dug my fingers in a little. Nothing I said was helping. I didn't have the words to take away his anxieties. Or mine. So instead I kissed him.

My hands grasped the back of his neck, moving up through his hair as his mouth worked mine with a dizzying desperation.

He groaned a masculine sound against my mouth and said, "*God, Anna.*" But there was so much more than lust in those words. The despairing grip of his hands on me said it all.

I could only whimper in response, causing his arms to tighten around me.

"What will I do?" He sounded in pain. "I can't lose you."

"Stop thinking that way. I can't fight them if you're not on board, Kai."

He looked at me, his forehead creased. I knew he was feeling selfish, wanting to keep me and keep our bubble of joy as long as we could, knowing it couldn't last. I knew he wanted to support me, and that he would when it came down to it. But right now he couldn't own it.

I tugged his face to mine and spoke against his lips. "You haven't lost me, Kai. I'm right here with you. Hold me."

He buried his face in my neck and did just as I asked, pulling me close and not letting go.

That night we cuddled in the backseat under a blanket—Kai leaning against the door and my back against his chest. His arms moved around my waist and I linked our fingers. The other cars eventually left. We stared out at the stars for a long time, both lost in thought.

I whispered, "The first time I came to Lookout Point—"

His fingers tightened around mine, almost painfully.

"Not with a guy!" I clarified, wanting to laugh as his grip loosened. "It was the day I got the postcard from you after the summit." Again I felt his whole body tense, maybe with guilt about how things had played out back then. I kept going. "I knew I had to let you go, and I knew there was something bigger coming." I turned, angling myself enough to look into his haunted eyes in the moonlight. "I never thought we'd get this time together. We're so lucky."

I unclasped one of our hands so I could reach up and stroke his face. He closed his eyes, the troubled tension never leaving his features.

"Kaidan, if anything happens to me—"

His eyes flew open and he yanked me closer. "Don't. Don't you dare finish that sentence. Nothing is going to happen to you."

I swallowed hard. We both knew that might not be the case.

His eyes seemed to burn in the reflected moonlight, impassioned.

"If we both, you know, end up down there . . ." I cleared my throat. "In hell. We can make it through together. We'll keep each other strong until it's time for our judgment."

He said nothing, and from the corner of my eye I saw his Adam's apple bob as he swallowed.

"I'll never leave your side," he whispered. "I swear it."

I sighed and snuggled down against his chest. In his arms I felt secure and stronger as the threads of our love twined together like a sturdy rope for us to hold tight to.

May we never let go.

A shift of the light woke me hours later, and I opened my eyes to the rays of a pink-tinged sunrise. We were scrunched in the seat, half sitting, half lying. My heart softened at the sight of Kaidan's sweet sleeping face with long waves of hair lying against his skin. He appeared gentle and innocent. At peace.

We must have both been exhausted last night. I couldn't recall falling asleep, but now a spike of fear pierced me at the thought of being seen together like this. I hated to wake Kai, but when I tried to sit up he sucked in a ragged breath and jolted upward, pulling me to his chest and searching around us.

"It's okay," I said.

He let out the breath and leaned back.

"We shouldn't have slept like that last night," I said, reaching into my purse for a mint.

"Yeah." He cracked his neck, which probably had a kink from how he'd slept. "Not our best idea."

"They could have caught us." What were we thinking? Whisperers were out hunting for me, and we fell asleep snuggling in public? How stupid!

Kaidan's face hardened and he stared out of the window, giving a shrug. I narrowed my eyes at him.

"What's that supposed to mean?" I mimicked his shrug.

"You're intent on being turned in anyhow."

"Yes, but on *our* terms. And I'm the only one getting turned in, not you. They have to trust you."

He continued to stare out at the great expanse past the cliff's edge. I knew he didn't like the idea of me being in danger "alone," and he hated pretending to be against me, but he was more valuable as an ally if Pharzuph trusted him.

I reached for his knee, needing to comfort him and make him see the importance of his role, but he shifted and my hand landed inside his thigh. I pulled away, but it was too late. His red badge expanded then snapped back to its normal size and began to throb. His head lowered and his blazing blue eyes rose to mine.

"Maybe we should take a break from talking," he said in a low voice.

The breath I'd been inhaling got stuck.

Bad, bad, dangerous boy.

"We can't." I tried to sound strong, but then he licked his

bottom lip and flicked his hair aside, and a burst of citrusy pheromones filled the car. My eyes fluttered a little, and I cursed my weakness for him. "Kai, don't. We seriously can't be caught in any compromising . . . you know . . ."

"Positions?" He sported a devilish half grin.

Yeah. That.

His hot hand reached for my hip, but I pushed the car door open and jumped out. The air was warm outside and already muggy, but when I felt him come up behind me I shivered with desire. I spun to face him, stepping back.

He looked half amused and half lusty as he lifted his palms in question. "You're running from me?"

Glad he could find humor in it.

"If you keep being all hot like that, then yes. It's not safe."

"To be hot?"

"To *do it*." I crossed my arms.

Kaidan's lips quirked upward. "Do what?"

"Be serious, Kai."

He stepped toward me again and I stepped farther back, running into his rental car.

"No more sex," I said in a rush.

A look of astonishment crossed his face.

"Just until after the summit," I added quickly.

All amusement vanished at the mention of the summit. Kaidan's face once again turned hard as he stared at me.

"Kaidan . . . ," I whispered.

He continued to stare, the mask in place to hide all emotions from me. I hated that mask. I wanted to yank it off and throw it over the cliff. I went to him and placed my hands on his shoulders. He made no move to touch me back. I lowered my hands down his arms and took his hands. When I spoke, I kept my tone gentle, but firm.

"You have to pretend not to like me. It sucks, but it's the smartest plan. If we're both going to survive this, which I really think we can, and *will*, this is our best bet. You're better at hiding your feelings than I am, but at this point it doesn't matter if they think I have feelings for you. You can even say you made me fall for you to lure me in. Your father trusts you to find me and get me to the summit on your own. That's huge. He has to think you're in his pocket until the very last minute. We'll have freedom to communicate with each other and warn the others. Do you really want to jeopardize one of the only things we have going for us?"

He closed his eyes and squeezed my hands. When he opened his eyes the mask slipped away.

"No, I don't. I'm sorry," he said. "I'll do whatever I have to do. Or *not* do."

I let out a relieved breath, trying to push back the waves of emotion. "Thank you. So, from here on out, no kissing, no holding hands or touching until this is all over. No doing anything that could be suspicious."

He nodded, lips pursed, and let my hands go. I felt an immediate loss. I missed him already.

CHAPTER TWENTY-FOUR

PRISONER

K ai and I went our separate ways that morning so I could hide while he took care of the estate business. I didn't want to go anywhere too populated where whisperers might be, so I drove around winding back roads, passing farms. When I stopped for gas I went into a nearby drugstore for a drink, tape, glue, and a large bag of candies.

The plan was to contact Pharzuph that afternoon, and that evening we'd be on a plane to wherever he demanded. I had to conceal the Sword of Righteousness when I flew. Hiding it in a bag of candies had worked for all my trips so far, since X-ray machines couldn't detect its celestial material. I parked in the back of a tiny church's lot under shade trees and set to work disguising the hilt, stuffing a piece of banana taffy into my mouth as I went.

After lunch I got a text from James Bond that said, *Done*.

My stomach constricted and I started the car to meet him at the car rental place as we'd discussed. I made it there in forty-five minutes and waited in the parking lot while he turned in the car. When he came out, I moved to the backseat and scrunched down while he took the driver's seat, setting a white box and some paperwork in the passenger seat, then adjusting the leg room and driving us away.

"Where are we going?" I asked.

"Back to my old home so you can shower and get ready."

My heart thumped. "Do you think it's safe?"

"My father's gone. The house is under contract, but it's still mine until the sale is final. If a whisperer shows, I'll let it know I'm in charge of you. It'll be fine."

"Okay." I hated the idea of setting foot in that lair, but we didn't have many options.

When we got there, Kaidan held my arm as if escorting me inside, in case any whisperers decided to show. Kaidan keyed in a code for the alarm and let me go when the door closed. The house was eerily quiet, and the sheets draped over the furniture made the place feel even spookier.

Kai led me down to the basement so I could use his shower. I glanced once at his giant king-size bed with its gray silky sheets, and I wanted to puke remembering Pharzuph's comment about the smell of lust. I couldn't smell anything, but still. The thought of how many girls had been in here made my stomach hurt with a vile intensity.

"Here." Kaidan handed me a fluffy black towel from the linen closet. I wasn't sure if his sudden gruffness was part of his captor act, or if being back in his old space felt as uncomfortable to him as it did to me.

I went into the bathroom and heard Kaidan's music turn on the moment I closed the door. Everything in the large restroom was black and shiny. Very masculine. I showered, using all his boy products, and kind of liking the idea of smelling like him all day. Though the products had nothing on the scent of his natural pheromones.

After brushing my hair and teeth, I dressed in a pair of shorts since I couldn't wear the hilt now that it was snug in its candy bed. I wouldn't have been able to wear it at the airport. My knife either. I'd have to change clothes and secure the hilt around my ankle again when we got to our destination—wherever that might be. When I opened the door, Kaidan was sitting on the edge of the bed with something silver in his hands and a grave expression on his face.

"It's not too late to run," he said. He turned the object in his hands and I recognized it as a pair of handcuffs. My tummy fluttered with trepidation.

"Yes, it is," I whispered.

I made no move when he stood and closed the distance between us. The dimmed lighting in his room, and the way he took his time moving toward me, made him seem almost sinister. My heart was beating harder than it should, given the fact that I wasn't in immediate danger. Without taking his eyes from me, he took the book bag from my hand and let it drop to the floor. I felt the cold metal as he clinked the cuffs over one of my wrists, then the other.

Heart rate. Too. High.

Breathing. Too. Fast.

Kaidan's eyes trailed down my body and he whispered, "Damn."

"What?" I breathed.

"You look amazing in handcuffs." Stormy eyes. Spinning, pulsing badge. "And you're officially my prisoner."

The true scent of Kaidan that drove me so crazy wafted around me now, urging my senses into a frenzy. He grasped the short chain between the cuffs and dragged me closer.

"We can't," I whispered, but there was no conviction behind my words, especially when he looked at me that way, all smoking-hot intensity. I forced myself to keep talking, to remind us both of the stakes and the fact that our current feeling of safety was only an illusion. "Remember, you told your father you don't like me. You're not supposed to want me, and the whisperers could find us any second. We can't lose our advantage."

My speech did nothing to calm his cloudy eyes.

"It's time to call him, Kai. Tell him you've found me. And then we'll call the others to let them know it's starting."

That cleared his head. "Not yet—"

"Yes. Now. Let's get it over with before we lose control and ruin everything."

His eyes dropped to the floor and I watched the thoughts and emotions warring inside him. With my bound hands I reached into his front pocket and pulled out his phone, holding it out.

"That was brave," he said.

"It's time," I whispered.

It hurt me to push him, knowing the horrors our futures forced him to face, but I couldn't let this drag out. The longer we waited, the more opportunity we'd have to mess up. He took the phone with reluctance, and it was the first time I'd ever seen his hand unsteady.

"I love you, Kai." I pushed up on my tiptoes and kissed his cheek. I kept my mouth close to his skin, closing my eyes and hoping he would feel my words as deeply as I did. "Let's bring them down. You and me and the others, together. We'll use our element of surprise while we have it. It's our time."

He rocked his jaw back and forth, mulling it over. I stayed silent, leaning against him. After what felt like an eternity, Kaidan finally nodded, clenching his jaw as he stared down at his phone, and then dialed.

His face was hardened when he brought the cell to his ear. I concentrated my Nephilim hearing on the phone to listen to their conversation. Pharzuph answered right away.

"Father." Kai clutched the phone tighter and his eyes hit mine, filled with more torment than I'd ever seen. "I've got her."

CHAPTER TWENTY-FIVE

JET RIDE

"You're kidding me." Pharzuph hooted with evil glee. He sounded young and euphoric—hyper even.

Kaidan looked like he might throw up.

"She's cuffed."

"Did you find the sword?"

"No, sir. I searched her and her belongings but found nothing."

Pharzuph swore. "She must have hidden it somewhere. Doesn't matter. We'll get her to tell us." His confidence rubbed at me like sandpaper, and I couldn't help but feel ill at the thought of their methods of torture. "Nice job, Kaidan. You accomplished what over five hundred prowling Legionnaires couldn't do last night. They searched damn near every bar, club, and hotel on the East Coast. Where the hell'd you find her?"

Kaidan wouldn't look at me. Everything about him screamed regret.

"She had a group of mates in her old town who always partied at a lake house. I thought perhaps she'd fall back on them, and I was right."

Pharzuph experienced another bout of creepy, proud laughter before getting ahold of himself. "Where are you now?"

"Our old house."

"Excellent. I'll call an immediate emergency summit in Vegas. It's our most secure location, and we're always looking for an excuse to visit Sin City, right?"

Kaidan let out a dry laugh and rolled his eyes. Weren't they just in Vegas? What could be so great about one city?

"All right," Pharzuph said. "Meet me at the Atlanta airport in two hours."

Kaïdan and I exchanged surprised, alarmed looks.

"Er, it's not necessary for you to fly down here, Father. I'll book our flights and deliver her to the summit."

"Oh, it's definitely necessary. I want to be the one to escort her into the summit tonight." I could hear the smile in his voice, and I realized this was about bragging rights for capturing me and bringing me in. "See you at the jet."

Three and a half hours on a plane with Pharzuph? I scratched my arms, which felt like they were crawling with spiders.

"We'll be there," Kaidan said, hanging up. He looked at me. "We're not going."

"Kaidan!"

He threw his phone on the bed and shoved his hands

roughly through his hair. "What have I done?"

I bent down to my book bag and took out my cell, then texted our planned emergency code to each of our allies to let them know the prophecy was starting. My hand trembled and I fumbled a little from the awkwardness of the handcuffs. I couldn't believe this was finally happening. Kaidan was freaking out enough for the both of us, so I had to keep my cool. Immediately I deleted the messages and tucked the phone in my pocket.

He turned to me, desperate. "Anna—"

"Stop!" I pinned him with a serious look. "No more. Get it out of your head, Kai! We are not running. This is happening whether you like it or not. It's time to get your game face on and get ready to kick some ass."

He stared at me, mouth open. I was kind of shocked myself. My dad would probably have beat his chest with pride if he'd heard me say all that.

I waited for Kai to argue again, but instead he swallowed and gave me a single nod.

"You're right." He stood there a moment longer, still a little stunned. Then he came forward, took me by the handcuffs, and led me into the bathroom, closing us in.

"It's more believable if I keep you in my sight," he explained. Then he began to take off his clothes as he headed to the shower and turned it on.

I backed myself against the cool sink and watched as every piece of cloth shed from his body to the floor. I should have looked away, or pretended not to be interested, but I couldn't. Kaidan was just . . . wow.

"You're testing my self-control, luv." He must have noticed my not-so-stealthy staring.

I looked away but said, "You're passing with flying colors."

He growled low in his throat, and my body tightened.

"You should really get in the shower," I told him.

At that, he finally slipped in, closing the cloudy glass door. I let out a breath and relaxed against the sink. A text came through to my cell, rocketing my body into high alert, but I relaxed when I saw Veronica's name. *On my way to Spain!!! And check out my view. . . .* She took a selfie pic and got the two guys next to her in the background—dark haired Spaniards, easy on the eyes. Hence her devious smile. I grinned, feeling emotional, and wrote back: *I hope Spain is ready for you. <3 Big hugs, xoxo.*

Delete.

I kept my eyes averted when Kai got out of the shower and dried off, though I could feel his gaze on me. I stayed in the bathroom while he went into the room and dressed, then I joined him.

He looked gorgeous in a pair of black trousers and a crisp button-up shirt, a pale shade of blue that brightened his eyes. The top two buttons were undone, and his hair was still damp.

"You look nice," I said, which was an understatement, but I was trying to take it easy.

He didn't respond or look at me as he busied himself tucking his wallet into his back pocket. His anxious, stiff demeanor gave him an angry-looking edge, which would hopefully work in his favor in front of Pharzuph.

Kaidan's gaze suddenly shot up, above my head, and I

spun. Two gaunt, hideous whisperers had flown in. When they saw how close they were to me, they both hissed and moved toward Kai. A look of annoyed disgust crossed his face at their nearness.

"We're leaving now. I don't need any damned escorts."

"Orders are orders," one of the spirits gurgled to us telepathically, giving me a suspicious glare.

Kaidan grumbled loudly and stuffed my book bag inside of his duffel bag along with a few travel things of his own. Then he grasped my upper arm and pulled me from the room. I knew I needed to play it up in front of the whisperers. I tried to shrug away from Kai.

"Let me go," I said.

He yanked me closer and pushed me forward in front of him. The two spirits circled us, watching me warily and seeming to enjoy the fact that I was cuffed and subdued by someone they believed was on their side.

"Seriously. Where are you taking me?"

"Shut it," Kai said. "Don't make me gag you."

I made a show of struggling now and then, glaring at Kaidan, who never looked at me.

The whisperers stayed with us until the doors were sealed shut on Pharzuph's personal jet, which was smaller than Blake's but still over-the-top luxurious. The leather furniture was crimson colored, offset by amber-shaded wood paneling and tables. Two oversize chairs faced the front of the plane, and in the back was a horseshoe-shaped couch with a table in the middle. Pharzuph sat on the couch with his arms spread wide and his feet up on the table. He was dressed similarly to

Kaidan, but he wore tan slacks and a white dress shirt, also unbuttoned at the top. He seemed older today in this setting and in that outfit—maybe a year or two older than Kai—not like the young college guy I'd first encountered.

Pharzuph's eyes flashed bright red when he saw me. He stood, never taking those freaky eyes off me.

"I had to leave the cuffs in the car," Kaidan explained. He obviously couldn't escort a handcuffed girl through the airport without getting questioned.

"That won't do," Pharzuph said coolly. He lifted a panel in the table and pulled out a thin rope, coming forward. "Hold her arms while I pat her down."

I hoped Pharzuph couldn't sense Kaidan's slight hesitation.

"I took care of that . . . Father." Yeah, it must've been weird for him to call this kid "Father."

"I said, hold her arms."

"I don't have anything—," I began, but Pharzuph cut me off in a low, deadly voice.

"Do not speak again. And don't you dare make a move."

Kai came up behind me and took my forearms in his hands while Pharzuph frisked me, touching me *everywhere*, though thank God it was only through my clothes. Kaidan's grip got harder and harder as his father touched me. I prayed he could hold himself together as I gritted my teeth and averted my eyes from Pharzuph's hate-filled eyes. Finally he stepped back, wiping his hands down his sides as if I were grotesque.

"Tie her up," he ordered.

Kaidan pointed to the closest seat and told me to sit.

With a slight huff I sank into the leather. Pharzuph leaned

over the back of my chair, nuzzling his mouth against my hair. I could feel his hot breath, and it took all my willpower not to pull away.

"I know who you are," he whispered, his voice deceptively sweet. "And I know what you're up to. But it won't work. You'll never win."

I tried to keep my voice steady as I lied. "I have no idea what you're talking about or what's going on. Why are you doing this?"

Pharzuph chuckled. "We'll see." To Kaidan he said again, "Tie her up."

As Kai knelt in front of me, I saw movement behind him in the front of the cabin. A beautiful woman in a flight attendant uniform came out of the galley with a glass of champagne in her hand. My eyes locked on the bubbling drink.

Champagne would be *really* great right about now. I took a deep breath to settle the grabby-handed longing inside me.

The woman stopped, seeming surprised at the sight of Kaidan preparing to tie me up, and her aura went from happy to nervous. Pharzuph chuckled from his seat behind us.

"Don't worry about them," he told her. "They're just having fun." He shot me a warning look.

The woman regarded me questioningly.

I gave her a little smile and held out my wrists to Kaidan. He began to tie them, never letting his eyes veer up to my face.

The flight attendant's nervousness lightened as she passed us to deliver Pharzuph's drink. She returned to the galley to finish her preflight prep. When Kaidan was done, Pharzuph sauntered up and tossed back the last of his drink. He ran his eyes over me like I was a pest about to be exterminated.

The plane's engines fired up, gently rumbling the cabin and surrounding us in white noise.

Pharzuph walked to the front to chat with the pilot in the cockpit. Then he stopped by the galley to return his glass to the flight attendant. I couldn't see her, but I had a perfect view of him inching closer, giving her a flirtatious smile as he said something that made her laugh. He reached out, maybe at her waist level, and his smile disappeared, his expression changing to a heated look of lust. When he spoke again, a blast of swirling red aura filled the space between them, coming from the woman. I dropped my eyes, feeling ill. Apparently the flight attendant wasn't just there to serve us drinks. The horror of it washed over me in sickening waves. Pharzuph was going to work right here in this small cabin space. Right in front of Kaidan and me.

A revolting thought occurred to me. Would he expect Kaidan to work? There were no other women in sight. No, this woman was for Pharzuph's pleasure only. She had to be.

The pilot announced it was time for everyone to take their seats. Pharzuph grinned and left the galley. As he made his way to the back of the plane, he stopped next to Kaidan and said, "You can have her after me. Or you could join us if you like."

Oh. My. Gosh.

Kaidan gave no reaction except a nod. "Thank you. Perhaps after you. I didn't sleep last night, so I might rest a bit first."

It could have been my imagination, but I swore Pharzuph

stiffened a little at Kaidan's lack of interest. Then his lips rose in a quick grin and he patted Kai's shoulder. "Rest up then. The Neph girl shouldn't be any trouble." He gave me a warning glance, and I dropped my eyes again.

My body was working against me. I felt light-headed and nauseous. What if Pharzuph pushed Kaidan to be with that woman? Kai would refuse. Our plan would be ruined.

And then I relaxed. Because just above Kaidan in the overhead compartment was my bag inside his bag with the Sword of Righteousness. Pharzuph had no idea it was on this plane. I would kill him if he pushed Kaidan to work. I might even enjoy it.

Of course then we'd have a dead body and a freaked-out flight attendant on our hands when we landed, but we could deal with that. I leaned back and closed my eyes.

Kaidan came over and buckled me. I kind of hoped he'd squeeze my hand, but he kept up the act, seeming repulsed by me. I felt sicker by the minute.

The flight attendant exited the galley and pulled down a jump seat next to the door across from me. She sat and buckled, a shimmer of red still present at the base of her aura. The entire takeoff process was uncomfortable with the woman staring between the seats at Pharzuph behind us. He had to be making eyes at her or something because she lit up like a red Christmas tree and rubbed her knees together, biting her bottom lip.

Please, God, let this flight go by quickly.

When we leveled out and the flight attendant stood to return to the galley, Kaidan got up and opened a wall panel, pushing buttons until a movie screen came down from the ceiling panel between us. I watched as he pulled out a pair of headphones from the armrest of his seat. He shot me a very quick glance. I angled myself enough to open my armrest and take out the headphones. It was difficult, but I got them unraveled, plugged in, and on my ears just as the woman was coming down the aisle.

Her flurry of lust disappeared when she approached me, looking at my bound hands.

"Anything to drink or eat, miss? We have turkey paninis and—"

"Nothing for her," Pharzuph said, sounding too close.

The woman looked up, surprised, then back down at me. "No beverage?"

The Dukes thought I was a lush, so I needed to act the part. "Rum and Coke?"

"She's underage," Pharzuph said from his lounging position behind me.

"Oh." She looked at me with a touch of exasperation. "How about a soda?"

I shook my head. "Nothing for me, thank you."

"Okay, sweetie." She definitely didn't know what to think about me and my predicament. I wondered how old she was. Younger than Patti. Maybe thirty.

She served Kaidan and Pharzuph their meal. Kaidan ate fast and looked as sick as I felt. He stood and pulled a small pillow from the overhead bin and sat again. The movie credits began just as a peal of feminine laughter sounded from behind us, followed by flirty bantering . . . a minute later, a quiet

277

moan. With as much discretion as possible I reached over and turned up the volume in my headphones as high as it would go.

I dared a glance at Kaidan, who was leaning against the window with his pillow. I knew he was pretending to sleep because his mouth was closed. His lips always parted the tiniest bit when he slept.

I stared at the movie in a tense daze, not daring to turn my head. The skin at my wrists burned. Time passed too slowly. When I finally felt our descent, I let my muscles slightly relax for the first time. Kaidan hadn't moved the entire trip. The flight attendant took her jump seat, staring blankly ahead and looking pale, her aura a blend of residual lust and fuzzy dark grays. I didn't want to pick apart her emotions.

Kaidan stared out his window as we hit the pavement in Vegas. The flight attendant rushed from the plane the moment the door opened.

I remained sitting as Kai stood and pulled out his bag. Pharzuph walked up from the back with his hands casually in his pockets, a neutral expression on his face.

"A car should be waiting for us," Pharzuph said to Kaidan. "Cover the girl."

Kaidan took a navy blanket from the overhead bin and put it around my shoulders, wrapping me enough to hide my hands. Then he put an arm around me and forcefully led me from the plane, down the stairs, into the waiting car and the sweltering dry heat of a Vegas evening.

CHAPTER TWENTY-SIX

SIN CITY

It was six p.m. when I got my first glimpse of the infamous Vegas Strip. Tall buildings and hotels crammed together in a tight cluster amid the arid landscape. I ignored my cravings at the sight of people walking the streets openly with alcohol, some carrying full cases of beer. I kept myself numb to the barrage of signs that advertised women for sale. Pharzuph chuckled from the driver's seat.

"It never gets old."

As we pulled up to The Venetian Hotel, Pharzuph turned to Kai, who sat next to me in the backseat. "Untie her, but hold her hand and don't let her out of your sight until you get to the room."

"Yes, sir."

Kaidan untied me, and I rubbed my wrists. He pulled me

from the car, taking my hand securely in his while he held his duffel bag in the other. A valet took the black sedan, and the three of us made our way inside the hotel. Though Kaidan came across as cold, his hand was warm and I was glad to be touching him.

Pharzuph bypassed a long line of people waiting to check in at the giant, fancy lobby. He smiled warmly, and nobody complained. It was amazing to watch his willful influence in action. The check-in clerk was blushing and laughing as she placed the key cards in his waiting hand.

He strolled handsomely back to us, winking at the tallest, slimmest woman I'd ever seen. She wore a silver, slinky dress and was on the arm of another man, who didn't notice as she turned and stared brazenly at her tempter. He was much younger than some of the women checking him out, but that only added to his allure—young, confident, handsome, built, and rich.

"I love this city," Pharzuph said to himself. He handed a key card to Kaidan. "Keep to your room. I'll send someone for you when it's time for the summit. It's likely to be late in the night before everyone gets here. We're planning for the witching hour—demon hour if we must." Pharzuph looked me up and down, a sneer on his lips. "She can't get into the club dressed in that. Find something more appropriate."

"Yes, Father."

Without another word, Pharzuph strode away. My back relaxed as distance was put between us, but I stretched my hearing to him, determined to listen to where he was going and what he was planning. I knew Kai would be listening, but

I wanted to hear for myself.

"Come on," Kaidan said, tugging my hand.

It was a relief to be out of Pharzuph's presence. I was quickly taken in by the hotel's ambience. It was like a hotel, high-end mall, and entertainment gallery combined. We walked down a wide corridor full of the diversity of humanity and the army of guardian-angel soldiers, who focused with total devotion on their jobs. I wondered if all of these angels knew the dangers that were in store for their humans' souls tonight. I still tried to keep tabs on Pharzuph, placing a bubble of my hearing around him, but I had to shift it every time he moved, and it took great concentration to focus on his voice and footsteps, especially with all the sensory distractions.

The Venetian was home to an indoor waterway that replicated a canal in Venice, Italy. There were gondola boats and singing "Italians" in red-and-white-striped shirts. The rounded ceilings were painted to look like a summer sky above the Piazza San Marco, as vivid as the real thing, if only the sounds didn't echo off the storefronts lining the walkways.

Kaidan tried to lead me into a boutique dress shop, but I noticed the window display in the next store and stopped.

Leather.

I bit my lip and pulled him in that direction. He made a face, confused, but took my lead and let us walk in. One look at the badass female mannequin in front of me and I knew. I was not wearing a dress tonight. Kaidan raised his eyebrows but didn't stop me as I approached the racks and made my purchases, hoping the clothes were true to size.

Back in the hall we had to squeeze through a ton of people

to get a better look at the waterway and sky scene. It was so crowded that we were well hidden from anyone who might be trying to get a look at us. I pulled my hand from his and signed a question to Kaidan, keeping my hands low: *What are the witching hour and demon hour?*

Witching hour is midnight. Demon hour is three a.m., he signed back. He again entwined his fingers through mine without looking at me. We could only stand there for a moment, pretending to be a normal couple, before it was time to get back to our room.

Knowing what would go down that night, it seemed like everything around us took on a strange distortion. The happy faces surrounding us were like mocking carnival masks. We shuffled quietly through the crowds, then elevators, and the long halls. The hotel felt like a maze, but Kaidan seemed to make sense of it.

I could still hear Pharzuph, his loud footsteps, and his occasional words. I was proud of myself for keeping up with him while we were on the move in such a busy, large place.

I listened as Pharzuph walked two floors above us down a quiet hall on the other side of the hotel. He had been silent for some time now, so I had to focus on the sound of his footsteps against the carpets. He stopped. Now I heard him knocking and the sound of a door opening.

Kaidan and I turned down our hall.

"Brother Pharzuph. Didn't I just see you on the slopes in Switzerland?" The man laughed, and I recognized the rough English accent as belonging to the Duke of Adultery. My stomach dropped. Kaidan's hand squeezed mine.

282

What was Astaroth doing in Vegas already? Coming from London would have taken at least ten hours. He must've been closer for some reason. Then it dawned on me—he probably headed to the U.S. when he heard about the Sword of Righteousness, knowing that if they caught me there'd be a summit.

"Ha," Pharzuph said. "Yeah, well, this summit's going to be much more enjoyable. Let me in."

Astaroth chuckled low as he let Pharzuph in and closed the door. "Do you have the sword?"

"No. She's hidden it. That's not why I'm here. I need a favor," Pharzuph said to him. Kaidan and I slowed our pace to listen better. "It will only take a moment. I'm curious about a possible bond between two people, though there's probably nothing there. I've just got a nagging feeling and I want to rule it out."

"Ah. A possible conquest?" Astaroth asked, sounding interested.

Pharzuph paused, and when he spoke again it was in fluent Russian.

Chill bumps flew across my skin.

Kaidan and I stopped where we were in the long hall and looked at each other, both listening to the foreign conversation taking place between the two Dukes now. I didn't know Russian, and I was guessing by Kai's wide eyes that he didn't either. Pharzuph had chosen to speak in a language he knew we wouldn't understand. There was only one reason he would've done that.

He didn't want us to know he was bringing Astaroth to our

room to check for a bond between us.

We forced ourselves not to run the short distance down the hall to our room, keeping our steps as light, but quick, as possible. Pharzuph would be listening, and our sudden rushing would only rouse his suspicion further. I followed Kaidan's lead until we were at the room, sliding through the door. What were we going to do? I felt caught, caged, one breath away from flipping out.

Kaidan strode fast past the bed, jumping over the three steps down into a sunken living room area, and tore open the small refrigerator on the floor. *Yes!* Alcohol would blur the bond between us! I rushed down and squatted next to him. He signed, *One of us has to stay sober to listen.*

I pointed to him. He was better at the listening. Even now, I'd lost Pharzuph in my panic and had no idea how close they were. But that would mean I had to drink. My heart thumped and my hands shook. I looked at the row of small bottles. I hadn't drunk in a long while. I wasn't sure how high or low my tolerance was now. I had to drink enough to hide the bond, taking into account the fact that my Nephilim blood would burn off the alcohol at a fast rate. But I couldn't drink so much that I might lose control and say something stupid. We couldn't afford a slipup. I would drink the absolute minimum amount to hide our bond, then they would leave and I could sober up quickly. I could handle that, couldn't I? I had to be stronger than the alcohol, and Kaidan would be there to make sure I didn't get out of hand.

He took a bottle of clear liqueur with golden flecks floating around, untwisted the cap, and passed it to me. I got a whiff of cinnamon as I brought it to my mouth and tipped back my head, chugging the thick, hot, sweet syrup. I blew out a long breath. Kaidan was ready with the next bottle. I could physically feel where the alcohol touched the inside of my body. It was on fire, down to my empty stomach.

I quickly drank the next bottle of liqueur he offered. It was too sweet. Kaidan's eyebrows were crinkled together as he looked at me. I was feeling nice and warm, even a tiny bit more relaxed. I tapped my wrist to see how much time we had. He made a three and a zero, thirty seconds. I was expecting to feel something more from two bottles. Alcohol usually hit me fast.

He tried to hand me the amaretto, but I shook my head and reached over his lap. No more sweet stuff. I grabbed the bottle of golden tequila, screwing off the top and draining it fast.

What if the bond was still visible? I was so nervous. What would Pharzuph do to us if Astaroth saw something? He wouldn't kill me because they needed me for the summit. Kaidan was a different story.

Fear struck and I stuck out my hand for another bottle, just to be on the safe side. He passed me the vodka and I made a face. I hated vodka, but I tilted my head back, slapping the carpet as the vodka burned its way down my throat. I held out my hand for another.

I stared at his hands as he signed, *Are you sure?*

It took me a second to comprehend what he'd said, and I nodded. He passed me the rum and I downed it, hardly feeling the burn this time.

I moved to adjust the way I was sitting, and swayed. Out

of nowhere a giggle escaped me, and Kaidan's eyes widened. Whoa, that was weird. I looked to the row of bottles, already wondering which I could have next, and he made a slashing movement of his hand across his throat to say I was cut off. A moment of panic overtook me. I realized, too late, that I'd had more than I probably needed. The alcohol was strong inside me, awakening and taunting the beast I worked so hard to keep tame.

Kaidan's head turned to the door five seconds before the knock came. He looked at me, pleading with his eyes, bringing a finger to his lips before he got up to let them in. I was feeling at ease, not nearly as nervous as I thought I'd be when they got here. I would sit like a good girl and be quiet until they were gone. That was my big, brilliant plan.

I sat there in front of the open fridge while they walked down into the living room area toward me. Pharzuph and Kaidan stood side by side, feet apart, arms crossed. I covered my mouth and looked up at Astaroth.

He was as rugged as ever with his romance-novel-cover long golden hair and face made of jutting angles. He looked between me and Kaidan, his eyes landing on me with a severe frown.

"This one's piss-drunk. I can't get a reading."

"A reading on what?" Kaidan asked in a hard voice. Nobody answered him.

I realized then that I should probably stand in the presence of the Dukes, but when I lifted myself from the floor, the alcohol hit me full force. *Holy Moses!* My balance was completely gone, and I tumbled into the arm of the couch, which was absolutely hilarious, and I couldn't hold back the laughter.

"You don't waste any time," Pharzuph said to me.

"There's more." I pointed to the open fridge. "I didn't drink it all. Want some?" It couldn't hurt to be nice. Patti would be so proud of me.

"I'll pass," Pharzuph said, "but I think *you* should have another." He smiled.

I smiled back because, well, that was awfully kind of him, and I agreed that another sounded like a wonderful idea.

I dropped to the floor in front of the mini fridge. I picked out two bottles, looking them over and finding the letters all sort of jumbled, so it took me a second to read them. I turned to the three men who were watching me. I wondered why Kaidan, my beautiful Kai, looked so friggin' mad. I smiled up at them.

"If you don't need me for anything else, I'll just be on my way," Astaroth said.

"Nothing more," Pharzuph told him. "Maybe later. Thank you, Brother."

Astaroth left the room.

"They need more tequila in these minibar fridge thing-amajigs," I said, settling on the gin.

Pharzuph laughed and looked at Kaidan, who was now leaning against the entertainment center with his arms crossed.

"I told you," Kaidan said to his father. "She's a lush. An idiot. I can't believe you'd think there'd be a *bond* between us."

Pharzuph chuckled at his son's anger, and his smile was handsome. "Eh, you can't really blame me for wondering when you wouldn't even screw the stewardess today. You're usually all about cougars."

"Eww!" I squealed. I wanted to claw those words from my ear canals.

"See," Kaidan said. "Completely immature."

I felt suddenly upset, though I couldn't place why. I unscrewed the bottle of gin.

"You're trashed," Kaidan said. "You don't need any more."

"Oh, shut up."

He tried to swipe my drink, but I yanked it back and took a glug.

"No touchie the drinkie. That's bad, bad, bad." I waggled a finger at him. "Why're you being so grumpy, anyways? We're in Vegas, baby!"

I stood up, grabbing the top of the fridge when I almost fell. A laugh erupted from my throat and I felt hyper. I wanted to jump on the bed and run down the halls!

"You are being obnoxious," Kaidan said through clenched teeth. "It's bad enough I have to babysit. I'm not holding your bloody hair if you puke."

He looked severely angry, which made me laugh again because I was pretty sure we were playing a game.

My words dragged out when I tried to talk. "It's funny to annoy you." I poked a finger into his chest, which was yummily hard. I leaned into him, even though I was trying to stand straight. "You're, like, sooo hot when you get mad."

"I'd watch it, if I were you," Pharzuph purred into my ear from behind. I jumped because I'd forgotten that he was still here—the guy who made me feel gross. I felt his hands on my waist and his mouth at my ear. "He can get pretty rough when he's upset."

Something inside me screamed that I was supposed to be careful and scared, but for the life of me I couldn't remember why. I pulled away from Pharzuph's embrace. Both of the guys were giving me menacing stares. I tipped back the rest of the gin and threw the empty bottle on the floor. These guys were getting annoying. I wanted to have fun.

"Whur's the music?" I spun, looking for a radio, and everything blurred.

Pharzuph stepped close, grabbing my arms and getting in my face. "Where's the sword?"

For some reason an image of the sword in the stone came to mind.

"I ain't got a swoooord, crazy ass." I laughed.

"Don't talk to him like that," Kaidan warned, moving toward us.

Pharzuph chuckled, but he didn't look happy. "We'll see, little girl."

"Yeah, we will!" I said, laughing gleefully and throwing myself onto the couch. I clutched my stomach as an onslaught of giggles overcame me. "What the heck are we even talkin' 'bout? I thought we were gonna dance." I rolled off the couch and crawled to the fridge. I needed another drink. And maybe I could make drinks for the guys since they weren't happy.

"I make the bestest drinks, guys. I'll make you sooo happy."

"Not likely," Kaidan mumbled.

Pharzuph slapped him on the shoulder and jutted his chin toward me. "Yeah, good luck with that. And be careful. I wouldn't put it past her to use your lust inclination as a distraction to escape. Don't let her get the upper hand, you know what I'm saying?" He winked, and Kaidan nodded. "Don't leave the room, and don't let her out of your sight."

"Yes, sir."

Pharzuph watched me again.

I cracked open a beer, throwing the bottle top with amazing accuracy at Kaidan's face, but he snatched it from the air before it hit him. I fell back onto the couch and kicked my legs in the air. Kaidan pressed his fingers to his forehead.

"Aw, c'mon, Kaidan Rowe, hottie-boom-bottie. Let's play."

Dang, I was funny.

"I see what you mean now," Pharzuph said to Kai, eyeing me with disgust. "It does seem ridiculous that she could be the one. Still. We need to find out what she knows."

Kaidan nodded. My head turned in slow motion as I watched Pharzuph leave. Kaidan raised his arms and shot both middle fingers up at the closed door. He then leaned back against the wooden entertainment center and crossed his arms. He looked angry. And sexy.

H-O-T-T.

I wet my lips, feeling bold and single-minded when I realized we were alone. He slowly shook his head back and forth at me. I set my beer on the coffee table, stood, and walked to him, wishing good riddance to the last shred of my inhibitions. I was invincible. I could do anything I wanted. But what I chose to do was the most dangerous thing of all.

CHAPTER TWENTY-SEVEN

ALLIES

I pressed my body against him.

He took my shoulders and tried to push me away, gently, shaking his head, but my busy hands were insistent on touching.

Nothing else in the world existed in that moment. Just us. Nothing else mattered. I wanted him. I loved him.

"Don't," I said when he tried to grab my hands. He quickly covered my mouth with his hard hand and spoke lowly against my ear.

"Shut. Up." And even that was sexy.

I wanted his hand on my mouth to be his lips. I stopped trying to push up against him and concentrated on his hand. I pressed my lips against his palm, looking up at him as I did it. His breathing went ragged. I took one of his fingers and slowly kissed it. He stepped back and I ran my tongue slowly over his fingertip.

"Ah, damn it," he whispered. There was flickering in his fiery eyes, and he yanked his hand from mine.

"Please," I urged. I reached up and pulled my ponytail holder out, dropping it and letting my hair fall around me.

"I will tie you up again if you don't behave," he warned.

"Oh, you'd like that, wouldn't you?"

In a flash he grabbed me, turning and crushing my back into the giant entertainment center's doors, making a superb racket, kissing me hard and pressing his whole body against mine. I welcomed his forceful hands and hot mouth. We made our way to the couch, where he fell on me and kissed me with a passion that obliterated all thought. I was lying on a cloud of bliss, my head a boggle of contentment, my body in its element against him. He was all I needed.

"We're about to have company," he said, but he didn't stop kissing me, kissing my neck, touching me everywhere.

Company? But that didn't mean we'd have to stop, did it? That would just be wrong.

There was a long string of insistent knocking on our door, but Kaidan mumbled for whoever was out there to go away. His hands were up my shirt, vibrant against my skin, making me gasp and moan.

"Oi!" shouted a familiar female voice. "Open the damn door."

"I'm busy." Kaidan bit my bottom lip with a nip, and a shiver rippled through me.

"The more the merrier," Blake said. His voice didn't sound completely right.

We paused and looked at each other. They were trying to stop us.

"Just ignore them," I said. I grabbed his shirt and pulled it up, lifting myself up to kiss the skin on his chest.

He moaned and was kissing me again.

"Don't let that skank take advantage of you when you're bored, son of Pharzuph."

Ginger! Anger stirred and I tried to sit up, but Kai pushed me back down. I yelled in the direction of the door, "Who you callin' a skank, you—"

Kai slapped a hand over my mouth and I struggled against him.

And then it was Kopano's temperate voice that spoke, seeming to clear Kaidan's head for the second it would take to pry him away from me and bring him back to his senses.

"Open up," was all that Kopano had to say.

Kaidan stood abruptly, shuddering as he took another look at me lying there, still wanting him. Then he went and leaned his forehead against the entertainment center for a long moment before going to the door. I couldn't move.

I heard the four guests pushing their way in and I felt furious at them for butting in. They looked upset with Kaidan—all of them were signing too fast for me, but I recognized *caution* and *stupid*.

Whatever.

I grabbed the beer from the coffee table and drank it all. Everyone was coming down into the living area. Their voices were excited, but when I turned to look, their faces were serious.

Kaidan looked at the empty bottle in my hand and clenched his jaw.

"Someone put on some music!" Marna said, stepping down

into the lower suite where I sat.

"Ezzactly!" I slurred. "I been trying to say that."

Marna pressed her lips together like she was trying not to laugh, but I didn't know what was funny.

Someone opened the curtains, giving us a superb view of the city. Loud music came on, and the sisters stood in front of the wall made entirely of glass, dancing for all Vegas to see. They were very good at keeping up appearances, considering that from the right angle outside the hotel, any Duke would be able to see us clearly with his extended sight.

"Come here." Marna's voice was seductive as she crooked her finger at me, and I went.

I didn't have to do too much, since Marna danced around me, rubbing against me, slinking all the way to the floor and back up effortlessly with her hands against the sides of my body. I put my hands under my hair and lifted it up, moving my hips to the beat. When I looked up at Kaidan standing at the railing with the other guys watching, I saw the fire still in his eyes.

Ginger went to the banister, grabbed Blake's hand, and pulled him down. She danced with him and it was, by far, the most sensual thing I'd ever seen. He kept looking like he wanted to kiss her, but she'd get within an inch of his mouth and cruelly turn, flipping her hair in his face. Marna came up behind Blake, and the twins danced with him in the middle. Their moves were so seamless that I swear they must have choreographed the dance. If these two sisters set their sights on a guy in a relationship, he didn't stand much of a chance.

Kaidan hit a button on the wall, and electronically controlled curtains began to move inward. The second they were closed, the dancing stopped, and the twins walked away, leaving Blake standing there with his arms held out at his sides, like "what's up with that?"

I laughed so hard I almost fell over. He came forward and stuck out his knuckles to me. I fumbled the first attempt but was eventually able to bump his fist with mine.

"Anyone want a drink?" I asked loudly over the music.

"What have you got?" Blake asked.

We opened the fridge and found that we were sadly running low on the adorable bottles of liquor. But there was plenty of beer and wine.

"Here, Blake," I said, "I know you want to party." I tried to toss him a bottle of the beer, but it fell short and broke, fizzing all over onto the floor. Like everything else, it was riotous in my eyes and worthy of laughter. Blake shook his head and *tsk*ed from the side of his mouth.

"I'll get my own this time." He reached over me and grabbed one out, twisting the top and flicking the cap at Kaidan, who kicked it aside. Kopano picked up the broken beer bottle and threw it away, then tossed a towel onto the spot.

I looked around for Zania, but she wasn't with them. I wanted to ask where she was, but something inexplicable kept me from speaking.

Ginger took a miniature bottle of wine. She, Blake, and I lifted up our drinks to give a cheer, and before my mouth was full with the first gulp, the bottle was snatched from my hand. I swallowed and gasped.

"Hey," I shouted, "Give that—" Kaidan's hand covered my mouth and he gave me a hard look. I wanted to throw a tantrum. Why was he being so mean? We were just trying to relax before . . . before what?

Ginger snorted, way too amused by the tiff between Kaidan and me. Was she laughing at me? Rage for all the nasty things she'd ever said made me lunge forward, but strong arms yanked me from behind. Kaidan still held me tight around the waist, and I kicked out, wanting to fight her. My only satisfaction was the pure surprise on her face and the fact that she wasn't laughing anymore.

"Calm. Down," Kai growled into my ear. I settled down but was still breathing hard.

Everyone stood there looking at us. Blake took Ginger's arm and pulled her farther away from me. Kaidan kicked the fridge shut and did that throat-slashing motion to the others, pointing at me. He went up the steps to the bedroom level that overlooked the suite. He seemed distressed. Was he mad at me? We shouldn't be fighting about . . . what *were* we fighting about? Why was I so angry?

The music blared, scrambling my thoughts even worse. For a moment I felt lost and confused, and all I wanted was Kaidan. I went up the steps and stopped in front of him, leaning against the railing. He looked down at me, unsmiling. I rubbed my hands across his chest and down his arms. He froze and closed his eyes. Someone took my arm.

Marna pulled me down into her lap on the bed and shook her head at me. What was that about? Why were her eyes so sad? She was a beautiful person. I wanted to tell her so. I opened my mouth to speak, but she quickly pinched my lips with two fingers.

The serious look in her eyes scratched at my brain, trying to unearth something I needed to remember. Something was coming soon. Something big. A meeting. Those men weren't very nice, and I was going to show them who was boss. Not me; I mean, of course I was not the boss, but the big guy was. The Big Guy. He could see me now, see what I'd done. I was a failure. I couldn't control my emotions as the shame overcame me, so I buried my face in Marna's shoulder. She rubbed my back. I could almost hear Patti's voice telling me not to cry. *Hush, baby, you're all right.*

When I finished my quiet bout of tears, we lay back on the bed and I felt lost in a fluffy sea of down. It was soft and I was warm all over and I wanted everyone to feel this cozy. I saw now that the music was blaring from the television. As I watched the images without really seeing them, I zoned out. My mind went blank. And blank, much like calm, was good. I lay there warm and numb and thoughtless for who knew how long. Then everything was black.

Sometime later I pushed my heavy eyes open, and the room started to spin. I sat up halfway and groaned. Wow, it was really spinning, round and round like a carnival ride. Ugh. I didn't feel so good. I covered my mouth.

"I think I'm going to take a shower," Ginger said, looking pointedly at me.

"Hells yeah!" Blake said. "Shower time."

Ginger pulled me up and put a finger sternly to my lips. Marna went to my other side to help me walk.

It was quieter in the bathroom with no music, then one of them switched on a television up in the corner of the giant marble bathroom. Why was there a TV in the bathroom? I wasn't able to ask. The spinning was turning to a rolling in my stomach.

We three girls turned to see Blake standing there, too. Ginger scowled and lifted her stilettoed heel impressively high, placing it in the middle of his chest and kicking him out. He stood outside of the bathroom with a grin, and Ginger shut the door in his face. Marna kissed my cheek softly and touched a finger to my lips to remind me to stay quiet. She stripped me down to my underwear while Ginger turned on the shower water.

I groaned, bending.

They quickly helped me into the shower stall. It was just in time. I went down on my hands and knees, vomiting hot liquor and stomach acid, vile and sweet, and when that was all gone, I still heaved. The hot water stung my sensitive skin. My temples pounded, and my mouth was sour and dry. I wanted to tip my head back and catch some water, but I didn't have the strength in my neck. My stomach was still churning. I heaved several more times and then started crying.

I looked up enough to see Kaidan come in. The sisters shook their heads at him and tried to push him back, but he swept past them and opened the shower door. They watched him warily for a moment as he unbuttoned his shirt, taking it off and throwing it across the sink.

Everything hurt. I moaned.

Kaidan sat outside of the shower stall on the marble floor and put an arm around my body, pulling my back up against him and holding me. I clung to his arm in front of me, resting my head on it as my body shuddered under the stream of hot water.

When most of the alcohol had burned from my body, and my mind was shifting back into the alertness of reality, I felt very naked and ashamed. I turned slightly and looked at Kaidan behind me. Our eyes met and he nodded. He pulled away and left the bathroom, wiping his soaked arm on the way out.

Marna came over with a towel for me and we turned off the shower. I was still shaky as I stood, and my stomach was not right. Physically, I felt weak. Mentally, I was more scared than I'd ever been. I started shivering with my hair dripping onto the floor. Marna took one of the fluffy white robes and wrapped it around me. It was huge. I tried to towel dry my hair. I could hardly sit up straight. Worst timing ever for a hangover.

I tried to think of everything that had happened, but there were many blank spots in my memory. Had I done or said anything that could incriminate us? I remembered dancing. When exactly had the other Neph shown up? I flashed to a memory of Kaidan kissing me on the couch, and I was horrified to recall how I'd baited him. I looked up at Marna and Ginger. They had saved us from ourselves. I could have ruined everything.

Marna sat me down at the vanity and took a brush from her bag, working it through my wet hair. Ginger filled a glass with water and set it in front of me. I emptied it all and gave her a small smile, which she did not return. I grabbed her hand and she stilled.

I'm sorry, I signed to her.

She surprised me by grinning. *You can be mean*, she signed. *It was nice to see.*

My face flushed and I shook my head. Ginger patted my shoulder with her free hand, then pulled the other hand from my grip to pick up the blow-dryer.

The hot air felt good on my head. My body shook every few seconds with tiny tremors. I was so tired.

"Order us some food, Kaidan," Ginger shouted at the door. "I think we've all worked up an appetite." My stomach growled at the mention of food, and I realized that I was completely famished.

I took Marna's wrist and looked at her watch. It was eleven o'clock. We had somewhere between one and four hours to prepare for hell on earth.

What was I going to do? I felt completely unprepared. How could I ready myself for a spiritual battle under these circumstances? What would Patti do?

Wait. That was it. I knew exactly what she would do.

I jumped from the chair and ran into the suite, leaving the twins with hairbrush and blow-dryer midair. I could feel all of their eyes on me in my oversize robe as I flung open each dresser drawer. All empty. *Oh no.* I turned and saw the nightstand. I ran to it, passing a confused Blake, and opened the tiny drawer.

There it was. The Holy Bible.

I took it out like a precious gem. It probably hadn't been opened once in all its years in this room. It was a funny thing, wasn't it?—the notion of keeping Bibles in hotel rooms. I

wondered how the tradition had started and why it had continued. Maybe superstition. Maybe for me and this very moment.

I looked up at everyone staring at me. The room was
wrapped in nervous tension.

Watch for spirits, I signed.

The others nodded their agreement. I climbed up to the
middle of the big bed and placed the book on the terrycloth
robe over my lap. Very slowly, very quietly, I opened to the
back and found the Dictionary/Concordance. It was hard to
concentrate with everyone on edge and the television blaring,
but I forced myself to focus. Kopano walked away from the
group, going to sit at the table in the living room area with his
eyes closed in mediation.

Marna climbed up and sat next to me. Blake and Ginger
watched television, or at least pretended to, and Kai paced
silently. I first looked up "demons." I knew there were a ton of
passages about them—this wasn't my first time looking—but
in the past none of it had stood out to me as very informative.
I guess the verses that stand out are the ones most relevant to
you at the moment you're reading them. Like poetry. I pointed
to the lines I was reading so Marna could follow.

For forty-five minutes I read the many accounts of demon
possessions. There were weird passages about suicidal, demon-
possessed pigs. I didn't have time to pick those ones apart. The
use of parables and lack of explanations had me dissecting for
meaning, something that I wasn't good at.

I nearly came out of my skin at the sound of a knock at the
door. Kaidan went to it, and I was flinging the puffy down
comforter over the Bible. Marna patted my arm to reassure

me. I tried to catch my breath and slow my heart when I saw it was only our room service. Kai had ordered a ton of food, and my mouth watered as the scent hit me.

Nobody else ate quite as enthusiastically as me. I barely took time to breathe as I downed an entire huge hamburger, then drank a soda. My stomach wobbled a little with nausea again, so I sat back on the bed. My full belly made me feel even sleepier. I patted my cheeks and pinched my cheekbones. *Get it together, Anna.*

I turned again to the Concordance and looked up "sword" this time, but it was all mostly symbolism for war, or proverbial lines like "reckless words pierce like a sword."

I read about angels and their jobs as messengers and guardians of souls. Kaidan paced the room again with his arms crossed over his chest, listening for danger, his face slightly pinched from absorbing so much sensory input at once. I chewed my fingernails while I read until Marna pulled my hand down.

My palms were starting to sweat. I wiped them on the robe absentmindedly.

Can you turn the air up in here, please? I signed to Blake.

He nodded, fiddling with the temperature gauge.

I couldn't stop peeking at the clock. It was after midnight. I wasn't even dressed yet! I knew Kaidan would warn me when it was time to get ready, but panic was fraying me around the edges. The Sword of Righteousness was still in my bag, and we needed to figure out who would carry it—obviously not me since I'd be patted down to the max if they had one of the Neph checking people as they came in like at the last summit. I grasped my head. I had too much to figure out still!

I flipped pages. There had to be something I could use. Kopano caught my gaze from across the room. I pleaded with my eyes. Did he know something that could help? He came over and sat next to me. I felt a rush of safety and hope from his nearness.

He signed, *What are you searching for, in particular?*

Anything to battle them and defeat them, I signed.

I held the book out to him, and he took it, flipping pages with quick assurance. He'd get to a passage, stop, shake his head, and flip again. After three times his face softened. *How about this?* He set the book in my lap and pointed to Ephesians 6:11–18. My heart stirred. I read it twice and my pulse quickened. I read it a third time and I knew this was it. Marna and I shared an elated glance. I gave Kope a grateful look before he stood. Kai pushed off the wall, his eyes wide, wondering what we'd found. I beamed at him. Kope took over keeping watch for whisperers while Kaidan came to my side. Together, we read.

The Whole Armor of God

Put on all of God's armor so that you will be able to stand firm against all strategies of the devil. For we are not fighting against flesh-and-blood enemies, but against evil rulers and authorities of the unseen world, against mighty powers in this dark world, and against evil spirits in the heavenly places.

Therefore, put on every piece of God's armor so you will be able to resist the enemy in the time of evil. Then after the battle you will still be standing firm. Stand your ground, putting on the belt of truth and the body armor of

God's righteousness. For shoes, put on the peace that comes
from the Good News so that you will be fully prepared. In
addition to all of these, hold up the shield of faith to stop the
fiery arrows of the devil. Put on salvation as your helmet,
and take the sword of the Spirit, which is the word of God.
    Pray in the Spirit at all times and on every occasion.
Stay alert and be persistent in your prayers. . . .

I smiled as I read it. Kaidan watched me with that boyish look he sometimes gave me when he was in awe, as if I was capable of amazing feats.

The Armor was all metaphorical imagery. With the exception of the sword, all of my primary available weapons and protection would have to come from *inside me.* I had been fully equipped all along.

Truth. Righteousness. Peace. Faith. Salvation. And prayer. That was it.

Overwhelmed with gratitude, I slid from the bed and fell to my knees, but still I felt too high. I pressed my forehead to the carpet and silently spoke the most important, fervent plea of my life. I lay there with my eyes closed, buzzing with the sureness of my arsenal.

"Daughter of Belial," I heard Kaidan say. He stood at Kopano's side.

I quickly pushed to standing and faced him.

He nodded, his eyes hard. "It's time."

CHAPTER TWENTY-EIGHT

GALAXY

At once Kaidan and Kopano became still, their eyes far away as they listened.

Oh, no. What were they hearing?

Kaidan's eyes darted around the floor, landing on his duffel bag by the closet. He ran to it, unzipping it and pulling out my book bag.

"Here's your bag. Get ready," he said roughly. But with his hands he signed, *Hide the hilt! The son of Shax is coming.*

Marek! Not good. He was a possible ally, but I couldn't take any chances.

I thought fast. As quietly as possible I removed the bag of candy from my backpack and put it in the trash. Then I took some napkins from the room service cart and threw them on top. Yuck.

When the knock came, my stomach dropped. Kaidan pointed for me to sit on the bed. I sat with the book bag in my lap as he opened the door. To my horror Marek came in, flanked by a whisperer. Marek was shorter than Kai, about Blake's height. I'd wondered if he was friendly before—he'd seemed like it compared to Caterina—but his face showed none of that friendliness now. His eyes were like ice as he pushed up the sleeves of his black dress shirt.

He stopped in front of me, and I wished I were dressed instead of wearing a stupid robe. My Neph friends stood in a tense semicircle around us.

"We meet again," Marek said. Without asking, he took my bag from me and began to riffle through it, tossing my underwear and shirts out.

"Hey!" I said, trying to seem indignant. "What are you doing?"

When the bag was emptied and he'd felt all the pockets, he glanced around the room.

"What did you take from the bag before I arrived?"

"What? Nothing—"

"I heard a sound! Like . . . crinkling. What was it?"

No, no, no.

"Oh," I said. "Just some candy I didn't want anymore."

He turned and scanned the floor until his eyes stopped on the trash can. No! Without hesitation he reached in.

"Ew, man," Blake said, but Marek was undeterred.

Panic flared like a rushing meteor inside me. Everyone stepped closer, faces hardened as if ready to fight.

Marek shook the trash off the candy bag and proceeded to

do what nobody from any of the airport security checks had done before. He ripped the bag open and dumped its contents onto the desk. I leaped from the bed and dived toward the exposed hilt, but I was too late. The whisperer hissed above us as Marek shoved me back, plucking off pieces of candy that I'd taped to it. Kaidan stepped forward, but Kope steadied him with a hand to the shoulder. I hoped Marek and the whisperer thought Kai was angry about what I'd hidden from him, and not the fact that the son of Shax was taking possession of it.

Marek didn't seem to notice any of this. He didn't act surprised or satisfied or . . . anything. He matter-of-factly opened the leather flap to reveal the shimmery heavenly metal underneath.

"Dude," Blake said. "What is that? What are you gonna do with it?"

The whisperer had plastered itself to the ceiling as far from the hilt as possible.

Marek closed the leather flap over the hilt and slid it into his pocket before answering Blake. "Don't worry about it."

I watched the wheels turning in Kaidan's mind. He looked prepared to attack. I gave him a tiny shake of my head, and Kope stepped slightly in front of him, as if signaling him not to make a move. As much as I wanted to jump on Marek and take the hilt back, I knew this was a pivotal moment. We could not yet let on that we were all allies. I needed to be the only threatening one until we had all the Dukes gathered. Then the Neph boys could take the hilt by force. If we tried to take it now, the whisperer would fly off and rat us out. Then we were trapped at a disadvantage.

We could still get it back. We had to.

Marek looked at Kaidan and nodded his head toward me. "She had it all along. Don't you know never to trust a pretty face? Don't let her out of your sight."

"I won't," Kaidan said, his eyes hitting mine. "Especially now."

Marek turned and headed to the door, seeming to speak to the air as he said, "I've got it." And he left the room with the whisperer trailing behind him.

We all stood there, stunned. This changed everything. For one, my guilt was now proven. I'd lost my biggest weapon. What was I going to do without the hilt? All at once I felt small, fragile, and useless. My breathing hitched, a panic attack approaching.

I grasped for something positive, trying to slow my heart rate. We still had the surprise of our Neph alliance, as small as it might be. And maybe other Neph would join us when they saw we were willing to fight. I couldn't pretend that a huge fraction of my confidence hadn't disappeared with the hilt, along with the hope that Marek might end up as an ally, but I didn't want the others to feel as desolate as I did.

We'll get it back, I signed.

I could tell from the fierceness in everyone's eyes that they agreed. Then both of the Ks widened their eyes at the same time.

Kope signed, *Shax just told Marek to dispose of the hilt.*

He said, "Bury it in the desert if you must," Kaidan added, his hands moving fast.

No! We had to get it back!

Kaidan's phone chimed with a text. He read it and slid the cell back into his pocket.

"Summit's in one hour. One of us needs to guard the door at all times so she can't escape."

"I'm on it," Blake said. He went to the door and leaned against it, crossing his arms.

"We'll stay with her while she gets ready," Marna said, guiding me to the bathroom.

I wanted the positive feeling of peace to return. If I was going to lead us into this battle, I had to have that hope. As I pulled on my new snug black leather pants, black tank top, and short leather jacket, I ran through the passage in my mind, reminding myself of the arsenal I had at hand. I told myself the Sword of Righteousness was just a crutch—I didn't really need it, but *crap*! I wanted it! It had been my one tangible weapon.

By the time I zipped on the black leather ankle boots and stood up, my confidence was wavering back and forth. The twins watched me, sort of agape at my outfit choice. Ginger had an impressed half smile as she looked me over.

I pulled my hair into a high ponytail and went to the mirror to do my makeup. The demons might have labeled me as a mercenary of heaven, but I wouldn't be wearing any white wings tonight. I darkened around my eyes with gray eyeliner and silvery shadow, blushed my cheekbones, and smoothed red lipstick over my mouth. The overall effect was even more powerful than I could've hoped. Over the tank top I placed Kai's gift, the turquoise necklace, the one splash of color I'd be wearing.

Blake came into the bathroom in a black suit with an

iridescent green tie. He wet his hair and helped himself to some spray gel, flicking pieces here and there. Ginger grabbed the spray gel from him and spritzed the back of his head, doing the same thing that he'd done to the front. I saw him visibly relax under her touch.

A speck of blue caught my eye in the mirror, and I looked up to see Kaidan leaning against the doorframe with his hands in his pockets. He also wore a black suit, but with a royal blue shirt underneath that made the sapphire of his eyes pop. I had to swallow. He ran a hand through his hair as he looked at me.

I will drink tonight, just enough to hide the bond, he signed to me, and I nodded.

I wanted to kiss him again. One last kiss. He must have been thinking the same thing because he was ready for me when I turned and went to him, running my hands over his strong shoulders.

His mouth was tender, and he tasted of sweet bourbon. Maybe it was wrong, but I didn't care if any of our Neph friends were watching or how they felt about it. The only thing that made me pull away was fear of whisperers flying in. Behind me I heard the twins and Blake walk out, flicking on the bathroom's television and turning up the volume before leaving us alone.

Kaidan pressed me against the sink, kissing me deeply.

I wanted to tell him that I loved him, but he held me close and wouldn't let me budge an inch away from him. I let my mind open wide, revealing the pinks in my emotional aura just long enough for him to see. He took me up into his arms.

When he set me down, he rested his forehead against mine, breathing hard. I knew he was scared. I could see it in his eyes. I lifted my hand and signed, *We're going to win this.* He looked down at the floor between us, running his tongue over his lips. When he raised his eyes again, he pulled the ponytail holder from my hair, causing the blond layers to tumble heavily over my shoulders.

Now you're ready, he signed, looking me over with dark-eyed appreciation.

I nodded. We needed his wits clear enough to be able to fight if it came to that. I watched as Kaidan leaned down, removing the knives from his pockets and fidgeting with the thick soles of his boots. He'd rigged tiny compartments to hide the blades.

Good thing he had such big feet.

When he stood, he took a small bottle of whiskey from his pocket and drank it, tossing the bottle into the trash afterward. The hot scent hit me and I shook with a moment of need, despite my lingering hangover.

My stomach plummeted at the sound of firm knocking on our room door. Kai and I stared at each other for a long moment before breaking apart. We met the others in the entryway, and Kopano answered the door.

My stomach flipped at the sight of the sons of Thamuz in the doorway, looking us over with disdain. Their long brown hair was pulled back in low ponytails and they wore brown suits. They were completely healed from the last time I'd seen them, but pure malice lived in their dark eyes. They all but snarled as they stared at me, promising pain and evil deeds

311

if given the chance. I fought to hold their stares and not back down.

Marna shuddered next to me and stepped back.

"Good evening, sons of Thamuz," Blake said with false politeness.

"It will be a good evening once the punishing begins," one of them said.

Fear coursed through me, thick and bitter for all the evil we'd have to face tonight. Marna made a pitiful sound. When the sons turned their eyes to her, Ginger stepped in front of her sister and crossed her arms with challenge. Ginger had given me a lot of stink eyes in the past but nothing close to the one she gave the sons of Thamuz now.

They sneered at her. Blake moved to Ginger's side and jutted out his chin at the newcomers.

"We leaving or not?" Blake asked.

One led the way out of the room while the other waited so he could walk behind us. The Dukes would be proud to see a brood of their children surrounding me to protect their fathers from a would-be mercenary.

When we stepped into the hall I spotted two whisperers dashing down the long space as if racing. As if this were all fun and games. I wished so much for my father at that moment. Where was he? Had he heard about this summit through one of his ally spirits? And what about Lucifer's spirit messenger, Azael, our unlikely ally? I wished we had more information, more allies, more time.

My body craved quiet peace so I could concentrate on the task, but making our way through levels of shopping and casinos was sensory overload, even at two o'clock in the morning. Whisperers were everywhere, darting through the spaces and whispering in unsuspecting ears. The noise was outrageous, like a dozen carnivals crammed into one massive building. Electronic games from the casino went crazy with overlapping bleeping and dinging. Hundreds of human voices fought to be heard. Their angel guardians were grim and on guard.

Each laughing face that we passed was a possible victim. I wanted to scream out to them all to leave, but it was a useless thought. The Dukes had been meeting here for as many years as Las Vegas had been popular. It hadn't gained its nickname of Sin City by accident.

I silently meditated as we left The Venetian and crossed over to an independent casino with a stairway on the side leading underground.

Music played, but it seemed to be coming from under our feet in gentle vibrations. At the bottom of the stairs, out of public sight, we stopped at a set of solid metal doors with a sign above the entrance that said GALAXY NIGHTCLUB. My heart sank to new depths at the sight of the Nephilim standing guard at the door. Marek. I forced myself not to look at Kaidan or do anything suspicious.

Marek ran a metal detector wand over one of the sons of Thamuz, then the twins, Kopano, and Blake, then patted them down. I felt a hard poke in my back and turned my head to the other son of Thamuz, who was staring down at me with angry impatience.

"*Move,*" he ordered.

313

I stepped forward, and Kaidan discreetly stepped between me and the angry Neph without looking at me. I faced Marek, who would not meet my eye.

"Lift your arms," he said.

I did everything he told me. When he was done with the metal detector, he patted me down, concentrating on my pockets. I heard Kaidan shift behind me and clear his throat when Marek's hands were feeling my back pockets. Thankfully he finished quickly, giving my ankles a pat and then standing and motioning me through.

"Thank you," I said softly. I wasn't sure why I thanked him—maybe just the years of manners ingrained in me, but it made him look at me, surprised. Maybe even a little shaken. I dropped my eyes and walked through the door to where the others waited in the darkened entrance with its low ceiling.

I moved to the side where I could see Marek waving the wand over a straight-faced Kaidan. It beeped at his waist, and Kai removed his belt, displaying the metal buckle as if bored. He put it back on when Marek nodded. More beeping sounded when the wand got to Kaidan's feet. He untied his boots and kicked them off, letting Marek step down to inspect them. I could see the bulge under Marek's shirt at his waistline where he packed a gun.

My heart pounded.

Marek was the son of Shax—known for clever tricks of thievery. He would know ways to hide things in shoes. How could Kaidan stand there acting so cool? My body was going crazy and I could hardly stay still. I watched as Marek's fingers ran along the edge of the thick heel, right where the secret compartment lay. His movements seemed to slow, then pause, and I watched Kaidan's jaw clench. Holding my breath, I felt like the wait dragged on forever.

Then Marek stood abruptly and gave Kai a nod, moving past him to begin running the wand over the son of Thamuz. All the breath left my lungs. Kaidan put his boots back on and joined me. His arm brushed against mine and I wanted to sing. Three knives between us weren't much compared to the guns we knew the Dukes had, but at least they were something.

At the end of the hall we went through another set of doors and down more steps into a gigantic, dark room blaring techno music. The loud sound seemed to cause all my senses to open up. I could smell the bodies—a mix of sweat and skin and perfumes. I smelled alcohol everywhere, fresh and in the cracks of every surface, and marijuana somewhere nearby. My body buzzed.

Kaidan's hand touched my lower back to urge me forward, and I sucked in a ragged breath at the wonderful feeling of the contact. He glanced at me with wide eyes, his badge giving a spin, and I realized even my sense of touch had been let loose. I needed to rein it all in. I focused, forcing every sense back to normal except my night vision, and moved forward.

We were in a warehouse-size underground club already packed with people. To the left was a DJ booth, which made me think of Jay with a pang. I hoped with all I had that he was okay. And Patti. It brought me joy to think that after tonight they might never have to hide again.

A long bar stretched the entire length of the room, with bartenders flipping bottles and shaking tumblers. Thamuz's two sons slithered straight to the bar, telling us the Dukes would get us when it was time, and telling Kaidan to watch me. They didn't seem to feel the need to babysit us anymore—probably because the entrance and exit were covered.

I peered around for other exits. It was hard to see exactly how high the room was because every surface in the club was painted black. The black ceiling and walls were dotted with tiny twinkling lights in an exact replica of the galaxy, like a planetarium.

"Where are we meeting?" I dared to ask Kaidan, having to shout.

"The VIP room," he said.

I nodded. We walked farther in, following where our friends had gone. When we were surrounded by people, I saw Kaidan stealthily bend down and mess with something. I glanced, trying not to be obvious, and saw him lifting the flaps in the soles of his boots and taking out the blades that had been hidden. I felt one being slipped into my pocket and I pressed my lips together to hold back a smile. We kept moving until we met up with our group, clustered by the bar. They all stared around the room, appearing calm, but on guard. I looked around, too.

Almost the entire room was a dance floor. I hadn't noticed at first, but along the walls, giant black cages hung from the ceiling with females inside—cage dancers—who used the bars to flip expertly or hang upside down before landing gracefully and dancing perfected individual routines.

As I watched, the already dimmed lighting seemed to waver in the room.

"Legionnaires," Marna murmured next to me.

Hundreds of demons swarmed above us. I held my breath, feeling helpless and ill at the sight of their attack on the room. Every few seconds one of the spirits would dart down and whisper in an unsuspecting ear. Within one minute there were more people flocking to the bar, and the dancing was steamier. Two guys got into a fight on the dance floor, and bouncers ran to break it up while people around them screamed.

Ginger and Marna looked at Kaidan and me, staring purposefully back and forth between the two of us—at our bond. *Crap!* Kaidan moved away from me and went straight to the bar. I gave the twins a nod to thank them for the heads-up, then turned when someone bumped me.

A girl, no older than twenty-one, staggered by and after she passed us she bent over and threw up. People around her screamed. Her puke splattered up on the heels of the couple nearest her, and they spun to face her. The offended woman's aura was dark with rage, worsened by a whisperer pouring its vile message into her head. She poured her drink over the girl's back, causing her to stumble to one knee. A demon swooped down on the man, who lifted his beer bottle as if to throw it at the girl.

"Don't!" I yelled.

The man looked up at me with haunted eyes.

"Don't you dare," I said breathlessly, going to the girl's side. The man slowly lowered his arm, seeing Kopano and Blake watching.

I helped her up by the arm. Yes, it was stupid of me, but my secret had already been revealed. I was working for the other

317

team, so these demons could just kiss my heavenly booty.

"Donna?" the drunken girl mumbled.

"No. Do you have a friend here named Donna?"

She looked around, bleary-eyed, without responding. I led her to the end of the bar, half carrying her, and reached over to take napkins from a pile. I wiped her face and dabbed at her hair. Another girl her age ran up to us, out of breath.

"Oh my gawd! There you are, you stupid hooch! I thought you were going to the bathroom. Rob keeps asking about you. He bought us another round. Come on."

"Are you Donna?" I asked.

"Yeah. Why?" She looked at me for the first time.

"Your friend just got sick. Maybe she should go back to her room."

"Excuse me? Who do you think you are, telling me—"

I didn't have time for this. I used my influence. *If you care for your friend, take her back to the room.*

She looked at me with big eyes as she dealt with her inner turmoil. Then she glared at me, pulling her friend's arm around her shoulder and walking off in the direction of the exit.

Oh, thank goodness. I sighed. A whisperer swooped down on me, then another, shouting their telepathic messages.

What was that? You disgust us!

Kopano sidled up, looking serious.

"Leave her," he told the whisperers in his low, ominous voice. "She'll get what she deserves soon enough."

It worked and they left me alone, a shiver rippling over my skin at the double meaning of Kope's words, whether he meant it or not. Would I survive this night?

The demons had to be destroyed. If it took my death to make that happen, so be it. It broke my heart to think of Kaidan left behind without me and how he would cope with that, but he *would* cope. And we'd be together again someday, in a different way, but together nonetheless. I tried to gain confidence from these thoughts, but my heart was too heavy.

My Neph friends had formed a box around me, and I wondered if they were trying to protect me from whisperers or keep me from helping any more humans. Whatever the reason, their close presence gave me strength.

Kaidan returned to us with a double shot of something amber-colored over ice. I got a strong whiff of bourbon, which made me want to kiss him again. His eyes captured mine and held them as he tipped back the glass until it was drained.

The sons of Thamuz returned to us, holding their drinks and looking repulsed by our presence. They signaled for us to move, and we followed. The music thumped through my whole body. The fierceness on the faces of my surrounding allies fueled me.

We came to a set of double doors with a sign saying LUNAR ROOM. My body was alight with adrenaline. In the Lunar Room of the Galaxy Nightclub, heaven and hell would meet.

Pharzuph practically burst through the doors, his avid eyes on me. He frowned.

"This isn't exactly what I had in mind when I said to get her different clothes," he said to Kaidan. Pharzuph grabbed my arm and pulled me forward, not caring to hear a response from his son. I met Kai's steely stare and knew those eyes would be on me all night.

With a deep breath in my chest, and a prayer in my heart, we entered the summit.

Life, although it may only be an accumulation of anguish, is dear to me, and I will defend it.

—*Mary Shelley,* Frankenstein

CHAPTER TWENTY-NINE

LUNAR ROOM

Nine sets of blood-red eyes landed on me, making adrenaline run a race through my body. Everyone was there except my dad, Rahab, and Jezebet. The nine Dukes present looked me over with complete disdain before nodding at Pharzuph with admiration for my capture.

Pharzuph shoved me forward, a proud look on his face, and said, "Go sit down until we're ready to deal with you."

I moved, sensing my allies close behind me, and took in our new surroundings. I'd never been able to picture this final summit—and now here we were. I wouldn't have imagined this most deadly fight taking place in a swanky VIP lounge.

The room was all black, like the main club, with similar stars twinkling overhead. The same music played, only at a lower volume. Tables shaped like phases of the moon and modern, black leather seats filled the floor space. The lounge area surrounded a circular dance floor with a gleaming black surface that reflected the ceiling's stars. Next to the entrance was a bar with a middle-aged male Neph bartender I didn't recognize. He ignored us and focused on the Dukes, who gathered around the bar, talking and laughing as if this gathering were nothing but a social event.

Long, black couches lined the walls of the room. We went to the end of the lounge and sat against the wall. Kaidan, me, Marna, then Ginger sat on a couch together. Blake and Kope sat on the next one. We didn't have to wait long for others to begin arriving. The Neph all came to this far side of the room, then spread out their numbers along the wall couches, acknowledging one another with nods but never talking.

Kopano's two older brothers approached and sat next to him. More allies! My hope grew at the sight of the three of them sitting on the next couch in stoic silence. His brothers had the same large body frame as him, but their eyes were deep brown.

A gross sensation slithered through my belly when Caterina came in, the tight bun in her hair looking like it would give a normal person a migraine. As she walked toward us and sat on a lone couch, she smiled at me—the creepiest smile I'd ever seen. I guessed she knew why we were gathered and was looking forward to it. I found the twins glaring murderously at her, so I gave Marna a discreet elbow to the arm to make her stop.

Duke Jezebet walked in then, and Caterina sat up taller, watching the Duke of Lies with adoring reverence. The stunning Russian woman in her crisp gray suit never even glanced at her daughter. Instead she scanned the Neph until she found me. Our eye contact lasted only a brief moment, but seeing the lack of hate in her eyes and knowing she was an ally lifted my spirits, while also making me long for my father.

I felt Kaidan stiffen next to me when Pharzuph and Astaroth looked our way. Then Astaroth gave a shake of his head and they went back to drinking. Marna inclined her face toward me and Kaidan, leaning forward enough to check our bond. She gave a small nod. We were good. Kai relaxed again. It made me wonder how long his buzz would last and hide the bond. Probably not long. All of our secrets would be revealed soon.

Watching the Dukes socialize, unconcerned about a so-called mercenary Neph girl, gave me a strange sense of resolve. They believed they were untouchable. They saw their enemy tonight as just one girl. One stupid girl who might be working with someone, but their complete lack of concern showed their weakest flaw.

Foolish pride. We would use it against them.

Though my resolve empowered me, my body still behaved with traitorous nerves when I thought about how I no longer had the sword, and no clue how else to physically get rid of these demons. Kaidan bumped his leg against mine when I started chewing my thumbnail. I dropped my hand. Okay. Nobody was going to try to kill us this very minute. I sat up straighter.

A young Asian man walked in with a green badge, looking like he could be a Chinese actor—Melchom, the Duke of Envy. His shiny black hair was a few inches long and he styled it much like Blake's. I glanced at Blake, who was staring at his father's new body with awestruck horror. He quickly schooled his facial expression when Melchom looked over and inclined his head. Blake returned the gesture.

While the Dukes warmed up, drinking and laughing, we all stared blankly around the room, doing our best not to draw any attention to ourselves. I counted ten of the twelve Dukes.

Then Duke Rahab entered with his deep purple badge, and a hush settled. I swear a chill swept the room as the Duke of Pride's eyes scanned us, flashing bright red for a whole second when he saw me until he composed himself. He turned to his comrades and smiled tightly. Someone turned off the music. Marek came through the doors behind Rahab and closed them, locking them from the inside and standing guard. The momentary silence was deafening.

Rahab nodded to the Dukes at the bar, and they all filed into the lounge, sitting at the small tables that circled the dance floor. Rahab made his way to the center of the black circle and stood with his hands clasped behind his back like a dictator. He seemed to have aged since I'd seen him a year and a half ago—his face looking gaunt and too dour to be handsome. He was tall and elegant, but too thin. I was surprised he hadn't opted for a new body yet. Maybe his over-abundance of pride caused him to hold out longer than the others.

He began speaking in his rich, loud, French-accented voice.

"Good evening, Brothers . . . and Sister," he said. "Thank you for your presence on such short notice. We hope to resolve a delicate issue as quickly as possible so that we can all move on to more pleasant things. Our favorite city awaits." Chuckles and smiles filled the lounge. "We begin by calling forth the messenger Azael to oversee this summit and report back to our Lord Lucifer at the conclusion of our events."

I braced myself as a frightening hissing filled the air. Azael with his lionlike features ascended up through the shining black floor right in front of Rahab. His wings spread wide for one moment before closing tight to his hazy back. The sight was jarring, but I was so glad to have Azael present.

"Thank you for joining us, Azael," Rahab said. "We hope not to keep you long."

The demon spirit inclined his head in a nod.

To the Dukes, Rahab said, "Let us summon the Legionnaires."

Again with the horrible cacophony of hisses. On cue, the black walls began to spew smoky spirits into the lounge from all directions. I couldn't wait for them to be gone. Forever.

The room dimmed as it filled with the spirits, and I turned my night vision on full.

When everyone was still, Rahab looked toward the doors.

"Son of Shax," he said to Marek. "You are in charge of listening for interferences during these proceedings. Tonight's events will require the full attention of the Dukes. Understand?"

"Yes, sir," Marek said, with a slight bow at the waist.

Regret filled me as I thought about our lost ally, Flynn, and how the door watch would have been his job. It would have been a huge advantage.

Rahab looked over the crowd, a scowl on his face as he

surveyed the hundred-plus Nephilim. When his eyes stopped on me, they turned a vivid red.

"Truly," he said, "I never believed this summit would be called. But alas . . . the great prophecy is upon us. We can thank Brother Pharzuph for his quick work in bringing a traitor to justice this night."

Murmurs erupted around the room, Dukes and Nephilim alike. Rahab motioned for Pharzuph to join him.

Instead of going to Rahab's side, Pharzuph bypassed the dance floor, strolling toward me with a cocky grin.

Here we go. My insides fell to my feet.

I sat up straight, not moving, keeping my eyes locked on Pharzuph's as he approached. When he got to me and saw that I wasn't going to cower, he grabbed my arm and yanked me to my feet.

"Think you're brave even without your weapon, huh?" He eyed me with disgust. "We'll see."

I kept up with him as he pulled me to the center of the room. My chest and face heated, but I worked not to show any fear. Pharzuph let me go, wiping his hand down his dress shirt and leaving me between the two of them. Rahab peered at me with sheer loathing.

"You can all see her badge," Rahab said. "We had hoped it was a by-product of being ignorant of her legacy for so long, but even after working these past two years, her badge still holds the white of *innocence*." He spat the word. "First the angels intervened to keep her alive, and then her father goes missing when we attempt to question him. But once we take care of his offspring we will find Belial, and he will be dealt with. He will burn for his traitorous ways."

I expected the Dukes to cheer at this, but they were quiet, watching with shocked faces as they digested the way they'd all been deceived by one of their own and his offspring.

"How can this be, Brother Rahab?" Blake's dad, Melchom, asked. "The prophecy was a myth! It called for a Nephilim of both light and darkness. We all know that is not possible."

"Really?" Rahab asked smoothly. "We have reason to believe that eighteen years ago a guardian angel broke ranks and possessed a human to be with a Duke. Some of you might recall the angel Mariantha and her *touching* bond with Belial?"

"The traitor!" bellowed Sonellion, Duke of Hatred. He slammed a fist against his table, making it rock. Sonellion's eyes lit up like glowing blood, along with several other sets of eyes among the Dukes. My breathing shallowed as their voices rose in anger toward my father. This was unscrupulous anger. There'd be no reasoning with these demons.

Breathe, I told myself. Just breathe. I looked above me where Azael hovered, watching me closely.

"Wait," called a smooth voice. Everyone turned to Alocer, Kope's father. "I am not sold on this so-called prophecy. How do we know it's true? What proof do we have?"

Rahab frowned. "As you know, I have always been in the confidence of our Prince of Darkness. He called to me himself to tell me of the prophecy spoken through the apostle Paul. Do you dare to doubt him?"

"Of course not," Alocer responded, narrowing his eyes at Rahab. "But I dare to doubt his source for this information.

329

Who was witness to this prophecy? Besides the guardian angel of the apostle?"

"A trusted whisperer." The Dukes broke out into groans, and Rahab had to raise his voice. "Our Lord took the prophecy with the utmost seriousness, and you should as well!"

"Tell us, Brother," Jezebet said. "Remind us once again of the words of the prophecy." She leaned on the table and tapped a French-manicured fingernail against her bottom lip.

"The prophecy stated," began Rahab, "that a Nephilim born of both an angel and a demon would be the instrument used for a treacherous end to our kind. It foretold that this child would send every dark angel into the chains of hell for the rest of eternity." His eyes were savage, and my head began to spin. "This . . . *infant* is the prophetic Nephilim sent by God to rid the earth of us! *This*"—he dramatically ran a hand up and down my profile—"is the best that God could do in His moment of desperation!"

A loud racket of shouting and laughter rose. I waited for Rahab to tell the rest of the prophecy, but he didn't. He only stood there looking smug. And then I wondered . . . did he even know the whole prophecy? The part about their possible redemption?

I glanced toward my allies, who were all sitting up straight on the edges of their seats. Kaidan looked ready. Kopano gave me the slightest nod, almost imperceptible. The intensity of their eyes on me was a push. It was time. A boldness took me by the vocal cords.

"There's more!" I loudly interrupted the Dukes. "You're all being given a second chance at heaven!"

I stumbled sideways to the floor at the force of Rahab's backhand to my face. My cheekbone throbbed with pain. I'd forgotten how much he loved to hit.

My allies were on their feet now, and sudden fear shot through me for Kaidan. He was poised to fight.

Rahab stood over me, staring down with pure malice.

"You. Will not. Speak!"

"What are we waiting for?" cried Thamuz. "Let's kill her! No angels to stop us this time."

Shouts of assent filled the air. I stayed on the floor, watching to see how it would play out.

"Wait!" hollered Melchom. "What is she talking about?"

"Lies against our Lord!" Rahab said.

"Let Jezebet decide if she's telling truths or not," Alocer suggested.

Grumbles sounded, but nobody stopped Jezebet as she stepped gracefully onto the circular floor in front of me. I stood, and she grasped my jaw in the thin fingers of one of her hands.

"Speak," she said, and watched my eyes.

I talked as loudly as I could with her nails digging into my skin, but I kept my eyes locked on her crystal blue ones so that she could sense my full honesty.

"There is more to the prophecy. God is willing to forgive you and take you back to heaven. But those who still choose to stand against him will be damned to hell forever, just as Rahab said."

The room was silent as Jezebet's eyes narrowed at me, but the whisperers above us shifted like storm clouds. She watched me as she spoke, loosening her hold and then letting go.

"She speaks the truth."

The Dukes rose to their feet now, yelling over one another about this new possibility. I looked over at Kaidan, who watched the scene unfold with a keen-eyed steadiness.

I'd been saved once from death at a summit. Who was I to doubt the same sort of miracle wouldn't happen again? And if it didn't? Then it was my time. Fear of death had no place in my heart anymore. I shed it, let it go, and allowed the confidence that stemmed from that freedom to pour through me.

"Thank you, Jezebet," Pharzuph said, motioning her to take her place again.

Jezebet took one last look into my eyes, no traces of wickedness in hers, and then went back to the other Dukes. They were turning to one another, voices becoming more frantic and impassioned.

"What if it's true?" asked Alocer. He looked toward his sons, who met his hopeful eyes.

"After all this time?" Melchom asked in disbelief.

"Who cares?" Kobal, the Duke of Gluttony, shouted. "I'm not going back there!"

"Why would you leave this out, Rahab?" Shax asked.

"I told you the entire prophecy as it was told to me." Rahab's patience was wearing thin.

I gasped as my head was yanked backward by the hair, pulled against Pharzuph's body with one hand on my throat while his other arm circled my rib cage, pinning my arms to my sides.

"Who gave you this information?" he demanded.

I could hardly breathe the words. "A nun—a Nephilim

descendant of the apostle Paul's angel."

"Impossible!" Rahab shouted. "We would know if there had been a descendant of old on earth." But his tone was marred by his own doubts. The crowd was beginning to unravel, and he had to know he was losing them. He threw his head back and let out a freaky hiss, calling one of his whispering spirits down to him.

"Is this true?" Rahab asked it. "Was there a Neph of light?" Everyone was quiet as the spirit whispered directly into Rahab's mind and he answered it out loud in return. "Oh, you didn't think it was important? *An unsupervised angelic Nephilim*? I don't give a damn how harmless she seemed, or if she never left the nunnery! Get away from me, you insipid idiot!" He threw out a hand, and the spirit shot back up into the dark cloud of Legionnaires.

"It doesn't matter now," Pharzuph said. "We have the girl. And what a rare treat it is to foil a plan of God."

Rahab addressed the Dukes louder now, as Pharzuph continued his tight hold on my neck and body.

"None of us here can enter heaven again unless we take it by force! This stupid girl is mistaken. Lucifer holds the power now. We have no loyalties to the weak one. He thought we might be fooled by this sweet face, but we have proof that she's out for our destruction! She was in possession of a flaming Sword of Righteousness. She killed three of our spirits just this week!"

There were gasps of horror and shrieks from above.

Pharzuph continued to hold me tightly against him as Rahab stood close.

"Where is it?" Sonellion asked.

Through clenched teeth, Pharzuph began, "It was retrieved—"

"By my son," Shax cut in proudly.

"And disposed of," Rahab finished. The Dukes and whisperers swelled with relief.

"How was she able to wield the sword?" asked Alocer.

Pharzuph huffed and shook his head. "We don't know. But she did. A whisperer witnessed it."

More murmurs and whispers as confusion and fear spread.

Thamuz's eyes glowed a sickening crimson as he looked me over. "Enough games. I want blood."

"Yes, Brother, there will be blood." Pharzuph chuckled. "We will savor her." He licked my earlobe and I cringed. "I won't even have her first," he graciously offered. "She's my little gift to you, Brothers. Just be careful not to kill her yet because she needs to suffer in every possible way. Heaven is watching. Let's give them a show."

I closed my eyes.

"Me first," one of the Dukes offered. I recognized that Australian accent.

"Of course *you* would say that, Mammon, you greedy bastard," said Pharzuph, and there was laughter.

I opened my eyes again, trying to see my allies. They were all still standing, Kaidan having moved forward, but the Dukes didn't seem to notice or care.

Mammon stepped into the circle, followed by Thamuz and Sonellion. Unadulterated hatred filled their red eyes.

Oh, God, please help me. I didn't know how much torture I could take. Would they cut me? Rape me? Burn me?

No. Kaidan and the others wouldn't let it get that far.

I stupidly struggled against Pharzuph's strong hold as he turned us toward the three Dukes.

"Father . . . ," Kaidan called from behind us. I recognized the warning in his voice.

Without turning, Pharzuph yelled, "Not now!"

It was a testament to how focused they were on their blood-lust that none of the Dukes seemed to care that a Neph had spoken out at this summit.

Mammon loomed over me like a salivating monster with a savage hunger and thrill in his eyes. His gold watch and neck-laces lacked any luster in the darkened room. He moved closer, unbuttoning his pants, which answered the question of what his chosen form of torture would be.

"No," I moaned.

"*Yes.*" Pharzuph chuckled.

Mammon reached out to pull me to him, and that was when it happened. In my periphery I saw a rapid twist of silver, end over end. There was a whir close by my face, and a wet, crunching *thunk*. One minute Mammon was a foot in front of me, and in the next moment he was staggering backward with a blade lodged deep in his eye.

His mouth was a round O, and he fell to his knees, leaning back as his shrieking, dark spirit fought to get out of the body. Pharzuph wrenched me backward by the neck and spun us in the direction of Kaidan. He turned on his son with rage that shook the room.

"What have you done?"

Kaidan squared off, standing his ground, another knife already in his hand. He spun it on his palm before gripping it again.

"Just a bit of holy water on the blade." He spoke casually, but his eyes were fearsome.

Mammon's face hit the floor with a *thud* and his spirit thrashed above the body as if on fire. *That's for your son, Flynn*, I thought.

"Return to hell, Brother," Rahab called to the spirit. "The holy effects will burn from you there."

Mammon's spirit dived through the floor, and the room filled with a dreadful silence.

"You," Pharzuph whispered to Kai. His eyes were bright red. He moved closer to his son, dragging me. "I trusted you."

"No, you didn't," Kai said.

Pharzuph's eyes widened, and the room gasped at Kai's audacity to talk back.

"You filthy, weak idiot! You had more potential than all my past sons combined! How could you let yourself be charmed, like a dog, by a Neph girl? You're a failure!"

Kaidan's face was pained for a fraction of a second.

"Kill him," Rahab demanded. My heart jumped hard in my chest. *No!* I tried to push away, but it wasn't necessary.

As Kaidan wove the blade through his fingers, nobody made a move.

Cowards, I thought. All of them. They could have taken Kaidan down if they had wanted, but they knew he would have time to kill one of them if they reached for their weapons, and none were willing to sacrifice themselves. Even Pharzuph used me as a shield, facing me toward Kaidan and keeping his face close against my head. What would Lucifer say if he could see his fearless leaders now?

Their selfish motives worked in our favor, and for that I was grateful. Kaidan watched me as his father moved us from side to side in a sickening dance.

"Brother Pharzuph," said the dapper Astaroth, "I'm afraid this is more dire than we thought. Your son and the traitor's daughter are quite . . . *in love.*"

"You jest," whispered Pharzuph, squeezing my throat harder.

"Not in the least," Astaroth said. "And they've acted on it. They're *married.*"

The Dukes let out scandalized sounds of disbelief. Even surrounding Neph gasped.

"So, that's how you did it," Pharzuph hissed.

In a careful voice Astaroth said, "Marna and Ginger, move away from the son of Pharzuph. You will have nothing more to do with him."

The girls stared at their father, unmoving.

"I said, get over here!" Astaroth commanded.

"No," Ginger told him.

Astaroth's stunned expression was priceless.

"What the hell is the problem here?" Thamuz snarled. "Andre, Ramón!" His two sons stepped forward, standing just outside the circle. "At least one of us can control our children!" Thamuz bragged to the Dukes, then looked at his sons. "Take care of him!"

Both of the guys turned toward Kaidan and hesitated.

"Do it!" Thamuz yelled.

"We have no weapons," one of them said.

Thamuz's eyes went wide with anger. "Since when do you need a weapon? Two of you against one knife is no contest. Kill him!"

As they moved toward Kaidan, panic welled up inside of me and I pressed my will out to them: *Do not harm him! You don't have to obey your father!* Their steps slowed and they stopped. I could not believe it. One of the sons grabbed his head as if it hurt.

Thamuz let out a terrible yell and punched his nearest son in the temple, knocking him out cold. The other one fell to the floor and cowered before him.

"I don't know what's happening, Father! I think we're being influenced!"

"*Idiota!* Your will to kill should be stronger than any influence."

Rahab shook his head. "No Duke would dare to influence you against your father's wishes, and no Neph is powerful enough—" He stopped, and his head slowly turned to me. Then all eyes were on me. Pharzuph's grip tightened to the point that I could barely breathe. It wouldn't be long before I passed out if he didn't loosen his hold.

"*You* did this!" Thamuz said to me. I was feeling so faint I could hardly manage an ounce of fear.

Until Rahab stepped in front of me.

"Do not forget with whom you are dealing, child," he said. His demon self came half out of the top of his body, leaning into my face like a wraith and shrieking. His gigantic horns twisted around the shadowy spirit head, making me shrink back into Pharzuph.

I felt Rahab pressing into my mind, and though I fought it, he was too strong. A chilling sense of evil filled me as his words rang out in my head. *"How does it feel to know you'll be burning in hell this very night as we bask in your suffering? You chose wrong when you chose against the stronger force."*

I remembered the peace of my mother, Mariantha, and her words of love.

"You're wrong about the stronger force," I silently said to him. *"Now, get out of my head!"* With huge effort I pushed my mind, like moving a brick wall, and I forced him out. His demonic eyes bore into mine, shocked that I was able to extract him. He pulled his soul completely back into his body. Pharzuph was clutching painfully hard around my throat. I grabbed his forearms, trying to pry him away or at least loosen his hold before I suffocated, but he didn't budge.

"Your feistiness was endearing at first, but it's starting to wear thin," Pharzuph said.

"Her mind and will are strong," said Rahab, "but there are ways to disable any person. Everyone has a weakness . . . something that makes them question their Maker."

I didn't like the way he was looking at me. Like he had some knowledge or secret that could "disable" me.

"Excuse me, Duke Rahab," called Marek from the doorway.

All heads spun to him.

"I apologize for the interruption, but I believe Duke Belial approaches."

Just then a loud knock sounded. The faces of the Dukes hardened, and my heart soared high above the summit.

"By all means," Rahab said. "Let him in."

The door was quickly opened, letting in a wash of sounds from the club, then closed and locked again as my father strode in wearing a navy blue pinstriped suit. His hair was neatly cut and he looked amazing. At his side was Zania in designer jeans and heels. She crossed her arms and glared at the Dukes. Her father, Sonellion, let out a growl.

"Now you just hurt my feelings," Dad said in that gloriously deep voice. "I didn't even get an invitation."

"Traitor!" Sonellion yelled. He looked poised to strangle my father, but neither he nor any of the other Dukes made a move to seize him. "You were behind all of this! You stole my daughter!"

Dad laughed at the ridiculousness of that.

"You came here to mock us?" Pharzuph demanded, and in his preoccupation with my father, I felt his hold on me loosen. My lungs filled with air, and a surge of energy accompanied the oxygen.

"I ain't here to mock you," my father said. "We got a lot to talk about. 'Cause I know I'm not the only one in this room who knew after the Fall we'd been used like a bunch of fools. Lucifer's the one who did us wrong—"

"How dare you!" Rahab said.

Sonellion reached into his jacket for a gun, and my dad pointed at him. "You'd better rethink that, my man. You see my son-in-law over there?" He nodded toward Kai. "That's right. He got damn good aim with that knife, as y'all have seen. And it's a straight shot to the back of your big ol' head."

Red eyes galore.

Dad went on like he hadn't been interrupted. "We served hell all this time out of fear, or maybe our own greed, and it didn't look like there was no option of anything better. But there is. Y'all know we can't stay on earth forever. But we don't have to go back down there either. I don't know about you, but I'm making the right choice this time."

The Dukes showed their frustration and anger as they tried to speak over one another. They didn't know what to believe. The Neph stood in silence, sidling closer together, farther from the Dukes. Kai had moved forward, getting closer and sizing up the scene. Rahab was shouting, trying to regain control. Pharzuph let go of me with one hand, and I gasped for air through my sore throat. He grasped me only by a wrist now as he stepped toward the mob to better be heard. Fierce arguing ensued, and eyes were bloodred in every direction. Kaidan caught my eye, then looked toward where Pharzuph held me. I could see the gears working in his mind as he tried to figure out how to free me.

I barely heard my name being called from the other side of the room in a familiar European lilt. When I turned toward Marek's voice, his hand was behind his back, and then a blur of glimmering metal was soaring into the air. Pharzuph turned at the sight of it, but he was too late. I snatched the hilt from the air with my free hand and felt a jolt go up my arm. Marek winked at me, and I smiled, more grateful than I'd ever been in my life. Kaidan moved into the circle at my side.

Blinding light shot from the end of the hilt and expanded

to reveal a shimmering blade of blue flames. It was huge, yet virtually weightless. Pharzuph leaped away from me and rushed to his fellow Dukes. The entire room turned toward the shocking light, and the demons hissed at the memories it invoked. More than six hundred dark spirits stirred in agitated fright above us.

The twins, Blake, Kopano and his brothers, Marek, Zania, and my father all joined the circle now. I grasped the hilt with both hands.

"You have thoroughly betrayed me." Pharzuph was incredulous as he looked at his son.

"We don't have to be divided," Kaidan said. "You were an angel of light once—"

"I will not return under these conditions to be the laughingstock of the heavenly realm!"

"Pride was Lucifer's downfall, too," my father said.

A handful of Dukes hissed at him, showing their bright red eyes. As scary as they were, I was happy that the spotlight was off Kaidan.

"I tried to warn you all about the Nephilim," Rahab said to the Dukes, though his eyes were on me. "They are the worst kind of beasts, willing to bite the very hands that feed them."

"We're not *beasts*," I said. "And we're tired of being fed lies. We don't belong to you."

While we spoke, my father, Zania, and Marek pulled out weapons and passed them down the row of Neph—several guns and knives, which were now aimed at the Dukes, who only had eyes for the Sword of Righteousness. They wouldn't go near its glowing blade, but I could see the ideas spinning through their evil eyes about how to take me down.

"You've underestimated us," Kaidan said, looking at his father.

Astaroth muttered something about a bloody uprising and spat on the floor.

Rahab stepped toward us, and I jutted the sword out in response.

"Now, hold on just a minute," he said, raising his palms. "That is no mere toy, child. Surely you are not prepared to commit murder here tonight?"

"That's not my intention, but I will if you make me. All I want is for everyone to listen." I spoke as calmly as I could manage. I looked around at the watching Dukes and up at the circling black cloud of spirits above. "You have all been deceived. Again. You don't have time to think it over. You have to make a decision tonight—"

"*Will we stand here*," interrupted Rahab, with boiling red eyes, "and allow this Nephilim to attempt to separate the ranks of our valiant leader?" His voice cracked with emotion. "Will we tremble in the presence of a solitary flaming sword wielded by a child?"

More tumultuous shouts sounded.

"Let's kill her!" bellowed Thamuz, rushing forward.

"Let her speak!" Jezebet pushed Thamuz back, stronger than she appeared.

"It's blasphemy!" someone cried.

"But what if it's true?" asked Melchom.

"I propose a test," Rahab said. The room hushed. "She would only be sent to do a task of this magnitude if she were of flawless faith. If we can get her doubts to surface, then she will lose the power of the sword."

Doubts? I didn't like the sound of this.

"How do you propose to test her faith?" Jezebet asked.

"I came prepared." Rahab grinned, and a shiver raced through me. He gave some sort of signal with his arm, and two Neph men entered from a back stairway with the bang of a metal door. The two Neph were holding someone between them. I nearly convulsed when I recognized the pinkish skin and wavy strawberry-blond hair. Her mouth was gagged, but her nurturing eyes stabbed at my gut.

"Mom!"

At the sound of my voice, love ballooned out from her aura, and when it burst, it was replaced by the lavender of peace. *Not her*, I begged, *please not her!*

The irony was not lost on me that the first time I called her *Mom* could be the last time we'd ever see each other.

Dad's eyes grew in dread and surprise.

Ginger's hand flew to her mouth to cover a strangled cry.

"Where's Jay?" Marna whispered, frantic. I looked around, but Jay definitely hadn't been brought in.

I adjusted the hilt in my hand, trying desperately to think of a way to get her out of this. *Let her go*, I willed to Rahab. His eyes tightened, and he turned.

"Is that you sending a thought into my mind? That may work on these worthless Nephilim toss-outs, but not me." His eyes shone at the unfolding of his evil plot. "Some humans are not afraid of death or suffering for themselves," he said. "But when those same people are forced to watch their loved ones

344

suffer and die, well . . . their faith wavers. Even disappears. I wonder? Are you one of those, Anna? Will you become bitter and angry as you watch us kill this woman? When your glorious savior doesn't save her?"

I wanted to scream, to cry. *Not Patti!* I didn't want this test. I silently begged for an army of angels to burst in like they'd done before. This atrocity couldn't be allowed to happen! She didn't deserve this. It wasn't fair.

I felt Kaidan beside me, raising an arm ever so slightly, at the ready.

No angels were coming. I felt panic welling. I needed to pass this. My faith was my shield. Their torture of Patti would be their flaming arrows at me.

I would have preferred actual arrows to this.

"You're not allowed to kill humans," I stammered in a last-ditch effort. As far as I knew, it was their only "rule."

"My dear, this is war!" Rahab laughed at me. "Normal rules no longer apply."

"Be strong, Anna," my father urged.

"Oh, shut up, Belial." Rahab cursed in French then nodded toward Thamuz. "You may do the honors."

Thamuz's black badge grew as he knelt down by the body of Mammon and pulled the knife from his eye. *Oh crap.* My allies stirred around me with apprehension, but I couldn't look away. Thamuz stalked toward Patti and grinned as he swiped her from temple to chin with the blade. I screamed in horror. She let out a small cry and slumped forward as blood seeped from her face, down her neck. Her guardian angel circled her in desperation.

"Stop it!" I screamed, shaking my head side to side. "No more!"

And then I noticed with amazement that her color never wavered. She was still at peace, so filled with love for me. My gut ached at Patti's willingness to sacrifice herself. As I looked at the lavender surrounding her, I knew Patti wouldn't have me choose any other way, but I hated it. I hated myself for not being able to save her.

"Pray for it to be stopped," Rahab teased. "See if it happens."

I'd never felt more desperate.

"Please, God," I begged. "Please, make it stop. Save her! *Please*."

The room stilled. I watched the walls, the ceiling. Nobody was coming. *Why?* My hope fizzled and I felt the beginnings of anger, frustration, and doubt creeping in. For one second the hilt dimmed. When Rahab smiled, I realized his plan was working.

He was baiting me to lose faith through an unanswered prayer. Patti would not be saved. I had to come to terms with that, and quickly. She was perfect in my eyes, but in the scheme of the world she was one woman. A woman who'd lived a good life and would be revered by all who'd known her. If this was her time to go, I had to find peace with that in order to preserve my faith. I had to believe there was a bigger reason for it all. But I didn't want her to suffer.

Inhale. Exhale. I smacked away horrid feelings of bitterness and unfairness and loss as they hurled themselves at my heart, threatening to break me.

It took every bit of my energy to speak. "You can see she's not afraid to die." I swallowed hard, trying not to cry. "And I am not afraid for her. I know where her soul will go."

"Well then." Rahab's eyes were maniacal. "Let's send her there now! First-class!"

Ginger shrieked, "Nooo!" She tried to rush forward, but Blake grabbed her tightly around the waist.

"Don't watch," Kaidan warned me, touching my face to try and turn my head to him, but I couldn't look away. Thamuz stabbed her brutally in the stomach once, twice, three times. *Oh, God,* I begged, *make it stop! Take her quickly!* I bent slightly at the waist and felt my stomach contracting in a heave, but I forced myself to stand straight again. Kaidan's arm went around me, holding me. I tried to focus on the freedom Patti would soon have, free of pain and tears. Fighting the urge to dive into a pit of angry vengeance at that moment was the hardest thing I'd ever done.

"Bastards," Kaidan whispered in anguish.

Thamuz lifted the knife again, and I'd had enough. She would die soon from the wounds he'd already inflicted, and anything more was superfluous cruelty.

"Stop him, Kai," I begged, which was exactly what he'd been waiting to hear.

In half a second Kaidan's knife was through the back of Thamuz's neck, and his soul was frantically retreating from the body with a screech. His evil spirit sped toward me, and I sliced the flaming blade through the air. He was gone in a bang of black particles.

"Papa!" hollered one of his sons. I looked at the two of them, both baring their teeth.

"Do not avenge your father," I willed to them out loud. "His ways don't have to be yours." They stopped, panting with emotion.

I addressed all of the Nephilim then, before the Dukes tried to retaliate. I knew several of them probably had guns, but none of them tried to reach for their weapons, knowing they were outnumbered and afraid of being turned on. The eyes of the Dukes followed my movements as I pointed the sword at them in turn and spoke to the Neph. My body shook and my voice was thick.

"For the first time ever, you all have a choice," I told them. "You can move to the side, or you can join us and fight against the Dukes. But no matter what you choose, your fathers *will* leave this earth tonight, and you *will* be free from them. Make your choice now."

A frenzy of whispers rose up. Nearly half of the Neph ran for the side of the room, circling around the back of us, out of the reach of the Dukes. I couldn't blame them for wanting to stay out of it, and I was glad to see the youngest among them dragged by one of the older women. They pushed against the side wall, behind the bar area, and crouched.

The other Neph looked around at the Dukes and then at one another before deciding. One by one they moved behind either me or the Dukes. The sons of Thamuz, Caterina, and about twenty others joined the Dukes. At least thirty piled behind me. But at the moment I didn't feel like cheering about our greater numbers.

Patti's body lay in a bloody heap.

"Daddy," I whispered.

Without a word, he moved to Patti. The Dukes glared at him but didn't try to stop him as he scooped her into his big arms and brought her to me. Her chest rose and fell in short, fast spurts. I couldn't let go of the sword, so I bent my head and kissed her damp forehead.

"I love you, Mom."

Her eyes fluttered open, and a faint smile crossed her bloodied lips. She whispered, and I had to lean closer to make out the gurgled words. "Love you, sweet girl." I kissed her again, my tears falling on her face. Kaidan's hand was heavy on my shoulder.

"I could save her," Dad said in a low, unsure voice.

My head snapped up to him.

"I could leave my body and try to heal her—"

"No!" Patti rasped. She reached a weak hand up to his arm and stuttered her impassioned words. "Don't. You need . . . your body. To protect Anna."

"Please!" I cried, but she only gave her head a stubborn, weak shake.

"You're all needed . . . to fight them."

I tried to plead with Dad through my eyes, but he shook his head sadly. He wouldn't do it without her permission. I lowered my cheek to hers.

"I'm not scared, honey," she said to me. "I'm ready."

Mom took a wet-sounding, wheezing breath and whispered, "Gin . . ."

Ginger pushed through to be at Patti's side next to me. She took her hand, tears streaking down her face. "Miss Patti."

"Beautiful girl . . . you will be . . . a good aunt. . . ." And with a shudder, Patti became still.

"No," I whispered.

Her guardian angel gathered her spirit in his arms as it rose

349

from her body, soft and gentle. With a nod at me, the angel shot upward, taking her home. I allowed the tears to fall down my face, making no move to wipe them. Dad stepped to the side and set her body against the wall with great gentleness, closing her eyes before coming to stand by me again.

"This cannot continue," Sonellion growled. "Playtime is over. This prophecy is a lie, and you're all about to pay." He reached behind his back, making my allies and me tense. If he pulled out a gun, the fighting would begin.

The spirit Azael flew down and hovered between our two groups, facing the Dukes. He spoke telepathically to the whole room, who were rapt to hear what Lucifer's messenger had to say.

"The prophecy is real. I myself possessed a human and destroyed the written prophecy at the command of Lucifer. The version given to Rahab was only partial truth. What the girl says is the full truth. We are being offered heaven. Lucifer knows there are those in his army who doubt him, and this prophecy would shrink his ranks even further for the final battle to come. The Nephilim child has proven herself. Let her proceed. I, myself, will choose the Lord of Light."

The Dukes were stunned. Most appeared outraged, while a few looked in awe.

I didn't know how many of the fallen angels in this room would return to heaven, but I did know most would not, and they wouldn't go down without a fight. They enjoyed earth and the power they held here. They didn't want to go back to heaven any more than they wanted to return to hell.

I glanced through my tears at my friends standing at my side. Ready. Outnumbering the Dukes.

"The Maker turned his back on us!" Sonellion shouted. "I will not run back to Him with my tail between my legs!"

"He's right," said Shax. "Besides, we can take earth and heaven on our own."

Pharzuph looked on the verge of panic. "We can't let the prophecy be fulfilled."

"Then she has to die," said Kobal. "Now."

"No!" Alocer moved to stand in front of me. "You'll have to pass through me first."

"Be reasonable, Alocer," Astaroth argued. "Do you want to spend eternity with angels looking down their noses at you?"

Jezebet stepped to Alocer's side. "We'll be treated fairly if we return; we all know it."

"That's your damned female hormones talking, Jez." Sonellion grabbed his crotch. "Grow some balls again."

She gave him a venomous look. "I have more clarity about the world in this body than I ever had with a set of balls."

He snarled at her, and Dad piped up.

"Enough. We were a bunch of idiots to think we could overthrow Him back then," he said. "And y'all are worse fools to think there's a chance of doing it in the future."

"Do not listen to these traitors!" Rahab shouted.

Pandemonium ensued. Lines were drawn and sides were taken. My eyes darted around, waiting for someone to pull the first weapon. Suit jackets and ties were flung to the ground. Only three of the ten remaining Dukes, including my father, stood to protect me.

"Work to disarm them," Dad yelled over his shoulder at the Neph.

Sonellion let out a snarling war cry and ran at Alocer. Behind him I saw Pharzuph and others reaching for their guns and heard shots fired as our Neph allies surged forward. I couldn't keep track of who went in which direction.

Kaidan and my father didn't leave my side. Another shot was fired, and Jezebet, who'd been right in front of me, screamed and grabbed her arm, shooting a murderous glare at Kobal just before he was tackled to the ground by Kopano.

I slashed and stabbed at every spirit that came near us. Everything was happening so fast, and the room was loud with shouts and cries. In my head, I ran through the description of the armor of God. What was left? There had to be a catalyst to send the fallen angels to their permanent places, but what? Of all my weapons, I only saw two of them as actions: faith and prayer. My faith had been put to the test. So that left prayer. Was that all I had to do? Just *ask*? It felt too simple, and as I'd learned many times over, I didn't always get what I wanted. But it was the only thing in my arsenal I had left.

One by one the Neph were taking the Dukes down, getting slashed and shot at as they fought, disarming them and holding them captive. Another round of gunfire rang out, and I heard Zania scream.

Kopano lay on his back, Zania pressing her hands against the hole in his chest, which was bright red.

"No!" I screamed. I started to run to him, but Kaidan pulled me back.

"You can't enter the fighting," he said.

Kope was lying right in the midst of the chaos.

Like a raging bull, Sonellion charged through the crowd,

heading straight for me. I took a lunging stance and prepared myself. Dad and Blake came at him from both sides when he was three feet away. They knocked his legs out from under him, and I stabbed the sword down through his chest. A dark fizzle rose from the wound, and his chest puffed as his soul was extinguished.

I stood again and looked toward Kopano. With a sinking feeling I acknowledged that he wasn't breathing. Alocer pushed his way past people and dropped to the floor next to his son, across from Zania.

Alocer was shaking his head. "It's not his time." And then he surprised us all. Half of the room stopped fighting to watch as Alocer's spirit left his body. Immediately his former body heaved in on itself, as if having a heart attack, and fell over, lifeless. Alocer's dark spirit hovered above Kopano's body, and then slowly settled himself downward, entering his son's skin.

Kopano was being possessed.

I held my breath. Zania was holding Kope's head, murmuring in Arabic. The possession caused his frame to jolt, but his soul didn't fight it—a sign of how far gone he was. And then Kope's chest rose with a sharp intake of breath.

Zania gasped and said, "He's healing!"

I let out a relieved laugh of joy, still holding the sword at the ready.

As Kope healed, his body began to jolt and thrash. His soul was fighting Alocer's soul. Before it could get too bad, Alocer pulled himself from his son's body and watched the scene from above. He'd saved him.

Several screams sounded from the other end of the room, and I looked to see Caterina clawing at Ginger while Marna tried to restrain the girl. She was like a wild animal, but the twins were able to get her down with the help of an older Neph woman who grabbed Caterina by the feet and held tight. When Caterina let out a screech and bit Marna's hand, Ginger punched her in the face, and the girl went limp.

The fighting grew and I couldn't believe the violence surrounding me. The blood. The screams. Weapons were being taken and tossed. Dukes, who weren't accustomed to losing, were going berserk as more and more of them and the opposing Nephilim were being detained.

"It's time," I whispered.

"Yes," Kaidan said. "Do what you have to do."

He pressed me back against the wall and blocked me as fighting continued in front of us.

I concentrated on the sword, unwilling to close my eyes with all the surrounding chaos. I began my prayer out loud for all to hear.

"Father"—my voice trembled with emotion—"let your will be done—"

Pharzuph charged for me, a complete madman with glowing red eyes and gelled hair flying out of place. Kaidan's knife arm went up, but before he could release, my father took Pharzuph down to the ground, crushing his windpipe and holding him there. Kaidan went to one knee next to them.

"It's too late, Father. This is your opportunity to make amends. Please consider it."

"I will not grovel at His feet!" Pharzuph choked out.

My heart hurt to see Kaidan's hope for his father, which was sure to be shattered.

Kaidan looked up at me, pained but resolute, and nodded for me to continue. I thought about Patti and Mariantha, and all the love I'd been given in my life. I focused on the love.

"I pray forgiveness for the souls who once betrayed you and have reconciled. Return them to their rightful home, and let those spirits who still harbor hatred be returned to hell—"

The room filled with terrifying shrieks that made me flinch down into a crouch and hold the blade higher. An over-powering warmth and lightness spread over me. The room, which had been so dark, was brightening.

"It's working!" Kaidan said. "Keep going!"

Kobal broke from the mob and rushed toward me with his teeth bared in fury. Blake and Kopano grabbed him, and Marek stood over him with a gun pointed to his face.

I prayed louder and faster now, and as the words left my mouth I felt a sense of . . . magic. I didn't know how else to explain it—as if I'd called upon something ancient and mys-tifying. There was going to be a reckoning here tonight, both sweet and terrible.

My voice shook with emotion as I spoke loudly. "Please, banish all the demons from earth!"

And then something else began shaking. *The ground.*

At the very last second, I knew there was one more ele-ment essential to my task—one more prayerful request that had nothing to do with the prophecy. I spoke faster as the earth rumbled ominously.

"I ask with all my heart that the demon stains be washed

from the souls of all Nephilim, both here on earth, and those who came before us. Please allow us a chance at redemption."

A furious gurgle came from the earth, and the room tilted, throwing us all off our feet. The sword flew from my hand, immediately extinguishing its glowing blade. It rolled and bounced into a giant crack in the floor, where the earth was opening. Leather chairs and tables were thrown around the room. The dark-winged angels were torn unwillingly from their places in the air, and from their human bodies, shrieking and flailing, being spiraled downward into the gaping hole. We watched as Pharzuph's soul was pulled by invisible arms out of his handsome young body and sucked down with the others. Kaidan stared at the hole where his father disappeared.

An army of heaven's angels flew in from all sides now, beautiful and magnificent, and the remaining dark angels moved, making space. A huge white cloud of vapor descended on the bright room, causing us to shield our eyes. Peace, whole and beautiful, settled over me, and the purest kind of love filled my heart.

"It is well," I heard whispered in my ear as I crouched on the tilted floor.

I turned to my father next to me. He motioned toward the other dark souls as they transformed from black to gray to gleaming snow, ascending lightly above us. My dad and I looked one last time at each other.

"You did good, baby girl." It was time for him to go. I squeezed him around the neck. He gave me a grateful smile as he let me go, and then his spirit rose from the body of Big Rotty. His shining soul flew above me, wings flapping.

"Good-bye," I whispered to him. But I couldn't be too sad, because I knew I'd see him again, and he was going to be with Mariantha. All the things that were so crazy on earth would shed away and cease to matter.

The angel army led the way up, and the newly brightened souls followed, rising through the ceiling to their long-lost home. Kaidan grabbed me in a tight hug. As we looked at each other, I felt a strange tug within me.

From our chests, where our badges appeared, dark smoke was expelled, dissipating into the air. We gasped to see each other's badges change to bursts of white.

And then a rushing of air made us turn to the opening in the earth. Souls of redeemed fallen angels and Nephilim from the underworld were flying upward by the thousands. We watched their ascent with pure amazement.

The building gave an ominous creak all around us, followed by a vicious quaking. Dust and dirt billowed up throughout the room.

"We have to get out of here!" Kaidan yelled.

Surrounding Neph grabbed hands and pulled one another up. We all ran as fast as we could, hurdling bodies on the ground, jumping over furniture and mounds of uprooted earth. Zania fell as the tremors under us increased, but Kaidan and Kopano pulled her up, and we ran to the back alley stairway, where we pushed through the heavy metal doors and sprinted upward, out into the Nevada summer night.

CHAPTER THIRTY

NEW LIFE

In the aftermath of Las Vegas's worst earthquake in recent history, humanity showed its best. The streets were crowded with people. In the midst of the mayhem, complete strangers were helping and comforting one another. Miraculously, only thirteen people were killed in the quake—an eclectic group from around the world, eleven men and two women, all in the Lunar Room of the Galaxy Nightclub, which sat directly above the fault line. Rumors flew about the scandal of Big Rotty and his "faked death" followed by his real one.

No part of the club was salvageable. Hundreds were injured, and there'd been minor structural damage to surrounding buildings, but otherwise the news called it a modern miracle.

When Galaxy's owner was interviewed, he said, "We cleared out the club as soon as the earthquake began, but the

Lunar Room was locked. We banged and banged, but nobody would answer, and we had to get out of there."

Reportedly, shots had been fired in the Lunar Room just before the quake began, but that was all speculation.

Kaidan never let go of my hand as we fled the nightclub as quickly as possible, pressing through the crowded streets of dusty chaos and back to the enormous lobby of The Venetian, where people talked animatedly about the quake. Lights from rescue squads flashed across the room through the glass doors.

He pulled me into a corner against the wall, where we were partially hidden by an ATM. Kaidan grasped my face and I held his waist. All we could do was stare at each other.

"We made it," he whispered, sounding disbelieving.

The truth of those words exploded inside me. It was over.

"We made it," I said back. "We really did."

He held my face, placing kisses across my skin—my nose, forehead, chin, and cheeks, then finally my lips. We were alive. I couldn't believe it. When he wrapped his arms around me, a terrible, gaping loss gripped my heart, and it felt like I was cracking into pieces. "Patti . . ."

Kaidan held me tight as I broke down.

"I'm so sorry, luv," he whispered. I felt him kiss my head as I clung to him, the memory of her death slicing through me.

Knowing she was at peace couldn't stop me from hurting for the fear she must've felt when she was captured, and the pain she experienced at the hands of an evil soul. And the fact that I would no longer feel her hugs or listen to her supportive words here on earth. I'd miss her every day of my life.

And then I thought of something. . . .

I pulled back from Kaidan with a frantic feeling inside me.

"Where's Jay?" I asked. How could I not have thought of him sooner?

I turned, searching the lobby until I saw our group of friends huddled close to the glass and looking out at the craziness in silence. Marna was on her phone. When we made eye contact, her arm shot into the air, waving me over, and she was smiling.

Pure, sweet relief rushed through me. He was okay.

I ran to Marna and we embraced.

"Where is he?"

"He's actually here in Vegas. He didn't know where we'd be, so he checked in at another hotel, but he's on his way over." She was beaming.

"How did he know to come here?" I asked. "What happened?"

"I texted him last night, but I don't know what happened on his end. Anna . . ." Her eyes softened. "I'm so sorry about your mum."

I swallowed back another bout of tears.

Marna took my hand and we went to the window, watching for Jay. Next to me, Kaidan wound his fingers through mine, and I looked up into his tired blue eyes. I wanted to be happy that we'd made it, and be joyous about our future, but first I needed to mourn.

I looked toward Ginger, also standing by the glass. Blake had his arm around her, holding her close, and she was wiping her eyes.

I went to her and put a hand on her shoulder. Ginger

turned, and when she saw it was me, she wrapped her arms around me and we cried together. Every negative thing that had ever been between us slipped away at that moment. She hadn't known Patti very long, but I knew Ginger saw what I saw—a loving woman who accepted us and believed in us.

"She was the closest thing to a mum I ever had," Ginger said. "I know that sounds silly. I barely knew her."

I let her go so I could see her face. "It doesn't sound silly at all. Patti loved you right away."

Ginger nodded. Her jaw trembled as she wiped her eyes again.

"Jay!"

We all turned toward Marna's voice. She ran from the hotel, crashing into Jay on the sidewalk. He lifted her off her feet in a giant hug that went on forever.

"He really does love her," Ginger whispered.

We all nodded and watched as Jay and Marna pulled apart, talking. His face fell and his demeanor changed, his aura turning dark blue, and I realized he was probably hearing about Patti. Again, my heart ached. I pressed a hand to my chest and wondered if the pain would always be with me.

As Jay and Marna made their way inside, he came straight to me and held me. I wanted to ask what had happened, but I didn't want to talk about it out in the open. I was just so glad he was okay. We held tight for a long time.

"I'm so sorry, Anna," he whispered.

I couldn't answer, and he seemed to understand.

Kopano and Zania joined us. Kope's shirt had a bloody hole in the middle, a sight that made me shiver as I remembered how we'd almost lost him. Looking around, I saw that every-one was a little worse for wear, bloodied and scraped, with torn clothing but, thankfully, no lasting injuries.

Kaidan and Kope gave each other a man hug, then Blake and Jay, too.

Jay pointed at Kopano's shirt, his eyes huge. "Dude!"

"Yeah, how you feeling, mate?" Kaidan asked.

Kope rubbed his chest. "It's tender and feels strange, but I am okay. It looks bad. . . . I need to change this shirt."

The way Zania watched him was endearing.

"Let's go back to the room," Kaidan suggested, and we all agreed.

As we made our way through the lobby, we stopped to thank other Nephilim who'd fought with us. It was weird to see everyone's badges turned white. I met Kopano's brothers and gave them hugs.

I found Marek watching out the window with his hands in his pockets, and I punched him in the arm. He turned, sur-prised when he saw me standing there with my hands on my hips.

"You scared me!"

Marek laughed. "I was working for your papa!"

Dad had been there all along, playing a hand in the events. I smiled. "Well, did you have to be such a good actor?"

"My plan was to tell you when we met, but that did not work out." His eyes lifted to someone behind me and he leaned closer to my ear. "So, you and the son of Pharzuph, eh? Good choice." He gave his eyebrows a playful lift.

"Um, thanks. . . ." I glanced over my shoulder at Kai, who

turned away from us with an amused smile. Yeah, it was too bad Kaidan didn't have a twin brother to appease the masses, because I wasn't sharing my man.

"You have my admiration in more ways than one, Daughter of Belial. Enjoy your life with that gorgeous husband. You deserve it." He winked.

I reached up and hugged Marek now, and he hugged me back.

"Keep in touch," I told him.

As he walked away, the back of a young girl caught my eye. She was watching out the window, her arms wrapped around herself. Her dark hair hung limp. Just a child. Was she separated from her parents? I had to find out.

"Excuse me," I said to her.

When she turned, I sucked in a breath. *Caterina*. Her eyes were bloodshot and distant. Her hair had come out of its neat bun.

"Where is she?" Caterina asked.

"Who? Oh . . . Jezebet?"

Caterina nodded.

I spoke with care. "She's in heaven."

The poor girl looked pitiful. Baffled. I actually felt sorry for her. Jezebet had been working for the opposite side for who knew how long, and Caterina had to feel betrayed.

"She couldn't tell you," I started to explain, but Caterina cut me off with a curt nod.

"She did not trust me."

I bit my lip. What could I say to that?

Caterina stared at my badge. "Is mine . . . ?"

"Yours is white now, too," I said.

"And what does that mean?"

I thought about it. "It means you're not automatically going to hell when you die. You're not cursed anymore just because of who your father was. You can choose how you want to live your life now. You're free."

She looked more frightened and childlike now. The girl had had no guidance except in evil.

"Caterina . . . where will you go now?"

She looked around, lost.

"You'll come with me," I heard, and turned to see Ginger eyeing Caterina.

The girl's eyes got big and she shook her head. "No. *Nu.* I will care for myself."

"Bollocks." Ginger stepped closer. She pushed the hair off Caterina's shoulder, and the girl flinched away. "I'll never hit you. But I'll also not put up with any lying or attitude."

Caterina shook her head, staring down at the floor. Ginger didn't bother with gentleness when she spoke to her. She was as frank as always, which made me think they were a good match for each other.

"How old are you?" Ginger asked.

"Thirteen."

"I know some of the things you've done," Ginger told her. "I've done a lot, too. But that's all going to change now. Come on." She held out her hand.

Caterina stared at her outstretched offering. Based on everything I'd witnessed from the girl, I couldn't imagine her taking it. But people were full of surprises. Caterina took her hand.

"Right then," Ginger said. She marched through our group, pulling Caterina behind her and leaving us all gaping in her wake.

"Unbelievable," Marna whispered.

Blake grinned. "I freaking *love* her." He jogged to catch up to Ginger.

I smiled up at Kaidan, who still seemed dumbstruck, and I twined my fingers with his.

I'd always considered myself a forgiving person, but when it came to Caterina it was hard to see past the evil things she'd done, and to remember she was young and badly nurtured. It was humbling to see Ginger being more open-minded than me in this matter. I thought she understood the girl's attitude in a way the rest of us couldn't.

It was nearly six in the morning when we made it to the room. We were dragging, and covered in a layer of dust. I couldn't believe we'd been in this room just five short hours ago, wondering if we'd live or die.

Caterina sat in a chair with her ankles crossed and her head down, looking nervous. Ginger tapped her shoulder and handed her a cola with ice.

"No need to be scared of anyone here. They know I'll kick their arses if they mess with you. Got it?"

Caterina nodded and stared down at her drink.

Kaidan dug a T-shirt from his bag and tossed it to Kopano. When Kope came out of the bathroom, he seemed uncomfortable. The shirt was tighter than anything he usually wore. I peeked at Zania, who was sitting on the floor cross-legged and staring hard at Kope. When she met my eye she tried to hold back a smile, because yeah . . . he looked really good.

"You tryin' to show me up, man?" Blake said to Kopano, flexing his lean biceps.

Everyone laughed and Kope gave his bashful smile, dimple and all, before he took a seat on the floor next to Zania.

Kaidan sat at the end of the couch and put his arm around me. I squished close next to him, taking his hand. This was weird. It was the first time ever that we could be affectionate without worry or fear. I smiled up at him. Wow.

We were all here. Alive. And our fathers were gone from earth forever. The quiet that settled over the room told me we were all thinking that same thing. It seemed unreal.

"So, what's it mean, Anna?" Blake asked, his eyes dropping to the supernatural badge on my chest. "They're all white."

"I don't know," I said. "I mean, I prayed that all Neph, alive or dead, would have a chance at heaven just like regular people."

Blake nodded, then got up and walked over to the mini fridge, opening it and pulling out a couple of small champagne bottles.

"Wanna celebrate?" he asked the room. I actually felt surprised when the dark urge stirred inside me and I longed to drink both those bottles and then some. Blake eyed me meaningfully. "Feel anything, Anna?"

I bit my lip and dropped my eyes, nodding. "It's still there."

"I could've told you that, mate," Kaidan muttered, making Jay and Blake laugh.

"And I still see the bonds," Marna said. Ginger agreed.

The auras and guardian angels were still there, too.

So our demon urges hadn't left us—only the stain that

made us damned. But we were strong. We'd proven that.

The room quieted as Blake put the drinks back in the fridge, and my mind switched gears. As much as I didn't want to get upset, and as morbid as it may have seemed, I needed the details about what Patti had been through.

"Jay?" I said quietly. "What happened?"

He didn't say anything at first. He rubbed Marna's knee and thought.

"She knew something was coming. I don't know how— intuition or something—but she made us separate. She kept hugging me and saying not to worry, she'd see me soon."

He got choked up, and I felt my eyes burning all over again.

"So we separated. Then I got a text from Marna saying y'all were going to Vegas. That things were going down. I couldn't get ahold of Patti, and I felt like I needed to be here, so I came. I'm sorry, Anna."

I grabbed his hand. "You don't need to be sorry."

"I keep thinking if I didn't leave her . . . if I made us stay together—"

"You wouldn't have been able to stop them," Kaidan said. "They would have killed you or tried to use you against Anna, as well. And if you'd been there, they would've seen your bond with Marna."

Jay looked down and shook his head.

Marna put her arm around him and kissed his cheek. "I think it had to happen the way it did, luv."

Her eyes darted to mine, a worried expression on her face about what she'd said. I nodded, because I no longer believed in coincidence.

Zania's voice was soft when she said, "She is my hero."

"Yes," Ginger whispered.

I tucked my face in the crook of Kaidan's arm, overcome.

"Hey, Kope," said Blake. "What your dad did for you? That was awesome. You were gone, man."

I lifted my eyes to see Kope incline his head.

"I cannot remember it. It was just . . . there was only pain and darkness, and then I was opening my eyes."

Zania shifted next to him, as if the memory was too much. Kope laid his hand on top of hers. After another stretch of silence, Blake spoke again, relieving the room's tension in the way only he could.

"So, how 'bout them exorcisms, Kaidan Rowe–style, eh?"

Kaidan huffed a laugh through his nose.

"Seriously, dude," Blake went on. "When you hit Mammon in the eye . . . I was, like, *dayum*!"

The energy in the room rose.

"That *was* amazing," Marna said.

"Good thinking with the holy water," Kopano added.

"I wasn't sure it would work," Kaidan admitted. "Bloody good thing it did."

We all angled toward one another, and for the next hour we talked about the events of the summit, rehashing every single detail, in awe at how things had turned out.

Caterina stayed put in her chair, trying to keep her head down, but periodically looking up with interest at something someone said before dropping her chin again. Ginger kept a close eye on her, seeming to study her and gauge her reactions and interests.

And then we began figuring out exactly which of the Dukes had chosen heaven. My father, Kopano's father, and Jezebet. Melchom, Pharzuph, and Astaroth had not. It was a solemn conversation. No tears were shed. The twins and Zania had no sentimental attachments to their fathers, and were glad to see them go. Kaidan hadn't said a word. I looked at him, but he kept his eyes averted.

"Your father showed interest in the beginning," I said to Blake. "I was hopeful."

"Yeah." He shook his head. "If it was just a choice between going to heaven or hell, I think he would have chosen heaven. But choosing between heaven and earth, he'd definitely wanna stay here. He thought they could stop the prophecy and stay on earth. Bad move."

I knew it bothered him, just like it bothered Kai. Kaidan leaned his head into my hand. His chest swelled and fell with a silent sigh.

"So, what's everyone gonna do now?" asked Jay.

Kaidan spoke up right away. "I know the first thing I'm going to do."

Surprised and curious, I leaned to the side so I could see his face better.

"I'm making an anonymous call to the police about Marissa and her trafficking ring."

"Yes!" I said. I threw my arms around him. Those words made me fall a million times more in love with him. He could bust the madam now with no fear of having it traced back to him.

"Nice," said Jay. "How 'bout you, Anna?"

Kaidan squeezed my hip. "Anna's a uni girl now."

I shook my head. "I'm already missing class by being here, and after all this, I think I need to take the semester off. I don't really care where I go to school. If you want to stay in L.A.," I said to Kaidan, "I'll transfer to a school out there."

He looked at me, his eyes all melty. "That'd be nice."

I smiled. It'd be *very* nice.

"And what about you, Jay?" Kai asked him. "I could hook you up with some people in the recording business or radio shows in L.A. Maybe we could write more music together."

"For real?" Jay's aura lit up like an orange firework, and we all laughed. "Dude. I'm there! What do you think, Marna? Wanna live in L.A.?"

"Sounds brilliant to me," she said. "As long as Blake and Ginger stay in California . . . at least until . . . you know, after the baby."

The mood of the room sank again. Ginger took her sister's hand and looked her in the eye.

"I'll be there."

Blake had turned, and appeared touched by their interaction. "Hey, Gin. Wanna join the married club while we're here in Vegas?" He waggled his eyebrows. Surely he was joking.

All eyes were on Ginger.

"No." Her voice was hard. "I'm never getting married."

Caterina sniggered. She stared down at her nails and said, "She means that."

Blake rubbed his chin, undeterred, then raised his pierced brow at her. "All right. Want to move in with me?"

Ginger narrowed her eyes at him, tapping her foot at his side. "You takin' the mick?"

"Nah. I'm serious."

"He is," Caterina muttered.

Ginger sniffed. "Fine."

"Sweet," Blake said with a grin.

"I'm not moving in with him!" Caterina crossed her arms and frowned. There was the girl I remembered. When she saw us all looking at her, she uncrossed her arms and dropped her head again.

Ginger smiled. I think she took Caterina's sassiness as a challenge. "When you see Blake's house, you might change your mind."

"What about you, Kope?" Marna asked, shifting the attention.

"I will finish my master's soon and return to Africa with my brothers. There is much that needs to be done there."

"And you're just the man to do it." Marna winked, and he gave a grateful smile.

I looked at Zania. "Where will you go, Z?"

She sort of shrugged and looked shy.

"You don't have to decide right now," I said, just as Kopano blurted, "You would love Malawi."

Then we all giggled and shifted, trying not to allow the moment to get too awkward. Zania gazed up at Kopano, who watched her with his signature intensity.

"Yes," she said. "I think I would love Malawi very much."

Marna clapped her hands.

Caterina made a disgusted sound and spoke fast in her

high-pitched little voice. "But . . . you're all Nephilim. And he is a human!" She pointed at Jay. "I don't understand this. Are all of you *in love*?"

We all looked around, taken aback by the question, an allegation that five hours ago would have scared us to death to hear out loud. And then in sync we burst into laughter, because *yes*. Yes, we were all in love. We'd defied the oppressive rules, fought back, and won. No more hiding. No more running. No more faking. No more fearing.

We were free.

EPILOGUE

Six Years Later ...

Malawi was everything Kopano had said it would be. Kai and I loved it from the moment we stepped off the plane, holding hands, smiling into the bright sunshine. Zania and Kopano met us at the doors of the orphanage. They'd been married five years now. Zania and I hugged first, while the guys shook hands.

"Your big day is finally here!" Zania said. She'd been working with us for the past year to make this happen.

Kaidan took my hand. We were both shaking a little. I was nervous and excited beyond belief to meet our boys—brothers.

We knew parenthood was hard. We'd been there for Jay after Marna's soul had passed during Anise's birth. She'd been taken despite our earnest hopes, but she'd made the most of her last months of freedom. I'd never seen anyone laugh and smile as much as Marna had. She radiated joy, and even Ginger softened under her ray of sunshine.

It was no surprise that Jay was the hippest rockstar single dad ever, but I knew he was tired, working full-time and then being the only parent for his baby girl.

Ginger and I spent a lot of time with Anise, keeping her whenever Jay had night-deejaying events for the L.A. radio station. Anise was a perfect combination of Marna's happiness and Ginger's divaness, walking around in her pink tutu with a hand on her hip. And Jay could do no wrong in his girl's eyes. She laughed at all his jokes and loved when he called her Short Stuff.

So. Cute.

But we all missed Marna.

For one extraordinary moment as Anise was born, I thought there would be a miracle. An angel of light had gently flown down and poised itself over Marna. But as Anise drew her first breath and Marna exhaled her last, the angel ushered her spirit from her body. With one glorious sweep of the room, Marna's loving soul rose with the angel, ascending home.

We followed Kope and Z inside the one-story building, a relatively new structure built with Alocer's funds, along with a library and medical facility in the small town.

We were led down a hall to a sparse room with chairs and toys.

"Let me get them," Kope said, leaving us.

Zania motioned for us to sit, but we declined. I clutched

Kai's hand, and Zania sighed happily.

"This is my favorite part. New parents are adorable." She rubbed my shoulder and I tried to smile through my nervousness.

When I heard footsteps coming down the hall and Kope's rumbling voice talking sweetly, my stomach clenched with anticipation.

The door opened and Kopano had a boy on each hip. They looked positively tiny in his arms, and I immediately teared up. *Don't cry*, I told myself. I didn't want to scare them. As we all moved closer, the eighteen-month-old boy, Mandala, held tighter to Kope, wary of us. Six-month-old Onani, on the other hand, let out a giant gurgling giggle and waved his arms up and down, making us all laugh.

I held out my hands, and Onani came to me with no qualms, obviously going to be our "people person." I checked out his skinny limbs, which somehow still managed to have soft dimples at the knees, elbows, ankles, and wrists. Despite being so thin, Onani's cheeks were chubby, and his head was a gorgeous mess of black curls.

I was in love and I couldn't stop smiling.

"Hi, Onani," I said softly.

He went a bit cross-eyed as he tried to focus on me, taking in every feature on my face with serious curiosity. Then he reached out and grabbed my hair, squealing happily while we all laughed and I unpried his little fingers. I looked at Kaidan and he was watching us in awe.

"I should have warned you," Z said. "He loves hair."

While I held Onani, adoring the weight of him in my arms, I watched as Kope and Kai both squatted on the floor.

Mandala leaned back against Kopano, still wary of Kaidan.

"I think I have something you might like," Kaidan said. From one pocket he pulled a cherry-red toy car.

This piqued Mandala's attention. He took a step toward Kaidan.

"It's yours, mate," Kai assured him. "I brought it just for you." He held out the car and our boy took it. He crouched down on the ground and rolled the car. Kaidan made a vrooming sound effect and Mandala smiled, making my heart flutter. Kai grinned up at me, and I swear . . . I had no idea I could love him more. But as I watched Kaidan lie on the floor and play with Mandala, my heart overflowed.

We spent the day at the orphanage, trying to get the boys as comfortable with us as possible before we took them to the hotel. Other children came in and out of the playroom where we stayed, and they all took an interest in us. Zania said I could give them candy, so I became quite popular among the kids, all the while watching Onani trying to crawl next to me.

"He's awful cute, isn't he?" Kaidan asked, grinning at me in wonder. Then Mandala sidled up close, holding his new toy, which nobody was allowed to touch, and he gently petted his baby brother's head, looking up at Kai for affirmation.

"You're a good boy," Kaidan said to him.

My heart officially melted.

Kaidan earned major hot points with me that day.

When a new group of kids came into the room, one of the little girls stood at the door and stared at us. Specifically, she stared at Kaidan. She looked about three, no older than four, with thick braids.

"Would you like one?" I asked her, holding out a lollipop.

She eyed the candy, considering, but then her eyes went back to Kaidan and she shook her head.

The auras of children were always interesting jumbles, because they couldn't process all those emotions. But this girl's were pretty clear and unwavering. Underneath, stirring like a low storm, were dark emotions. When I opened myself to her I felt fear, and it made me gasp. I pulled back and watched her, surprised. Because on top of that fear was pure, light pink love, swirled with light gray apprehension, and sparks of orange excitement. It was the love she was so clearly feeling as she stared at Kaidan that I couldn't quite understand. Zania and Kope came back into the room after some time, and they noticed the girl right away. They looked back and forth between her and Kaidan, who hadn't noticed what was happening yet.

"Are you all right?" Zania asked, crouching next to her.

She looked up at Zania with big, dark eyes and nodded, then looked back at Kai. Something strange was going on.

"Kai," I said softly. "I think someone wants to meet you."

He sat up from where he'd been lying, playing, and his eyes went to the girl. He looked confused as he took in her colors, but he smiled at her.

"Hi there. What's your name?"

Her voice was soft but rich when she answered, "Bambo."

We looked at Zania, who appeared perplexed, and she looked up at Kope.

He crouched down now, too.

"Her name is Alile." He said it like *Ah-LEE-leh*. "It means 'she weeps.'"

She weeps. What a sad, beautiful name.

"Alile," Kopano said to the girl. "*Zikuyenda bwanji?*"

Z whispered to Kaidan and me, "She speaks Chichewa."

Alile gave Kope a small smile but didn't answer. In that moment her guardian angel leaned down to whisper, and her apprehension disappeared, which showed me she was very in tune with her angel. In slow movements she went to Kaidan. He stayed very still as she touched his face and searched his eyes. In fact, he was searching hers in return. And then she sat right in his lap as if it were her home. She looked up at Kai and again said, "Bambo." The moment felt delicate and precious. Kaidan stayed very still with his palms on the floor next to him as if afraid to touch her.

"What does *bambo* mean?" I whispered.

The four of us stared at one another, still crouching.

"It's a word for 'father,'" Kopano said.

Kaidan's chest rose and fell faster as he looked down at the girl in his lap.

And then Zania signed to us, *She came to us from another orphanage that shut down because of sexual abuse.*

Kaidan looked at me with big eyes, and I knew the same appalling feelings coursed through us both. What had this poor girl been through? I watched Kaidan's jaw clench just thinking about it.

Kopano spoke to her again in Chichewa. I heard him say Kaidan's name.

"He tells her Kaidan is his friend and wants to know why she calls him father," Z whispered.

The girl answered, causing Kope and Z to go still.

"What did she say?" I asked. Kaidan was looking a little green, like he'd rather not know at this point.

Kope cleared his throat. "She says, 'In my dream, he was my daddy.'"

Goose bumps broke out across my skin.

Kaidan's eyes met mine and we stared.

And then something happened that I thought I'd never see. Kaidan and I had been through so much together, but one thing he'd never, ever done was cry.

At that moment, as he looked down at Alile, and his arms circled her, pulling her closer, I watched the first tear streak down Kaidan's cheek, followed by another. His face grew serious and his entire demeanor surrounding Alile shouted fierce protectiveness.

No daughters, Kaidan had told me so many years ago. Over the years I learned that having a girl would force him to face down his invisible demons who whispered of inadequacy. But I knew at that moment that Alile would be our daughter, and Kai would beat his fears. Nobody would *ever* hurt this little girl again and get away with it. Because she had a daddy now.

I reached out for Kaidan's hand and he took it, holding it tight.

Life was often so cruel, so ugly. And then, in the midst of all the madness, a precious gift would be placed in your lap.

Because life could also be so sweet.

DUKE NAMES AND JOB DESCRIPTIONS INDEX

Duke Name: Job Description: Their Children
(Neph we meet)

Pharzuph (Far-zuf), *Lust*: craving for carnal pleasures of the body; sexual desire outside of marriage: Kaidan (Ky-den)

Rahab (Rā-hab), *Pride*: excessive belief in one's own abilities; vanity; the sin from which others arise

Melchom (Mel-kom), *Envy*: desire for others' traits, status, abilities, or situations; jealousy; coveting: Blake

Mammon, *Greed*: desire for earthly material gain; avarice; selfish ambition: Flynn (deceased)

Alocer (Al-ō-sehr), *Wrath*: spurning love, opting for destruction; quick to anger; unforgiving: Kopano (Kō-pah-nō)

Kobal (Kō-bal), *Gluttony*: consumption of more than one's body needs. *Sloth*: avoidance of physical or spiritual work; laziness; apathy: Gerlinda (deceased)

Astaroth, *Adultery*: breaking marriage vows; cheating on one's spouse: Ginger and Marna

Jezebet, *Lies*: being dishonest or deceptive: Caterina

Thamuz (Thā-muz), *Murder*: taking the life of another person: Andre and Ramón

Shax, *Theft*: stealing: Marek

Belial (Beh-leel), *Substance Abuse*: physical addictions, primarily drugs and alcohol: Anna

Sonellion, *Hatred*: promotes prejudices, ill will toward others, hostility: Zania

ACKNOWLEDGMENTS

I can't believe it's over.

I first want to thank my readers, my "sweeties," who push me daily to do my best—whether you Sigh for Kai, Hope for Kope, or Ache for Blake—I thank you for the constant stream of encouraging messages. I read every single one and soak in the love, though I cannot always respond. Your enthusiasm is much needed and appreciated. I heart you something fierce.

Thank you to my loving and supportive family, near and far, for sharing me with the Nephilim world these past four years, and being interested in every detail of my journey. I could not have done it without you. I mean that. My husband, Nathan. Our kids, Autumn and Cayden. Our parents, Nancy and Dave Parry, Jim and Ilka Hornback, and Bill and

Jane Higgins. Our siblings, Frank Hornback, Dan Parry, Jeff Parry, Lucy Hornback, Bryan Higgins, Andrew Higgins, and all of their wonderful spouses.

Thank you to Manassas Baptist Church and Preschool for allowing me to use their facilities to write while the little guy was in class.

A huge cup of overflowing gratitude to my hardworking agent, Jill Corcoran.

Thank you so much to my team at Harper! I must say, I am in serious awe of my editors. A huge thanks to my lovely editor, Alyson Day, my marketer, Jenna Lisanti, and those amazing behind-the-scenes copy editors who polish the story into something so much worthier. Lastly, a big hug to Alana Whitman for always going above and beyond to make me smile.

To the cover-design team—thank you Tom Forget, Howard Huang, the gorgeous model Alexa Benk, and everyone who had a hand in the three Sweet covers. Such fun! (PS, if you know who the mystery male model is, I'd love to know, too, ha-ha. It's *not* Wade Poezyn, but I do want to thank him for being a great sport about all this book stuff. ☺)

A world of gratitude goes out to my friends (many of whom are early readers whose feedback rocked my writing world): Kelley Vitollo (aka Nyrae Dawn), Jolene Perry, Evie J, Carrie McRae, Jen Armentrout, Chanelle Gray, Courtney Fetchko, Jill Chamberlin Powell, Brooke Leicht, Carol Marcum, Jill Wilson, Hilary Mahalchick, Holly Andrzejewski, Christine Jones, Danielle Daniels, Valerie Friend, Meghan Lublin, Ann Kulakowski, Joanne Hazlett, Janelle Harris (and Jimmy, for more drummer jokes), Daniela Meilinger, Sam Wilson, and Carolee Noury.

And back to where it all began, thank you, Google, and thank you, God.

It's been a wild ride. Thanks for swooning, laughing, and crying with me. I'm not sure what's next, but I'm sure looking forward to finding out.

ROMANCE, TEMPTATION, AND HIGH-STAKES DRAMA...

BOOK 1

BOOK 2

BOOK 3

WILL GOOD DEFEAT EVIL?
Find out in the Sweet Evil series from Wendy Higgins.